M000168349

TO
have
& TO
hold

BOOK TWO IN **THE PASTOR MAGGIE SERIES**

Copyright © 2017 by Barbara Edema

All rights reserved. No part of this book may be used or reproduced in any
manner, including electronic storage and retrieval systems, except by explicit
written permission from the publisher. Brief passages excerpted for review
purposes are excepted.

This novel is a work of fiction. Names, characters, places, and incidents are
either the product of the author's imagination or are used fictitiously.

ISBN: 978-1-68313-083-3

First Edition
Printed and bound in the U.S.A.

Cover design by Kelsey Rice
Interior design by Kelsey Rice
Cover photo: jodie777/Love is Patient/Thinkstock

TO have & TO hold

BOOK TWO IN **THE PASTOR MAGGIE SERIES**

BARBARA EDEMA

Pen-L Publishing
Fayetteville, Arkansas
Pen-L.com

Books by Barbara Edema:

THE PASTOR MAGGIE SERIES

To Love and To Cherish

To Have and To Hold

This book is dedicated to my children
Elise, Lauren, Alana, and Wesley.
You inspired this book and reside in these pages
as well as in my heart.

In memory of Kenneth Walter.
You are greatly missed and lovingly remembered.

Sonnet 116

William Shakespeare

Let me not to the marriage of true minds
Admit impediments; love is not love
Which alters when it alteration finds,
Or bends with the remover to remove.
O no, it is an ever-fixed mark
That looks on tempests and is never shaken;
It is the star to every wand'ring bark,
Whose worth's unknown, although his highth be taken.
Love's not Time's fool, though rosy lips and cheeks
Within his bending sickle's compass come,
Love alters not with his brief hours and weeks,
But bears it out even to the edge of doom.
  If this be error and upon me proved,
  I never writ, nor no man ever loved.

We all have something we love that cannot be altered. It may be a person or a thing. A virtue or a vice. Our hearts are completely entwined with this true love. It is obvious, not just by our words, but also our very actions give us away. We show what, or who, is our ever-fixed mark.

—BARBARA EDEMA

List of Characters

RESIDENTS OF CHERISH, MICHIGAN

Pastor Maggie Elzinga – Pastor of Loving the Lord Community Church

Hank Arthur – Administrative Assistant at LTLCC, married to Pamela Arthur, hospital volunteer

Doris Walters – Custodian at LTLCC, married to Chester Walters

Irena Dalca – Organist at LTLCC, fan of miniskirts and vodka

Marla Wiggins – Sunday school superintendent, married to Tom Wiggins, owner of The Cherish Hardware Store; mother of Jason and Addie

Howard and Verna Baker – Recent newlyweds

Chief Charlotte Tuggle – Cherish Chief of Police, married to gravel pit owner Fred Tuggle; mother of twins, Brock and Mason, and daughter, Liz

Officer Bernie Bumble – Charlotte's inexperienced deputy

Martha – Nosy police dispatcher

Cate Carlson – Maggie worshiper and a student at the University of Michigan

Cole Porter – Owner and proprietor of The Porter Funeral Home; husband of Lynn Porter, and father of Penny, Molly, and Samuel

Harold Brinkmeyer – Successful young lawyer

Dr. Jack Elliot – Family practice doctor on the staff of Heal Thyself Community Hospital

Ellen Bright – Nurse at Heal Thyself; good friend of Pastor Maggie; Jack Elliot's cousin

Sylvia Baxter – Owner of The Garden Shop, married to Bill Baxter, handyman and master of construction

Mrs. Polly Popkin – Owner and proprietress of The Sugarplum Bakery

Cassandra Moffet – Distracted mother of Carrie and Carl, her two small children

Jennifer and Beth Becker – Sisters and owners of The Page Turner Book Shop

Redford Johnson – Financial planner and slimy character

Max Solomon – Always sits in the last pew

Julia Benson – Reporter for *The Cherish Life and Times*

Lacey Campbell – Owner of We Work Miracles Beauty Salon

New Members Class at Loving the Lord Community Church

William and Mary Ellington – Owners and proprietors of The Grange, a local bed and breakfast

Dr. Dana Drake – Veterinarian at Cherish Your Pets Animal Hospital

Winston Chatsworth – Friend of Howard Baker; can't seem to comb his hair

Dr. Ethan Kessler– African studies professor at the U of M, married to Charlene; father of Kay and Shawn

Dr. Charlene Kessler – Family practice doctor and partner of Jack Elliot; mother of Kay and Shawn.

Skylar Breese – Owner of Pretty, Pretty Petals Flower Shop; friend of Sylvia Baxter and total flake. Or so it appears.

Shut-ins in Cherish, Michigan

Katharine Smits – Sylvia Baxter's mother

Marvin Green – Hates women ministers, supposedly

Various other old darlings

Resident of Ann Arbor, Michigan

Detective Keith Crunch

Residents of Blissfield and Detroit, Michigan

Ken and Bonnie Elliot – Jack's parents

Anne Hubbell – Jack's older sister in Detroit, married to Peter; mother of Gretchen and Garrett

Andrew Elliot – Jack's younger brother; prepared to take over the family farm along with his girlfriend, Brynn

Leigh Elliot – Jack's younger sister; owner of the maternity shop Kanga and Roo in downtown Blissfield

Nathan – Jack's youngest brother; student at the U of M

RESIDENTS OF ZEELAND, MICHIGAN

Dirk and Mimi Elzinga – Maggie's parents

RESIDENTS OF HOLLAND, MICHIGAN

Joanna James – Widow of Ed James

Dan and Nora Wellman – Maggie's best friends from seminary

Mike and Kristy Brown – Parents of baby Matthew

RESIDENTS OF SAN FRANCISCO, CALIFORNIA, AND BAWJIASE, GHANA

Bryan Elzinga – Maggie's brother

Joy Nelson – Founder and CEO of Africa Hope, Bryan's boss

RESIDENT OF BIG SKY, MONTANA

Clara Abbott – Runs the front desk at the Mountain Peak Lodge

OTHERS

Abe Jones and his daughter, Melissa

Prologue

The whispers continued. They had begun years before on a foreign hillside and now were a common occurrence in her everyday life. Sometimes they happened when she was out running down the dirt road, a gust of wind coming from nowhere. Sometimes it was the sun blazing through the branches of a tree. Occasionally, she heard a whisper right in the middle of a sermon on a Sunday morning. She would stop, catch her breath, and find her sermon going a different direction than previously planned.

Sometimes the whispers came while sitting on the lakeshore. God showed up in nature, probably because he created it all. One time in particular, she'd heard him as she was holding a baby boy, baptizing him with drops of Lake Michigan water. A shiver went through her when God got too close and blew in her ear.

Sometimes the whispers came as she argued over hymns with Irena or tussled with Marvin, who pretended to dislike her, or when she took a bite of a particularly delicious donut. She was learning to be attuned to God's whispers and direction.

Once, the whisper came through the exhaust of a dirty old car.

God seemed to show up everywhere. Even gas stations.

1

Maggie heard the click of the gas pump. She topped off her tank, replaced the gas cap, and that's when she saw him.

He came out from under a car parked at the opposite pump and walked toward her. He was small and appeared to be completely gray, looking up at her with huge green eyes rimmed in black.

Maggie looked down at the kitten and gasped with a rush of pity and jaw-clenching anger. *How did this little creature end up at a gas station, near a highway, under a car?* In the midst of her mental assault on these injustices, she heard a tiny mew.

"Hi, little guy," she said softly as she knelt down and gave him a pet.

A mix of dirt and oil was matted into his fur. He mewed again and pushed into her hand.

"Oh, no, no, no!" Maggie said. "I can't do this again. I'm sorry, little one."

The car engine at the opposite pump roared to life, and the kitten leapt onto Maggie's bent knee and clung to her with all his little claws. Maggie held a protective hand over his head as the car pulled away.

Oh, good grief!

Maggie left the Lansing, Michigan, gas station with the little gray bag of bones and whiskers in her lap. He smelled of oil, dirt, and gas fumes. As she was driving, she noticed the kitten had curled into a ball and fallen asleep. She sent a curse out into the world against all those who would hurt or abandon an animal. Her most vehement curse was meant for anyone who would ever hurt, neglect, or abandon a child.

Pastor Maggie had no patience for any form or variation of those evils. She would be quite un-pastor-like if she ever met an abuser face-to-face. But for now, what was she going to do with the little waif? She already had two cats in the parsonage. How could she add another? One year ago, she had been given permission to bring her cat, Marmalade, a large orange tomcat, to the parsonage. That was when she had accepted the call to be pastor of Loving the Lord Community Church in Cherish, Michigan. But shortly after her arrival, she'd adopted an orphaned female kitten, Cheerio. There had been quite a fight in the church council over the new addition. Maggie had won. She'd then found homes—possibly by force—for Cheerio's two siblings.

With her current rescue in her lap, she took the off-ramp to Cherish, drove down Main Street, and turned right onto Middle Street. When she pulled into the parsonage driveway and turned off the engine, the gray ball remained asleep. *Now what?* She sat for a moment, thinking of how her impulsiveness almost always got her into trouble. *Drat.* She finally opened the door and carried her little bundle into the parsonage.

First things first. He must be bathed. He was probably full of fleas. She filled the kitchen sink with warm water and ran upstairs for her shampoo. Then she ran back downstairs to the kitchen, carrying the kitten the whole way. Finally, she carefully placed him in the water. He was so weak, he didn't have enough energy to fight being drenched and bubbled. Maggie carefully washed him and slowly discovered four white-not-gray paws and a white-not-gray tummy. He had gray, tan, and black Tabby markings on his head, back, and tail. She tried to get the gray splotch off his nose with the shampoo but discovered it actually belonged there.

After wrapping him in a towel and drying him off, she put him by the food bowl. He jumped right in and ate with gusto. It was at that particular moment Marmalade and Cheerio smelled something new in their house. When they got to the kitchen, they both fluffed out like angry chickens. What was in their food bowl? Howls and yowls began, with much hissing thrown in for good measure. The new kitten paid no attention. He had been in worse spots than that before. He ate until he fell asleep on top of the remaining food, all four limbs spread out over the bowl.

That was how Maggie Elzinga's second summer of ministry at Loving the Lord Community Church was winding down. For the past fifteen months, Maggie had been pastor of the small church just west of Ann Arbor. She had earned her place as pastor by trial, error, and occasional success. Being a woman, and a small woman at that—five foot three and one hundred fifteen pounds—did not make her an overpowering presence. She looked up to everyone. Except the elementary Sunday school class.

Maggie's first year of ministry had been what it should have: full of surprises and a lot of firsts. First funeral, first baptism, first wedding. And each one had been unpredictable in every way. She discovered ministry was like life. The difference was, in ministry the pastor was part of everyone else's life, which meant being part of everyone else's surprises as well as her own. Maggie's impetuous and emotional personality had drawn her completely into the lives of her parishioners. She had also sustained a personal loss on Valentine's Day that could still bring her to tears at the drop of a hat or someone's kind word.

Now, watching the new kitten sleep, Maggie was suddenly invaded by a horrific thought. *How will I tell the church council about it?* The church owned her house and made the rules. She envisioned the obvious reason why she would not be allowed to keep the little orphan in the church parsonage: supposedly, no pets, though they had already allowed her two. At times like that, she could see the advantage of having her own home. She looked once more at the kitten lying on the bowl, as if guarding the food with his pathetic little life, and knew she would keep him. She was in love.

"Come on, little one," Maggie whispered as she gently picked up the Tabby. He showed no resistance. "It's to the doctor with you."

She got into her car, put the kitten on her lap again, and drove to Cherish Your Pets Animal Hospital, just north of town past the beautiful old clock tower.

Maggie opened the door into the lobby of the animal hospital, and immediately the smell of antiseptic overlaying the unmistakable smell of animal urine wafted through the air and up her nose. Maggie thought of all the poor pups that had lost control of their bladders once being walked, or dragged, into the veterinarian's office.

Dr. Dana Drake ran a lively business caring for all of the pets in Cherish. Maggie liked Dana a lot and had been hoping she might join Loving the Lord as a new member. Dana was a tall, thin, African-American woman. She had been number one in her class at the Michigan State University veterinary school. Her hair was always pulled back in a tight ponytail, and her cocoa eyes and black lashes gave her the gift of never having to wear makeup, which she wouldn't have done anyway. Dana was as comfortable in a field caring for large farm animals as she was in her bright-yellow office caring for the smallest of God's animal kingdom. Although Dana was a few years older than Maggie, they had forged a fast bond due to their mutual love of cats.

Dana was at the front desk with one of her assistants when Maggie walked through the door. She glanced up at Maggie, but her eyes immediately went to the little bundle in Maggie's arms.

"Oh, Pastor Maggie. Now who do you have there?"

Dana carefully took the kitten from Maggie.

"I found him about an hour and a half ago at a gas station in Lansing. Can you believe someone just dumped him there with all those cars? And so near the highway?" Maggie's voice rose in tandem with her anger.

"I can believe it," Dana said quietly. "People can be so cruel. Animals, especially baby animals, don't have a chance when they are abandoned like this. Let's take him back and see what we see."

Maggie obediently followed Dana to one of the examination rooms. Dana listened to the kitten's heart and lungs with her stethoscope.

Then she took his temperature. Although it was embarrassing, the kitten didn't complain.

"I would say he's just about two months old," she said, looking at his teeth.

Then she took him to the back of the medical area and did a little blood test, and after about twenty minutes, Dana finally returned with the kitten.

"Pastor Maggie, you have quite a sick little guy here. His blood count is so low that I'm surprised he can even stand. I can let you take him home with some medicine, or I can keep him here for a couple of days. If you take him home, along with the medicine, I suggest giving him one small slice of raw beef liver every day with his regular cat food. That will help get his blood count up."

Maggie thought and then said, "I'll take him home, if you really think that's okay with the other cats there."

"You should keep them separated until this one gets stronger," Dana said. "How are Marmalade and Cheerio?"

"Hilarious. And perturbed about this new infidel." Maggie smiled.

"I'll get the pills for him. I gave him an antibiotic injection, but we'll wait on the other shots until he's stronger. By the way, what's his name?"

Maggie looked quizzically at Dana. "I don't know. I hadn't thought about it. I guess, with Marmalade and Cheerio, I'll call this one . . . mmm . . . Fruit Loop."

Dana laughed. "Hi, Fruit Loop. We're going to have to get you healthy and fattened up, my little friend."

Dana went to get the medicine while Maggie cuddled Fruit Loop. He was still able to purr, even though he was so close to losing one of his nine lives. Maggie felt a rush of relief that one more little life was spared.

When Dana returned, Maggie said, "You have done your job, now I'll do mine. I would love you to join the new members class at church. Any chance you would be interested? We meet this Sunday right after church for a chat about Loving the Lord. The classes are each of the next four Sundays."

"I was already planning on it, Pastor Maggie, ma'am," Dana said with a serious nod of her head. "When I heard you did an animal blessing service last fall, I knew you would be the kind of pastor I could get along with. Most of your type bore me to tears. I was raised Baptist, and it sort of messed me up."

"Great!" Maggie said too excitedly, making Fruit Loop jump. "I promise, no Baptist guilt at Loving the Lord, but someday I want to know how it messed you up. I like hearing stories about what doesn't work in churches so that I won't do those things at ours."

"Fine. Someday over lunch. Now, as far as little Fruit Loop is concerned, here are his pills. They will get rid of his worms. If you want, you can smash them into the cow's liver. He won't notice. Bring him back here in one week. Okay?"

"We'll be here," Maggie said as she took the pills.

She brought Fruit Loop home and fixed up a space for him in her parsonage study. She put down a small bed, food and water dishes, and a litter box—nice and close so he would be sure to see it. She also left a few toys for when he was feeling stronger. Then she headed off to buy a very disgusting piece of cow's liver and silently apologized to the cow as she did so.

2

When Maggie returned to the parsonage, it was five o'clock. It was the last Friday of August, and it felt as if the month had gone on forever. After Ed James's death on Valentine's Day, Maggie had suffered the residual effects of losing a loved one. Ed had been her professor, mentor, and trusted friend. When he'd died suddenly of a heart attack, Maggie questioned every inch of her faith. For a while, she didn't know how she could continue with ministry. God had stolen a great man. She briefly believed God could not be forgiven for that.

Family, friends, her congregation, and Ed's widow, Jo, had surrounded Maggie in a variety of ways until her faith found her again. Jo, in the throes of her own deep suffering, had been the most helpful. She'd put Maggie on to a letter writing challenge: creating letters from herself to Ed and then Ed's responses to her pain and questioning. Since Maggie had to write Ed's responses, her weary and broken heart had begun to heal.

When Maggie looked back at that, she marveled at Jo. She, who had suffered so much, had taken the time to help Maggie heal. Maggie felt more than a little guilt over her own self-centeredness. Since Ed's death, Maggie had made regular trips over to Holland, where she and Jo drank pots of tea and ate peanut butter cookies.

But still, the summer had felt like a bad dream. She had been able to work and carry out all of her responsibilities. She had laughed and smiled appropriately, even when she really wanted to scream or cry, but she had been reminded daily of how much she had relied on Ed's wisdom, direction, sense of humor, and constant encouragement. She wanted the bad dream to end, or at least to lessen a little bit.

So Maggie had tried to focus on the two highlights of her summer. The first had been officiating the wedding of her two best friends. On July fourth, Nora Drew and Dan Wellman became wife and husband. And thanks to the city of Holland, free fireworks over Lake Macatawa celebrated the nuptials of these two dear friends. Both Nora and Dan worked at the Holland megachurch Jesus Lives and So Do We! Maggie had put her heart and soul into the wedding. The planning and preparation had been a joyous respite from grief.

A half-hour before the wedding, Maggie'd had an idea. She found Dan with his groomsmen and pulled him aside. Then she opened her small, black wedding notebook and pulled out a pen and an index card.

"Dan, tell me what you love about Nora," she said, looking him straight in the eye.

"What?" Dan was confused, along with being a nervous groom.

"Just tell me. What do you love about Nora? Why are you marrying her in a half-hour?" Maggie persisted. "Is she nice? Is she pretty? Is she good at volleyball? Is she great with the youth group?"

Finally, Dan began to speak. He poured out everything that came to mind. Maggie wrote furiously to keep up with him. She filled out both sides of the index card.

Next, she'd gone to the bride's dressing room and found Nora. It had been only fifteen minutes before the wedding. Maggie had another index card already in her hand.

"Nora, what do you love about Dan?" Maggie asked.

Nora was mute.

"Nora, why are you going to walk down the aisle to Dan in fifteen minutes? What is it about him?"

Nora's eyes had filled with tears. They spilled onto her foundationed and blushed cheeks. She made a choking sound and whispered, "Everything. I love everything about Dan."

"Be more specific. Like what? His smile? His love of pancakes?" Maggie sounded like a drill sergeant.

Nora sniffed loudly and began her love litany.

The wedding had begun ten minutes late due to Nora having to reapply her makeup.

Right before Nora and Dan had shared their vows, Maggie said, "Before the wedding, I had a chance to ask each of you a question. Dan, I asked you what you love about Nora. And Nora, I asked you why you are walking down the aisle to Dan today. What do you love about him? Let me tell you what you had to say about each other."

Then Maggie had read what Dan and Nora said. There wasn't a dry eye anywhere. Not even the wedding planners, who were standing quietly in the back. It had been a magical, holy day.

Maggie had decided she would do that for all future weddings. It was the most meaningful part of the entire ceremony. She also held on to the index cards. She would send them to Dan and Nora on their first anniversary.

The second highlight of Maggie's summer had been being asked to baptize a tiny gentleman named Matthew. He had been born to a couple Maggie had only met once—in the Holland hospital. They had met on the horrific day the couple lost their first child to stillbirth. Unbeknownst to Maggie, the couple, Mike and Kristy Brown, had worked hard to find out where Maggie had moved after seminary. They just had to find her and tell her about the birth of their son, Matthew, after losing baby Anna Lee.

Maggie had made a point of visiting the Brown family whenever she made a trip back to Holland. It was on one of those visits that Kristy quietly asked, "We would love you to baptize our little Matthew. Would you be able to do that somehow?"

Maggie had been taken aback. She knew Mike and Kristy didn't belong to a church, and it was curious that they wanted Matthew baptized. But then she'd smiled.

"I would love to baptize him," she said, giving Kristy a hug and thereby smushing Matthew, who was fast asleep in his mother's arms.

"We know Sunday mornings are kind of busy for you," Kristy said. "So we were thinking maybe later in the afternoon on a Sunday. Is that okay?"

"Yes," Maggie said, thinking quickly. "It would take me two and a half hours to get here. Our church service is over at eleven. I could easily leave by noon. Where do you want to have Matthew baptized?"

"We were thinking on the shores of Lake Michigan. We both grew up on that lake and hope Matthew does too. Our parents have put quite a bit of pressure on us to have him baptized."

Kristy looked embarrassed.

"It's up to you and Mike. However, I think baptism is a lovely sign and seal of God's love and promise. It's your choice."

Maggie had stopped herself there. If baptizing Matthew on the sandy shores of Lake Michigan brought a small bit of comfort to Mike and Kristy, Maggie would happily participate. She knew some pastors talked about baptizing only in a church and the importance of regular attendance and participation. Maggie suspected Mike and Kristy hadn't forgiven God yet for the loss of Anna Lee. She understood a variation on that sentiment since Ed's death.

And so, on the shore of Lake Michigan one warm July Sunday afternoon, surrounded by family and friends, Maggie had read the baptism liturgy and gently sprinkled Matthew with water from the lake. His tiny nose had wrinkled as the water slid down each side of his small face. Then he sneezed. Then he began to cry. He had been having such a nice nap before all the lake wind and water permeated his small being. So Maggie had quickly handed him back to his mother, whose familiar smell and soft noises calmed Matthew immediately.

As Kristy held Matthew and Mike held Kristy, Maggie had finished the service.

"Today God has made a promise to Mike, Kristy, and Matthew." She looked at the parents, who were looking at their son. "Matthew is yours to have and to hold, but he belongs to God. Just as Anna Lee does." Maggie reached behind the sand grass and brought out a small pink rose in a vase. She handed it to Mike. "This is a day of celebration and a day of remembrance. God holds this day and all our days."

Following the service, Maggie had given Mike and Kristy Matthew's baptismal certificate.

"Thank you for remembering Anna Lee."

Kristy trembled as she hugged Maggie.

"She will always be remembered," Maggie said. "Her story is your story. And God's story."

Maggie had trailed off at that last part. She was uncertain about how far to go with that line of thought.

But Kristy smiled and kissed Matthew on his small nose.

"I might actually believe that one of these days," she said.

But at the end of that hot last Friday in August, Maggie's long drive home from Holland, finding the kitten at the gas station, the vet visit, and her shopping trip, were all taking their toll. She sat down and poured a glass of iced tea to sip on.

She and Jack had a dinner date set for that night. She picked up her phone and dialed his cell number. After the first ring, he picked up.

"Reverend Highness?" Jack said in mock seriousness.

Oh, gorgeous voice! Maggie could listen to him talk all day long.

"Hi, Jack," she said. "How are you?"

"Fine, now that I've heard your voice," he said lightly. "Also, happy that I have a date tonight with a beautiful woman. What are you doing?"

"Oh, you know, bits and bobs, odds and ends, this and that."

That was often Maggie's response when she didn't want to reveal what she was doing or if she wanted to avoid small talk.

"I see." Jack smiled, wondering what she was up to.

"About that date you mentioned. Instead of going out, would you mind eating at the parsonage tonight?"

"It's my favorite place to eat. What's on the menu?"

"Nothing. I'm inviting you to buy dinner and bring it here." Maggie laughed. "I have had a very, very, very busy and important day. All you did was save humans. Would you please bring me dinner? A salmon salad? From the Cherish Café? And dessert? Mounds of chocolate?"

Jack laughed. "Ahh . . . Yes, Your Reverend Highness. I shall hunt and gather and lay my bounty at your adorable little feet."

"Soon?"

"Within the hour. Farewell." Jack clicked off.

Maggie knew, if people heard the way she and Jack talked to each other, they would cringe and then gag. She didn't care. She loved being in love.

Dr. Jack Elliot was a local family doctor in Cherish and a faithful church member. Maggie and Jack had gotten to know each other through shared work: his doctoring and her pastoring. Jack fell in love with the loving new pastor, even though she dressed like a ragbag. Maggie fell in love with the charming doctor—for the first time in her life. She fell in love with Jack's heart, initially, but his tall, dark, handsomeness hadn't hurt one bit. At six foot three inches, Jack was exactly one foot taller than Maggie. His thick, dark-brown hair and chocolaty-brown eyes were the *dark* part of tall, dark, and handsome.

Both Jack and Maggie enjoyed physical activity. Jack regularly used the health center connected to the hospital for workouts. Whereas Maggie loved to run down her dirt road. Jack liked an indoor workout, and his physique showed the effort he put into those workouts.

Maggie remembered in high school asking a boyfriend if she could have one of his T-shirts. All the girls did that with their boyfriends. It was a badge of honor to have a young man's shirt to cuddle with and smell at night. But now, being the mature pastor that she was, she had not asked Jack for a shirt to smell—rather, an entire bottle of his cologne. Jack wore Claiborne for Men. Maggie sprayed it everywhere. Like air freshener. Somehow the scents of basil, lemon, black pepper, coriander, grapefruit, pineapple, rich amber, and sandalwood blended perfectly into the "scent of Jack." It also sounded like a decent salad. Minus the sandalwood. The only reason Maggie knew the list of ingredients of Jack's cologne was because she looked it up online. Thank heaven for Google. Maggie caught her breath every time her blue eyes looked into Jack's brown eyes and whenever her nose got a whiff of his scent. Fortunately, the feeling was mutual. Of course, Maggie always smelled exotically of Dove soap.

Jack and Maggie had tiptoed into a relationship during the past autumn. Romantic dinners and long conversations in the parsonage had begun to cement their love for one another. After the death of Ed James, Maggie had left Cherish and gone home to grieve. It was then that Jack knew he couldn't let her go for good. He'd sent a bouquet of bright-red carnations, her favorite flower, to Maggie each day she was away. It took Maggie a little longer, but she came to the realization that she loved Jack too.

They'd spent the late spring and summer enjoying romantic dinners and conversations but also creating a more comfortable pattern with one another. They had unwittingly begun to try on the feelings and actions of a more permanent relationship. They all fit very nicely. New love was like that. The differences in their personalities hadn't collided. Yet. Maggie had continued to work through her grief over Ed, and Jack had allowed her to do so. Maggie began to smile again. Jack encouraged her to laugh. Maggie's heart had begun to change direction. The direction was Jack.

Before he arrived to fulfill her dinner demands, Maggie took the cow's liver out of the packaging and stifled the urge to be sick. She took a sharp knife and cut the liver into small slices. *Disgusting!* If it wasn't going to save a life, she would stuff the whole thing down the garbage disposal and be done with it. Instead, she held her breath and cut away. She placed one thin slice on a paper plate and put the rest of the slimy pieces into a Ziploc bag. After scrubbing her hands like a surgeon, she brought Fruit Loop his first taste of liver with one of Dr. Dana's pills smashed into it. It was gone in seven seconds. Then he crawled into her lap, washed his face, and fell asleep. He stayed there, even when the Westminster chimes rang at the front door.

Maggie carried her sleeping charge to the door. She greeted Jack with a kiss.

Her eyes were on the bag of food he was holding. His were on the kitten.

"Did Marmalade have another kitten?" he asked.

"No. He hates this pathetic little thing. So does Cheerio. She didn't even try to like him."

"I would like to hear the story of this one," Jack said.

"I would like to eat everything in that bag," Maggie countered. "I'll talk while we eat. I will be very rude and talk with my mouth full. My mother would be appalled."

"It's a good thing I like you a lot, or I might take my bag of food and leave you, you crazy cat pastor lady with no manners."

"What you say, 'tis true, 'tis true, and, yes, true 'tis. Give me my dinner, peasant!"

They went into the kitchen, and Maggie set out dishes while Jack opened a bottle of wine. Maggie told him the whole story of finding Fruit Loop at the gas station and their visit to Dr. Dana.

Jack was appropriately sympathetic to the plight of Fruit Loop. Jack's love of animals and his natural tendency to care for any kind of suffering—human and otherwise—were just two of the thousands of reasons Maggie was in love with him.

They ate some of their dinner and then freed Marmalade and Cheerio from the family room. Marmalade was a big orange-and-white tomcat. He had thought he ruled the parsonage, until Maggie brought home the orphaned Cheerio. After three days of despicable behavior, Marmalade took Cheerio to be his very own kitten, and he had raised her well. She was now a large, fluffy calico. Fruit Loop looked like an acorn next to those beasts. He hissed a pathetic little hiss. Everyone sniffed and growled. Then they were separated once again for the night.

"Okay," Maggie said, taking a large bite of salmon salad, "tell me about your day, although I'm sure it couldn't have been as exciting as mine." She giggled.

"Of course not. I saw several patients this morning, as usual. Then this afternoon I was called in for one of my OB patients who was trying to deliver a baby that didn't want to be born."

Jack buttered a Cherish Café roll and popped it into his mouth. Maggie stopped chewing.

"What happened?" she asked, her mouth full of salad, her eyes wide.

"We got her ready for a C-section once we found the baby to be in distress. We were just beginning the surgery when the father, who was holding the hand of his wife, went right down. He hit his head on the side of the delivery bed on his way to the floor. He was bleeding everywhere." Jack shook his head.

"What did you do?"

Maggie thought listening to Jack's stories was often better than television. Jack sipped his wine.

"I had to continue with the surgery. Ellen and one of the other nurses dragged him out."

Ellen Bright, Jack's cousin and one of Maggie's best friends, was a nurse at Heal Thyself. She was not just efficient but had a great sense of humor. She had no-nonsense, short, dark hair, but it was her doe-like brown eyes and gentle demeanor that comforted almost any patient. Maggie and Ellen had spent many Sunday evenings with a bowl of popcorn, an extreme amount of talking and laughing, and the occasional movie.

"The mother was screaming for her husband to stand up and watch his son being born," Jack continued. "But he was face down as he was dragged out the door by the two nurses. She was so mad. I don't know if he will ever live down the humiliation."

"Oh dear," Maggie sighed. "I feel sorry for the mother *and* the father. You must see every possible response in situations like that. Did the father finally come to?"

"I checked in on them before coming here. The family of three were all together, awake, and exhaustedly thrilled. The father had a bag of ice pressed to the front of his head, but the mother was holding her baby as if God had dropped an angel in her lap. All's well that ends well."

Maggie always liked to hear Jack's happy-ending stories. He had plenty that weren't. Because so many of his patients were her parishioners, they often dovetailed their different brands of care at the hospital. Although he regularly broke HIPAA laws by telling her things reserved only for family, she was able to do her job better when she knew what the facts were. She never broke his confidence, and he knew her discretion was complete.

Jack left at midnight. They were both tired and always hated saying goodbye.

As he drove home, Jack began thinking of how to end the late-night goodbyes for good. He was crazy about his crazy, cat-loving pastor. He wanted her for keeps.

3

On weekdays and Saturdays, Maggie's schedule rarely varied. She got up at five thirty, gulped down a cup of coffee, and then set off for a five-mile run. Upon her return, she would shower, dress, and—along with two more cups of coffee—eat a bowl of oatmeal covered with sliced banana and pure maple syrup drizzled over all. On Sundays, the whole routine began at four thirty in the morning.

Yes, she exercised every day. Yes, many people told her she shouldn't. Maggie never liked being told she "shouldn't" or that she "should" do anything. She tended to do the opposite of what she was told. The only time she chose to skip a run was when she had been up all night with a sick or dying parishioner.

She finished her oatmeal that lovely Saturday morning, completed her cat duties, and made sure Fruit Loop was safe in the study before she went to church. Living in the parsonage meant her commute to work was a walk across the lawn. She could hear Irena playing the organ as soon as she stepped out of her home. Irena practiced part of every day, but she camped out all day on Saturdays as she prepared for Sunday. Maggie usually enjoyed Irena's music as she worked at church. Occasionally, Irena had to be asked to tone it down a bit, which she rarely did.

Irena Dalca—*dalca* meaning lightning in her native Romanian—was the organist at Loving the Lord. Standing four feet eight inches and weighing around eighty pounds, Irena was a powerhouse of the miniature size. Irena and Maggie had gone around and around at the beginning of their relationship and had settled into their respective roles. Irena liked to play loudly—for every kind of church service, especially funerals—and she could somehow wear skintight miniskirts and four-inch stiletto heels as she sat at the organ and played the music of heaven. Added to her miniskirts and heels were fishnet stockings, plunging necklines, brightly colored push-up bras, and makeup and hair to frighten the bravest of souls. Irena dyed her own hair over her kitchen sink. The outcome was never normal or good. Her makeup looked as if she had gone to clown school to study eye shadow, rouge, and lipstick. Her combinations were frighteningly dazzling. Maggie had also learned of Irena's capacity for vodka, brandy, or any other liquor. It was quite breathtaking. Visitors of Loving the Lord were always shocked when they saw Irena colorfully perched on her organ bench. Everyone else loved and feared her.

That day, Irena's hair was dyed the color of purple onions.

"Good morning, Irena," Maggie said as she walked to the side of the organ.

Without taking her eyes off the music, Irena responded, "Goood moorrning, Pastoorr Maggie. I'm beezy. Pleeeese go avay."

Maggie rolled her eyes as she walked through the gathering area and into the offices. Hank was busy covering his desk with his blue tarpaulin in preparation for Sunday's service and coffee time. Hank was LTLCC's helpful, happy assistant.

"Good morning, Hank," Maggie said cheerfully. "May I help you with your tarp?"

Hank looked up and smiled. "Good morning, Pastor Maggie. And yessireebob, if you could just take that end and set some hymnals on top to keep it in place, I would appreciate it."

Maggie secured the tarp just as Doris, the church janitor, pushed her rolling trash can into Hank's office. She was wrapped in her huge yellow apron with the many pockets, all stuffed with cleaning supplies. Doris was round, gray-haired, opinionated, and ferociously clean. She and her husband, Chester, were faithful members of Loving the Lord. Doris's head was wrapped in a green bandana, and she had a smudge of dirt on her nose. Maggie wondered where Doris could have found the dirt. The church was so clean, anyone could eat right off the floors, probably even the toilet seats.

"Good morning, Doris," Hank and Maggie said in unison.

"Good morning." Doris wasn't smiling. "Someone has been in this church since last night and left footprints of dirt and mud on the basement floor. Was it one of you?"

Doris gave both Hank and Maggie a withering glare.

"Nosireebob! It wasn't me," Hank said emphatically. "I was home with Pamela. You can call her." Hank sounded as if he were being interrogated by the police.

Hank was one of the few people who had the right to be in the church any time he wanted. He squared his shoulders and sent Doris an evil scowl.

"I wasn't here last night either, Doris," Maggie said more calmly. "I was in the parsonage, but I didn't notice anyone around the church. Was the basement door to the outside unlocked?"

That stumped Doris.

"Well, I hadn't actually checked the door."

The three of them trooped downstairs to check out the possible entryway of the mud vandal. The basement door was locked, but Maggie and Hank could see the mud prints on the floor.

"This is strange," Maggie said. "Why would anyone want to come down here? Did you find any other dirt or mud marks in the church?"

"Believe you me, I have searched on my hands and knees by every door and window. Not another trace of filth. No one's going to pull the wool under my nose," Doris said, sounding a tiny bit like Hercule Poirot.

Hank walked over to the windows that flanked each side of the basement door. He pushed up. The right window was locked down tightly, but the left window lifted straight up.

"Well, looky here," Hank said.

Immediately, Doris said, "Hank, you crawl through there and see if you fit."

"What? Nosireebob, Doris. I'm not crawling through that window. I've got a bad back." Hank sounded highly insulted.

"I can't do it," said Doris. "I'm too fat. Plus, I'd have to take off my apron."

Maggie didn't know why that was an issue.

"I'll do it," she said.

She kicked off her sandals and wrapped her white gauze skirt around her legs. She grabbed a folding chair, unfolded it, and climbed up. Then she grasped the window frame and easily pulled herself through.

"I did it!"

"Of course you did," Doris said with disdain. "You're twenty-seven and as small as a child."

Sometimes Maggie wanted to smack Doris with her own mop.

Maggie slid back into the window frame.

"But there is plenty of room. Don't you think there is enough room for someone larger?"

"Easily," said Hank. "That's a large window there."

They heard two sets of feet coming down the basement stairs. The first set was the click-clack of Irena's high heels. The second set was much quieter.

Irena and Marla, the church Sunday school superintendent, appeared at the door. Their eyes immediately went to Maggie hanging in the window frame.

Maggie was just ready to jump down when she saw the two women. Distracted, her foot slipped and went through the back opening of the folding chair. The chair collapsed on her leg, she was pulled out of the window frame, and then fell face first onto the cement floor. Her gauze skirt floated around her like a jellyfish.

As she lay face down on the hard floor, she wondered if they could all see her underpants.

Everyone gasped at once. Maggie groaned.

"Pastor Maggie! Are you all right?" Marla rushed in first.

Hank was quick to follow. Maggie's underpants *were* on full display. He carefully averted his eyes, but not before he saw the pink and red hearts sprinkled all over her bottom.

"Pastor Maggie, let me help you up. Are you hurt?"

He pulled the folding chair from her leg with his eyes closed.

Marla grabbed Maggie's skirt and pulled it down to cover the pink and red hearts. Then Hank and Marla each took one of Maggie's arms and lifted her to a standing position.

Irena stood with arms crossed, staring from the doorway. Her latest disaster at the kitchen sink, combined with the sunlight through the basement windows, rendered her hair a glowing purple orb. She watched the commotion through narrowed eyes as Hank and Marla helped get Maggie to her feet. Doris was also watching, but only because she was completely dumbfounded.

Maggie got her balance, blonde hair hanging in her face and more embarrassed than she had been in a very long time. She could feel a sharp pain in her right ankle where her leg had been caught and twisted in the folding chair, and her right cheek and eye were aching from where they had hit the cement floor.

Finally, Doris came to life.

"Pastor Maggie, your ankle doesn't look so good. You better sit down."

She unfolded the chair for Maggie to sit on. Irena stepped forward.

"No! No! No! Do not seet een dat deth trrup! Git herr up de stairs."

"Let me sit for a minute, Irena," Maggie whined.

Irena was so bossy.

"Qviet, you!" Irena hissed. "Git herr out ov herre."

She glowered at Hank. So he and Marla helped Maggie limp over to the stairs and then painstakingly make her way up one step at a time. Doris shut the window and made sure it was locked. She would just have to wait to come back down and clean up the dirt and mud, which now had been spread all over the floor.

"What a disaster," she grumbled to herself.

"Carrfuull!" Irena shouted as Maggie took each new step.

Her screaming was giving everyone a headache.

Once they were all settled in Maggie's office and her swollen ankle was resting on a chair, the questions began.

"What were you three doing in the basement?" Marla asked. "I didn't think anyone went into that back room. It reminds me of a jail cell."

Doris decided it was time for her two cents. "I was cleaning in the dining room and went into the back room, like I always do. But then . . ." Her voice got dramatic, at least for Doris. "I saw them. All over the floor!"

"You saw what?" asked Marla.

"Muddy footprints."

Marla's eyes grew large. Nothing like that had ever happened before at Loving the Lord.

Hank, tired of the drama, continued with the story.

"One of the windows was unlatched, although the door and other window were locked tight. Pastor Maggie lifted herself through the window—"

"Because you wouldn't, you big chicken," Doris piped in. "Now Pastor Maggie probably has a broken leg, and it's all because of you."

Maggie jumped in before Hank and Doris worked themselves into a church brawl.

"I wanted to see if a person could easily fit through the opened window. As I was coming back inside, my foot got caught in the folding chair, and I fell. You saw it all."

Unfortunately, I saw a little too much, thought Hank.

Maggie continued. "I think I should make an announcement in church tomorrow and see if anyone has an easy explanation for the open window and footprints. It is strange the footprints went no farther than the back room. What's that room for, by the way?"

"It used to be a storage room," Marla said. "But a few years ago we had a church rummage sale and cleaned out the entire space. We found it was really just full of junk. It had been almost twenty years since anyone had taken notice. Most of it went straight to the dump. Remember, Doris?"

"It was a good day, yes, indeed," Doris said dreamily.

"No! No! No! You ubsolutlee vill not mek announcement in church." Irena's face was as purple as her hair. "Den you vill let de villain know ve know! Ve must trup heem."

Maggie's ankle and cheek were both throbbing now. Irena's intensity was too much.

"What do you mean, 'We must trap him'?"

"Een my country ov Romania, ve know all about de bad gys. To find dem, ve lay de trup."

"What kind of trap?" asked Hank.

He was enjoying the idea of espionage. Life at Loving the Lord could be a little boring at times.

"First, ve dunt mention anyting to anybudy. Okey? Den, only ve five know vat has happened. Okey? Den, ve vatch and vait for anudder incidunt. Okey? Den, ve ketch de villain. Okey?"

Irena's facial animation, along with her ridiculous green, orange, and red makeup, was enough to give the Dalai Lama a seizure.

"Yes! I get it, Irena," Hank said. "We won't let the villain know that we are on to him *or* her. It could be a woman, you know. We will see if they try to break in again. So we need to make some kind of a secret pact, right? Just among the five of us?"

"No!" said all four women at the same time.

"Okay," he said, a little more subdued. "But we don't want word to get around, so we'll keep it quiet, right?"

"Yes," the women agreed.

"So we'll have 'sort of a pact,' right?" Hank pleaded.

The women sighed and nodded. Men were such boys.

Marla piped in. "I do think we should call Chief Tuggle. Someone broke into our church, and that is against the law. If we don't say something, we might be accomplices."

Irena was violently shaking her head *no*, but before she could begin another excruciating tirade, Maggie spoke.

"You're right, Marla. Hank, get Charlotte on the phone, please. Try to bypass Martha at the desk. She'll put this on the police radio for the whole world to hear. Say it's just church office business."

"Yesireebob! Pastor Maggie, I'm on it."

Hank went to his desk and called the Cherish Police Department.

The others watched Hank through the open door as he said, "Hi, Martha. This is Hank Arthur over at Loving the Lord. Is Chief Tuggle in please? . . . No, I don't want to leave a message . . . No, I'm not reporting anything . . ." Hank grimaced. "It's just church office business . . . Martha, is she in or not?" Long pause. "Hello, Chief Tuggle. This is Hank at church. We would like you to come down here for a little visit as soon as possible . . . No, I'd rather not say over the phone." Then he whispered loudly, "We don't want Martha to know . . . Okay, we'll see you soon."

Hank hung up the phone. He was sweating as he walked back into Maggie's office. Maybe this espionage stuff really wasn't his thing.

"Hank, on another matter." Maggie quickly switched gears. "I need you to send an email to the council members for a quick meeting tomorrow after the service. Please ask them to meet in my office."

"The last council meeting was just two nights ago. Why another meeting?" Hank asked.

"An issue," Maggie said with a slight edge to her voice.

"Is it that new cat yours?" Doris asked.

"What? How did you know?"

Maggie felt the pain in her foot and face and was now also just plain perturbed.

"I didn't. Just made a guess. So you've got another one, eh?"

"Yes. I do," Maggie said haltingly. "I found it abandoned at a gas station. It's very sick."

She was justifying her guilty self already.

"Ve eet de cats in Romania," Irena contributed, staring at her fingernail nonchalantly.

She mainly said it for shock value. It worked. Marla was appalled.

"Well, we don't eat cats here, Irena. Don't even think about it."

"If we're making a sort of a pact about the footprints," Maggie said, "can we please include the new kitten in the pact? Let me tell the council tomorrow, and then you can tell anyone you want."

Maggie wanted to get home and find her ibuprofen. She began to stand, but her ankle wouldn't let her.

"Ouch!" She immediately sat back down. *Drat!*

4

Charlotte Tuggle had been the police chief of Cherish for the past ten years. She was over six feet tall, weighed about two hundred fifty pounds, was fifty-seven years old, and was not to be messed with. She, along with her second officer, Bernie Bumble, did their best to keep Cherish crime free.

Charlotte arrived in her squad car but had the decency not to use the light or siren. She thumped into the church office, creaking from the leather of her gun holster and night stick strap. Her gold badge was proudly pinned to her chest, and her police hat was perched forebodingly on her head.

"Why in the world did I have to drive over here, Hank? I am an officer of the law. I don't have time for 'little visits' when I'm on duty." She turned to the rest of the crowd. "Good morning, Pastor Maggie, Doris, Marla, Irena. What's up?"

"Well, it appears there has been—" Maggie began.

"Mud everywhere!" Doris yelped.

"Ve vill ketch de villain," Irena chimed in.

"It was all very scary," Marla whispered.

"It's been quite a morning around here," Hank's low voice added.

All Charlotte heard was a cacophony of unintelligible words and voices.

"Halt!" Charlotte bellowed. "Pastor Maggie, you seem to be injured. Tell me why I'm really here."

Maggie was feeling a little sick to her stomach from the pain in her ankle and her face.

"Charlotte, it appears someone broke into the church. Doris found footprints in the basement that weren't there yesterday. One of the windows was unlocked." Maggie briefly finished the story, skimming through her fall through the folding chair. "We didn't want it to be in a public report. We are hoping to watch and see if it happens again." Then Maggie pandered a bit. "But we knew it was very important that *you* should know, Charlotte, because you are the police." Maggie sounded simpering and ridiculous, but apparently only to herself.

"You were right in calling me." Charlotte's ego was appropriately bolstered. "I'd like to take a look at the crime scene, if you please."

Charlotte was now in complete control.

Everyone except Maggie trooped back down to the basement. Charlotte examined the mud and the window. Unfortunately, after Maggie fell through the chair and everyone scrambled to help her, the footprints had been scattered in all directions. It just looked like a dirty floor. Charlotte wrote notes that no one could see on her ticket pad. Hank explained the "sort of pact" they had made in order to try and quietly catch the perpetrator.

"Well, let's all keep our eyes open around here," Charlotte said unnecessarily.

What else are we going to do? Keep our eyes closed? thought Doris.

"I'll write up a report, but I'll keep it under lock and key in my own desk. It won't get on the police radio, I guarantee it. Martha is vigilant about getting police news out to the masses. She thinks it helps curb crime." She looked around the cement room again. "Maybe this is the beginning and the end of it."

They all marched back upstairs.

"I'll be leaving now," Charlotte said. "See you all in church tomorrow."

She creaked out of the sanctuary door. The others went back to the office, glad to have Charlotte out of the way. They really felt they could handle it on their own.

Maggie had laid her head on her desk. Her ankle was aching even more now. The others turned their attention from Charlotte and footprints to their pastor.

"Pastor Maggie," Marla said gently, "maybe you should have your ankle looked at, don't you think? May I bring you to the emergency room?"

"No," Maggie said a little too harshly. "It's not an emergency."

"How about Dr. Elliot's office?" Marla persisted, determined to help the pastor she adored.

Maggie shook her head, although seeing Jack was all she wanted to do.

Against her will, kind of, they bundled Maggie into Marla's car. Hank, Doris, and Irena crammed themselves into the backseat as Marla drove over to Jack's office. Hank had already called Jack to give him a heads-up.

"Dr. Elliot said to meet him at his office. Because it's Saturday, the office is closed, so no one will see us sneak Pastor Maggie inside."

Hank reported this in low, serious tones. Maggie was beginning to think this sort of a pact idea might be going a little over the top.

Once they had snuck her inside the office building, Jack met them and kept his professional face in place as he checked Maggie's ankle. After hearing the how and why of the accident, he had to be let in on the sort of a pact too.

He wrapped Maggie's ankle, which was badly sprained. She felt an unexplainable embarrassment when the others saw Jack touch her, even if it was just her ankle. Jack was in total doctor-mode as he found her the right sized crutches from the storage room of his office. He also looked at the darkening bruise on her face and her now black eye. Those would take time to heal, as well as her ankle. He saved his personal comments for later in the parsonage and looked at the crowd in his office.

"So what's the story in church tomorrow as to why Pastor Maggie is battered and bruised? You can't tell people the real reason. You might tip off the villain."

He almost laughed as he said it, but he held it together. Who used the word *villain* anymore?

That got everyone thinking and talking at the same time. Again.

"We could say Pastor Maggie tripped over Marmalade and fell down the parsonage steps. Everyone knows how clumsy she is." That came from Hank.

"Maybe she was returning a wayward baby bird back to its nest and fell out of a tree." Doris contributed that fine piece of imagination.

"Well, we could say she stepped in a pothole on her run this morning, then tripped and fell." Marla spoke carefully, but it was obvious it went against her very core to tell a lie. Plus, she couldn't bear to think of Pastor Maggie hurt in any way.

"Ve cood say Doctoorr Juck hit herr in de fez. And pooshed herr," Irena said bluntly.

"Shut it, Irena!" Maggie barked.

By then the pain medication Jack had given Maggie was kicking in. She'd had enough of her workmates and the idiocy of the day, and she was ready to smack Irena in the "fez." Maggie never felt guilty about those feelings towards Irena. They were mutual, although each woman would walk through fire for the other if the need arose.

Jack said, "Maggie slipped at church and took a tumble. That's all that needs to be said. If people get nosy, just say, 'Using a folding chair as a stepping stool is a bad idea.' We will all be around in the morning to keep the gossips at bay. It's part of the sort of a pact. Now, I'll take Pastor Maggie home, and the rest of you practice your espionage faces for tomorrow."

"May I bring you some supper tonight, Pastor Maggie?" Marla asked, her small brown eyes searching earnestly.

Maggie could have cried at the kindness. Marla was one of those people who set aside her own life to care for others, whether they be friends or strangers. Occasionally, she could be taken advantage of.

"I'll take care of supper, but thank you, Marla," Jack said matter-of-factly.

Maggie grabbed Marla and whispered, "You are good for my soul, Marla. Thank you."

Jack got Maggie settled in the living room of the parsonage on the once-white-now-gray velvet couch. Marmalade and Cheerio, who had complete run of the house except for the study, were very curious about the large bandage on Maggie's ankle and even more curious about the crutches. Their noses went into overdrive.

Maggie was starting to feel sleepy. She cuddled into the couch with her blanket and pillow.

"I'll be back tonight with dinner," Jack said. "This is the second night in a row that I am bringing you dinner. Please remember this once you awake from your drug-induced sleep. I am a wonderful boyfriend."

"Yesh. You are . . . a . . . wonderful . . . husband." She drifted off to sleep.

Jack almost sat on Marmalade when he heard Maggie's last word. Husband.

Back at the church office, Hank, Doris, Marla, and Irena were hashing over the events of the morning. They had stopped at The Sugarplum Bakery across the street to gather sustenance of the heart-disease kind. Mrs. Polly Popkin owned and operated The Sugarplum. She was a solid five feet and nearly as round as she was tall. Her philosophy was, "If you can eat a donut, why wouldn't you?"

Mrs. Popkin greeted one and all with her own crazy catch phrase.

"Well, hokey tooters!" she had bellowed as the church crowd entered the bakery. "What are you folks up to? You don't often travel in a herd."

They'd told her about Pastor Maggie's fall, staying very vague about the details, and then changed the subject to what was in the pastry case. They ended up with a box of fat, calories, and deliciousness—a nice mix of maple donuts, cranberry bars, blueberry scones, banana cake, and frosted chocolate brownies.

Then they'd all settled in Hank's office, drinking a fresh pot of coffee as they ate their treats with deserved and satisfied gusto.

"It all goes back to whoever left those footprints on the floor," Doris said as she bit through the thick layer of chocolate butter frosting covering her brownie. "How did they get the window open from the outside? And why didn't they go any farther than the storage room?" Her teeth were covered in brown goo.

"Maybe they did," Marla said dramatically. "Maybe they saw the mud from their shoes and then took their shoes off before they went through the rest of the church. Have we looked to see if anything is missing?"

That brand-new line of thinking had them all in a kerfuffle.

"I was only looking for more dirt when I searched the church this morning," Doris said. "I didn't look to see if anything was actually missing. It never occurred to me."

"We should check the safe first," said Hank, standing up with his mouth full of banana cake.

They all marched to the closet in the back of Pastor Maggie's office. That was where the safe was kept and where the weekly offerings were held before they were taken to the bank on Monday. Hank quickly opened the lock on the safe. Only Hank, Harold Brinkmeyer (the chair of the council), Charlotte (the clerk of the council, as well as the police chief), and Redford Johnson (the chair of finance) knew the combination. Not even Pastor Maggie knew what it was, and she liked it that way.

As expected, the safe was empty because it was Saturday. The church offerings would have been brought to the bank the past Monday.

"We'll have to check again this coming Monday before Harold takes the money to the bank," Hank said. "But your idea is good, Irena. We won't let anyone know we are aware there's been an intruder. We'll catch whoever it is."

Unfortunately, Hank said this just loudly enough for the person standing outside the office door to hear. No one was there when the four accomplices returned to Hank's office a few moments later.

Maggie woke up to the sound of meowing. She was a little fuzzy in her brain, but she sat up, then tried to stand up before remembering she couldn't walk on her right foot.

"Ouch!" she cried and sat back down on the once-white-now-gray couch.

She could still hear the pitiful meowing. She reached for her crutches and hobbled over to the study door. Marmalade and Cheerio were both glued to the bottom of the door, growling at the meowing Fruit Loop on the other side. Maggie none-too-gently pushed them aside with her crutch. Then she opened the study door and watched Fruit Loop slowly creep out, tail down and ears up. Marmalade made a leap at him and was surprised to get a paw in the face. Fruit Loop gave a brave hiss. Maybe the liver and his medicine were doing some good. Maggie decided to let them all figure out their new life together. She was too tired, and in too much pain, to sort it out. The discussion of cat hierarchy commenced.

She crutched her way into the kitchen and was going to try to get upstairs to brush her teeth when she heard Jack come in through the back door. He was carrying a pizza box from It's Not Your Mama's Pizza pizza parlor. It smelled delicious. Maggie hadn't eaten anything since her oatmeal that morning.

"Pizza!" Her cranky mood changed immediately. "I'd kiss you, but I really need to brush my teeth. I just woke up, and now we have the cat Hunger Games going on around here."

Jack didn't get the connection between teeth brushing and cat Hunger Games because there wasn't one. He was learning about Maggie and her sometimes scattered thought processes.

"I'm kissing you anyway," Jack said nonchalantly as he carefully grabbed her and kissed her twice. "How are you feeling?"

"My ankle hurts. And so does my face," she said pathetically.

"I'm sure they do. It will take a few days for you to feel better, longer for your ankle. Are you up for preaching tomorrow?"

"Yes. I may cut it a bit short, but I can do it. I want to get the special council meeting over with after church and find out how much trouble I'm in for getting another kitten."

"Being on crutches will certainly help your cause. Just make sure to wince now and then, especially if Verna gets mouthy."

He laughed and grabbed plates and napkins from the cupboard, totally at ease in the parsonage kitchen.

Maggie and Jack feasted on pizza and Diet Coke. As they ate, they listened to the three felines hiss and chase their way to a truce of sorts. Maggie hoped it wouldn't take too long for peace to reign.

"Hey," Jack said, looking at Maggie's battered cheek and swollen eye. "You said something interesting when I was leaving today. Do you remember?"

"I have no idea," Maggie said, finishing her last bit of pizza crust. "Did I confess all of my darkest sins? It couldn't have been very exciting. I don't have a lot to report on that front."

"No, you didn't confess any sins. You maybe confessed something else. You said, uh . . ." He felt nervous all of a sudden, which wasn't normal for him. "You called me a wonderful *husband*."

Maggie didn't look embarrassed at all. Jack didn't know why he had expected her to.

"And?" she said, completely nonplussed.

"Uh . . . well . . . wow! I really don't know what to say." He was as ruffled as she had ever seen him.

"Does that make you nervous, Jack?" she said with a sly smile.

He took a deep breath. "No. Actually, it doesn't," he said. "Does it make you nervous?"

"No. Not at all. I haven't been nervous with you one single time since the very first evening we spent together after Mrs. Abernathy, I mean Mrs. Baker, tore the stitches in her back. You have always been comfortable to be with. I have been excited but never nervous. And now I feel like I know you. I know you so well that maybe I don't want to be your girlfriend anymore. A *girlfriend* is so high school, isn't it?" She laughed. "Maybe I would like to be more than a girlfriend. And maybe I would like it if you didn't have to go home after every one of our dates. Maybe I would like to be your wonderful *wife*. I already know you would be a wonderful husband."

"Maggie, are you proposing to me?" Jack asked, grinning.

5

When Maggie awoke Sunday morning, she once again forgot she didn't have two working ankles. She remembered when she put both feet on the floor and her right ankle screamed at her. She had set her alarm for six instead of four thirty, knowing she would not be able to run. Marmalade and Cheerio were on her bed, as usual. Fruit Loop was on her chair in the corner. At least they were all in the same room.

Maggie hobbled downstairs, brewed a Keurig Cup, and felt the pain in her face as she took the first swallow. *Drat!* She wondered what her cheek and eye looked like. She didn't want to check quite yet, so she made her oatmeal and banana and ate in pain.

Three yawning, stretching cats slunk into the kitchen. Fruit Loop didn't know exactly why he was there, but the other two knew it was breakfast time. Maggie filled their dishes, and Fruit Loop ate with typical relish. She also gave him his piece of liver with one of his pills smashed into it, which he slurped down before the other cats could even get curious.

Once tummies were full, Fruit Loop made a mad leap onto Cheerio's face. He then grabbed her with all four paws and rolled her over and over in lopsided somersaults. Cheerio screeched and hissed to no avail. Marmalade stared and then washed his face.

Maggie left the kitchen and the mini-war and slowly went back upstairs. The first look in the mirror showed a large purple bruise on her right cheek. Her right eye was also swollen. She washed her face, tried to use makeup to hide the bruise, and finally got dressed for the day. Then she limped pathetically downstairs with her crutches and went to her study to look over her sermon notes and her Sunday school lesson. After Sunday school and the church service, she would have the (hopefully) brief council meeting and then her first new members class. The day was already feeling too long.

Her Sunday school class would arrive at nine a.m., expecting donuts, and she planned to swear them all to secrecy regarding Fruit Loop. She wanted to be the one to tell the council—*ask* the council—about keeping the new kitten.

The Westminster chimes rang from the front door.

"Coming!" Maggie shouted as she crutched her way down the hallway.

The door opened, and Ellen stepped in carrying a large bakery box.

"Hi, Ellen," Maggie said, almost squealing.

"Pastor Maggie, I heard all about your tumble. I thought it might be easier if I brought donuts to you and your high schoolers rather than you trying to pick them up yourself. There are too many people at The Sugarplum, and they are a nosy bunch, as you well know. I couldn't see how you would be able to maneuver crutches and carry a bakery box, even though you are remarkable."

Ellen laughed. Maggie thought her friend's face made the world a nicer place.

"Thanks, Ellen. I was actually going to ask one of the kids to go get them. These crutches are a pain. Did Jack fill you in on everything?"

Maggie ushered Ellen into the family room/Sunday school room. Being cousins, and working in the same hospital, allowed Jack and Ellen to share just about everything. Ellen was secretly hoping to hear about an engagement between her cousin and her pastor (and dear friend) soon, but that morning it seemed she was unaware of the possibility of such news.

"So," Ellen said, "someone broke into the church. Folding chairs are dangerous weapons. The church staff has a sacred secret pact to catch the villain who has perpetrated this hooliganism." Ellen spoke melodramatically, and she and Maggie laughed at how ridiculous it all sounded.

"I have to say, I don't like the break-in part," Maggie said, "but we will be watching carefully now. You would have wet your pants listening to Irena as she set forth our undercover activities."

Maggie lifted the lid of the bakery box and snuck a maple donut. She pushed the box to Ellen, who also helped herself.

"How much are you going to tell the council?" Ellen asked.

"To be honest, I don't want to say too much, mainly because of Redford. I feel guilty for judging without cause, but I don't want him to know what's going on. I think we might be able to catch whoever it is if we wait. Irena was right about that."

"You won't have to worry about Redford today," Ellen responded. "He's gone for at least three weeks. He was bragging to Harold and me about some big fly-fishing trip he was leaving for, in Montana or Wyoming or someplace. I wasn't really paying attention. Redford is such an ass."

"Harold and you?" Maggie's one good eye widened.

Harold Brinkmeyer was an excellent lawyer and in high demand in Cherish. He was in his mid-thirties and had the sandy-blond, blue-eyed good looks of Ryan Gosling. He had a smile of perfect, pearly-white teeth that were swoon-worthy. Harold was the chairperson of the council and utterly reliable. His crush on Maggie last summer was never made public, so when Maggie told him she wasn't interested, they were able to keep their friendship and their working relationship intact. Harold was one person Maggie wanted to find a match for. Partly because she thought he was a nice guy, partly out of guilt for turning him down.

Ellen laughed. "Yes, oh nosy one. Harold and I had lunch on Wednesday at O'Leary's. Redford was there, drinking his lunch, as usual. He came over to our table, interrupted our lunch, and made a rude comment."

Maggie looked at her quizzically.

Ellen sighed. "He said if Harold couldn't have you, he might as well settle for me. Then he bragged about his stupid fishing trip and stumbled away. That's my sweet, Christian Love take on it." Ellen sounded a little more rueful now.

Harold must have told Ellen about his crush on Maggie last summer, and Redford had seen them eating lunch at O'Leary's the day Maggie was arrested for too many parking tickets.

Oops. Oh, well. Good for Harold. He is honest.

"Everything Redford says is poison," Maggie said, moving right along. "I'm glad you and Harold had lunch. Whatever that means for you two. I hope it means something couple-ish. He's wonderful and intelligent, and he looks like Bradley Cooper. He's not Jack, of course, but who is?" Maggie smiled.

Ellen knew Harold had done his best to win Maggie's attention and affection last year, but Maggie was never interested. Ellen had found Harold to be all the things Maggie said he was. She wouldn't say no to another lunch invitation.

"Anyway," Ellen said. "Redford left on Thursday, I think, and won't be back until the end of September. It will be nice not to have him creeping around."

Maggie agreed. The past January, Redford had crashed her surprise birthday party at the church. He interrupted the festivities by coming into the church drunk and spewing vulgarities in front of the entire congregation, Maggie's family, and Ed and Jo—not to mention making not-so-thinly veiled threats to sexually assault her later in her home. He wanted to scare her, and he succeeded. Maggie had avoided him as much as possible since that time. It was difficult just to see him around town. Those were the times she needed Ed and his wisdom.

Maggie jumped to another thought.

"If Redford left on Thursday, there's no way he could have made the muddy footprints in the church on Friday night. I have to admit, he was my first suspect in this whole thing. Bad Maggie!"

"He would have been my first suspect too, but he wasn't even in Cherish. Maybe more of the council should know the story since he's gone for a while."

"You're right," Maggie said thoughtfully.

Just then, Fruit Loop chased Cheerio into the room. Cheerio's fur was completely catawampus as she tried to get away from her furry little mugger, who was having the time of his life.

"Oh my gosh! Who is this?" Ellen gasped.

"Oh, that's Fruit Loop. That's the original reason we are having a quick council meeting after church. I found him at a gas station on Friday. He could hardly move then, but he has found another one of his nine lives it seems."

Maggie smiled at the little kitten lovingly, always a pushover when it came to animals.

"He looks like Tabby," Ellen said.

Ellen was the proud owner of Cheerio's little brother, Tabby. Their mother had been killed by a car the year before. Maggie took Cheerio, then forced Verna (Abernathy) Baker to take the other little calico— oddly named Caroline by Verna herself.

"Yes, he does. I want to keep him, so I thought I should just bite the bullet and have a meeting right away before the gossip starts," Maggie said with resignation.

Fruit Loop had a hold of Cheerio's back leg and gave it a bite. Cheerio squealed, hissed, and ran out of the room looking for her absent foster "mother," Marmalade. What was the kitty world coming to?

Maggie and Ellen heard the high school students come through the back door, so Ellen rose to leave.

"Maybe we can talk more this afternoon," she said.

"Do you want to come over for popcorn tonight?"

"I'll be here at six o'clock."

Ellen left through the front door to avoid the teenagers.

Maggie's original students were Addie and Jason Wiggins—Marla's children—along with Chief Charlotte Tuggle's three: twin boys, Brock and Mason, and daughter, Liz. But word had gotten out that Pastor Maggie did a cool animal blessing service in the fall and her sermons weren't too long. Most importantly, she had donuts every week at Sunday school. That good news meant friends of her students were now joining the Sunday school class and participating in church services. There had been new, non-feline additions to her Sunday school class in the last year.

Maggie was having her class prepare for a youth Sunday in the fall. It had been a successful service the past year, and Maggie decided to make it an annual event. It was also her sneaky way of getting the parents of the new students to come to church. If the parents enjoyed youth Sunday, they might come back. Maggie felt the unfair pressure to "grow the church," but she was really the only one putting on the pressure.

Sunday school that day went well because of the distraction of the new kitten. Her students knew Maggie was an animal freak, but they all liked the cats in the manse.

"Oh, look!" squealed Addie when Fruit Loop had come tearing through the Sunday school room as soon as they arrived. "Pastor Maggie, who is that?"

Addie Wiggins was a senior at Cherish High School. She was a beautiful girl, tall and athletic, and was a captain on the girls' tennis team. She had deep-brown eyes rimmed with an abundance of black lashes, and her long, wavy, brown hair was always brushed neatly into a ponytail that hung down her back. Like her mother, Marla, Addie loved children and was a favorite babysitter for many families in Cherish. Addie's gentle demeanor, creativity, and basic good manners made her stand out from other high school students. Maggie was already mourning the fact that it would be Addie's last year in Sunday school. A year from that fall, Addie would begin college and a whole new life.

Even the groggiest students were alert as the kitties jumped and rolled their way into the room. All eyes were on Fruit Loop.

"That is a big secret, and I need you to take a blood oath that you won't tell your parents until after the council meeting today," Maggie said.

No one had seemed to notice her bandaged ankle or her crutches. Or even her face.

"But who is it?" demanded Liz.

"His name is Fruit Loop. That's all you need to know. But I haven't told the council yet. Did you all hear me say that?" Maggie asked a little more loudly.

"Yes, yes, yes," they all mumbled as they watched Fruit Loop jump into the bakery box.

Maggie deftly removed him by the scruff of his neck and set him on the floor, but he jumped back in.

"Addie, could you please put him in my study?" Maggie asked.

That's when they all noticed her incapacitation.

"Pastor Maggie, what happened to you?" Brock asked, staring at her ankle.

"And what happened to your face?" asked Mason.

Everyone was staring now.

Addie quickly put the kitten in Maggie's study. She and Jason already knew the story, at least part of it. Their mother had told them and their father last night at dinner. Charlotte's children were clueless. She never shared police or church business with them.

"I fell through a folding chair, sprained my ankle, and bashed my face. That's it."

Maggie attempted a laughed. Then she quickly dove into the Sunday school lesson.

Following Sunday school, Maggie crutched her way across the lawn to church. She got to her office before having to stop and talk with anyone. She was sure the Cherish phone lines had been on fire the night before as news of Pastor Maggie falling through a folding chair and spraining her ankle made the rounds.

When Irena finished her prelude—a fanfare on "Joyful, Joyful We Adore Thee," one which she composed herself—Maggie stood up with her crutches and faced her congregation.

"This is the day the Lord has made. Let us rejoice and be glad in it!" she said with too much exuberance. "I believe you have all heard how I fell through a folding chair yesterday and sprained my ankle. I'll be moving a little more slowly for the next few days, but there is no permanent damage."

She made her way through the service, shortened her sermon, and at ten fifty, instead of eleven o'clock, the service was finished. She announced the special council meeting to be held in her office immediately after the service and then hobbled her way through the "secret" door attaching the sanctuary to the church offices—at least she liked to pretend it was a secret door to add some intrigue to her life.

Sitting in her office, she could hear Irena belting out the postlude as the congregation made their way to the table of cookies, coffee, and punch. Slowly, the council members trickled into her office. Sylvia Baxter, Marla, and her husband, Tom, were the first to arrive. Verna Baker was next, followed by Harold, Charlotte, Ellen, and Jack.

Once they were all together, Maggie asked, "Charlotte, are you taking minutes?"

"Of course, Pastor Maggie. Ready to write."

Charlotte gave Maggie a knowing and conspiratorial nod. She was holding something that looked like her ticket pad, but it was filled with blank paper instead of tickets. Her pen was poised.

Harold began the meeting with condolences for Maggie's ankle. Then he turned it over to her. She was sitting while everyone else was standing, and she didn't like feeling shorter than usual.

"There are two issues to discuss today. Jack, would you please shut the door?"

He complied, and Maggie dove right in.

"The first issue is this: I would like permission to add a kitten to the parsonage. I found another little victim at a gas station on Friday."

She held her breath. Everyone slyly turned their eyes toward Verna.

Verna looked at the quiet council members and then turned her gaze on Maggie.

"Apparently, this council has gone mute. What is your new cat's name?"

Maggie nearly choked in surprise. That was the last thing she had expected from Verna. Maggie slowly realized she was looking at an ally, not an adversary.

"His name is Fruit . . . Loop." Maggie heard herself and cringed. *What a ridiculous name.*

Verna kept her composure, but Maggie could see the hint of a smile in her eyes.

"Why do you name your animals after food?" Verna asked.

"I . . . uhh . . . think it's cute," Maggie said, fighting back a laugh.

"It is," Verna said. "So, what is the second issue?"

Now everyone laughed. Verna had played them all. She seemed to enjoy having that kind of power. Pretending to be the church crank was fun.

Maggie reigned in her smile to move on to the second topic.

"This next issue must remain highly confidential. Irena, Hank, and Doris know of it because they were here yesterday. Charlotte knows because she is our chief of police, and we called her right away."

Maggie glanced quickly at Marla, who smiled and nodded. Charlotte also nodded gravely.

"It appears someone broke into the church sometime Friday night or early Saturday morning. One of the windows in the basement storage room was unlocked, although the other window and the door were secured. Muddy footprints were found only on the floor in the storage room."

Charlotte picked up the narrative. "Nothing seems to be missing from the church. We are keeping this quiet for now, but we will watch and see if there are any more incidents. Again, please don't mention this to anyone. I will give you updates, if there are any."

The council members were quiet. Then Tom Wiggins spoke.

"I recommend changing all locks on the doors and windows of the church and parsonage. It may seem excessive, but I know there are spare keys floating around in the congregation. We also know Pastor Maggie received a threat from a person on this council who is not present here today. I will donate the locks and see if Bill Baxter will help me get the work done."

"Thanks for that, Tom," Harold said. "Both the idea and your generosity. What do you all think? Discussion?"

Sylvia, newlywed wife of Bill Baxter and owner of The Garden Shop, spoke first.

"I hear it's never good to volunteer your spouse for anything. However, I know Bill will be happy to help. Also, once we have a set number of new keys, there should be a system for those not on staff or on the council to access a key and therefore the church. I think we have always been so trusting around here that most of the parishioners have a key in a junk drawer somewhere, whether they know it or not. It's too bad this has marred that trust."

Everyone felt the same way. It had been a violation of their church and their church family.

Verna coughed and said, "I think the work of changing the locks should be done undercover, so to speak. I realize people drop by the church office at all times, but the fewer people, or should I say, the less *a specific person* knows about what we're doing, the better."

This is so G.M. Malliet! thought Maggie with a little thrill. Then she returned to reality and said, "Charlotte, how does that sound to you? We'll casually replace the locks and also keep our eyes open for anything suspicious."

"Good work, that's what this is," Charlotte said, looking appreciatively around the room. "Officer Bumble and I will make our regular drives around town in the squad car but also do extra reconnaissance here at the church. If someone is up to mischief, we'll find them. I recommend this council report does not get circulated. Pastor Maggie, I'll give you a copy. That's it for now."

"Where is Redford Johnson today?" Verna asked.

Ellen briefly told everyone about Redford's fishing trip out West. She tried not to look at Harold while she was talking but couldn't help it. She gave him a quick smile and then looked away.

"So, Redford should be out of town for at least the next three weeks," Ellen concluded.

"We all heard Redford threaten Pastor Maggie at her birthday party," Verna said. "He hasn't been in church for weeks, and it seems he's not even carrying out his financial duties now that Harold and Fred

Tuggle are assisting him. I support the lock changes and add this: Redford should not receive a new key until we know his intentions regarding church membership and the carrying out of his council responsibilities. I must say, it's providential he's out of town for a few weeks while we get this lock business taken care of." She gave a terse nod of her head.

Everyone quietly agreed. The difficulty was this: how was the church supposed to love one of its members who made it as difficult as Redford did?

"All in favor of the new lock plan, say aye." Harold was back in charge.

Everyone said, "Aye."

Jack spoke up. "Harold, would it be smart to take this morning's offering and put it in a different safe, perhaps in your office, until you can get to the bank tomorrow morning?"

"Good idea, Jack," Harold agreed. "Ellen, will you count the offerings with me now?"

Church policy said that there always needed to be two people when counting the money. Somehow the council had let that slide over the last year or so. Redford had been counting alone for several months. That was worrisome since some church members gave their offerings in cash.

They all left the meeting a little subdued.

Jack quietly told Tom he would work on the locks in the parsonage.

"I'm there regularly. It won't look so suspicious."

Tom agreed. He wanted to get the job done, but he wondered what the intruder was up to. He believed none of the staff should be alone in the church until the locks were changed.

Tom found Bill at the cookie table in the gathering area.

"I need your help with a project around here," he said.

"My wife just whispered something in my ear. And it wasn't romantic," Bill said.

"Can you come by my store sometime tomorrow?"

"I'll be there when you open the door in the morning."

6

The day before Maggie rescued Fruit Loop in Lansing, Michigan, Clara Abbott was running the front desk of the Mountain Peak Lodge in Big Sky, Montana. It had been her summer job the past three years as she worked her way through college. Now that she was a graduate, she was staying on for the year to hone her hospitality skills. Clara had become a favorite of the owners of the lodge during her first summer there. When the other college students spent a little too much time at the bar and not enough time making sure the guests were properly cared for, Clara picked up extra shifts and covered for the immaturity of her peers. She also had the gift of remembering names. Guests were amazed, and their egos boosted, when Clara greeted them by name after checking them in the day before.

That last Thursday afternoon of August was particularly busy as people were enjoying their final vacations before the end of summer. Clara's short, brown hair looked tousled as she worked to check people in and out of the lodge. She had been on duty for ten hours that day already, thanks to the hangover of another college employee, but her blue eyes were bright, and her mouth knew how to smile, even when she was exhausted.

"May I help you, sir?" Clara asked the next guest.

She looked up to see a disheveled man with dark hair, eyes that seemed to swim in their sockets, and breath that smelled like a mini-distillery.

"Johnson," he slurred.

He seemed to be trying to make eye contact but failed miserably.

"Welcome to the lodge, Mr. Johnson," Clara said with forced hospitality. "Let me look up your reservation." Clara's fingers typed rapidly until she found it. "You are booked into the Fisherman's Delight cabin, right on the river. And you're here for over three weeks. What a nice vacation for you. I'll have a porter bring your luggage and fishing gear to the cabin for you. Now I just need your driver's license and a credit card."

"I don't need a porter." He growled.

His hand dug into his pocket so fiercely, Clara thought it might go all the way through. He haphazardly dropped his credit card on the counter while fumbling for his license, slid it across the counter too fast for Clara to catch, and the card flew onto the floor. He laughed as she retrieved the card.

He had a mean laugh.

"Oh, I see you're from Michigan," Clara said, smiling. "I know a little bit about Michigan."

She was ready to elaborate when she looked up at Mr. Johnson's surly face, so she remained quiet.

Clara ran the credit card and watched the machine. She swiped the card again and watched. Then she looked up and said in a low voice, "Mr. Johnson, I'm afraid your card has been declined. Would you like to try a different card?"

"No. I'll pay cash," he said gruffly.

"Well, our policy is to have a credit card on file for incidentals."

Clara smiled, but her voice was serious. She had dealt with that issue several times with other guests over the summers.

Mr. Johnson dug through his wallet and threw down another card. "Here. Use this."

Clara looked at the card. It couldn't be right, but she ran it through the machine, and it was accepted. Her smile faded as she handed Mr. Johnson his key card and a map of the lodge and surrounding areas.

"Have a pleasant stay," she said, feeling confused and annoyed all at the same time.

"Where's the bar?" he asked, breathing noxious fumes into her face.

"In the restaurant, sir. It's the large building just outside the lobby door and to the right."

She put her head down and held her breath, in case he spoke again or just breathed in her direction.

Mr. Johnson took both his credit card and key without looking up. He left the map on the counter and staggered out of the lobby, narrowly missing the woman standing behind him.

Clara sighed deeply. The day needed to end. But before she helped the next guest, Clara quickly jotted down the information she remembered from the credit card. She would check into that later.

Redford Johnson had found his way to his Fisherman's Delight cabin. It took a while because of his detour to the bar. He topped off the drinks he'd had on the plane with a few more for good measure and effortlessly charged them to his cabin. He might as well live it up.

"How long are you here for?" the bartender had asked.

"Three and half weeksh," Redford mumbled.

"Are you here to fish?"

"I'm *here* to drink." Redford pushed his glass across the bar for another whiskey.

After Sunday's worship and the council meeting, before Maggie could get to the new members class, Jack gently took her elbow.

"How are you feeling?" he asked.

"Rushed. Minor pain in my ankle and face. Sad about the break-in."

"I'll have lunch ready at the parsonage when you finish this class. We'll talk more then."

Jack gently squeezed her hand and left.

Maggie crutched her way to the nursery where the new class was gathering. When she got there, she saw two of her favorite people.

"Pasto Maggie, Pasto Maggie!"

Carl Moffet came running from the toys and almost barreled right into Maggie. Four-year-old Carl was followed closely by his big sister,

Carrie, who was six. Carrie and Carl were both blonde-haired, blue-eyed little munchkins full of giggles. They melted Maggie's heart on sight.

Carrie, Carl, and their mother, Cassandra, lived on Maggie's running route. Cassandra was a large woman who wore flowing blouses or bulky sweaters. She had a mane of unruly, long, blonde hair, which looked like it had never seen a brush, and she wore no makeup. She often looked as if she had just tussled with a small tornado. The tornado always seemed to have won.

Over time, Maggie had come to see that Cassandra was a "distracted" mother. Cassandra had accepted Maggie's initial invitation to come to church over a year ago, but since then it seemed to have turned into a convenient childcare center for her children.

At last year's Christmas pageant, the whole church was horrified when Carrie's sheep costume had caught fire from one of the Advent candles, and she'd suffered terrible burns to her scalp and ear. Her ear had been left permanently deformed. The church had surrounded the family with food, toys, and care, and Cassandra had come to depend on the church to watch over, discipline, and adore her children. Although Carrie and Carl were adorable, they reacted to the lack of mothering, as children often do, by acting out and running a bit wild.

Maggie and her parishioners were in the difficult position of being "the church." They loved Carrie, in her tutus and tiaras, and little Carl, whose shyness endeared him to everyone. But a dilemma arose. Cassandra had begun to need free babysitters regularly. The parishioners had a hard time saying no. How was the church supposed to deal with such a challenging situation? Marla seemed to take the brunt of Cassandra's requests. Carrie and Carl were regular fixtures at Marla's home and were often with her at church while she was working.

Seeing them in the nursery that morning, and wondering who was in charge of them at that moment, made Maggie wish for Ed's guidance. He would know exactly what to do. A pang in her heart overrode the pain in her ankle. There were still times when remembering his death could take her breath away. If Ed were alive, Maggie would let him know that the seminary had never taught her how to deal with that kind of Cassandra situation. Maggie had a running list of what seminary didn't teach her.

What she didn't understand was that no seminary could totally prepare a future pastor for what would come in each unique ministerial experience. The Redfords and Cassandras of the world were in every church. They came in a wide variety of shapes and personalities.

For Maggie, loving the unlovable was a difficult challenge, especially when the unlovable hurt or used the rest of the flock. When she tried to make sense of that, it was as if her soul were on crutches.

As the children ran to greet her, Maggie bent forward awkwardly before Carrie and Carl could knock her over.

"Hi, you two," she said, kissing each one of the top of their heads.

"Pastor Maggie, does your leg hurt?" Carrie asked.

"Yes. It's my ankle, actually. But Dr. Elliot gave me these crutches, so I feel a little better."

"Dr. Elliot made me all better after my head got burned," Carrie said solemnly.

Carl nodded. It had been quite traumatic for him when his sister was in the hospital and then came home with a huge, white gauze bandage on her head. Dr. Elliot was a hero in their eyes.

"Dr. Elliot is a wonderful doctor, isn't he?" Maggie smiled as she thought of Jack.

"Yes, he is. He gave me yummy medicine."

Carrie smiled and twirled. She was an excellent twirler.

Maggie could see her new members class gathered in a circle of chairs behind the children.

"I need to begin a class right now," she said. "Maybe you should find your mommy."

"We're going home with Mrs. Wiggins today," Carrier reported. "We're having lunch there and watching a movie with Addie. *Frozen!*"

Maggie smiled wanly. "Well, lucky you. Where is your mommy?"

She wasn't above using the children to find out what Cassandra was up to.

"She's busy," was Carrie's unhelpful answer.

7

The children bounced out of the nursery like happy little flyaway bubbles when they saw Addie.

Maggie couldn't think about the Cassandra problem right then. She hobbled her way across the room, feeling pain not only in her ankle and cheek but now in her unsuspecting armpits, which were not used to being jammed repeatedly by rubber-covered wood.

She sat down and smiled at the circle of faces staring expectantly at her. She was happy to see three familiar faces among the larger group. Dr. Dana Drake was there, as were Ethan and Charlene Kessler. Ethan was a professor, and Charlene was one of Jack's family practice partners.

As a pastor, Maggie was thrilled to have a group of seven people spend part of their Sunday sitting in the church nursery for the sole purpose of wanting to join the church. Hurrah for church growth! Although she felt preoccupied with the break-in, her future with Jack, and her physical pain, she just had to "shake it off," as Taylor Swift commanded. So she did.

"Hi, everyone. I'm Pastor Maggie, and I'm so thrilled you're here today. I apologize for the delay, but let's get started. This first week we will get to know each other. We'll continue to meet for the next three weeks—same place, same time. We will have our new members service and reception at the end of September."

Maggie felt as if she were talking too fast, sounding like Alvin the Chipmunk. She took a deep breath.

She gave a little personal background and went on to talk enthusiastically about the new church ministry she was most excited about. Loving the Lord would be partnering with the non-profit organization her brother, Bryan, worked for called Africa Hope. She explained that Africa Hope set up sustainable projects in several African countries and communities.

"Our church is raising money to send to different projects. We are forming a small group of our parishioners to make an actual trip to Ghana to work in an orphanage and hopefully build a school for the children of the community. We are gathering supplies to take to Ghana and also for Bryan to bring to other countries. These are items unavailable for purchase in those countries."

Maggie took another deep breath.

"I'm happy to answer questions you may have about any of this, but I've talked enough. Let's go around the circle and get to know everyone else."

Maggie smiled again, having forgotten about the pain in her various body parts. She looked at Dana.

"Hi. I'm Dana Drake. I am a vet here in town at Cherish Your Pets Animal Hospital. I've lived and worked in Cherish the past six years. I haven't been in a church in a long time, but I was intrigued when I heard that Pastor Maggie did an animal blessing service last fall. It took me awhile, but here I am."

Dana smiled, tossing her black ponytail, and looked to her left.

A couple, who appeared to be in their mid-fifties, smiled at the circle around them. He spoke first.

"We are William and Mary Ellington. We own The Grange, a bed and breakfast just east of town. It had always been a dream of ours to have our own bed and breakfast, and once our children were out on their own, we quit our jobs, moved to Cherish from Ann Arbor, and made our dream come true."

He looked at his wife. Mary continued.

"We've been running The Grange for the last four years. It's a lot of work, but worth it. Our only struggle will be getting to church when we have guests staying for the weekend. But you will see us here at every opportunity."

She dimpled, which immediately made everyone else smile, but Maggie saw something in Mary's eyes. They didn't smile when her mouth did.

Next to Mary was an elderly gentleman. Maggie guessed he was in his seventies. He had a full head of thick, white hair, all standing up on end. Maggie desperately wanted a comb and a tube of hair gel to get it under control. *Oh, well.* He had pale-blue eyes set in a long, thin face. His teeth were slightly crooked, which gave him a lopsided, cheerful look.

"I'm Winston Chatsworth. My friend Howard Baker invited me to worship because he said the pastor was pretty." He laughed. "Howard was right, of course, but he forgot to say that she could preach like nobody's business. My dad was a Lutheran minister, and I've heard it all. I heard so much when I was young that I decided to take a break for a few decades. Now I'm back. My wife died almost ten years ago. She was the love of my life." Winston took out an oversized hanky and wiped his nose with a sniff. "She had always wanted me to get back to church. I was a mean old coot and wouldn't do it. I hope she's smiling now because here I am."

He honked into his hanky and then put his head down.

"I'm so glad you're here," Maggie said, feeling his embarrassment and wanting to make it disappear immediately. "Howard is a handful. I will appreciate any help you can give me to keep him in line."

Winston looked up.

"I'll keep an eye on him, Pastor Maggie. Although I think that new wife of his definitely gives him his marching orders, not to mention keeping him in line."

Maggie smiled to herself when she thought of Verna keeping Howard "in line." Howard had surprised Verna the past spring by falling in love with her. Howard, the "church flirt," had decided it was time

Verna, the "church crank," should be un-cranked. He had been just the man to do it.

Ethan and Charlene Kessler had been coming regularly for the last few months. In fact, it had been Charlene who asked when Maggie would be leading a new members class. Of course, Maggie hadn't even thought of doing such a thing. Drat the seminary, once again. Charlene was a spunky brunette and Jack's partner at the doctor's office. She was loved by her patients and coworkers. Maggie liked her sense of humor.

Ethan was an African studies professor at the University of Michigan. He enjoyed teaching, and Maggie had heard from Cate Carlson, a soon-to-be sophomore at the U of M and a huge Pastor Maggie fan, that he "wasn't even boring!"

Ethan and Charlene had a twelve-year-old daughter, Kay, and a ten-year-old son, Shawn. From Maggie's perspective, Ethan and Charlene were excellent parents. They seemed to be in complete and consistent control, but able to have lots of fun with their children. Maggie loved watching them in action on the several occasions she and Jack spent time with them. Maybe Charlene could give Cassandra some mothering tips.

"We are excited for the mission trip to Ghana," Charlene said. "We're both planning to go. I'll help Dr. Elliot with a small medical clinic."

"And I want to learn about the new school they're building for the children at the orphanage," Ethan added.

Neither Ethan nor Charlene took themselves too seriously. They believed being a professor and a medical doctor were not elite badges to wear, but a responsibility to do as much good in the world as possible. They took their work and their faith seriously. The mission trip had caught their attention immediately when Maggie and Jack first mentioned it to them last winter. Maggie knew they would be crucial members of the team due to their skills and their temperaments.

Maggie also knew that Marla was just about having kittens trying to figure out what to do with Kay and Shawn for Sunday school. They were too old for Marla's elementary class and too young for Maggie's high school class. Maggie thought that was a nice problem to have.

The last person in the circle introduced herself. Her voice was light, airy, and a little dreamy. She looked as if she were over six feet tall, the way her long legs were wrapped around each other, and as if she weighed one hundred pounds soaking wet.

"Hi," the woman said melodically, if one syllable can be melodic. "My name is Skylar Breese."

Willowy was the only word to describe her. She had curly, blonde hair cascading in a perfect waterfall down her back, almond-shaped gray eyes, and perfectly straight, chemically whitened teeth. She also looked as if she were completely dressed in scarves, though it was actually a dress.

Maggie immediately and desperately coveted a shorter version of that dress. She wondered what it was like to be that tall, that thin, and that lovely.

The delicate fairy woman spoke again.

"I own the Pretty, Pretty Petals Flower Shop, down Main Street past the hair salon. Mmmm . . . Sylvia Smits and I have known each other since high school. Oops, I mean Sylvia Baxter." Sky laughed, and it sounded like wind chimes on a gentle breeze. "I moved away for a while to go to school and mmm . . . see the world." As she spoke, Skylar looked upward, which gave everyone the opportunity to see her incredibly long eyelashes. "Recently, Sylvia told me about her garden shop, but . . . mmm . . . she didn't seem to have enough time to grow everything and then sell and deliver flowers too. I do that part . . . mmm." Her sentence faded away on a breathy cloud of distraction. "Oh!" She came back to life. "You can call me Sky."

"Hello, Sky, and welcome to Loving the Lord." Maggie thought that sounded a bit like an AA meeting. "Did Sylvia invite you to church?"

"What? Oh . . . oh, yes, she did. I like it here."

She was off again in some other world.

"Well, I want to welcome you all here today. As I said at the beginning, we will continue to meet over the next three Sundays and get to know each other and the church better. I'm glad you have found Loving the Lord a good place to be. It is certainly my hope that you will continue to do so."

They closed the first session with each person sharing a story of their happiest birthday remembrance. Maggie had thought that might be a fun way for a group of strangers to get to know each other. She was right. There was much laughing over the individual remembrances. By the end of it all, Maggie was worn out. She was happy to bid the new members class farewell, say a prayer of thanksgiving, lock the sanctuary doors, and hobble her way to the parsonage and Jack.

Jack had picked up sandwiches and fruit salad at the deli and had set the table. When Maggie hobbled through the door, he handed her three ibuprofen tablets and a glass of water. She looked at the table and saw a large bouquet of red carnations.

"Carnations? Thank you, Jack," she said with a tired smile. She buried her nose in the spicy smell of the flowers. "Hey, are you always perfect? I don't think I can keep up with a perfect man, having so many deficits myself."

"Take your ibuprofen and sit down. No, I am not perfect. I just hide my very few flaws from you, which is easy because you are so gullible and obviously think I'm flawless."

"Yes. That is true. I guess you are flawless. Now tell me the truth. Do you have any faults at all? Have you ever had a bad day?"

Jack sighed. "Okay. Here it is. I get frustrated with patients who don't do what their doctor tells them to do. I get angry when cardiologists and orthopedic surgeons think they rule the world. My sister Anne would tell you that I'm not always good at expressing my feelings. I hate messes. When I begin a project, I like to finish it without interruption. Now sit down, woman, and put your ankle on this chair. Did you not hear my first fault?" Jack led her to the table and propped her ankle on one of the kitchen chairs with a pillow. "Now eat!"

Maggie laughed. Every one of his deficits seemed like a charm on a bracelet to her. She wondered if that would ever change.

"By the way, *you* don't have any deficits," he said as he unwrapped the sandwiches.

Fortunately, only the cats overheard the interchange. Anyone else would have been completely nauseated.

"How was the new members class?" he asked, opening a bag of potato chips.

"It was great. I had no idea there would be so many in the class." She told him about the four people he didn't know. "I think they will all fit into our funny little church."

"It makes a lot of work for you, but it's good for the church and for the new members themselves. They have no idea what fun they're in for under your leadership."

She didn't notice he was looking at her intensely. She just wanted to eat.

As Maggie reached for half of her turkey and cucumber sandwich, she took a gulp of Diet Coke. Jack put his hand on hers.

"About last night. Let's talk about your proposal," Jack said abruptly.

Maggie almost sent Diet Coke through her nostrils with a gigantic snort. She wiped her mouth and nose with a napkin and looked Jack in the eyes.

"Wasn't it mutual?" she asked. "Didn't we sort of propose together?"

"Contrary to what my family might believe possible, I'm going to completely express my feelings now," he said very carefully. "I love you, Maggie. I don't want to be your boyfriend anymore. I'm tired of having a clumsy, emotional, badly dressed girlfriend. I want a clumsy, emotional, badly dressed wife. Maggie Elzinga, will you marry me?"

Maggie dropped her sandwich. She looked at Jack and saw just the smallest evidence of a tear forming in his left eye. Her eyes filled rapidly and her bottom lip quivered ever so slightly.

"I thought I, uh, didn't have any deficits?" she said, smiling as she blinked away her tears. Then she wriggled her way out of her chair and onto Jack's lap. "I will marry you, Jack. And here are my vows. I vow to be overly disappointed in patients who don't follow your orders. I vow to look with disdain upon all cardiologists and orthopedic surgeons who think they're God. I will help you try on different emotions and then guide you into succinctly expressing them to me. I vow to make messes for you to clean up, in order to give you a sense of purpose. And I vow not to interrupt you, unless absolutely necessary, while you're completing a project."

She ended her vows with a sniff and a kiss, which was returned in kind.

Jack carefully moved her back onto her chair and replaced her ankle on the pillow.

"Would you like some fruit?" he asked, breaking the mood.

"Sure," she said, confused at the abrupt change.

He passed her a round, plastic container. She pulled off the lid and took a deep breath. There sat a small velvet box. She was not prepared for the sharp pang of emotion that hit her heart when she held the box in her hand. Their proposal conversation had been lighthearted, bordering on goofball, although they both knew it was underpinned by the true meaning of what their future would be together.

She stared at the small box. That was just plain romance. She opened the lid.

Nestled in the velvet was a ring she knew she would wear for the rest of her life. That fact meant more to her than the beauty of the extraordinary diamond sparkling up at her. Jack took it out of the box and slid it onto her ring finger. The tears in her eyes made it look even sparklier.

Maggie looked at Jack as he cleaned up after their lunch.

"I'm so happy right now," she said. "Bryan's coming to stay for a week, the mysteries of Ghana await, and I'm getting married. Have I mentioned that? Because, I am! I am getting married. I am an engaged person."

Marmalade, Cheerio, and Fruit Loop had all been hanging around the kitchen, hoping for something out of the lunch bag. They weren't fighting at the moment.

"Look, kitties. Look at my pretty ring!"

The kitties, who were hoping for cat treats from the proffered hand, were extremely unimpressed by the ring.

Jack looked at her and said, "You're a nut. I love you."

"So . . ." she began.

Jack held his breath. He knew what was coming.

"Who shall we tell first? Do we want to tell anyone yet? What kind of wedding ceremony would you like to have? Short? Long? Should we write our own vows or use traditional? I like the traditional vows. When would you like to be married? Who is going to marry us? Will your parents be happy? Can we go on a honeymoon? Oh, dear! Where are we going to live? Here in the parsonage, or in your condo? Maybe both? Maybe our mission trip to Ghana should be our honeymoon. How should we tell the church? Shall we tell the council first? The staff?" She paused. "I'm feeling a little tired."

"Good. We will have time to answer every question. Just not all of them today. Would you like to call your parents, or would you rather tell them in person?"

Jack sat back down at the table near her. Maggie sighed with happy thoughts.

"To be honest, I can't imagine driving over to Zeeland with this ankle. Should we just keep it our own delicious secret for a bit?"

"Sure. I think you'll be up and around in a week or so, if you keep your ankle elevated as much as possible. This is going to be fun," he said with a grin. "We'll keep it just between us until your ankle is healed. Then we can tell our families first, in person, and see where it goes from there. I'm sure you would like to tell Jo James in person too, right?"

"Oh, yes. We'll tell her when we tell my folks."

Then grief surprised her once again. Maggie was so tired of those wicked stabs of emotion. *We won't be telling Ed. We won't be telling Ed. He would have married us.*

Jack saw the shadow cross her face.

"Ed would have loved this news," he said quietly. "I'm sorry he won't be marrying us."

Maggie looked at him.

"Thank you for saying that out loud. You help me get some of these thoughts out of my brain. Ed would have laughed and hugged us both, and then he would have wished us the same kind of happiness that he and Jo shared throughout their marriage. And then he would have pulled out some chocolate from a secret hiding place that Jo had no clue of and passed it around like champagne," Maggie said, remembering Ed's chocoholism.

"We can tell Nora and Dan the same day."

Maggie smiled into Jack's eyes. The shadow was gone.

"After that, we can head down to Blissfield and tell my family," he said. "My mom will go crazy."

"Were you actually going to propose this weekend?"

"I was. You made it easy on me last night. You asked first," he said, grabbing her hand.

"I didn't ask anything. I just made a few declarations. You asked the question. This is all on you, Dr. Elliot." She squeezed his hand and watched her ring dance. "I suppose I'll have to take this lovely ring off during the day. But I'm going to wear it every night."

8

When Ellen walked into the parsonage at six o'clock, Jack was gone, as was the ring from Maggie's finger. The two women enjoyed a big bowl of popcorn and watched *The Notebook* instead of the usual Disney movie. They laughed and cried and each woman thought of her own personal love story and all the goo that went with it.

After the movie, Maggie wanted so badly to tell Ellen about Jack and the engagement. What would that hurt? Ellen was an extraordinary secret keeper. She was a nurse, for heaven's sake.

Instead, Maggie said, "So tell me about Harold."

Ellen laughed. "I like him. I like him a lot. It's so funny, when you have known someone for a long time, worked with them at church, and suddenly, one day, you look at them in a totally different way. All I ever thought before was, 'There's Harold the lawyer. Nice guy. Nothing special.' How did I ever think that? Our lunch was so nice, except for Redford. We are getting to know each other better. This coming Friday, we're having dinner in Ann Arbor." Ellen actually giggled.

Maggie was now excruciatingly dying to tell Ellen about the engagement. It was complete and utter torture. *What if I have a stroke keeping all this good news trapped inside?*

"So what about you and my handsome cousin?" Ellen asked.

"He's taking very good care of my sprained ankle," Maggie said, wanting to scream: *We're engaged! We're engaged! We're engaged!*

"And?"

"And I love him, and he loves me, and it's magical. That's it."

Maggie put a huge handful of popcorn in her mouth to keep herself from speaking further.

Just then, Cheerio came screeching into the room, with Fruit Loop following close behind. He did his little trick of rolling Cheerio over like a lopsided ball. Cheerio hissed, growled, and spat. Fruit Loop pounced. He was once again having the time of his pathetic little life.

Marmalade sauntered in and watched the proceedings while washing his paws. His whiskers were impeccable. Cheerio slammed into him before he saw her coming. More hissing, growling, and spitting.

"I better give these beasts their treats for the night," Maggie said, hoisting herself up on her crutches. Her armpits were killing her.

"I'll do it," Ellen said quickly.

She went to the kitchen and shook the treat container. All three cats came running. She put little piles of treats on the floor, and the felines settled in to a crunchfest.

"Maggie, can I do anything else for you before I go?" Ellen called out.

"I don't think so," Maggie said as she hobbled into the kitchen. "I'm ready for bed."

Ellen gave her friend a hug and left out the back door.

Maggie was about to lock the door when Ellen burst back in, gasping for air.

"Maggie . . . [breath, breath] There's someone at the . . . [breath, breath] back of the church [breath, breath]," Ellen said shakily.

"What do you mean 'the back of the church'? Are they inside or outside?"

Ellen took a very deep breath. "Outside. Someone is walking around the back of the church. I saw their shadow. It's creepy. Whoever it is is dressed in all black. I saw the person as they came back around to the parsonage side. I couldn't see a face." She took another deep breath.

Thinking fast, Maggie turned off the kitchen lights. The two women made their way to the unlit family room. They ducked down and then peeked over the window sill. The family room had the largest window facing the church. They were absolutely silent.

Suddenly, Maggie gasped. Ellen squeezed her hand. They both saw a figure dressed in black stealthily walking around the east side of the church. When the figure got to the sanctuary door, he or she quickly opened it and disappeared inside.

"What do we do now?" Ellen scream whispered.

Maggie couldn't believe what she was seeing.

"Drat these crutches!" she said. "We better call Charlotte. Part of me wants to go right in there and see who it is, but I'm sure they would hear me coming on crutches. I wouldn't be able to chase anyone anyway."

"Maggie, let's call Charlotte right now," Ellen said before Maggie could ask *her* to go. She had no desire to be anywhere near the sanctuary after what they had seen.

Maggie pulled her phone out of her pocket. She dialed Charlotte's cell phone as she glanced at the clock. It was ten o'clock, but she answered after the second ring.

"Police Chief Charlotte Tuggle speaking," Charlotte said in her most police-ish voice.

"Charlotte, this is Maggie and Ellen. We're at the parsonage. Just now Ellen was leaving when she saw a figure in black walking around the back of the church. We both saw whoever it is go into the sanctuary."

Maggie stopped. She knew Charlotte would know what to do. She didn't have to tell her.

"I'll be right there." Charlotte clicked off.

Maggie and Ellen stayed in the family room, watching the sanctuary door. Fewer than ten minutes later, the lightless squad car slid silently up to the curb across the street from church. Everyone knew that Charlotte kept one of the two Cherish squad cars in her own driveway at night for just such emergencies, of which there had been none.

Charlotte's large frame was visible in the streetlight as she crossed to the church. She was in her full police uniform, including hat.

"How in the world did she get her whole uniform on so fast?" Ellen whispered.

"I was just wondering the same thing."

Maggie couldn't help giggling. It seemed very surreal.

Charlotte disappeared into the church.

At first, Maggie and Ellen saw the occasional glimmer of Charlotte's flashlight. After about fifteen minutes, they saw one light after another come on in the church. Charlotte was going room by room and turning on all the lights. Maggie and Ellen had their eyes glued to the sanctuary door.

When it finally opened, Charlotte stepped out in the shadow of the sanctuary light. She made her way across the lawn to the back door of the parsonage. Maggie and Ellen were right there waiting.

"Pastor Maggie, Ellen, I've checked the entire church. Whoever got in through the sanctuary door got out through the basement window used for the first break-in. He must have headed west if you didn't see him. Or her."

"We kept our eyes on the church. We didn't see anyone," Maggie said.

"Can you give me any kind of description?" Charlotte asked, pulling out her ticket pad of paper and a pen.

Ellen said, "All I could see was the person dressed in black. The person was maybe close to six feet tall and slim. It was kind of hard to tell because, okay, this sounds silly, but they were stealthily slinking around the building. You know, the way you would see in an old-time detective movie."

Ellen began to move in slow motion, arms and knees moving up and down in exaggeration.

"That's helpful." Charlotte scratched on her pad of paper. "Now, Pastor Maggie, I'm sure no locks have been changed on the parsonage yet. Do you want to stay here tonight?"

Maggie thought for a moment. "Yes. I have a feeling our intruder was surprised when you showed up. He or she probably won't try to make any more trouble tonight. I'll leave a few lights on, just in case."

"I can stay with you," Ellen said hesitantly.

Maggie could see Ellen was shaken up, more so than she herself.

"No, you head home, Ellen. You have an early morning at the hospital, and I really will be fine."

"If you're sure," Ellen said, looking relieved.

Finally, Maggie got both women out of the parsonage. Charlotte said she would be on duty for the night and would stay close to the church.

Maggie left a lamp on in her study, one in the living room, and the overhead kitchen light. She also took two kitchen chairs, dragging one to the front door and putting the back of the chair under the door knob. She did the same thing with the back door. Maybe she was a little more nervous than she'd thought.

Does that chair/doorknob thing even work?

She realized that she had tried to sound calm about the whole break-in situation for Ellen's sake, but she wasn't. She wanted her mom and dad. She wanted Jack.

Maggie finally shambled upstairs. Looking in the bathroom mirror, she saw that the bruise on her face was a little darker. Her eye was swollen and an unattractive shade of purple. It hurt, her ankle throbbed, and her armpits were raw. She felt as if she had been through a hamburger grinder.

How in the world did Jack propose today when I look like an unfortunate Roller Derby mishap?

She carefully brushed her teeth, put on her pajamas, and crawled into bed. Marmalade and Cheerio were on her pillow, curled into an orange and calico ball. She gave them a little shove to make room for own head. Fruit Loop was back on the chair.

Before she turned out the light, she took the velvet box from her nightstand. She slipped the diamond onto her finger. It felt foreign and familiar and wonderful.

Maggie was startled awake in the middle of the night when she heard noises downstairs in the parsonage. It sounded as if someone was pushing chairs across the kitchen floor, then opening and slamming the kitchen cupboards.

Maggie went cold with fear. She was just about to get out of bed to hide in her closet and call Charlotte when she heard footsteps pounding up the stairs. She tried to roll out of bed and onto the floor but got tangled in her sheets, her ankle twisted, then shooting pain. She looked up.

The person in black was standing in her doorway. She could see the outline of the figure by the streetlights. The intruder was massive, filling the doorframe, but Maggie couldn't see the face. It appeared to be covered in a mask. Maggie screamed as loudly as she could, but he moved across the room and covered her mouth. The other hand grabbed for her and tried to wrench the diamond ring off her finger. She tried to scream, "No! It's from Jack! Let me go!"

Maggie jumped and woke herself up. Her heart was racing, and she was soaked with sweat. It had only been a nightmare.

She quickly turned on her nightstand lamp and looked at the clock. Two forty-seven. She sat up and saw her hands shaking. The kitties all blinked at her with sleepy eyes. Was it time for breakfast?

She sat and waited for her heart to slow down. Her diamond was benignly and cheerfully sparkling in the lamplight. How funny that in her nightmare the black figure was only trying to steal her ring. No one even knew she had a ring.

What should she do next? She wasn't in any danger. If she called Charlotte, what would she say? She had a dream that someone tried to steal her engagement ring? She didn't want to call Jack. He had a busy day ahead. Poor Ellen would just be terrified.

She finally reached for her crutches and painfully hobbled down to the kitchen for a cup of Lady Grey tea in her favorite yellow happy face mug to cheer herself up. She checked to see that her chairs were still in place by the two doors. The parsonage seemed too big. She thought of all the places someone could hide: the bathroom in her study, the extra bedrooms and bathroom upstairs, the many closets, and the attic, which she had never even seen herself. She felt small.

Maggie looked up. There was a face in the kitchen window.

She screamed and dropped her mug on the floor. It cracked in two, and the tea made a steaming puddle at her feet. She stared back at the window and saw a hand wave. It was Charlotte.

Maggie got to the back door on her crutches, pulled the chair away from the doorknob, and let Charlotte in.

"I didn't mean to startle you, Pastor Maggie," Charlotte said in her controlled-but-too-loud police voice. "I have been watching the church and the parsonage tonight. I saw your bedroom light come on a bit ago and thought I'd make sure you were okay."

"Thank you, Charlotte," Maggie said, without feeling any thanksgiving whatsoever. "Come on in."

Maggie grabbed a kitchen towel on her way back to the table and began to sop up the spilled tea. Charlotte bent down next to her and helped pick up the pieces of the mug.

"Why, Pastor Maggie! What's that on your hand there?" Charlotte actually sounded like a woman. Almost girlish.

Drat! "It's an engagement ring," Maggie said resignedly. "Dr. Elliot and I are engaged."

"Well, it's about time. I was worried he was just going to hang around being his pleasant self till kingdom come. But it looks like he finally had the nerve and good sense to propose. Congratulations!"

Charlotte did something very un-Charlotte-like and gave Maggie a hug. Her inflamed armpits rebelled in freakishly raw pain.

"Oww . . . ohhh . . . thank you, Charlotte," Maggie said hoarsely as she wriggled out of the hug. "Would you like a cup of tea?"

"That would hit the spot."

Charlotte sat herself down and allowed Maggie to do all the tea preparations on her crutches.

Maggie poured the tea and served it with some oatmeal nutmeg cookies out of the freezer. Charlotte heartily enjoyed the middle-of-the-night snack. She put away six cookies in no time flat.

"Who do you think is messing with our church?" Maggie asked.

"I have no idea. Yet. But we'll catch him. He isn't that clever. Or she. What I want to know is, what's the motive? We have no valuables in the church to steal. It's someone just being mean and stupid," Charlotte said unprofessionally as she dipped another cookie into her tea.

"It doesn't make sense," Maggie said thoughtfully. "I admit, I thought it was Redford. He's the only one who seems to have a grudge against the church. And life in general."

"And *you!*" Charlotte declared with her mouth full of cookie. "I suspect he's one of those men who can't handle women in authority. Mommy issues, I presume."

Charlotte's psychological musings were completely depleted with that sentence. Psychology and church break-ins were beyond her Cherish police experience.

Just when Maggie didn't think the night could get any stranger, the Westminster chimes rang out from the front door.

"What in the world?" Charlotte whispered loudly, then tried to furtively make her way to the front door.

She was much too big. She reminded Maggie of the dancing hippos in the Disney movie *Fantasia*. Maggie had to stifle a giggle.

Charlotte removed the chair from under the doorknob, peeked through the eyehole, and then opened the door.

Mrs. Popkin stood on the front porch, apronless.

"Hokey tooters, Charlotte! What are all the lights doing on over here? And why are you here? It's almost four in the morning."

Mrs. Popkin pushed her way right on through and into the parsonage.

"Hello, Polly," Charlotte said. "I'm here on official police business. I know exactly what time it is. I suppose you're opening up The Sugarplum right about now."

"I am, indeedy," Mrs. Popkin said, trying to see around Charlotte and into the kitchen.

Maggie limped out.

"Hi, Mrs. Popkin. Would you like a cup of tea?"

"Pastor Maggie, what's going on around here?"

Mrs. Popkin knew she had a better chance of getting an answer from Pastor Maggie than from Charlotte, who thought there were certain things not meant for public consumption, which was absolutely ridiculous. Mrs. Popkin believed the police department newsfeed should be run like The Sugarplum: everyone should have as much as they wanted, whether it be gossip or donuts.

The three women made their way into the kitchen. After Charlotte thought about it for a second, she realized Mrs. Popkin could be a help with the intruder issue. The Sugarplum was directly across from the church, and Polly got there every morning between three thirty and four. Also, Polly was nosy. Perfect.

Charlotte and Maggie filled Mrs. Popkin in on the person in black. They also told her the whole truth about Maggie's accident and the footprints in the basement of the church.

"Well, hokey tooters!" Mrs. Popkin thundered. "We better get to the bottom of these little shenanigans."

She helped herself to a third cookie.

"Agreed," Charlotte replied.

"To be honest, and I hate to say this," Mrs. Popkin said, not hating it at all, "I would bet a box of donuts it's Redford Johnson doing these vicious things. We've all seen and heard his venom."

"Redford left earlier this week for a fishing trip out West somewhere. He won't be back until the end of September," Maggie reported.

"Well, that's good news anyway," said Mrs. Popkin. "We can be thankful for small mercies."

She took a sip of tea, then noticed something catch the light.

"Wait! Wait just one frosted-cookie minute! What is that on your hand, Pastor Maggie?!"

Mrs. Popkin looked like her eyes might actually pop right out of her face.

Drat! Why didn't I take it off before Charlotte opened the door?

"It's an engagement ring," Maggie said plainly. Again. *So much for the sweet secret.*

"Yep. Dr. Elliot finally got the lead out and scraped enough money together to buy Pastor Maggie a ring."

Charlotte laughed hysterically at herself, as if Dr. Elliot had to scrape anything together besides his courage.

"Hokey tooters! Congratulations, Pastor Maggie," said Mrs. Popkin, not taking her eyes off the ring. "I'm just going to say right now that I'm baking your wedding cake for free. Yes, yes, I am."

She helped herself to another cookie in celebration.

"Thank you, Mrs. Popkin. That is so generous of you. I hadn't even thought about a cake yet."

Maggie actually felt a warm little pool of happiness growing in her heart region. Or maybe it was just the tea and cookies in her tummy. Nevertheless, she was going to get to plan a wedding. With Jack. And Mrs. Popkin. And Irena. And Ellen. And Marla. And Hank. And Doris and . . .

Because of her discombobulated night, muddled mind, and mainly her youth, Maggie was unable to see the two older women looking at her with hope and joy. Mrs. Popkin had been happily married before she lost her husband a decade ago. Charlotte and Fred had the comfort of a marriage never fraught with cruel arguments, lies, or apathy. They had grown into an easy and contented lockstep with one another.

Both Charlotte and Polly Popkin knew Pastor Maggie and Dr. Elliot would care for one another and maneuver through the future days of sweetness and sorrow as one.

"Ladies, I better take my leave, as much as I hate to. But the bread won't bake itself over at The Sugarplum."

Mrs. Popkin got up. Maggie limped with her to the door.

"Dr. Elliot and I were hoping to keep the engagement a little secret until we see our families." Maggie was almost pleading.

"Yes, indeed! Your secret is safe with me."

Mrs. Popkin unknowingly inflicted a painful hug on Maggie before she left.

Charlotte met her at the door.

"I'm going home to get a little sleep, but I'll be calling Officer Bumble and get him up to speed. Rest assured, Pastor Maggie, he will continue the watch."

Charlotte gave a curt nod as she headed out the front door. Maggie nodded mutely.

She knew her secret was not safe. It would be hurled out into the world by two goodhearted women who couldn't keep their mouths shut when there was something so happily and delightfully enchanting to talk about.

She needed some ibuprofen.

9

At six o'clock, after not going back to sleep, Maggie called Jack and poured out the whole story.

Jack was more concerned with the black figure creeping around the church than he was with the engagement being leaked.

"This is getting a little more serious," he said. "I'm not sure you staying at the parsonage is such a good idea."

"I will stay. I'm not going to let this joker scare me out of my home," Maggie said, sounding braver than she actually felt. "Plus, I have the cats."

"I'll call Tom Wiggins this morning and see when I can get the new locks for the parsonage. I'll be over right after work," Jack said. "We can talk more about everything then. I suppose we should make some calls to our families." And then, completely switching gears, he said, "How are you feeling, Reverend Highness? Your ankle, et cetera?"

"I think I'm high on adrenaline right now. My armpits hurt worse than anything. When can I get rid of these crutches?"

"As soon as your armpits get used to them, you'll be ready to toss them," Jack said practically. "I'll see you tonight. Love you."

Maggie took her time getting ready, mainly because she moved like a turtle. She removed her engagement ring and put it back in the velvet box, then slipped the box into her nightstand drawer. She would have to wait until that night to wear it again. Finally, she left the parsonage, cats full of treats, plus liver and smashed pill for Fruit Loop. She skipped her oatmeal because she was full of middle-of-the-night tea and cookies. She walked over to church, hobbled through the sanctuary doors, and was greeted by the delectable smell she knew would be in her nostrils for the next few months: vegetable soup.

Sylvia Baxter, owner of The Garden Shop, began her vegetable and flower plantings in a hot house in February. Last year, thanks to Sylvia's generosity, Maggie had been given copious amounts of vegetables piled almost daily on her desk, bookshelves, work table, and even the floor of her office. Maggie tried to encourage Sylvia to "share the wealth," but to no avail. Finally, when Sylvia married Bill, he came up with the soup idea. They could make the vegetables into soup and bring the soup to shut-ins and other interested parishioners. It could also be served at church suppers.

Mondays and Thursdays were soup days with the purpose of using the vegetables while they were freshest, so the whole church smelled of frying onions as the ingredients were being prepared. Although Doris raised a preposterous ruckus at first about "dirtying up the kitchen," she couldn't complain once about the lack of cleanliness in the kitchen at the end of each soup-making day. Plus, she was invited to eat as much as she wanted, as was the whole staff.

Maggie's nose filled with the kitchen smells, while her ears were assaulted by Irena's amazingly bombastic organ music. Irena's purple, red-onion-colored hair flowed down her back. She moved to the music dramatically, as if in a trance.

Maggie thought she could sneak by and just get to her office unnoticed. Unfortunately, crutches have an amazing way of keeping someone from sneaking.

"Pastoorr Maggie!" The organ abruptly ceased as Irena sharply screeched Maggie's name.

"Good morning, Irena. I didn't want to disturb you," Maggie said defensively.

"Pastoorr Maggie! I beleaf you hev someting to tell to me?"

"What?" Maggie asked, wondering if Irena had heard about the intruder in black.

"Vat? Vat, you say? You insult me." Irena climbed off the organ bench and tottered over to Maggie on her very high heels. She was dressed in purple from head to toe. It clashed with the purple of her hair. "I hearrr der ees news. I not hearrr it frum you. I hearr it frum Hunk."

She turned back to the organ bench. Maggie decided she would rather be on crutches than in Irena's heels. Irena began rifling through her large stack of music. She pulled out a piece and climbed back up onto the bench. Irena never changed from her stilettos into proper organ shoes.

Just as Irena was ready to attack the first note of her music, Hank's door opened. Hank, carrying a bakery box—along with Doris, Marla, Sylvia, Bill, Winston, Verna, and Howard—came into the sanctuary. Everyone but Hank was wearing an apron. It was the soup committee. Before Maggie could say anything, Irena's hands came down with a flourish.

She was playing the "Wedding March."

The others all came and gathered around Maggie. Hank opened the bakery box to reveal sixteen pale-pink cupcakes. Fourteen of the cupcakes had a letter piped in dark-pink icing on top.

HAPPY BETORTHAL.

The other two cupcakes had exclamation points. Mrs. Popkin must have forgotten her promise to keep the engagement a secret. After all, it had been all of five hours.

Good grief! Maggie thought. Her next thought came hot on the heels of the first. *I have to call Jack.*

When Irena finally stopped playing, there was a round of applause and many sly glances at Maggie's ring finger, which was ringless.

"Well, what can I say?" Maggie said, looking around. "Except that the O and the R in your cupcakes might need to be switched." She gave a fake little chuckle.

Hank looked at the cupcakes. "Well, looky there! BETORTHAL. Ha!"

Suddenly, everyone was speaking at once. Marla and Sylvia both had tears of joy in their eyes. *Oh dear, it looks like Hank does too.* Irena was glaring and smiling at the same time. It made her looked grotesquely possessed.

Verna patted Maggie on the shoulder and said, "Congratulations, Pastor Maggie, and Godspeed."

Maggie smiled wanly.

"What did your mother have to say about it all?" Verna continued.

At this question everyone quieted down to listen.

"My mother?" Maggie said dazed. "My mother doesn't even know yet. Jack and I were going to tell our families when my leg is better. No one was supposed to know." Maggie bit her lip hard to keep from crying. She took a deep breath. "Thank you, all of you, for this . . . this . . . thoughtfulness. I have a feeling Mrs. Popkin helped spread our good news. Please, eat a cupcake. I know you will understand when I say I need to call Jack right away and let him know the cat's out of the bag, so to speak."

She tried to smile but couldn't quite pull it off.

Verna saw exactly what was going on. She took control of the situation quickly.

"Pastor Maggie, we celebrate your good news. We will now return to the basement and continue making soup. You better get to your office, shut the door, and make the necessary phone calls. None of us will be bothering you. Hank, guard her door," Verna ordered and then gave Maggie a little wink.

Maggie nodded and crutched her way as fast as she could to her office. She closed the door, practically fell into her chair, and began dialing the phone. Jack didn't pick up. She dialed his cell phone again. And again. And finally, on her fourth attempt, he picked up.

"My goodness, you're a pest! I'm seeing patients this morning. What's up?" Jack sounded ever so slightly annoyed.

That was it. Jack's ever-so-slight-annoyance pushed her over the edge. After her unreal last night, minimal sleep, and BETORTHAL cupcakes, Maggie burst into tears.

Jack snapped out of his annoyance.

"Maggie, what is it?"

"Find . . . Ellen . . . [*sniff*] . . . she . . . deserves . . . to . . . [*sniff*] . . . know. Everyone . . . knows. Find Ellen . . . [*sniff*] . . . and tell her."

"Everyone knows what? About the person breaking into the church?" Jack asked, confused. He knew Ellen knew all about it.

"Our engagement!" Maggie cried. "Everyone knows except for our families. I actually lied to Ellen last night when she asked about us. You have to find her and tell her before she hears it from someone else."

"Okay. I'll track her down. How did it get out?" He didn't sound angry, just puzzled.

"I had my ring on last night when Charlotte and Mrs. Popkin were over. I asked them to keep it a secret. I guess I should have defined the word 'secret' before they left." She grabbed a tissue and blew her nose with one hand. "I have to call my parents and Bryan. I feel as if I've betrayed them all."

"It's okay. This is all going to work out, and in fifty, maybe sixty years, we'll be laughing about it. I'll find Ellen. You call your family. It's going to be fine. I still get to marry you. I love you, Maggie."

She was smiling and sniffling when they hung up.

She sat at her desk and marveled at the psychology of the church community. Everyone's business was everyone's business. She limped out into Hank's office. It was obvious he had blown his nose because it was red. He was overjoyed for his pastor. He looked expectantly at Maggie, ready to slay a dragon for her.

She smiled and asked, "May I have a cupcake?"

He lifted the box of remaining cupcakes to her.

She took a cupcake with an exclamation point on top.

It was early Monday morning, and Clara Abbott was beginning her shift at the front desk of the lodge. Sunday had been her day off, and unfortunately, the college student responsible for last night's shift had left the desk a mess. Not only trash from all the junk food he or she was eating but check-in receipts and maps cluttered the entire surface.

Clara began the cleanup, throwing trash away and sopping up spilled coffee. Then she found her own note from the previous Friday buried under the refuse. She had been so busy Friday and Saturday with new check-ins that she'd forgotten all about Mr. Johnson's credit card. She had seen him on Saturday afternoon at the restaurant bar. He had the same bleary-eyed look he'd had the day she checked him in.

She had to find out about the credit card. It was the responsible thing to do. Just as she was preparing to dial the phone, a family of four walked wearily to the desk.

"Good morning," Clara said as she surveyed the tired family.

They must have flown on a very early morning flight to look so bad. The dad handed over the required credit card and driver's license. The two children looked to be under the age of ten. The little boy was holding his mother's hand while using his other hand to rub his blanket under his nose.

"Where are you visiting us from?" Clara asked brightly.

"Johnson City, Tennessee," the father said with a pleasing drawl. "We drove straight through. I hope you have a place ready for us to settle into. We're wiped."

Oh. They drove. That explains it. "Yes, of course. I'll change your cabin immediately to one that's not in use. So, Johnson City?" Clara said, a little startled since she was just thinking of Mr. Johnson. "Well, you're trading one beautiful mountain range for another, aren't you?"

The father smiled. He was too tired for the cheerful banter.

Clara began the process of checking them in as she slipped the note from Friday into her pocket. She would have to check into Mr. Johnson later. She had to find out about that credit card.

10

Maggie ate her cupcake. It was unsatisfactory because her nose was stuffed from crying. She couldn't taste all the sugar, butter, and vanilla. She put the last bite in her mouth right when her phone rang.

"Hewo?" she mumbled through the cake.

"Hi, Maggie! It's me, Ellen. I just spoke with Jack. Congratulations! I am so happy for you both, and I'm sorry the secret escaped before you wanted it to. I think Hank must have told Pamela. I saw her talking with Jack very animatedly. I don't think it was about delivering flowers to patients." Ellen laughed.

Hank's wife, Pamela, volunteered at Heal Thyself Community Hospital, delivering flowers and gifts to those unfortunate enough to have to stay in the hospital for longer than a couple of days.

"Ellen, I'm sorry you didn't know before other people here at church. I had no idea the news would spread so fast. I wish I would have told you last night over popcorn."

Maggie was relieved. What had she been thinking? That Ellen would scream and yell? Or cry? Ellen understood small towns and small churches. Ellen knew how to be happy for the people around her, no matter what.

"The point is, this is great news. I'm sure the whole church will know by lunchtime. If you can, try to enjoy it, Maggie. We all love you so much. I've got to go."

Ellen clicked off.

Maggie felt much better. She dialed her parents' number and got their voicemail, as she expected. She left a brief message, then hung up.

Her phone rang again.

"Hello?"

"Hi, fiancé. It's me, your future husband." Jack almost sounded giddy. Very un-Jack-like. "Have you spoken with my delightful cousin?"

"Yes. And she is delightful and understanding and wonderful." Maggie let out a deep sigh. "I also want you to know that we are betorthed. I read it on some cupcakes."

"Well, happy betorthal to us!" Jack laughed. "Pamela just cornered me. Hank gave her a call earlier this morning. Our little bit of news is making people very happy, it seems. For tonight, how about this. I'll come to the parsonage after work. I will have the new locks for the doors, you will fix me dinner, and we'll call our families together."

Jack said this purposefully. Maggie knew that Jack liked to problem solve. Jack knew that Maggie needed a plan. It worked.

"I will have dinner ready for you," Maggie said. "Thanks for telling Ellen. I love you."

"Good." Jack hung up.

Maggie pulled herself out of the shock of the morning and smelled soup simmering in the basement. She made her way slowly down the steps, cursing her crutches as she went.

"It smells delicious down here," she said.

The soup committee members grinned at her.

"Pastor Maggie," Howard said. "I think we startled you earlier. It's great news, and I'm sorry, but we will all want to know each and every detail as it becomes available. You belong to us, you know."

"I'm so glad I belong to you," Maggie said. "It's a brand-new feeling, being engaged. We are going to tell our families tonight. Then we will see how things go. I want you to know how much I appreciate your happy thoughts and the cupcakes. I don't think I thanked you the way I should have before. My mother would hang her head in shame."

"You were taken off guard," Verna said practically. "We should have been a little less enthusiastic."

Winston, with his hair standing up, looked like a mad scientist.

"I'll just say this—I'm sorry you're out of the running, Pastor Maggie. I thought I might have had a chance." He was smiling like a goofball.

"Thank you, Winston. I'm sorry to disappoint you, but Jack has completely stolen my heart. Please stay in the new members class, however." Maggie smiled.

Sylvia quickly handed Maggie a plastic container of vegetable soup.

"You'll have to tell us how you like it," she said.

"Jack and I will have this for dinner tonight. Thank you," Maggie said, readjusting her crutches. Her armpits were still raw.

Marla took the container and slowly followed Maggie upstairs.

"I can put this in the parsonage for you," she said.

"Let's go over together. I locked it all up this morning."

They headed toward the back door of the parsonage, but then both women stopped and stood perfectly still.

The door was standing wide open.

"Oh, no! The cats!" Maggie cried. "I can't believe it. I forgot to lock the door!"

Marla was first through the open door. She put the soup on the kitchen counter and began calling for the cats.

"Marmalade? Cheerio? Fruit Loop? Here kitty, kitty, kitty!"

Maggie followed her to the kitchen. All of the kitchen cupboards stood open. Pots and pans were pulled out helter-skelter. One of the kitchen chairs was lying on its side. She hobbled to the living room. Pillows from the once-white-now-gray couch and love seat were on the floor. Papers and books in Maggie's study were strewn in a messy pile. Maggie was grateful to see her computer was still on her desk.

Marla dashed up the stairs two at a time.

"Maggie, I found them! They're in your room!"

Maggie hobbled as fast as she could. All three cats were in her bedroom. Her comforter and bed pillows were on the floor. She had never felt so violated. Then she gasped.

The ring!

She made her way over and opened the drawer. The velvet box was there. Maggie hadn't realized she had stopped breathing. She opened the box. The diamond winked up at her, and she let out a huge sigh. She took the ring out and slipped it onto her shaky finger, silently vowing to never take it off again.

Then she looked at the cats. They looked frightened, but Maggie guessed it was the abrupt entrance of Marla and herself that scared them.

"Oh, Pastor Maggie, what a beautiful ring." Marla gently held Maggie's hand to get a better look. "And how lucky no one knew it was here. But poor kitties." She switched her attention to the felines.

"I'm going to call Charlotte."

She tried to pick up her pillows and comforter while simultaneously reaching for her phone.

"I'll put your bed back together," Marla said and began gathering pillows off the floor.

Maggie sat on her corner chair next to Fruit Loop. Marmalade and Cheerio hopped in her lap, making the situation very crowded but very comforting.

"Charlotte, this is Maggie. We've had another break-in. This time it was the parsonage. It seems someone just wanted to let me know they were here. They threw pillows and books around. They really made a mess of the place. Okay . . . I'm here with Marla. We'll wait right here."

Maggie gave the cats a distracted pet. She dialed her phone again and left a message on Jack's voicemail.

"Jack, someone broke into the parsonage. Marla and I are waiting for Charlotte. I think someone just wanted me to know they could get in. The cats are fine. My ring is beautiful."

Marla borrowed Maggie's phone and called Tom. She told him the whole story then reported Tom's message back to Maggie.

"Bill Baxter has all the new locks at church. He began installing them this morning while all the soup-making was going on. Less chance of being noticed when the church looks busy. Bill also has the locks for the parsonage. He was going to leave them here for Jack to change."

"Good. I hope new locks work," Maggie said doubtfully.

Maggie and Marla went downstairs, followed by the three curious ones. Marla wanted to continue putting the parsonage back in order, but Maggie told her Charlotte should get a look at it first.

Charlotte arrived within minutes and carefully went through each room. Maggie and Marla told her about the lock situation.

"Those locks have to be changed immediately," Charlotte said in her professional voice. "When will Jack get here?"

"He isn't coming over until after work," Maggie said.

"Marla, will you please go get Bill. Let him know the locks here take priority over the church for now," Charlotte ordered.

Marla quickly left to fetch Bill.

"I don't understand what this intruder is up to," Charlotte said, more to herself than to Maggie. "He or she seems to want to scare us, without doing serious damage. But why?"

It felt like the same conversation they'd had earlier in the morning. Maggie felt the lack of sleep catching up with her.

"I don't know," Maggie sighed. She rested her head in her hands for a moment.

Bill and Marla were at the parsonage within minutes. Bill had his tool box and the new locks. His face was tense. Maggie knew the whole break-in situation was causing too many people—too many *good* people—a great deal of stress, and that made her angry.

"Thanks, Bill. I'm sorry for this," she said.

Marla put the parsonage back together again, while Charlotte looked on. Each woman lost in her own thoughts. Nothing like it had ever happened in sleepy Cherish or at Loving the Lord. It was such a violation.

Bill said quietly, "Pastor Maggie, I'm going to get all the locks changed today. I thought Jack and I could do it without people noticing, but we can't wait around. This intruder must be stopped now."

He was looking at the ground, but Maggie could see his face suffused in red.

The parsonage phone rang.

"Pastor Maggie," Hank said in his professional voice, "there is a reporter here in the office from *The Cherish Life and Times*. Are you available for an interview?"

"Oh, Hank! Does he know about the break-ins? We don't want this in the paper."

Maggie was overwhelmed with worry. Again.

"No, no, no, Pastor Maggie, nothing like that," Hank said quickly. "The paper wants an article about what it's like to be a female pastor here in Cherish."

"Oh. Okay. I see. He wants to do the interview right now?" Maggie asked, feeling the pain in her ankle begin to throb.

"Yes, *she* does. She said she could walk over to the parsonage if that's easier for you." Hank spoke in a staccato voice to warn Maggie.

"No! I understand Hank. I will be right over. Just put her in my office and keep an eye on her until I get there," Maggie said conspiratorially.

She told the others what was going on. She would go to the church and do the interview as quickly as possible.

"We'll stay put right here," said Charlotte. "Marla, how about some tea?"

Marla mutely filled the tea kettle and put it on the stove as Charlotte settled herself at the kitchen table.

Maggie got to Hank's office and watched as he made wild hand gestures and pointed to her office. She had no idea what he was trying to tell her. Everyone seemed to be on edge and suspicious, but with good reason. She smiled at Hank and went through to her office.

She saw the back of a tall, slender, dark-haired woman sitting on one of the chairs meant for visitors. The woman stood and turned when she heard Maggie enter. She was plain-looking and slightly disheveled, but Maggie could see she had the natural beauty to be attractive. She would need to put a little effort into it, however. The woman was wearing no makeup or jewelry. She looked like a blank canvas. No, she looked wary and tired. Maggie noticed the woman's ill-fitting brown suit, which did nothing for her pale complexion, and scuffed brown boots with mud around the edges. Maggie wasn't judging, just observing. She herself had no interest in clothes or makeup or jewelry. Except the thrill of her new engagement ring and her gold cross, a Christmas gift from Jack.

Maggie held out her hand, scraping her right armpit, and then winced when she meant to smile.

"Hi. I'm Maggie Elzinga," she said. "I'm sorry for the delay. I'm a little slow these days." She gave a halfhearted laugh.

The woman shook Maggie's hand limply.

"I'm Julia Benson from *The Cherish Life and Times*. We would like to do a story on you and your church."

Maggie went around her desk and sat in her chair. Often, when someone was in her office, she would purposefully sit in one of the two visitor chairs. She didn't like the feel of her desk separating her from someone who needed to chat. But Maggie was not feeling calm in her soul at the moment. Or chatty. And the woman was there to pry. At least that's how it felt to Maggie.

Julia pulled out a pad of paper and a pen.

"You've been here for over a year now, is that right?" Julia asked without preamble and very matter-of-factly.

"Yes. It was one year on June first."

"Where are you from, originally?" Julia asked. She stared at her pad of paper, ready to write.

"I'm from a small town on the west side of the state called Zeeland."

She tried to make eye contact, but Julia did not look up from her pad of paper.

The interview went on for thirty minutes. Julia asked a mix of personal questions about Maggie's family, questions about Loving the Lord, and the highlights of Maggie's first year.

Maggie answered each question as briefly as possible. She talked about her family and the different services that were highpoints for her in the past year.

"We had an animal blessing service last October. We have a lot of animal lovers around here. Many in the congregation brought their pets and filled our sanctuary with interesting, joyful noises."

Maggie thought that was clever.

Julia looked bored as she continued writing.

Maggie soldiered on. "All the animals received a blessing. We will have another animal blessing this coming October. Do you have a pet?"

She was trying to find out a little more about Julia. Just like her cats, Maggie was curious by nature.

"Actually, I haven't lived here very long. I took a job with the paper and moved here recently. So, no pets," Julia said. "What were some of the other highlights?"

Maggie felt the abruptness of the question. Julia didn't want to be chummy. Maggie wondered if it was insecurity or inexperience. She didn't seem to be much older than Maggie herself.

Maggie described some of the other happenings of the last fifteen months. It sounded as dull as Julia Benson looked.

Julia sighed, looked up at the ceiling for a moment, then scribbled more on her pad. Maggie didn't think she had said enough to produce so much writing.

Maggie dove into the plans for the mission trip to Ghana and the other work the church was planning to do for a village there. She was on a roll, and Julia really had to write furiously to keep up. Maggie did not mention Ed's death or her brief hiatus from Cherish last February. That was too personal, and she did not want it smeared in the local paper. Just thinking about Ed's death made the interview seem completely trivial.

Finally, Julia asked her about being a female pastor. Maggie's first impulse was to say it didn't make a difference at all. She felt respected and accepted by all. But then she remembered her war with Verna Abernathy when she had first arrived in Cherish. She remembered harsh words from Marvin Green at the Friendly Elder Care nursing home, just because she was a woman. And a shadow crossed her face as she remembered Redford Johnson's threats and degrading behavior, things he never would have said or done to a male pastor.

The most humiliating encounter had been when the pastor of the Baptist church in town came by to "say hello" and then, once in

Maggie's office, launched into a long litany of sins regarding a woman's place in the church. It certainly was not in the pulpit. Hank had overheard the tirade from his office and quickly knocked on Maggie's door to end the rant. Once the man was out the door, Maggie and Hank had sat and talked about the Baptist pastor behind his back until the sting of his visit dissipated.

Maggie had been protected in seminary. The professors believed the students were all called by God to serve in ministry. God wasn't sexist. God was an equal opportunity employer. Maggie hadn't been prepared for the negativity of some toward her ministry just because she wore a skirt.

Maggie chased those shadows away.

"I think there may have been a time of adjustment for a couple of our members, but I can say that I truly feel like the *pastor* of Loving the Lord, not the *female* pastor. The pastor. This is an incredible congregation."

"You look kind of beat up. What about the bruise on your face and those crutches?" Julia asked, moving past the *incredible congregation* comment.

Like most journalists, Julia wanted some controversy, not the lovey-dovey garbage. Maggie was caught off guard for just a second.

"I was using a folding chair as a stepping stool, and I slipped. I sprained my ankle and hit my face on the basement floor. I hope you're not planning on taking a picture or anything."

Maggie chortled uncomfortably, desperately hoping Julia was not going to whip out her cell phone camera.

When is this going to end?

Maggie wished she could get a handle on Julia's abruptness. Julia could have gotten a lot more information out of Maggie if she would have smiled a little and made eye contact once or twice.

"No pictures. So do you have any difficult parishioners? They can't all be nice."

The question was unprofessional. Maggie had had enough.

"No. They are all delightful. All the time."

Maggie tried to hide her sarcasm, but it peeked out.

"I see you're engaged," Julia snapped.

Maggie's sharp intake of breath surprised even her. The woman was obnoxious.

"Yes. I am. And I'm very excited about it," Maggie said, sounding robotic.

"May I have a tour of the church?"

Again, that was completely unexpected. Maggie thought quickly and figured Bill Baxter was still changing the locks at the parsonage, so Julia wouldn't see anything that might bring an unwanted question about door locks.

"Sure. It's not a large church, so it won't take long," Maggie said.

The two women moved out of the office and into the sanctuary. It was quiet due to the lack of Irena. Maggie looked up at the stained glass rose window and was awestruck, as always. Julia looked around at the other stained glass windows and the beautiful wooden pews. They smelled of Murphy's Oil Soap. Maggie heard Julia sigh deeply.

"It's beautiful, isn't it?" Maggie said quietly.

"Yes," Julia replied, almost in a whisper.

Maggie waited until Julia moved. Then she continued the tour. When they got to the basement, the soup committee—along with Hank, Doris, and Irena—were seated around a table, eating soup and a basket of yeast rolls from The Sugarplum.

"Would you like some soup?" Maggie asked, hoping Julia would say no.

"No. I need to get back to the office," Julia said as she noticed gazes from around the table glued on her. Everyone was smiling, except for Irena, who was eating as though it were her last meal.

Sylvia got up and went into the kitchen. She came back with a plastic container and handed it to Julia and said, "Well, you must take this home with you. We make soup every Monday and Thursday. It's for our shut-ins and anybody else who wants it."

Julia took the soup only because Sylvia let go of it once she put it in her hands. She looked too stunned to say thank you, although Maggie thought Julia's mouth wasn't familiar with those two words.

Maggie hobbled up the stairs with Julia. She was pleased that Sylvia had been so pleasantly forceful. It had put Julia at a momentary disadvantage. Maggie spoke without looking at Julia.

"I'd like to invite you to church this coming Sunday. Our service is at ten o'clock. You would be very welcome, Julia."

"I don't believe in church," Julia said without further explanation. "Thank you for the interview. I don't know exactly which week it will be in the paper. That will be up to our editor."

With that, Julia walked out the sanctuary doors.

When Maggie turned to go back to her office, she saw Julia's container of soup sitting on the organ bench.

It was Monday morning, and Redford made his way back to the restaurant. His head was pounding from the perpetual hangover he lived with, but what else was there to do but drink in that stinking place? He would get some breakfast and then wait until the bar opened at noon.

He sat in a corner booth and opened the menu. A waitress came to the booth with a coffee pot.

"Coffee, sir?" she asked cheerfully.

Redford pushed his cup toward her without looking up.

She filled the cup and pulled out her order pad.

"What can I get you?"

"Two eggs over easy. Pancakes. Bacon. Orange juice." Redford pulled his cabin key card out of his pocket. "Then take this and wait in my cabin. I have something for you." Redford looked up and sneered.

At first, the waitress didn't understand. When it sunk in, she turned immediately and walked away. It took fewer than two minutes for the manager of the restaurant to make her way to Redford's table.

"Sir, you're here for breakfast, correct?" Her words were clipped, all business.

Redford looked up contemptuously without answering.

"If you harass any of the wait staff in this restaurant, I'll call the police. We have zero tolerance for any kind of harassment from our employees or our guests. Do you understand?" It was obvious she had done it before. She had no time for idiots when she had a restaurant to run. She towered over him and asked again, "Do you understand?"

"Go to hell," Redford growled as he got up and pushed past the manager, shoving her shoulder hard with his.

"No, thank you," the manager said to Redford's back.

Redford pushed through the glass doors, enraged. He made his way back to his cabin. Once inside, he picked up a lamp and threw it across the room. It shattered into the log wall and fell to the floor.

His rage was unleashed. He tore pictures off the wall and threw chairs until they splintered. He ripped the sheets off the bed and shoved the mattress onto the floor. Then he took a knife from the kitchenette, slit the mattress, and shredded the sheets. He smashed every dish in the cupboards. He was spinning out of control, ripping and tearing and throwing everything he could get his hands on. His next destructive act was pulling the phone cord out of the wall and then smashing the phone onto the floor. But he wasn't quite finished with his damage.

Redford completely destroyed everything inside the lovely Fisherman's Delight cabin, which sat in the serene shadow of Lone Mountain.

Clara quickly made her way back to the hotel lobby. She had heard through the grapevine that Mr. Johnson had caused a scene in the restaurant at breakfast. It was only his fifth day at the lodge, and he had run up a high bill at the bar and now the disgusting behavior at the restaurant. It was going to be a very long three weeks.

Earlier that morning, Clara had called the credit card company used by Mr. Johnson. It was a church credit card for Loving the Lord Community Church in Cherish, Michigan. Mr. Johnson couldn't possibly be a pastor. At least she hoped he wasn't. The woman at the credit card company assured Clara she was going to call the church to verify the card's use. Clara wasn't the type to interfere, but she was curious as to whether the card was stolen or not. It had been a couple of hours since she called the first time, so she dialed the credit card company again.

As Clara was receiving information about Mr. Johnson's account, one of the maids came bursting into the lobby. Fortunately, no guests were mingling around since she was quite hysterical.

"Clara!" the maid shouted.

Clara put up a hand to quiet the maid, even as she received news she didn't want to hear. The credit card was suspended for questionable use—both the out-of-state charges and unusual hotel charge—until someone at the church could confirm it. She thanked the person on the phone and hung up. She would have to get to the Fisherman's Delight cabin and ask Mr. Johnson to leave. She would also demand cash for his bar tab.

"Clara! I have to tell you something!"

The maid's face was red, and her hands were trembling. She smelled like lavender cleanser. And sweat.

"What is it?" Clara was completely distracted as she picked up the phone to call the head manager.

"The Fisherman's Delight cabin is destroyed!" the maid shrieked.

Clara hung up the phone and came from around the desk. She grabbed the maid and dragged her out to the golf cart used by the cleaning staff to go from cabin to cabin. Clara got behind the wheel and took off toward Fisherman's Delight. They were there in under five minutes. Clara saw the door standing open. Ripped pillows and broken dishes were just visible over the threshold. One of the mullioned windows was shattered.

Clara ran to the cabin and through the door. Then she stopped. She gasped, tried to move in farther, then stopped again. There was no place to step. The floor was covered in debris. Everything that could be broken was smashed or torn. It was a crime scene.

Then the smell hit her—the stink of urine and feces. Mr. Johnson had left repulsive parting gifts on the expensive mattress and torn sheets. Clara thought she might vomit. She hustled the maid away from the cabin and back into the golf cart. Then she sped back to the reception office and picked up the phone, dialing 911.

The police arrived at the lodge within twenty minutes, which barely gave Clara's heart time to calm down. The officers followed Clara back to the cabin. As the forensic team got to work gathering evidence inside and outside the cabin, Clara answered as many questions as she could. In the three years she had worked at the lodge, she had never seen anything like it.

What kind of person could be so destructive?

Monday evening, Maggie and Jack each ate two bowls of vegetable soup, croissants from The Sugarplum, and slices of cinnamon pecan pie.

"I can't believe you made a pie today," Jack said, shaking his head. "You are a horrible patient."

"It's one of the easiest pies in the world to make. I needed to do something after that wretched interview. And just so you know, after the pie was out of the oven, I took a two-hour nap. So there. You are an evil and wicked doctor," Maggie said, putting a forkful of pie in her mouth, savoring the cinnamon.

She had told him about Julia Benson's interview and all that had happened following the parsonage break-in. Bill had not only changed the locks on the doors, he had also put metal rods in the windows to keep them from being opened. Maggie could open them from the inside if she needed some air, but they would be securely locked at night.

Jack was grateful that Bill had changed the parsonage locks. He had also spent the afternoon at church, changing every lock on the outer doors and putting rods in every window of the building. Charlotte had overseen the proceedings and declared the parsonage and church to be safe and sound.

Everyone hoped she was right.

11

Maggie's parents thought they knew what they were going to hear from their daughter after listening to the cryptic message she left on their answering machine earlier in the day. Once they were both home on Monday evening, they called the parsonage in Cherish.

"Hi, parents," Maggie said when she heard their voices.

Jack was listening on the speakerphone as he finished his piece of pie.

"Hello, Maggie," Mimi said.

"Hi, sweetheart," Dirk said at the same time.

"You left us a mysterious message earlier today," Mimi said.

Maggie's message had been: "Mom, Dad, this is Maggie. Oh, of course it's Maggie. Anyway, when you are home together, please give me a call. It's not an emergency, but sort of . . . but not bad. Anyway, call me. Love you!"

"Yes, I did," she admitted. "Jack is here, by the way. We wanted you to know we're engaged. He proposed last night."

"She proposed the night before," Jack chimed in.

Maggie put more pie in his mouth to shut him up.

"Congratulations to you both," Mimi said practically. "Jack, we are happy to welcome you into our family."

Maggie could hear her dad chuckling in the background.

"Anyway, we are happily engaged. Also, I sprained my ankle and smashed my face on a cement floor. We have a prowler hanging around the church and parsonage, and I have a new kitten named Fruit Loop. It's been a busy weekend. Oh, and I was interviewed by a reporter from *The Cherish Life and Times.* Bill Baxter spent the day changing the locks on the parsonage doors and the church doors. We were all hoping to be a little more subtle than that, but it just had to be done. Right now, only Hank, Doris, Irena, Marla, and I have keys to either place."

Maggie went on to describe all the events that had compressed themselves into three days. Her parents were appropriately horrified about the intruder, pleased with the council's decisions, proud of Maggie for keeping an uncommonly cool head, worried about Maggie's ankle and face, shocked at the third cat, and ecstatic about the engagement.

"Have you told Bryan yet?" Mimi asked. "I suppose you could tell him in person on Monday when he flies in to Detroit."

Mimi knew Bryan and Maggie would spend most of his Michigan time together. She would never let them know how much she missed them both. Although one hundred percent Dutch, Mimi was opposed to Dutch guilt.

"I think I'll call him," Maggie said. "I don't want to wait. He'll be called right after Jack's parents. We both feel bad that the whole church knew before we could tell our families. I'll call Jo and Nora and Dan tonight too."

"Congratulations tonight and in the future," Dirk said. "We can finally put that wedding fund to use." He laughed at himself.

"I didn't even know there was a wedding fund." Maggie laughed back. "Well, now, maybe we should get married in Italy or something. What's that called?"

"A destination wedding. Absolutely not," Mimi pronounced, but Maggie knew her mother was smiling over the phone. "And Maggie, you must get your cat issues under control. Maybe you should see a professional."

"I am," said Maggie, gazing at Jack. "Bye, Mom. Bye, Dad. I love you!"

"Goodbye, Dirk and Mimi," Jack chimed in. "We'll look forward to seeing you soon, in person, as soon as Maggie's ankle is better."

"We are glad to have you in the family, Jack," Mimi said.

A very high compliment from a woman who spoke the truth without embellishment.

They ended their conversation, and Jack dialed his parents' number.

Maggie had met Ken and Bonnie Elliot once at their home in Blissfield and a few more times at dinners, usually in Ann Arbor with Jack. Jack's parents made it easy to see how Jack turned out to be nearly perfect. Ken had been a farmer his entire life. He and Bonnie, a stay-at-home mom, raised their five children with these ingredients: love, responsibility, accountability, honesty, and plain good morals. Each of their children had become successful in different areas of life, which surprised Maggie. She would have expected to see one dud in such a large litter.

"Hello, Bonnie speaking."

Jack heard his mother's voice and smiled.

"Hi, Mom. It's Jack."

"Yes, dear, I know. I recognize your voice."

Bonnie giggled. She never mixed up her children's voices. It was something she was very proud of since Ken couldn't tell any of them apart.

"I'm here with Maggie," Jack continued, sounding nervous. "And we would like to tell you and Dad something. Is he around?"

Jack gave a slight cough, and Maggie locked her index finger around his. He took a breath and smiled at her.

"Hi, Jack," Ken said. "I'm on the speakerphone thingamabob."

"Hi, Dad. Maggie and I are getting married," Jack said quickly. "We got engaged yesterday, and we are very excited."

Giggles from Bonnie, and a loud "Well, I'll be!" from Ken.

"We haven't picked a date yet, but we will let you know as soon as we do."

Jack was being very manlike: brief. Maggie slid the phone from his hand.

"Hi, Ken and Bonnie. This is Maggie. Your son is very romantic, and I have something very pretty and sparkly on my ring finger. I would love to show it to you."

She knew that would make Bonnie happy.

"Oh, yes!" Bonnie giggled more. "Can the two of you come down for dinner this weekend?"

Jack looked at Maggie, who nodded effusively. He took the phone back.

"Yes. How about Friday night? We could be there by six thirty."

Jack was all business.

"We'll plan on that. Are you calling your sisters and brothers?" Bonnie asked.

"Yes. We're making our way through the list," Jack said.

"Well, Leigh and Nathan are here and have heard everything already."

There were loud whoops of laughter in the background.

Jack's two youngest siblings lived at home. Leigh ran a maternity shop in downtown Blissfield called Kanga and Roo. Nathan was just getting ready for his senior year at U of M.

"Congratulations!" Leigh and Nathan shouted in surround sound.

Bonnie chimed in with her own cheery congratulations, and then Ken followed suit. He said, "Andrew is out with Brynn tonight. We thought we'd hear this kind of announcement from him long before you, Jack. Good for you."

Andrew was two years younger than Jack. He was pleasing his father immensely by taking over the family farm. His girlfriend, Brynn, was already regarded as part of the family.

After hanging up with his parents, Jack and Maggie continued their phone calls to their family and friends. Jack's oldest sibling, sister Anne, was happily surprised and wanted to know the unknown date.

"We really don't have a date yet," Jack insisted.

"Well, don't waste too much time figuring it out. You're getting old."

Anne's abruptness made Jack and Maggie laugh. Anne and her family lived near Detroit, where she worked with emotionally impaired students in an inner-city Detroit high school. She was no fuss, no drama. Maggie was in awe of Anne and also a little afraid of her.

The waves of happiness swept over Maggie and Jack with each phone call. For one delightful evening, they completely forgot about break-ins and new door locks.

Maggie's brother, Bryan, was thrilled.

"So when is this thing going to happen?" he asked.

"We don't know yet, but we'll make sure you're not wandering around Africa at the time. You are probably the only person we need to consult with, now that I think about it." Maggie laughed. "We'll look at calendars, okay?"

She glanced at Jack, hoping it was okay. Jack grinned back. He would marry her tomorrow morning if she wanted.

It was late in the evening when Maggie and Jack called the last names on their list.

Maggie hesitated slightly as she began to dial Jo's number. Her friend would greet the good news with joy, but they would all be thinking of how Ed had meant to officiate Maggie's wedding.

"Hi, Jo," Maggie said. "It's Maggie and Jack. I hope we're not calling too late."

"Of course not, Maggie," Jo said clearly. "How are you both?"

Maggie's giddiness had dissipated.

"We are great. We wanted you to be one of the first to know we are engaged."

"What perfect news. I am thrilled for you both." Jo's happiness was genuine. "And you know Ed would have been thrilled too. He thought Jack was absolutely top drawer. A real class act. Those were his very words."

Jo's voice on speakerphone filled the parsonage kitchen with warmth.

"Thank you, Jo," Jack said. "That means a lot to me. I had only the highest respect for Ed."

"Thank you, Jack. Now, have you two picked a date? After Dan and Nora's lovely wedding, yours will be the next big thing."

Jo's heart wasn't so broken that she couldn't enjoy the love stories of other couples. After all, no couple could top the love story she and Ed had shared. She was utterly convinced of that.

"We don't have a date, but we'll be working on it and will let you know," Maggie said. "The next time we are on that side of the state, we'll call you, and maybe you'll invite us over for tea."

Maggie smiled.

"The tea will be ready, my dear."

They happily said their good-nights, looking forward to sharing a pot of tea in the near future.

Dan and Nora were last on the list.

"It looks like Jack and I will be joining you in the nuptial department," Maggie said when they were all on speakerphone. "We don't have a date yet, so we'll keep watching you two for a while and see how it goes."

Nora squealed uncharacteristically. She was a tomboy at heart, but being a bride, and now a wife, had softened her a little. She had shocked all who knew her by wearing makeup to her wedding. Still, Maggie would never participate in any sporting event involving Nora. Nora was a beast when it came to sports.

"This is the best news since our engagement."

Nora laughed, remembering how she and Dan had driven out to Cherish to tell Maggie in person and ask her to officiate their wedding.

"Hey, Jack, congratulations!" Dan chimed in. "You've got quite a fiancé there, except for her cat addiction."

All three cats were curled up on the kitchen floor in the little beds Maggie had bought them.

"I'm thinking of putting her in a twelve-step program to deal with her issue," said Jack.

"Say what you wish, you horrible men. It doesn't matter because I'm engaged, my fiancé is handsome, and I have cats," Maggie trilled.

They finally said their good-nights. Maggie noticed it was almost ten o'clock. She was exhausted.

"I think I need a little bit of sleep." She yawned.

"I agree. A pain pill probably wouldn't hurt either," Jack said, cleaning up the dishes.

"When can I get rid of these crutches?"

"A few more days. We'll try you with a cane at the end of the week. Okay?"

"Mmmm . . . that's a long time from now." Maggie yawned again.

Jack gave her a happy engagement kiss and then listened for the slide of the new deadbolt behind him as he left from the back door of the parsonage. He didn't like leaving Maggie alone but knew the locks would keep her safely protected. If only they could find the perpetrator of the break-ins.

As Jack walked to his car, he did not notice the figure in black watching him from the shadows outside the sanctuary doors.

12

Maggie awoke on Tuesday morning feeling as if she had only just closed her eyes to sleep the night before. She stretched and accidentally kicked a cat onto the floor.

"Sorry, Cheerio," she said while simultaneously feeling the pain in her ankle rise up. She also felt the bruise on her face.

When she looked in the mirror, she saw the bruise was turning a lovely golden green. *Drat!* But at least there had been no break-ins or scary people creeping around last night. As far as she knew, anyway.

As she hobbled around the parsonage—eating her oatmeal, banana, and pure maple syrup—she fed the cats and began getting ready for work. As she did so, she relived the night before and the phone calls she and Jack had made.

It was true! She was really getting married! She was getting married to Jack. She looked at her ring and took a long, deep breath of self-centered joy.

When she left the parsonage, Maggie carefully locked the back door with her new key. She crutched herself over to church and found Irena on the organ bench, purple hair flying, arms and hands flailing, and her tiny feet working the pedals as if she were on a bicycle. As soon as there was a break in this extravaganza, Maggie tapped Irena on the shoulder.

"Good morning, Irena. That was quite impressive. Are you practicing for Sunday?"

"No," Irena said.

"What for then?" Maggie asked, looking past Irena and into Hank's office, where he was busily typing something.

"Forr your vedding, ov coorse," Irena said as she shifted her music.

Maggie brought her eyes to Irena's brightly colored face and just stared.

"What?" Maggie asked.

"I prractice forr your vedding. It vill be magnificent! I hev all de pieces peeked out for your cerremony. Yes, eets no prroblem. Yourr velcome."

Irena lifted her hands to play. Maggie grabbed both of Irena's small hands in her own.

"Irena, don't you think we should talk about it first? Jack and I don't even have a date yet."

Maggie could feel a small ball of panic begin to unfurl itself in the middle of her oatmealed stomach.

Irena pulled her little claws out of Maggie's grasp. Maggie opened her mouth to speak but chose to reposition her crutches instead and move on. The conversation was going nowhere but bad.

"Thank you, Irena, for your work on this. We can talk about it later."

Irena's hands went down on the keys as she said, "Vy? You know notting aboot musick."

Maggie tried to move on in a dignified manner. Alas, she was on crutches. She hobbled her way into Hank's office.

"Good morning, Hank. How are things this morning? Any signs of our creepy intruder?"

"Pastor Maggie, there were no signs whatsoever. Doris and I made the rounds to each door and window. Everything's locked up as tight as your grandma's suitcase, yesireebob!" Hank was obviously relieved.

"Good," Maggie said, having no idea what her grandma's suitcase had to do with anything. "I will have a sermon title for you this morning.

Maybe today will be quieter with no soup committee and the brand-new locks installed."

"The only doors unlocked right now are the sanctuary doors. And with Irena, the Romanian wolfhound, on the organ bench, no one will get in without notice or inquisition. Doris is also on watch, ready to spray Raid on any intruder."

Hank turned back to his computer.

Maggie went into her office, amazed at the beauty of it, as she often was. She always felt as if she were walking straight into a daffodil. When she had been gone for a few weeks the past winter—after Ed's sudden death and her overwhelming grief—Maggie's delightful congregation worked together to completely redo the cavelike office she had inherited from her all-male predecessors. The congregation had decorated her office with pale-yellow walls, new seafoam-green carpet, and beautiful cream-colored furniture. She had been thrilled and still was.

Maggie sat and carefully set her crutches aside. Her armpits were still sore but were getting a little better. She pulled out her copy of *The Lectionary Bible* and began studying the passages for Sunday. It was now the long season after Pentecost, roughly June to November. Maggie was already bored. She began reading and writing down words that halfheartedly caught her eye when there was a light knock on the door. Hank popped his head in.

"Sorry to bother you, Pastor Maggie, but a Skylar Breese is here?" He raised one eyebrow questioningly. "Do you have time to see her?" Another question. Then quickly came a third. "I also just received a strange phone call from our church's credit card company. I need to tell you something. Is that okay?"

"Of course, Hank. Tell her just a minute and come back in here."

Hank did so.

When he returned, he shut Maggie's door with a horrified look on his face and whispered loudly, "Redford Johnson has used the church credit card to pay for his trip to Montana, or at least his stay there." Hank's eyes were practically bugging right out of his head. "The credit card company tried calling here yesterday, but no one answered. So they called again just now."

Maggie's mouth dropped open. She couldn't seem to close it. She also couldn't seem to breathe. What was Redford doing?

Hank spoke quickly. "I have already told them to stop payment on the card. Even though he has a card with his name on it as head of the finance committee, I told them it was invalid."

Maggie finally caught her elusive breath and asked, "How did they ever find out about this?" She was flatly astonished.

"Someone from the resort where he is staying thought it was odd when he used a church credit card. Whoever it was informed the credit card company to be safe rather than sorry. The credit card company put a hold on the card until they were able to speak with one of us here at LTLCC. God bless whoever caught that credit card discrepancy. Redford won't be charging anything to this church, nosireebob!" Hank said with zest, brushing his hands together, as if wiping Redford out of existence. "But anyhoo, this Skylar Breese is waiting for you. We can talk about this later. Who is she? She sure is tall."

"She's in the new members class. She was in church on Sunday," Maggie answered mechanically. She couldn't get over Redford's shameless use of the church credit card as quickly as Hank. Finally, she looked at him and said, "Please show Sky in, Hank. And thank you for stopping the credit card. That was good thinking."

Hank beamed.

He opened the door, and Skylar Breese breezed in. Her long, lean loveliness was accentuated by high-heeled sandals. She was wearing white harem pants and a pastel-pink lace blouse. She really was breathtaking.

"Hi, Sky."

Maggie tried to stand, but her ankle forced her back down. She picked up her crutches and made her way to one of the cream-colored visitor chairs while pointing at the other one for Sky. Maggie had to look straight up to make eye contact.

"Hi, Pastor Maggie," Sky said in her ethereal voice. "I just wanted to stop by for . . . mmm . . . a minute."

"That's great. Please stop in anytime. If I'm not here, I'm usually next door at the parsonage. I love to visit."

Maggie was fascinated by the blonde willow tree sitting next to her. Redford left her thoughts for the time being.

"Sky, I have to say it, you are just lovely. What can I do for you today?"

"Mmm . . . well, I was hoping I could do something for you." Sky gazed around Maggie's office, obviously forgetting her original purpose. "This is so pretty. You must love working here."

Maggie almost giggled. How in the world did this woman run the Pretty, Pretty Petals Flower Shop?

"I do love it," Maggie said. "I feel as if I'm in a flower all day long."

"Oh, yes. Flowers. That's what I've come to see you about. I was wondering if I could help with your wedding flowers. I heard yesterday from Sylvia that you and Dr. Elliot are engaged. Mmm . . . so sweet." Sky's eyes glowed. "Yes . . . congratulations. Weddings are so . . . mmm . . . yummy. I already offered the fresh flowers for your wedding cake. Mrs. . . . mmm . . . Popkin asked if I could help. She makes the most delicious donuts, doesn't she?"

Maggie could hardly believe what she was hearing.

"Yes, she does. And thank you. Dr. Elliot and I are very happy. Thank you also for your offer. When the time comes, we would love to know your suggestions for flowers."

Sky's gaze had already wandered off, and Maggie felt awkward. Sky seemed to have one long leg—or at least half her brain—planted in another world. Maggie soldiered on.

"If I may change the subject, I was so glad to have you in the new members class on Sunday. I hope Loving the Lord is a church where you find fellowship and a positive spiritual life."

"Oh, I love Loving the Lord. Sylvia told me I would, and I do. Except for that Verna Baker. She won't let me bring flowers on Sundays. All she grows, apparently, are zinnias. I won't even sell zinnias at Pretty,

Pretty Petals. They're too harsh, and they smell ... mmm ... skunky, you know?" Sky looked at Maggie.

"You and I completely agree on that," Maggie said, feeling as if she had finally made a connection with the dreamy woman. Too bad it was at Verna's expense.

A commotion started in Hank's office.

"Pastor Maggie is with someone right now!" Hank was using his authoritative voice.

"Okay, Hank. I'll wait. No big deal," Maggie heard Cate Carlson say.

Cate! Maggie had forgotten to tell Cate about the engagement. Cate and Maggie had hit it off when Maggie first arrived in Cherish. Cate was now going to be a sophomore at the University of Michigan, but she still liked to spend time with Maggie when she wasn't working at The Sugarplum. Cate was also long-distance dating Maggie's brother, Bryan. Maggie couldn't have been happier about that development. She didn't know how it would work when Bryan was in Africa. It was hard enough just having him in San Francisco. But it was working for Bryan and Cate so far.

"Well, Sky, is there anything else I can do for you?"

Maggie wondered if Sky was planning on spending the day. Plus, she really wanted to talk with Cate.

"No ... no ... I just wanted to stop by with my flower offering."

Sky smiled and looked right into Maggie's eyes for only the second time during their visit. She rose to leave and once again towered over Maggie.

"I really appreciate your offer, Sky. Thank you."

Maggie knew she could like Sky, if only she could keep her focused for a complete conversation.

As Sky left, Cate entered, smiling. She carefully threw her arms around Maggie.

"Pastor Maggie, I'm so sorry about your ankle and that ugly bruise on your face, but I'm so happy for you and Dr. Elliot. Congratulations!" Cate oozed with twenty-year-old enthusiasm. "Here, sit back down, get off your ankle. Was that Skylar Breese? She's the talk of the town with her new flower store. She grew up here but then left for school or something. Now she's back in good ole Cherish. Isn't she beautiful? I've never seen such a tall woman before. She dresses like one of those fairies in *Fantasia*, don't you think?"

Maggie laughed. "Cate, you are so good for my soul."

Cate grinned. "Ditto."

"Okay, where did you hear about the engagement? I want to apologize for not calling you myself. It seems that the news leaked out without our permission. All of a sudden, everyone in Cherish knew."

"I first heard it in The Sugarplum. I saw Mrs. Popkin decorating your BETROTHAL cupcakes," Cate began.

"You mean BETORTHAL." Maggie giggled.

"Is that how they showed up in the box?" Cate chortled. "Oops! Anyway, last night I talked to Bryan. He had already talked with you and Dr. Elliot. We are both so excited for you."

"Thank you. We are excited too. I have to say, it is a little overwhelming to have so many people knowing so fast. It seems everyone has something to offer us for the wedding."

"I've already seen your wedding cake," Cate said enthusiastically, not really hearing herself. "Mrs. Popkin showed all of us yesterday. She has a whole book filled with pictures of wedding cakes. It's really pretty. It's chocolate and has a raspberry custard filling. She's going to put fresh flowers on it."

"Oh. How nice."

Maggie felt a little dizzy. Other couples could plan and prepare their wedding in their own time and way. It seemed that Maggie's wedding would be planned by everyone but her.

"Anyway," Cate continued, completely unaware of the cake bomb she had just dropped, "Bryan will be here Monday. I can't wait to see him."

Maggie was thrilled to change the conversation to that subject.

"Yahoo! We'll all get to work on the Ghana project for a few days. Will you come back and forth from the U while he's here?"

Maggie already knew the answer. Cate would be in Cherish as much as she could while Bryan was in town.

"I've got some news on that too," Cate said, wriggling in her cream-colored chair. "The U has a study abroad program. Ghana is one of the countries offered. Ha! I'm going second semester this year. It's offered through the nursing program. I'm considering nursing or a public health degree. I'd like to do some good in this world."

Maggie felt the sting in her eyes before the tears actually showed up. Cate astounded her.

"You already do good, Cate. Your huge heart, profound mind, and strong imagination will get you to where you need to be to change the world." Maggie sniffed. "The timing is providential, isn't it? January is our Ghana mission trip, and Bryan will be there too."

Maggie gave Cate a sly look. Cate had planned it perfectly.

"It will be the best," Cate enthused. "All things are working together for good, as St. Paul says. Loving the Lord is actually busy loving the Lord. I'm so excited!" Cate was catching Maggie's emotion.

Suddenly, Maggie's office door burst open. Maggie inhaled, wondering what was going on now. It seemed non-stop that day. Actually, every day seemed to be like that.

Hank had tried to stop it, but Carrie and Carl were too quick for him. They ran right into Maggie, throwing their small arms around her neck, stepping on her sprained ankle, and knocking her crutches to the floor.

"Pasto Maggie! Pasto Maggie!" Carl cried. "We at church!"

Cate stared at the little angel/demons as Maggie attempted to settle them.

"Hi, Carrie and Carl. What are you doing here today?" she asked, hugging both children and feeling her ankle throb once again.

Marla came rushing through the door.

"Carrie, Carl, Pastor Maggie is very busy. I already told you that. Please come back out here, and we will go to the nursery." She looked at Maggie and Cate in exasperation. "I'm so sorry. I thought they were right with me, then POOF! They were gone."

"Why? What? So . . ." Maggie stammered as she looked to Marla for direction.

"Cassandra called me this morning and asked if I could take care of Carrie and Carl. She had something to do. She said she would pick them up here later today. So I picked them up at their house and brought them with me. I have some Sunday school work to do. I thought they could play in the nursery. I'm sorry they interrupted you."

Marla looked miserable.

"I see," Maggie said. She turned to the children. "Carrie and Carl, it's very important you do what Mrs. Wiggins asks you to do today. Will you please stay in the nursery until your mommy picks you up?"

They both nodded, but not as if they meant it. Marla took each child by the hand.

The babysitting situation was really getting out of control, and Maggie knew she would have to talk to Cassandra about "dumping" her children on the church for the impromptu, although all-too-regular, childcare.

"I apologize again, Pastor Maggie and Cate. We'll get back to the nursery." Marla looked at Carrie and Carl, who were all smiles and giggles. "By the way," Marla said, "do you know why Skylar Breese was here?"

"She stopped by to talk about . . ." Maggie tried to remember exactly. It had been such a scattered conversation. "Flowers. Why?"

"I just wondered why she was in the basement. I found her down there when I was looking for the children." Marla turned to lead Carrie and Carl out of the office. "She seemed surprised, but she went upstairs when she saw me. I waited until I saw her leave."

Maggie was dumbfounded. *Why would Skylar be in the basement?*

13

Thursday night, Jack was at the parsonage for dinner. He had brought Maggie the romantic gift of a cane. As they ate their soup from the day's yield at church, they caught up on each other's day.

"So far, so good with the new locks," Maggie said. "There has been no evidence of a break-in all week. We hope it's done and over with. Tomorrow Fruit Loop goes to Dr. Dana for shots and a tiny surgery to remove unneeded bits and pieces. Maybe then he won't be such a terror to the others."

Jack laughed. "Poor Fruit Loop. He doesn't know what he's in for tomorrow. But back to the locks, I hope whoever the intruder is has been thoroughly frustrated. You, the staff, and we on the council have done a great job of not letting the story leak. The congregation at large doesn't have a clue that we have changed the locks. We'll try to keep it that way. Now, finish your soup. I want to look at your ankle and see if you're ready for this cane."

"Yes, master."

Maggie stuck out her tongue.

After dinner, Jack unwrapped her ankle.

"Well, it looks like you have been a good girl and have given it plenty of rest. The swelling is down, and the bruise on your face is barely visible. I might even be able to take you out in public again one of these days."

Maggie ignored him and reached eagerly for the cane.

"My armpits got the worst of this whole deal."

Grabbing the cane, she stood gingerly on her feet, favoring her right. She stepped down on her left foot and let the cane take most of the pressure for her right foot.

"Hey! Looky. I can walk!"

"Don't go crazy, you nut," Jack said practically. "You'll be back on crutches if you overdo this."

"I'll behave. No more crutches for Maggie."

She walked slowly around the kitchen. It hadn't been a week since the accident. She knew it would still be a while before she would be able to resume her morning runs, and she missed how much they cleared her mind each day. Fortunately, she had the incredible metabolism of a twenty-seven-year-old, so the extra cookies and cupcakes weren't manifesting themselves on her thighs. It was nice to be young and fit.

"What time are you picking me up to go to your parents' tomorrow night?" Maggie asked as she traversed the kitchen with her new cane one more time.

"Five thirty. The whole family will be there, so get ready to be hugged and have everyone talking to you at once."

"No problem. Just sounds like another church coffee time."

Maggie was all smiles.

That night, Maggie fell into a dream, like Alice down the rabbit hole. She was at church, where everything was decorated with white and pink flowers. A ridiculous, eight-tiered cake covered in fresh flowers was sitting on the pulpit. Suddenly, the organ sounded. Maggie looked to the back of the church where Irena was perched on the organ bench, her hair an astounding shade of blue. She was playing "Zip-a-Dee-Doo-Dah."

Jack came through the secret door carrying a white cane.

"Here, my Maggie, a wedding gift for you." He smiled into her eyes.

"But, I . . . I . . ." Maggie stammered, not wanting to be ungrateful. "I don't need a cane, Jack. My ankle is all better."

"No, you will always need a cane," Jack said, putting it in her hand.

"What are we doing here?"

"The wedding," Jack said. "Did you forget about the wedding?"

The entire congregation filed in. Everyone was dressed in white. The children were scattering flower petals. The youth were walking in, looking bored and lifeless. The new members class walked in and sat in one pew. Skylar was carrying bouquets of flowers and began passing them out to everyone. Mrs. Popkin held another cake. She was so round, she looked like a wedding cake herself. Her satin baker's hat looked like a swirl of meringue on top of her head.

Maggie looked at Jack. "What are they doing here?"

"It's their wedding, remember? It's everyone's wedding, Maggie," he said, smiling.

"What about our wedding, Jack?"

Maggie wanted to cry.

"We can't have a wedding. Someone broke into the church and stole it. No wedding for Jack and Maggie."

Jack turned and left through the secret door.

Maggie woke up.

She couldn't find any air. Finally, she exhaled and took a deep breath. It was just a dream, but perhaps there was a little too much truth in it.

Friday morning, Maggie loaded Fruit Loop into a cat carrier. It was a relief. His daily portion of liver and pills had turned him into a feline superhero. All he needed was a cape. He flew through the air with the greatest of ease, constantly landing on Cheerio's head. Occasionally, he would give Marmalade's tail a chomp, but then Marmalade's large white paw would land hard on Fruit Loop's nose. Marmalade was still the "mama."

The Westminster chimes rang. Maggie walked with her newly beloved cane to the front door where Marla stood. She was there to drive

Maggie and Fruit Loop to Cherish Your Pets. Carrie and Carl were standing with Marla, wearing big grins on their faces.

"Pasto Maggie!" Carl said elatedly.

It looked like Marla had stopped at The Sugarplum before heading to the parsonage. Both Carl and Carrie had colored sprinkles attached to their faces with white icing as the glue.

Maggie looked at Marla, who shrugged resignedly.

Maggie looked back at the children.

"Hi, you two. I'm so happy to see you. Are you spending this morning with Mrs. Wiggins again?"

"No," said Carrie, who was dressed to the nines in a yellow leotard, golden tutu, and green, sparkly crown. "We get to spend all day with her. And tonight too."

"Really? Well, my goodness," was all Maggie could muster.

Something has to be done about this situation.

Marla carried Fruit Loop to the car in his carrier. He was too energetic these days to sit quietly in a lap. Carrie and Carl hopped in the backseat. Maggie noticed that Marla had car seats for both of them.

A short while later, the foursome walked into Cherish Your Pets and sat down to wait their turn. Carrie and Carl looked at the other animals in the waiting room.

Carrie whispered, "Pastor Maggie, may we pet that dog?" She was pointing to a golden cocker spaniel.

Maggie looked up at the older gentleman holding the leash of the dog. He smiled and said, "Sure. Sophie loves being petted."

Carrie and Carl shyly walked over to pet Sophie. Maggie was glad to see some semblance of manners in the two waifs. At least they weren't tearing around the waiting room the way they did at church.

Finally, it was time to bring Fruit Loop back to an examining room. Dr. Dana took him out of the carrier and laughed.

"Well, I don't think you're the same kitten I saw a week ago." Fruit Loop tried to squirm out of her hands to start sniffing the strange place. Dana wrangled him back in the carrier and said, "You can pick him up tomorrow afternoon. He'll need a little quiet time for a couple of days."

"Good," said Maggie. "He hasn't been quiet all week."

"By the way," Dana said, "I really enjoyed the new members class on Sunday. I can't wait for this week. And I personally love being the 'diversity person' at Loving the Lord." She smiled with beautiful white teeth.

Maggie laughed. "We have to work on that. Cherish doesn't have a deep well to draw from on the diversity front. Of course, we have Irena. She's your diversity buddy."

Both women rolled their eyes, and then Maggie gave Fruit Loop a wave goodbye and went out to the waiting room.

As Maggie and Marla left with the children, Maggie whispered to Marla, "Where is Cassandra today?"

"I'm not sure. She asked if I could keep them until tomorrow morning," Marla said grimly. "It's my own fault. I keep saying yes."

"I'll talk to her," Maggie said. "I'll just say I've noticed them around church a lot, blah, blah, blah."

Marla smiled but was doubtful it would do any good.

When they all returned to church, Maggie said goodbye to Marla and the children and hobbled around the corner from church and down one block to the We Work Miracles beauty salon.

Lacey Campbell owned and operated the only salon in town. Maggie had started going to Lacey after she realized that going back to Zeeland to get her hair cut was foolish. Even though she always worked in a visit with her parents or Jo or Dan and Nora, she knew she needed to find a local salon to get her hair trimmed. Lacey always made Maggie smile.

Lacey had shoulder-length, auburn hair, dark eyes, and wore bright-red lipstick. Maggie thought she was exotic and must live a very exciting secret life, like being a member of the CIA while posing as a hairdresser. Lacey had a delicate gold ring in the side of her nose, which added to her glamorous mystery.

Maggie was often refreshed in Lacey's no-nonsense presence. Lacey owned a boa constrictor named Evelyn, two cats named Ned and Ted, and a Chihuahua named Benedict. Maggie was hoping to get Lacey to this year's animal blessing service, minus Evelyn. Maggie was terrified of snakes.

"Hi, Lacey."

Maggie grinned as she came through the door. She always enjoyed getting her hair trimmed. She also liked going to the dentist. Anytime she could sit and let someone clean her teeth or wash her hair, she felt completely luxurious.

"Well, Pastor Maggie, I've been looking forward to seeing you today. So who do you think is breaking into the church?" Lacey said casually as she wrapped a plastic smock around Maggie's neck and snapped it together.

Maggie was tired of the surprise questions that seemed to suck all the oxygen out of the world. Once again, she stopped breathing.

"Lacey," Maggie finally gasped, "how did you know about the break-ins?"

Lacey looked at Maggie shrewdly. She was only five years older than Maggie but had the common sense and practical wisdom of a sage.

"Because I am who I am," Lacey said as she leaned Maggie's head back into the sink and began spraying it with warm water. "People come in here and tell me everything. They confess to me way more than they do to you, and that's the truth of the matter. By the way, your face doesn't look bad at all. Not like people are saying. And it's nice to see you have graduated to a cane."

Lacey scrubbed Maggie's head with shampoo, but she was not enjoying the hair washing one little bit. She was on the verge of giving a vague answer about the church when Lacey struck again.

"So, about your wedding. I'll do your hair for free. Are you going to wear it up or down? Most brides want up-dos, but I think your hair would look best down with big, soft curls. How about we put in a few highlights to brighten you up for the big day? When is the big day?"

Lacey was now slathering conditioner on Maggie's golden locks. Maggie pretended she couldn't hear as the water rinsed the conditioner out of her hair and into her ears. Then Lacey commenced wrapping Maggie's head in a soft, warm towel. Maggie just wanted to keep breathing.

Dinner with Jack's family was a chaotic delight. Everyone was there. Anne and her husband, Peter, with their two children—Gretchen (ten) and Garrett (eight)—along with Andrew, Brynn, Leigh, and youngest brother, Nathan. Ken and Bonnie seemed as if they would explode from sheer joy at having the entire family around their large dining table, but all eyes were on Maggie.

Having grown up with one sibling and quiet, cerebral parents—although loving and supportive in every way—Maggie took in Jack's family voraciously. She loved people as a rule, enjoyed figuring out what made them tick and act the way they did, and she had a sense of humor. Watching Jack and his siblings talk over each other, laugh, tease, and reminisce, caused a swirl of warmth and connectedness for Maggie. They were going to be *her* family. There would be stories that would begin, "Remember when Jack and Maggie . . . ?" She couldn't wait.

"You know, Maggie," Anne said, "Jack used to suck his thumb when he was little. We have so many pictures of him with his thumb in his mouth. I think we could use those for a wedding video. What do you think?"

Jack groaned at his big sister. She could still be such a pain. But then he laughed and punched Anne in the arm.

"Well," Maggie said, becoming less afraid of Anne and more in love with Jack, "I have several pictures that will match. I was a thumb sucker too. I was actually ambidextrous. I sucked both thumbs—not at the same time, of course—until I was ten."

She gave Jack a wink.

"That's how old I am," Gretchen said, appalled. "Gross!"

Everyone looked at Maggie. She smiled at Gretchen.

"My mother would agree with you, Gretchen. She tried everything to get me to stop. Nothing worked until I went to a sleepover at a friend's house. I put my thumb in my mouth without even thinking."

Gretchen's face and voice softened immediately. "What happened?"

"The other girls laughed at me. They all put their thumbs in their mouths and danced around saying, 'Look, we're Maggie. We thuck our thumbs.' On Monday, they told everyone at school. It was embarrassing." Maggie said all of it simply, which made it all the more devastating to listen to. "I never sucked my thumb again."

The dinner table became uncomfortably quiet. Maggie looked around at each face.

"I really am over it," she said, laughing. "I stopped crying about it days ago, truly."

Gretchen smiled, and then everyone erupted in laughter.

Jack impulsively leaned over and kissed Maggie on the cheek. The laughter quickly died down, and everyone stared, round eyed. Who was this new Jack?

Andrew jumped in. "We've been waiting for Jack to find a girlfriend. He seemed to think being in medical school precluded him from dating. But it looks like he may have pulled his head out of . . . the books . . . and found a wife."

Jack just smiled.

Bonnie asked hopefully, "Have you thought any more about a possible date?"

She began passing salads and the plate of barbecued chicken so that no one could see exactly how much she wanted an answer to her question.

Maggie looked at Jack. She was tired of the question but didn't want to hurt Bonnie's feelings.

Jack said, "We haven't. It's kind of different with Maggie being the pastor of a church. It seems everyone has already begun the planning, but they don't appear to think we need to be part of it." Jack sounded a bit more rueful now.

"Why don't you elope?" Anne asked practically as she helped herself to a large spoonful of potato salad.

∞

Jack dropped Maggie off at the parsonage at ten thirty after the dinner with his family. It had been a lively evening, but both Jack and Maggie were feeling a little "over-peopled."

Anne's surprising comment about an elopement had stopped everyone in their tracks. Bonnie looked absolutely stricken at the thought. She really wanted to be "The Mother of the Groom" and wear a beige dress, as all mothers of grooms were meant to do.

Jack and Maggie had talked about it on the drive home from Blissfield.

"I really don't know how we could get away with it," Maggie began. "I think everyone at church would feel betrayed if we eloped. But . . . it is getting so crazy with everyone's opinions and plans. It won't even be our wedding."

"What would you like it to be?" Jack asked.

He just wanted to marry her. The wedding could be in a church jammed with flowers and cake or in Dan and Nora's living room. They had at least made that one decision. Dan and Nora would co-officiate their wedding.

"I would like to be married in Loving the Lord because it's the greatest church on the planet, but I don't want other people's plans to make it a wedding I don't recognize. I don't want to be a spectator at our wedding."

Maggie had said this with a flair of the dramatic, remembering her dream of the stolen wedding.

"What if we sit down this weekend and make a list of what we would like our wedding to be? Let's even try to pick a date, which we can do by finding out when Bryan will be around. I think we can slowly make our way to the people who have made plans for us already and change things around if needed."

Jack spoke calmly but earnestly. Maggie thought that was exactly how he must sound when he was helping a confused patient stick to a health plan of some sort.

"Oh, it will definitely be needed. I'll let you deal with Irena. The music she was playing the other day sounded like something for a Halloween haunted house."

Both Maggie and Jack laughed, knowing Irena would be the biggest hurdle.

"We'll take back control of our wedding, Maggie, I promise. But you need sleep tonight. I think it would be smart to take another pain pill. It will help you sleep, and that will keep your ankle still. Just a suggestion. I'll call you in the morning after I make rounds at the hospital."

When they had arrived back in Cherish, Jack walked while Maggie hobbled up the sidewalk and around the west side of the parsonage. Jack kissed her at the back door.

"The wedding will be perfect because it will be our day. No matter what."

Maggie smiled and unlocked the door.

"Thanks, Jack. I don't know. Maybe an elopement would be the best thing after all."

"Tomorrow we'll plan."

He waited to hear the deadbolt slide into place and then walked to his car.

He didn't see the person hiding in the shadows, listening intently to their back-door conversation.

14

Having taken Jack's suggestion of swallowing a pain pill, Maggie awoke the next morning to the ring of her phone. It was nine thirty. Even in high school, Maggie had never been one to sleep in. "Early to bed early to rise . . ." Sleeping in that late felt lazy. She rolled over and grabbed her phone.

"Hello?" she said sleepily.

"Did I wake you up?" It was Jack.

"Yes. I'm so glad you did. What a lazy daisy I am. I never sleep this late."

Maggie sat up and saw Marmalade and Cheerio staring at her with the patience of martyrs. It was hours past breakfast.

"I'm glad you slept. I'm sure it was especially good for your ankle. I have just finished rounding. How about some oatmeal?"

"Absolutely, yes."

They hung up, and Maggie began to move. He would be there within minutes, and it would never do for him to see her first thing after waking up until he was legally her husband and couldn't back out.

She pulled on her jeans and a T-shirt, grabbed her cane, and got to the bathroom in seconds. Teeth and hair brushed, face washed, swipes of mascara, and a brush of blush were completed in record time. She was in the kitchen putting oatmeal in the microwave when Jack rapped on the back door.

She opened it and saw a shocked look on his face. *What?* Had she smeared her mascara? Was her T-shirt on inside out?

"Jack, what's the matter?" she asked.

Maggie grabbed her cane as Jack led her out the door. They both stared.

The two sanctuary doors were standing wide open, banging slightly in the wind.

The couple made their way to the front steps. The gently banging doors looked awry. They were strong, heavy oak, historical doors. They were not meant to wave to and fro like a broken garden gate.

"Okay," Maggie said shakily, "maybe someone is here. It could be Doris cleaning, or Hank organizing, or Marla doing something for Sunday school." But she knew none of them would leave the doors open without the brick stoppers.

"It could be," said Jack, "but we won't know until we go inside."

Jack noticed the broken wood around the lock about five seconds before Maggie. The doors had been pried open.

Maggie did not want to walk through those doors. She felt a chill. They walked in together, Maggie limping with her cane. They checked all areas of the church, but found no one.

Finally, Maggie hobbled to her office to call Charlotte. Jack sat down in one of the visitor chairs. As she waited for Charlotte to pick up, Maggie saw an envelope on her desk. There was nothing written on the outside. Maggie opened it and pulled out a white sheet of computer paper. Scrawled in red crayon were the words *AN ELOPEMENT? HOW SWEET.*

Maggie dropped the paper like it burnt her fingers. She was so taken aback, she couldn't respond to Charlotte's voice at first.

Finally, she said, "Charlotte, this is Maggie. We've had another break-in at church. Can you come over? Jack and I are here in my office."

"I'm on my way," Charlotte barked and clicked off.

"Do we show Charlotte this note?" Maggie asked, pointing a finger at the crayoned paper. "I know this is evidence, but that's one more possible secret out of the bag. Who could have possibly overheard us? Someone must have been outside the parsonage last night when you dropped me off."

Jack's anger rose. The crayoned letter was a taunt.

"We'll see what Charlotte has to say. It is evidence."

Before Charlotte could get there, Jack and Maggie heard the trip-trap of Irena's high heels. Her small body entered Maggie's office like a well-aimed bullet.

"Vat's going on vit dees doors? Vhy dey banging? Who deedn't poot de brricks in place?"

Irena fired off her questions with precision. Then her eyes were drawn to the red scrawled paper on Maggie's desk. Irena stepped forward until the two women were toe-to-toe. Maggie was still an inch taller, even though she was in flats.

"Vat ees dees?"

Irena must have had martini soup for dinner the night before, or breakfast perhaps, because the smell of it wafted out of her mouth in a pungent cloud. Maggie wanted to step back but didn't.

"Irena, this was left on my desk by whomever it was who broke into the church. That is the bigger issue, don't you think?"

"No. I dun't. Are you and Juck eluping?"

Irena stared out of her small, dark eyes, which were completely engulfed in lime-green eye shadow and long, fake eyelashes.

Maggie looked over Irena's unwavering shoulder at Jack. He just smiled and shrugged his shoulders. *So helpful.*

"Irena, Jack and I haven't made any plans yet. At all. I don't know who wrote this or how they got into the church. We still seem to be vulnerable to the villain, whoever he or she may be. Do you understand me?" Maggie said this last bit as if she were speaking to a small child.

Irena opened her mouth to speak, emitting more toxic martini fumes, but Charlotte could be heard thumping and creaking her way toward Maggie's office. She had made the three-block drive in a flash.

Everyone turned when she, followed by a much quieter Officer Bernie Bumble, walked purposefully through the door.

Not wasting any time, Charlotte began, "The doors were obviously wrenched apart with something like a crowbar. Officer Bumble will dust for fingerprints, but our criminal seems to be cleverer than I'd like to admit. What else happened? Start from the beginning."

Jack and Maggie took turns filling in the few details of the last thirty minutes. Since Irena's discovery of the crayoned note most likely made it public domain, Maggie showed Charlotte and Bernie. Charlotte tried as hard as she could to stay professional but couldn't quite manage it. Her eyes lit up, and her voice became less harsh.

"Uh . . . Are you two really going to elope? . . . ahem," she stammered.

"Dat's zactly vat I asked dem," Irena roared, dying for the chance to speak.

Maggie took a deep breath, inhaling martini billows accidently.

"No. We are not going to elope. I didn't write this note. Whoever broke into the church also came into my office and left this delightful little gift. Don't you think we should concentrate on the break-in? Even our new locks can't keep us safe."

Charlotte pulled herself together. "You are right, Pastor Maggie. Did you happen to hear anything last night or this morning? A strange noise that could pinpoint the break-in?"

"I didn't. I'm sorry. I took a pain pill for my ankle and slept in this morning. I was really out," Maggie said, feeling guilty, then feeling frustrated for feeling guilty.

More footsteps were heard coming toward the church offices. Not surprisingly, Hank and Doris came through and stopped still when they saw the gathering in Maggie's office.

Charlotte took over. "Hank, Doris, there has been another break-in. The front doors were pried open, and a crude note was left on Pastor Maggie's desk."

Both Doris and Hank leaned in to stare at the note. Maggie braced herself, then decided to be proactive.

"I did not write this. It was left on my desk by the villain. We are not eloping."

Doris and Hank seemed to assimilate each statement and, after a moment, had relieved and satisfied expressions resting on their faces.

Why is everyone so wigged out about an elopement? Maggie wondered, frustrated. *Doesn't anyone see the bigger issue?*

"Now what?" Maggie asked a little too harshly.

"Officer Bumble and I will search the rest of the church and look for any clues. If the rest of you could wait here until we've finished, it would be much appreciated. And call Bill Baxter, if you please. We need the sanctuary doors repaired ASAP."

Charlotte turned and went out the door. Bernie, who had been scribbling down every word on his pad of paper, turned and accidentally walked into the wall. He shook his head a little and walked out the door without looking back.

Hank got on the phone to Bill Baxter, who said he would pick up the needed supplies and head to church right away.

While Jack, Maggie, Irena, Doris, and Hank were all sitting back in Maggie's office, Doris seemed agitated.

"I'm sorry, but we need more help," she said disconcertedly. "Our intruder is running circles around our police, and locks aren't helping. It seemed to goad the person into more destruction."

Irena, looking smug, agreed. "I told you dis. Ve hev to tek mutters into our own arms. So, I say, ve need a plen. Onverrds and forrverds!"

Onwards and forwards? Oh dear! Maggie thought.

Although she was quite spirited and animated, Irena had no real plan. None of them did. Like a litter of orphaned kittens, they kept verbally crawling around each other, hoping and waiting for their mother to come back and make everything all right.

By the time Charlotte gave them the "all clear" after finding no sign of the intruder anywhere else in the church and taking the crayoned note in as evidence, Bill Baxter had shown up with a new lock. Irena crawled up onto the organ bench and took out her frustrations of the morning on the poor organ keys and pedals. Hank pulled out his blue tarpaulin and began covering his desk to avert the trash dumpers at coffee time the next day. Doris's vacuum could be heard in the nursery. Jack and Maggie went back to the parsonage. Maggie made two cups of Lady Grey tea, completely forgetting about the oatmeal congealing in the microwave.

"I don't understand *why*," Maggie said after burning her tongue absentmindedly with a gulp of hot tea. "Why would someone want to damage a church? And scare so many good people?"

Jack blew on his tea before taking a sip.

"I wish I knew," he said quietly. "It seems like vengeance. But for what?"

15

Jack and Maggie went to Cherish Your Pets Animal Hospital to collect Fruit Loop right after noon. By the sound of his purr, he seemed happy to see them.

"He should be fine if you keep him quiet for a couple of days," said Dana. "Maybe with this surgery he'll lose a little of his vim and vigor." She smiled.

No such luck. As soon as Fruit Loop was let loose in the parsonage, he began a holy crusade of pouncing, leaping, and chomping on his two feline roommates. They were not pleased. As the three inmates howled and yowled up and down the stairs, Jack and Maggie ate gooey, grilled peanut butter and jelly sandwiches at the kitchen table.

"What do you think needs to be done about the break-ins?" Maggie asked, her mouth full of sandwich, peanut butter oozing out of the grilled bread.

"I agree with Doris. There isn't enough being done. This is beyond Charlotte's expertise. I'm more concerned with you being here alone. I don't think you're safe. The new locks can't keep this lunatic out. I believe we were overheard last night at the back door, which means the person was too close. Why, what are you thinking?"

His turn for a bite of sandwich.

"I agree with you and Doris," Maggie said. "Neither the church nor the parsonage seems safe. Bryan will get here on Monday. He'll stay here all of next week. That makes me feel a little safer. But unless the villain is caught by the time he leaves, I don't know what to do. You can't stay here, Jack. It would look bad. Ellen would stay if I asked her, but she would be terrified."

"That is very true. Ellen was always the easiest one to scare when we were kids. We were actually kind of mean to her. I should probably apologize to her for that," he said, amused and ashamed all at the same time.

"Yes, you definitely should. What a meany you were to that sweet girl. At least now I can add another fault to your list of deficits."

She finished her sandwich and wiped messy peanut butter and jelly fingers on her napkin.

"I think we need another council meeting tomorrow," she said, "but I don't want to announce it in church. I'm beginning to feel our intruder is someone in the pews."

"Let's call the council members now. We'll each take half the list and let them know."

Jack pulled out his phone while unwittingly smearing peanut butter across the screen. Maggie handed him another napkin.

"Good. If I have to leave for the new members class, you can finish the meeting and tell me at lunch what they all think."

She didn't want to be late again for her new members.

"What if we ask people to come this afternoon?" Jack asked, considering the timeliness. "I realize some may have other plans because it's the Labor Day weekend, but this isn't an issue to be rushed through in a stand-up meeting after church."

"Good idea. I think the staff should come too. We seem to be the ones who hang out in the church the most."

Maggie smiled, thinking of the blissful hours of Irena's ear-splitting organ extravaganzas and the snippy fights between Hank and Doris. Oh, for the good old days when those were her biggest problems.

The phone calls were made, and all the members were onboard for the secret council meeting that afternoon. It was a testament to the boring lives led by the council members and church staff alike. None of them had plans for the holiday weekend.

Jack and Maggie did the few dishes from lunch after their phone calls. The cats were fast asleep in their beds, Fruit Loop having launched mini-attacks on Marmalade and Cheerio for an hour prior. No quiet days for him.

At three o'clock, council and staff members gathered in the church nursery, where Jack and Maggie had set out a circle of chairs.

Harold opened the meeting quickly, then sat down next to Ellen and let Maggie take over.

"Thank you for coming on such short notice," she began. "We had another break-in last night or early this morning. The sanctuary doors were pried open, and someone was in my office. Bill has replaced the locks on the doors. Thanks, Bill."

Bill just looked at her soberly. Maggie continued.

"We aren't making any headway with our destructive visitor. In fact, he or she seems to be getting the best of us. Charlotte, you and Bernie have been wonderful in gathering evidence and watching the church," Maggie lied ever so slightly, "but I wonder if we need some more professional help? It's a huge job to guard this place night and day, and there are only two of you."

Maggie hoped she sounded sincere and that feelings weren't being mutilated in the wake of her obvious message.

"We absolutely need more help." Verna Baker sat in her chair, straight as a ramrod, face looking pinched and annoyed, as in days gone by. "Both the church and the parsonage are being damaged when locks are broken and doors are splintered. How much more is this scoundrel going to get away with? Our church is a historical building." She looked around but did not get the response she was looking for. "Our church is registered with the Historical Society. We must protect it. No offense, Charlotte, but you don't seem to be up for the job."

Doris jumped in, speaking a little too loudly. "I completely agree. One hundred and ten percent."

Charlotte was utterly and completely offended. Bernie just hung his large, dark, buzzcut head.

"Verna Baker," Charlotte said in her most official police voice, completely ignoring Doris, "you have no idea what Officer Bumble and I have been doing to guard this church. We have sent evidence to the Washtenaw County Crime Lab and are awaiting results. When did you have *your* last training at the police academy?"

"If you were doing everything to guard this church, it wouldn't have been broken into. Again!" Verna glared at her.

The fact that no one was going to speak up on behalf of the Cherish Police Force was abundantly clear.

"I have to say something." Bernie Bumble spoke while looking at his own feet. "I have to admit that this week I fell asleep on duty when it was my shift to be guarding the church. Twice."

Maggie thought he was going to cry. Then she heard Charlotte's deep intake of breath and knew she had to act fast.

"Officer Bumble," Maggie said quickly, "we all make little mistakes. I believe our intruder is very clever, and even if you had been sitting on the front steps of the church, he or she would have made their way in. I think I can speak for the council when I say we just want you and Chief Tuggle to have all the backup you need until this person is caught."

"And kilt." Irena picked something out of her dark-red fingernail.

"What?" asked many voices at once.

"And kilt," Irena repeated. She looked up from her fire-engine red nail. "In my countrry, you know, Romania, we mek sure de villain, he ees caught and kilt. Okey?" She rubbed her two small, clawed hands together like a brightly painted evil scientist. "Done and done and ded."

Bill Baxter raised his hand, as if he were in elementary school.

"Yes, Bill?" Maggie squeaked. She wasn't quite over the "kilt" comment.

"I think the person we're dealing with has had some experience with breaking and entering. This morning, I found the doors definitely damaged, but the lock had been opened cleanly. There wasn't a scratch on any part of the lock at all. It seemed like the damage to the wood of the door was done to make it look more violent than it really was. Almost as an afterthought."

Bill sat back, and Sylvia slipped her hand into his. She couldn't get over how smart and brilliant her husband was, even as she was completely missing his point. His comment caused an immediate hush to fall on the little circle.

Finally, Hank spoke up. "Do the staff members still have their new keys to the church? I think we should double-check that we all have our keys. If the lock wasn't damaged . . ."

Hank, Doris, Irena, Marla, and Maggie pulled out their key rings. It sounded like a cheery little Christmas concert. Until there was one loud gasp.

"Oh, no!" It was Marla. "My key is gone. It's not on my ring."

"When was the last time you used it?" asked Charlotte, trying desperately to stitch her reputation as police chief back together.

Marla thought. "I haven't used it at all. Every time I have come to church, someone has been here. The doors were open. I've had a bit of a different schedule this week while taking care of Carrie and Carl Moffet. I've come to church with them a little later in the morning."

I have got to go speak to Cassandra, Maggie remembered. She could hardly stand the look on Marla's stricken face.

"I put it right on my key ring when Bill gave it to me," Marla continued.

Maggie was thinking of all the times Marla had Carrie and Carl with her lately, and how she was usually chasing them all over the church. Her purse and keys might have been lying around for anyone to pilfer.

"Is there anything else missing from your purse, Marla?" Maggie asked.

Marla began to look through the contents of her purse. She looked up.

"That's strange. My pocket calendar is missing. Who would want to steal that?"

"What did you use it for? Was it your personal calendar, or did you use it for everything?" Charlotte asked a little awkwardly.

"I used it for everything. Appointments, my kids' schedules, church meetings, birthday reminders, everything. It's not my only calendar. I have a wall calendar and a desk calendar as well."

"Well, now the intruder knows what the church schedule is going to be in the foreseeable future," Charlotte snapped.

"They could know that anyway, Charlotte," Maggie said with a sigh. "All anyone has to do is pick up a weekly bulletin lying around here. We always have a monthly calendar inside. It's more significant that Marla's key was taken. That explains how the lock was untouched by the damage of the crowbar, or whatever it was. Our intruder just opened the lock with Marla's key and then bashed the wood of the doors for effect."

"There is one other thing we must discuss." Maggie hadn't wanted to bring it up now but knew she had to. "The church credit card has been cancelled. I know most of you have a card. Redford did also, and he misused it on his trip to Montana. I won't go into details. Please cut up your cards or leave them on Hank's desk, and he'll take care of them." Maggie looked down at the floor and exhaled.

A sense of weariness descended on the small gathering.

"I'm wondering if we could find a little extra help from the volunteer fire department?" Jack asked. He wanted to get the subject back to watching the church and not slip down the sinkhole of Redford and the credit card. "If we could have more people watching over the church, the burden wouldn't be so heavy on Chief Tuggle and Officer Bumble."

Maggie smiled. What a great and simple idea. *Oh, Jack.*

"Who is the head of the volunteer fire department?" she asked in complete ignorance. She probably should have made a point of meeting the person sometime in the past year.

Everyone looked at her, puzzled.

Finally, Charlotte spoke. "My husband, Fred."

Maggie kept the smile glued on her face. Meanwhile, her head was feeling dizzy. So, the police and the fire department were both run by the Tuggles. Of course. That made perfect sense for crazy little Cherish.

"Dr. Elliot, what exactly were you thinking?" Charlotte asked, pulling out her phone to call her husband, the fire chief.

"I was thinking of shifts. Different people watching the church each night," Jack said practically.

Harold joined in. "I would recommend two people at a time. Our intruder obviously used something to break the wood on the doors. He could be more violent."

"Good idea," Bill said.

"Who's in the department?" Maggie began to get her scattered wits back together.

Bill said, "Well, I am, and William Ellington. You know, he owns The Grange bed and breakfast with his wife, Mary. Chester Walters, Doris's husband, Tom Wiggins, right over there." Bill gave Tom a nod. "And Winston Chatsworth and Dana Drake."

"Dr. Dana Drake? Winston Chatsworth? Are you sure?" Maggie thought maybe Bill was playing a joke on her. "I can't imagine Dr. Dana out fighting fires. And Winston, well, he's just too old."

Maggie didn't care if she sounded rude. She was going to say something about Chester but quickly remembered Doris was sitting there. Maggie stopped her mouth just in time.

So that was the fire department. What a ragtag bunch. It reminded her of Jesus' disciples.

"Ask how many fires there have been in the last five years," Ellen said with a twinkle in her eye.

"How many?"

"Zip, zero, nada," Ellen said.

At least that brought a chuckle to the group.

Well, then what do these people actually do? Maggie felt there needed to be something actually done now to protect the church.

"How about a roster?" she suggested. "Shall we put names on a list? Do we need to call the members of the fire department? Shall we begin tonight?"

Why did she feel as if they were all trekking through molasses? They needed a plan.

Maggie noticed Doris sitting tensely in her chair. She seemed to be in another world. Then Doris purposely scribbled something on a notepad. Maggie watched as Doris's lips tightened, her entire face focused on her writing. Then Doris took a deep breath and sat back, looking satisfied.

"Are you okay, Doris?" Maggie asked.

Doris jumped slightly and glanced around at everyone.

"I'll talk to Chester about this tonight. Don't you worry. That will give us time tomorrow to put a list together. Tonight is covered," she said firmly.

"Thanks, Doris," Maggie said.

"Charlotte." Harold took control. "Would you and Fred please put together a list of volunteers to cover the next two weeks? It would be best if there were two per night, but even one would do. You may add my name to the list. I know you and Bernie will continue with your surveillance, which is crucial, but we will all take part. Once our intruder realizes the fun is over, he'll either disappear or we'll apprehend him. Or her."

"You can add me to the list too," Hank chimed in. "I have no problem doing reconnaissance when it comes to battling this kind of malevolence."

"Fred and I will take care of the list," Charlotte said, "and Officer Bumble and I will continue surveillance. I will also speak with Polly Popkin. She arrives at The Sugarplum every morning between three and four a.m. She can take a peek out her window now and again. Although I suspect our trespasser knows this and does his mischief before Polly shows up."

Maggie felt better. There was some sort of plan in the making, as nutty as it sounded.

"Shall we meet at the parsonage tomorrow afternoon to go over the list?" Maggie asked. "I realize you are giving a lot of your time to this problem, but how about three o'clock? We'll try to keep it short."

Everyone agreed.

16

Doris walked home from the meeting to Chester. He was preparing meatloaf and mashed potatoes, along with fresh green beans from their garden. Doris sat down in the spotless kitchen and told him about the meeting and the new plan of surveillance.

"So, the fire department is in on it too now?" Chester asked. "Well, it's about time we have something to do around here. Driving down Main Street for parades and teaching fire safety in the parking lot at the high school doesn't seem to fill up much of our time and, I might add, our expertise."

He grinned at his wife, who did not grin back.

"I've never seen anything like this before, Chester," Doris said seriously, snapping green beans automatically. "Someone is doing this just to show he can. Nothing has been stolen, except for Marla's key and calendar. He's just breaking in to cause a ruckus. Why?"

Chester had no idea. He and Doris had belonged to Loving the Lord since the day they were wed at its altar. They had seen pastors come and go, but they had never seen anything like the vandalism that was taking place now. It was a conundrum.

Doris went on to tell him the plan for watching the church that night. He was a little surprised, but if the council said so, then so be it. He'd be the last to argue with the powers that be.

They ate their supper quietly, not really tasting anything. Then they washed the dishes together, as they did every night. But once it was dark, the first watchman headed to church.

Maggie, Jack, Ellen, and Harold had a lighthearted evening once they shook off the heaviness of the afternoon and the council meeting. They had decided to have dinner and do something a little more carefree. Pizza was delivered, wine was opened, and they sat down and played The Farming Game. It was one of Maggie's favorites from childhood, which, of course, gave her an amazing advantage. As they each tried to buy more land, cows, and fruit trees, it became clear that Maggie had a secret strategy to winning the game, which she did quite handily.

"I haven't played board games since I was about ten," said Harold, who had lost all of his hay and corn by the end of the game.

"That's a bummer," said winner Maggie with a grin. "You might have done better tonight if you had kept up your skills."

"We have to do this again," Ellen said.

She was very competitive and absolutely had to beat Maggie at that game.

"Any time," Maggie said.

Both Harold and Jack laughed.

Playing the game had taken the seriousness out of life and chased the doldrums away for a bit. Loving the Lord had been a place of joy and laughter and creative worship, especially since Maggie had arrived. Now the church had been violated, attacked. Worry had made its way onto so many parishioners' faces. And even worse, a sense of sadness. Maggie wanted the sadness banished.

Harold and Ellen left at ten o'clock. Jack stayed until midnight. He watched Maggie sleep on the couch. She hadn't meant to fall asleep. She was actually dreading sleep after the vivid dreams she'd been having. Maggie had always been a dreamer, remembered her dreams, and seen the connections to her real life. She had been that way since she was a child. It was something that had intrigued her mother, the psychologist, who'd always listened to Maggie's dreams and found them fascinating. Maggie had told Jack about her recent dreams. It wasn't hard to see the way her subconscious was making its way to the surface.

Jack didn't want to leave Maggie alone in the parsonage. Finally, he gently woke her up and waited at the back door until she sleepily locked it behind him. He walked around the entire parsonage and then the church but saw nothing. He finally got into his car and saw Maggie's bedroom light go out.

Jack sat in his car in front of the church until two a.m., which was when he saw Charlotte drive up in the squad car. He hadn't seen anyone on guard before then but knew Chester must be watching from inside the church.

"Hi, Charlotte," he said when she came alongside his window. "I guess I'm a little anxious after the day's events. I've just been keeping an eye on the church and parsonage. Some things are worth protecting, if you know what I mean." He smiled wanly. "Is Chester Walters supposed to be here tonight?"

"Yes, I believe he is. You probably just didn't see him. Go home and get some sleep, Doc," Charlotte said more kindly than normal. "I'll stay parked here for the rest of the night. We do have much to protect. I agree with you on that, for sure."

Jack drove to his condo and practically fell into bed.

That night, Maggie dreamed again. She was standing in the pulpit on Sunday morning. As she was preaching, Carrie and Carl began racing up and down the center aisle yelling, "You can't catch me! You can't catch me!" Maggie spoke louder, trying to be heard over the children, but soon Carrie and Carl had drowned out her voice completely. Then their voices changed, and it was a man's voice. He came out of the secret door. He was dressed in black.

"You can't catch me! Ha!" he yelled at Maggie and came toward her with a crowbar. "And you can't stop me!"

Maggie tried to run, but her feet were stuck in a bucket of peanut butter and jelly behind the pulpit. She couldn't move. She searched the congregation for Jack, but the entire congregation was covered in ashes. Maggie knew they were dead.

She awoke with a start when her alarm went off. Her heart was pounding, and she was covered in sweat. *Another nightmare.* She turned on her lamp and sat up in bed, trying to catch her breath and shake off the bad dream. The kitties, who had been rudely awakened by the alarm, were now readjusting themselves to finish napping. Marmalade smashed himself under her less sore arm.

Maggie reached for her cane and hobbled downstairs to the kitchen. She brewed a cup of coffee, went into her study, and looked out the floor-to-ceiling window. The three beautiful pine trees were standing at attention, with the summer flowers in the little red wagon gallantly holding their own. The weather would become cooler by the end of the month. Maggie could hardly believe it was Labor Day weekend already. That usually meant a small crowd in church, with everyone gone for one last hurrah of summer. But as she found out yesterday, apparently not at Loving the Lord.

It was the first morning in days Maggie had awakened and had not thought about her engagement. Someone was trying to harm the church. Someone was trying to scare her and everyone else. Prying the sanctuary doors open was a violent act, and it brought angry tears to Maggie's eyes. There was no reason for the senseless violence. Sadness, fear, and anger swirled in her head. She had seen the same emotions on the faces of the staff and council members yesterday afternoon.

Maggie looked at her sermon notes. She would be preaching that morning about a time when Jesus cast out demons from both a little girl and a deaf man. With just his words, Jesus took topsy-turvy lives and restored them right-side up. Maggie didn't believe in demons, but she did believe in evil. The problem was, she had no idea what to do about it. She wanted the topsy-turviness of life to be right-side up again.

She took a deep breath, smelling the familiar aromas of her parsonage study: pine furniture, dust, and a slight odor of new carpet. For over a year, it had been a sanctuary for her. She read and studied and contemplated there. She wrote sermons and planned Sunday school lessons. She prayed.

Maggie reached for a sheet of stationary from the pink box in her top desk drawer.

> Dear Ed,
>
> I don't know what to do again. Someone is doing bad things here at Loving the Lord. Break-ins, scare tactics, taunts. Our dear Chief Charlotte is doing her best, but I really don't think she's equipped to handle this level of malevolence, as Hank calls it. We decided to invite the Fire Department to help. I'm not hopeful. What I really don't like is the way it's disrupting everyone's lives. Everyone except Irena looks like they're waiting for a bomb to drop on the church. It's tense. How do I help? I'm scared too.
>
> I know God is reading this over your shoulder. Maybe you two could come up with a plan.
>
> I need a whisper.
>
> Love,
> Maggie

There was a loud knock on the back door of the parsonage. Maggie grabbed her cane and limped as fast as she could to the door. Chester stood there, looking absolutely frantic.

"Pastor Maggie, I'm sorry to bother you, but it's about Doris. She never came back last night. I woke up early this morning, and she wasn't back. I can't get into the church, but I know she's in there. That's where she said she'd be, you know?"

Chester's brown eyes were wide, and his voice tense with emotion.

His thin, gray hair hadn't been combed, and wisps were blowing in the gentle breeze. His church shirt, buttoned incorrectly, was hanging lopsidedly across his hips.

"Chester, what are you talking about?" Maggie's confusion grew into panic. "Doris wasn't at church last night. She said *you* were going to keep guard. Then later today we'll have a regular list of volunteers from Charlotte and Fred."

"No, Pastor Maggie." Chester looked back at the church. "Doris said she was supposed to be the first guard. It didn't make sense to me, but she said Chief Tuggle would be there too. I don't see Charlotte anywhere."

Maggie grabbed her keys. She was still wearing her pajamas—cotton pants and a top covered in orange kittens. They had been a seminary graduation gift from Nora.

When Maggie and Chester got to the sanctuary doors, she slipped her key into the lock and opened the door. The two walked inside the sanctuary, and Chester immediately began calling Doris's name. They looked through the entire sanctuary, the offices, nursery, dining room, and kitchen. Then they made their way into the basement back room where the first break-in had occurred.

The windows were wide open, and the rods meant to lock them were leaning against the wall.

Chester let out a choked gasp.

Doris was lying on the floor, absolutely still. Then Maggie saw the blood.

17

It was Monday morning, and Maggie sat at her desk in her church office. Cole Porter sat across from her. Cole and his wife, Lynn, owned and operated The Porter Funeral Home in Cherish.

Maggie's day had begun early as she woke before her alarm clock went off. She knew today she would pick up her brother, Bryan, in Detroit. But instead of the excitement she usually harbored when she was going to see her brother, the morning felt heavy, surreal. She couldn't shake off the events of the day before.

"The funeral is set for Thursday at the funeral home," Cole said. "A daughter is coming into town on Wednesday, but I think she would like to speak with you on the phone before then."

Maggie nodded her head. She tried hard to stay focused on Cole. She and Cole had worked together on several funerals her first year in Cherish. She trusted him implicitly and relied on him completely for all things funereal. Cole and Lynn lived just down the street from the parsonage. Maggie believed Cole and Lynn did more for the town of Cherish than any pastor ever could.

"I would be happy to talk with her. Wait, *happy* isn't the right word, is it?" Maggie felt like she was wandering around in a jar of marshmallow cream. "Give her my cell number, and I'll make sure I'm available. Do you know anything else? Any other details?"

"I don't. This funeral is a difficult one, but we'll get through it. This is an odd compliment, but you do beautiful funerals." Cole smiled.

"Thanks, Cole. I'll never forget how you got me through Rupert Solomon's funeral. That seems like a million years ago."

Maggie felt tired just thinking about the funeral coming on Thursday. With all the trouble at church, the break-ins, the shock of yesterday, and the fact that she had to pick up Bryan in three hours, Maggie's emotions were ragged. The problem was, so were the emotions of everyone else. They were all looking to her for answers, strength, and hope. She was all out of those things.

"Let me know if there is anything else I can do," Cole said kindly. "I'll print the obituary and send you a copy this morning." He rose to leave. "Hang in there, Maggie."

Maggie smiled unenthusiastically.

Cole left, and just as Maggie's head was dropping into her hands, there was a knock on her open door. Maggie looked up to see Mary Ellington. William and Mary had been at the second new members class the day before. The class had been abbreviated after the announcement in church about the break-in and Doris. Everyone was stunned and saddened by the news. Maggie had powered through the morning on autopilot, which was how everyone felt.

She quickly rearranged her face and abruptly stood up without using her cane or holding on to the edge of her desk. Her ankle let her know how stupid that was.

"Hi, Mary," Maggie said with a grimace. "Come on in. I seem to have forgotten, once again, that I sprained my ankle."

Maggie grabbed her cane and hobbled around to sit next to Mary. As she did so, she tried hard to refocus her attention. She was learning that her emotions had to be kept under control as she transitioned from a difficult situation to a joyous one, at times within minutes. She needed to learn to move smoothly from one situation to the next in order to be fully present for each parishioner. Maggie took a breath and looked into Mary's tired face.

"It's nice to see you. What are you doing here on a Monday morning?"

Mary closed Maggie's office door before she sat down.

"Hank wasn't at his desk. I hope it's all right for me to stop in."

"Any time. And feel free to come to the parsonage if you don't find me here."

Maggie did not say that to everyone. She had learned the hard way that some people had no boundaries when it came to her personal space.

"How are you, Mary?"

"Pastor Maggie." Mary looked at her hands as she absently twisted her wedding ring. "I'm just going to get to the point. I can't come back to Loving the Lord. I don't like church. I can hardly stand to walk into this place. I am in the new members class because it means so much to William, but I can't continue coming on a regular basis."

She looked up and stared straight at the pastor. Maggie could see the tears brimming over and falling softly onto Mary's cheeks. She grabbed the Kleenex box on her desk and gently held it out to the older woman. Mary took the box, pulled out a Kleenex, and wiped her eyes and nose. She let out a slight sob, then looked back at her hands.

"Mary, I don't know what to say. If you're not comfortable here, you shouldn't come. Church shouldn't be a place that makes you cry or causes you stress."

As Maggie spoke, she realized that was exactly what church was doing to her and so many others lately. She grabbed her cane and stood up.

"Come on, Mary. Let's go have some tea."

They slowly made their way across the lawn between the church and the parsonage. Once in the parsonage, Maggie led Mary to the kitchen and pointed to a chair.

Mary sat, crying softly, holding a wad of wet Kleenex in her hand. Maggie took the tissues, threw them in the trash, put the teapot on, got down mugs, pulled a bag of Best Cookies out of the freezer, and got

Mary some fresh tissues. After the Lady Grey tea was sitting in front of them, Mary spoke.

"I thought I was ready. I thought I could come back to church. But I can't. William tries to understand, but it's different for him."

Mary took a shaky sip of her tea. Maggie mirrored Mary by sipping her own tea, waiting for her to speak again. Mary took a deep breath and finally, unwaveringly, looked Maggie in the eyes.

"We lost our second oldest son almost five years ago. He was eighteen. It was the summer after his graduation from high school, and we were getting him ready to go to the U of M."

She lifted her mug and took another sip of her tea. If it was too hot, she didn't show it.

"He was driving home from his orientation in Ann Arbor. He had a brand-new cell phone and was talking while he was driving. He drove straight through a red light and slammed into another car, hitting the driver at full speed. The other driver lived for about a day in the hospital after the accident, but our son died at the scene."

Mary told the story as if it were a well-worn sweater. She just slipped it on. It seemed to give her an odd, familiar comfort as she spoke, retelling an old horror story.

"That's terrible," Maggie whispered.

"That's not the worst part," Mary said wearily. "I was the one who called him while he was driving. We were talking about orientation and what he wanted for dinner that night to celebrate. He was laughing when he ran into the other car. I heard the crash. Every single sound. So you see, I killed him. I killed my son. And I killed the other driver."

Maggie felt a cold chill run down her back. She clasped her hands together in her lap to keep them from shaking. What could she possibly say to her? Mary was obviously walking through life completely shredded. Maggie's inexperience and wild emotion kicked in.

"You can't believe that, Mary. You didn't kill him, uh, them."

Maggie was desperate to force Mary to believe her.

"Please don't," Mary said. "If I wouldn't have called him, he would have made it home. That's that. There's no one else to blame. I hate church because that's where I saw him last. In his casket. I hate organ music because that's what I heard on that horrible day he was buried. I thought I might be ready. William finds comfort in church, in this church. But I don't."

"What was your son's name?" Maggie asked, on the very edge of containing her own emotions.

"Michael."

Maggie took a deep breath and tried to compose herself.

"Mary, don't come to church. Don't come back to the new members class. What a torture for you. No one needs to know why." Maggie paused with the profound realization that the church had the capability of hurting people just by being the church. She looked into Mary's reddened eyes and said softly, "Tell me something."

Mary looked up. "What?"

"Is there anything that brings you comfort? Anything at all?"

"Nothing," Mary said.

"Nothing at all?"

"Well, my grandchildren. I love spending time with them. It's different being a grandma." Mary couldn't help smiling.

"This may be out of line," Maggie said, certain she was in deeper waters than she should be swimming, "but have you had any professional help?"

"Yes. I went to a grief counselor for about two years after Michael died. I stopped going because every session was the same. He would ask, 'How are you are you feeling this week, Mary?' 'Like hell,' I would answer. It never changed. So I decided to just be angry. Then I decided that was too much work. So now I stay busy at The Grange and wait to see my grandchildren."

"I don't blame you," Maggie said. "I don't have any professional training in therapy. I won't pretend I do. But instead of coming to church, how about you and I have a standing tea date? Once a week? We can meet here one week and The Grange the next. I would love to see what you and William do for your guests. We don't have to talk about Michael, or we can. Whatever you want. I'm guessing you're an excellent baker, so I would expect something delicious like muffins or cake or scones when we meet at your place. You'll most likely get frozen cookies when you come here. Maybe pie."

Mary actually smiled. Just then, Cheerio came flying into the kitchen with Fruit Loop galloping behind. He leaped into the air and landed directly on Cheerio's head, as planned. Now Mary laughed quietly.

"And when you come here," Maggie continued, "you will most likely see cat antics."

"Maggie, thank you," Mary said simply. "Tea would be nice. Next week at The Grange?"

"Yes. Can we make it for Tuesday? Then my brother will be on the other side of the state."

"Tuesday it is. Ten o'clock?"

"I'll be there," Maggie said.

Maggie saw Mary to the door and watched her leave. She remembered how Ed had told her: *we never know the baggage other people are carrying.* She thought back to the last two weeks, and even the Sundays before that when William and Mary had been to church. Mary had been so conversational and bright at the classes. She spoke easily of The Grange, her children, and grandchildren. Just one name hadn't been mentioned: Michael's. Maggie never would have guessed Mary and William Ellington were walking around with such huge, ragged holes in their hearts.

After Maggie cleaned up the tea things, she called Hank.

"I'm heading to the hospital, then to the airport to pick up Bryan."

"Yesireebob, Pastor Maggie," Hank said without his usual gusto. "I'll hold down the fort. Let me know how she is, will you? I'll stop by later this afternoon."

"I will. How does the church smell?" Maggie asked, knowing the soup committee would be in the kitchen.

"I'm sure heaven couldn't smell any better, even though there are only two of them down there. Just Bill and Sylvia today. I'll tell them to put your soup in the refrigerator. You can pick it up later."

"Thanks. I'll call you in a while."

Maggie hung up and grabbed her keys and cane. Jack had told her she could drive, as long as her ankle didn't hurt. That bit of good news made her feel like a bird let out of a cage.

She drove over to Heal Thyself Community Hospital, parked in a spot that felt a million miles away, wondered why the hospital didn't have clergy parking, and then limped with her cane through the sliding glass doors at the main entrance.

Maggie smiled at the small, gray-haired lady sitting at the information desk. Maggie saw her almost every time she came to the hospital.

"Hi, Gertie," Maggie said.

"Good morning, Pastor Maggie. Do you know where you're going this morning?"

Gertie was ready to look up names and room numbers.

"I sure do. I was here last night. But thank you, ma'am."

Maggie gave a little bow and kept limping down the corridor.

She turned in to room one thirteen and caught her breath at the sight. There stood Verna and Howard, Verna holding a large vase of zinnias. Winston was at the foot of the bed, telling a story. Ellen was on one side of the bed, trying to get a temperature, but everyone was laughing too hard. Chester was on the other side of the bed, holding Doris's hand.

Doris was sitting up in bed with a large white bandage wrapped unstylishly around her head. She was laughing at Winston's story while holding the back of her head, as if trying not to laugh her bandage off.

"Mrs. Walters, I need to get your temperature," Ellen said, looking at Winston and bursting into a fit of giggles.

Winston was a consummate story teller. He embellished shamelessly, which everyone knew and loved.

"And then there was Nurse Marie," Winston continued. "She couldn't help herself. She walked into my room, took one look at me, and right then and there professed her everlasting love. Alas, I had to break her heart. She, Annie, Madelyn, Jennifer, and Babs all left their shifts at the hospital utterly devastated." Winston shook his head sadly.

"There just wasn't enough Winston to go around. Plus, I had just had a heart attack. Not that that made me any less desirable."

Winston ran his hand through his white hair and made it stand on end even more than usual.

Maggie came through the door with her cane amidst peals of laughter.

"What is all this hilarity about?" she said, smiling.

Winston twinkled his bright-blue eyes at Maggie.

"Pastor Maggie, another one of my brokenhearted loves. Are you over me yet?"

"Winston, I desperately want to comb your hair," Maggie said as she made her way to Doris.

Winston smiled. "See?"

Ellen put the thermometer in Doris's mouth just as Maggie said, "How are you feeling this morning, Doris?"

Doris was still holding the back of her head, but her eyes were smiling. She took Maggie's hand, uncharacteristically, and mumbled, "Better."

Maggie stayed near Doris as Ellen finished her short exam.

"Mrs. Walters, can you tell me what day it is?" Ellen asked.

"Monday, September seventh. Labor Day," Doris said with a sigh. She had been asked that question regularly throughout the night and morning.

"And who is the president of the United States?"

"Barack Obama."

"How many fingers am I holding up?" asked Ellen, holding up four digits.

"Four," Doris responded obediently.

"And why are you here?"

"I was hit over the head by some idiot in the church basement," Doris said ruefully.

"And whose fault was that?" Chester chimed in.

He was still a little shaken from seeing his wife on the cement floor the previous morning.

"My very own fault," Doris said, looking at Chester and feeling horrible for her stupidity. And for lying to him about who was supposed to be watching the church. She'd wanted to do the job herself and be the hero who caught the bad guy, especially since he had left mud all over her floor.

Ellen smiled at Doris and patted Chester on the shoulder.

"All's well that ends well!" she said brightly.

"But let's not forget, it could have ended very badly," said Verna, putting her vase of zinnias on Doris's rolling tray. They smelled like a skunk. "It's a good thing we have the Ann Arbor police involved. Now something will get done." She pursed her lips. "We have certainly had enough of the Cherish Police ineptitude. I know I'll be sleeping easier at night."

"Of course you will. Remember, you sleep with me," Howard said and slapped her on the bottom.

Verna's severe face gave way under the spank.

"Howard, stop it. This is very serious."

"And as you said, my love, the Ann Arbor police are now in control. No need for any more consternation."

Howard gave her a playful hug. Maggie couldn't watch. All that lovey-dovey stuff between Howard and Verna was too much. She almost missed crabby, bossy Verna at times like that. Almost.

They all turned toward the door as they heard the trip-trap of spiky high heels. Irena entered carrying a bottle of vodka with a sticky premade Christmas bow stuck to the front.

Everyone looked startled. Those in the hospital room were startled because Irena was always startling, especially in broad daylight. Irena was startled because she hadn't expected to see so many people in Doris's room. It made her cross.

"Vat you all doing heerre?" she snapped.

She was wearing glittery-gold eye shadow instead of her usual horrendous green. She looked like a wildcat ready to pounce.

"Irena," Maggie said. "How nice of you to visit Doris. That's why we're all here too."

Maggie smiled. Irena did not respond in kind.

"I am heeerre to see dat Dorrees ees not kilt. Vit my own eyes."

Doris never would have believed she would be happy to see Irena, but she was. She stretched out her arms toward the crazy organist.

Irena trip-trapped across the room, pushing Maggie out of the way to get to Doris.

"You all, git out!" Irena barked to the other visitors.

They obeyed the tiny tyrant as they gave Doris hugs and waves and finally left the room. Only Chester was allowed to remain.

In the hallway, Maggie and Ellen laughed at Irena's wielding of her monumental power—and also the bottle of vodka she brought as a gift.

Verna was less impressed. *How in the world did we ever let that little foreigner into our church?*

"Let's go home, Howard. It's time for lunch," she clipped. "Are you coming, Winston?"

Winston was at Verna and Howard's more than he wasn't. He ran his fingers through his hair as he stared back into the hospital room at Irena. He wasn't usually afraid of women, but in the case of Irena, it was an even mix of confusion and terror.

"Yes, I'm coming. What's for lunch?"

"Soup, of course," was Verna's terse reply.

The three elderly people walked down the hallway in silence.

Behind the now closed hospital room door, Irena shoved the bottle into Doris's open arms.

"Dorrees, dis ees for you. You arre a verry brafe voman. You deed vat vas right. Sorry you got basht on de head. I'm glat you not got kilt."

Doris set the bottle down on the bed, reached up, and put her arms around Irena's scrawny neck. She pulled Irena in close, making her totter on her high heels. Then Doris gave Irena a kiss on her painted cheek.

"Irena, you are good for my soul, as Pastor Maggie would say."

Irena was surprised at the bout of affection. Mainly because she had never been on the receiving end of affection ever in her life. And also, she counted on Doris to be pushy and rude. It was their bond. She pulled back from Doris's embrace.

"Vell, dat's nice," she mumbled. Then she looked at Chester. "Chester, let's hev a drrink, yes?"

Chester was about to protest but then thought a drink might be nice right about then. The past twenty-four hours had taken a toll on poor Chester.

Irena opened the bottle of vodka and found two plastic cups on the rolling tray. They both had water in them. Irena took them and poured them into the sink in the bathroom. Then she poured two generous cups of vodka.

"Dorrees, you vant some?"

"I don't think that would mix well with my pain pills or my concussion," Doris said with a smirk.

"Yerr choice," Irena said with a shrug.

Then she tossed back her cup of vodka. And poured another.

"Ve hev to talk about de churrch," she said, fixing her gold-plated eyes on Doris.

18

Maggie had never been so frightened in her life as she had been the previous morning when she saw Doris on the basement floor at church. Especially when she saw the blood coming from Doris's head. Chester was on his knees instantly, holding Doris, his tears falling on her face. Maggie had run/hobbled upstairs to the office and dialed 911.

Doris had been hit over the head with a saucepan from the church kitchen. The pan was lying near her when Chester and Maggie found her on the floor. As Chester held Doris, he and Maggie received their first wave of relief. Doris whimpered.

She's not dead! Maggie had thought thankfully.

Doris didn't open her eyes, but her whimpers continued.

Chester held her carefully, repeating, "It's okay, Dorrie. It's okay," until the medics arrived and began to check her vital signs and assess the seriousness of her injury.

Finally, after wrapping a temporary bandage around her head, they strapped her onto the rolling stretcher. All Maggie had wanted was to see Doris with her large trash can and her yellow apron stuffed full of cleaning supplies and to hear her yelling at Hank about a mess he hadn't made. Maggie had stood in her kitty pajamas and watch helplessly as they took the stretcher up the stairs.

Charlotte, who was white as a ghost as she'd watched Doris being wheeled out on a stretcher, had arrived shortly after the medics.

Chester crawled into the ambulance, holding Doris's hand.

Chief Charlotte Tuggle had carefully placed the blood-stained pan in a plastic bag. After the evidence was in the squad car, Charlotte found Maggie coming up from the basement.

"Pastor Maggie," Charlotte said with a shaky voice, "I'm so, so sorry about what has happened in this place."

Maggie had sensed the mix of embarrassment and confusion as Charlotte slowly shook her head. She seemed to be replaying the scene in the church basement. Maggie knew that none of them, Charlotte included, were prepared to effectively deal with that kind of violence.

"Charlotte, we have someone dangerous on our hands. I don't think any of us would have suspected something this violent would happen. Especially to one of our own. You have been working tirelessly guarding the church, and we all know it."

Charlotte looked at her pastor. She had done her best, and she had failed. Now Doris was on her way to the hospital.

"Pastor Maggie," Charlotte said with a small voice, "I would like to call in a detective from Ann Arbor, if that's okay. I need some backup here."

"Of course, Charlotte," Maggie said, secretly relieved. "You know what's best, and I trust you to handle this." Partial lie.

Charlotte breathed a sigh of relief. It was time to bring in the big guns, so to speak.

After the ambulance had left, Maggie had called Jack and poured out the whole horrific story. Then Maggie had shakily gotten ready for church while Jack went straight to the hospital. Later, Jack told Maggie that Doris had slowly regained consciousness, and as she did so, had felt excruciating pain in the back of her head. She had a severe concussion, along with several stitches to sew up the gash made by the saucepan. Jack was able to find out the approximate time of the assault. He told Maggie that Doris remembered looking at her watch at three a.m., when she heard sounds coming from the church kitchen. She remembered nothing after that.

Maggie had felt sick when Jack told her the news. All she could think of was Doris lying on the cold cement floor of the church basement for hours.

Following the abbreviated new members class, Charlotte had introduced Maggie to Detective Keith Crunch from Ann Arbor. Charlotte had the good sense to be grateful for Detective Crunch and not feel threatened. He had the wisdom to treat Charlotte as an equal.

"Pastor Maggie, it's good to meet you." Detective Crunch held out his hand.

Keith Crunch was maybe five feet ten inches, at most, and he was muscular and fit. He looked to be in his late-forties or early-fifties. His brown hair was lightly flecked with gray but perfectly combed and sprayed, and he had vivid-blue eyes that sparkled with intelligence, a breathtaking smile, and immaculate fingernails.

Maggie liked him immediately. His light-gray suit, royal-blue shirt, and gray silk tie were of high quality. Maggie thought he should be on television with his George Clooney good looks. She discovered quickly that he was also an excellent detective. He dove right in with questions about the destructive happenings at Loving the Lord.

Charlotte, Maggie, Harold, and Ellen had met with Detective Crunch in the parsonage. He listened to the details of each break-in, especially to what had happened earlier that morning with Doris. Ellen gave her unhelpful description of the "figure in black" she had seen lurking around the church.

"The person seemed to be tall and thin, but the color black does that to people, doesn't it?" Ellen asked hesitantly. "He or she also seemed to be slinking around the church."

Thankfully, Ellen didn't do her slinking impression.

Charlotte jumped in. "We've changed the locks on the church doors, but then one of the staff had their key stolen. We suspect our intruder took it."

That sounded obvious. It seemed no one had anything helpful for the detective.

Detective Crunch said they were *very* helpful.

"From what you've described, the intruder is an amateur, unskilled. These break-ins are simplistic, at best. I see high school students doing this kind of thing." He smiled. "After I spoke with Chief Tuggle, I sent out a statewide message to see if there are any other church break-ins going on, particularly in this area."

He's brilliant! Maggie thought.

"And are there?" she asked.

"No. Nothing like this anywhere around here," he said, shaking his head. "So that tells me Loving the Lord is being singularly targeted. Have you thought about possible suspects, someone from the inside?"

Harold hesitated slightly but then spoke.

"We have had some difficulty with one of our parishioners in the past few months. His name is Redford Johnson. He has disrupted meetings and even threatened Pastor Maggie. The thing is, he's out of the state now on a fishing trip. Otherwise," Harold looked at the rest of the group, "there doesn't seem to be anyone in the church who would do this kind of damage."

"How can I verify where Redford Johnson is right now?" Detective Crunch asked.

"He's somewhere in Montana," Harold offered.

"Wait," said Maggie, her eyes lighting up. "We had a call from the credit card company because Redford tried to use the church credit card to pay for the resort where he is staying. I bet Hank would know."

"Who is Hank?" Detective Crunch asked.

"The church administrative assistant," Maggie replied.

"Let's get Hank on the phone. Then the first thing we'll do is send in our forensic team. They will look for any clues left by the perpetrator. Next, we'll install surveillance cameras inside the church. We'll put them in clocks and other places that won't be spotted. I'll have one of my team monitoring the cameras at all times, particularly at night. It's too bad the church doors have been repaired, but I'll still try to get an impression from the doors as to what kind of tool was used for the last break-in."

Detective Keith Crunch was in complete control.

"What about the parsonage?" Charlotte asked, nodding to the detective collegially.

Detective Crunch was thoughtful.

"We can install a silent alarm in the parsonage. Cameras would be a little too intrusive." He smiled at Maggie. "There will be a code for you to punch whenever you leave and at night before you go to sleep. It's a nuisance, but necessary."

"No problem," Maggie said. "Also, my brother will be staying with me all week. I won't be alone."

"Good. My team will get started. It was a pleasure to meet all of you. We'll get to the bottom of this. Chief Tuggle, may I speak with you?" Detective Crunch led Charlotte into the church. "Let's find Hank right away."

Charlotte pulled out her cell phone and dialed Hank's number. She had him on speed dial ever since all the shenanigans at church began.

The rest of the little group gave a communal sigh of relief. They were beginning to feel safer. It had been the most memorable Sunday Loving the Lord had ever known. And also one of the unhappiest. Many prayers were said for Doris that day.

Maggie had been relieved to see Doris the next morning in the hospital, even though it felt like a circus had stopped by to visit the same time she had. Maggie had a jolt of pure love for her parishioners. Just seeing Chester, Verna, Howard, Winston, and Ellen in Doris's room reminded Maggie of why she loved ministry and why she loved her community. What a crazy, devoted, caring bunch of people. Irena had put the exclamation point on that thought when she exploded into the room with her bottle of vodka.

On Monday afternoon, Maggie was in the parsonage when her cell phone rang.

"Hello?"

"Is this Pastor Maggie?"

"Yes, it is."

"This is Melissa Jones. I'm the daughter of Abe Jones."

It took Maggie a moment to get her brain in gear. Then it clicked: her conversation with Cole Porter earlier that morning. Melissa must be the daughter of the dead man Cole had told Maggie about. For having just lost her father, her voice was clear, and Maggie noticed there was no emotion in Melissa's words.

"Oh, yes. Hello, Melissa."

Maggie was too enthusiastic and felt her cheeks become hot.

"Mr. Porter told me I could call you about my father's funeral," Melissa said in her monotone voice, sounding like a robot.

Maggie had learned how difficult it was to officiate funerals for people (and families) she had never met, but that was part of her ministry. Maggie knew Cole Porter was called in, not just to bury the people he had grown up with, but strangers as well. Cole received his calls, and then Cole called Maggie. Without knowing much background, they carefully navigated burying the dead.

Maggie knew everyone dealt with grief differently. Melissa sounded as if she were still in shock.

"Yes. I'm so sorry about your father. How are you doing?"

"I'm fine," she said abruptly. "I'm flying in late Wednesday night. Mr. Porter said the funeral could be done in the funeral home on Thursday at ten o'clock. Is that correct?"

"Yes. Would you like to meet ahead of time?"

Maggie suspected the answer.

"No, thank you. How long will the funeral take? I'm trying to book my ticket home," Melissa asked, sounding as if she were checking her texts or painting her toenails.

"Well, as long as you wish. Did your father have any favorite Bible verses or hymns or poems? Would you or other family members like to speak and share remembrances? Is there a passage that would bring you and your family comfort?"

Maggie felt as if she should get every question in before the woman hung up on her.

"No, nothing like that. He just needs to be put in the ground," was Melissa's startling answer. "I'll book a return ticket for late Thursday afternoon."

Melissa must have been doing so at precisely that moment. Maggie could hear clicking on computer keys.

"Fine. I look forward to meeting you at The Porter Funeral Home on Thursday morning."

Maggie was running out of enthusiasm. They said their goodbyes and hung up. Maggie would have to plan the funeral with only the obituary for help.

19

Maggie had wanted to say a prayer with Doris at the hospital that morning, but Irena's command to leave the room had bullied everyone out, Maggie included. As she drove home, she wondered when she would ever feel like the real pastor of the congregation. Except for Irena, no one was malicious about usurping Maggie's leadership, but it seemed that Maggie's youth and inexperience gave others an excuse to take over. Once again, she needed Ed. She needed a whisper.

Maggie drove down Main Street to Middle Street, and instead of turning right toward the parsonage, she turned left. She went down Middle and pulled into Cate Carlson's driveway.

Cate had come home from the University of Michigan for the Labor Day weekend for the sole purpose of seeing Bryan. She would have to drive back to school after dinner but would have the rest of the day to be with Bryan. And Pastor Maggie.

Before she could even turn off the engine, Maggie saw Cate bounding out the front door. She was wearing skinny jeans, a pale-blue T-shirt, and a cream-colored cotton scarf wound loosely around her neck. She flip-flopped her way to the car, long hair flying behind her, running and bouncing at the same time.

"Hi, Pastor Maggie," Cate said breathlessly as she got into the car. "Oh! I'm so excited!"

"Really? I couldn't tell. You're always so sedate."

Maggie laughed as she pulled out of the driveway. Then they were on their way to pick up Bryan from the Detroit airport.

"Thank you for letting me come along," Cate said once she calmed down.

She reminded Maggie of a beautiful, blonde golden retriever—all excitement and affection.

"Bryan is going to be thrilled to see you. As much as I wish he was coming here just to be with his big sister, I'm quite certain that's not the case. We'll all have a fun dinner tonight."

Maggie smiled. If she didn't have her own true love, she doubted she would be so generous with Bryan's time.

Cate began gnawing on her thumb, until she remembered she wasn't supposed to do that. Maggie smacked her hand.

"Stop chewing on yourself, you weirdo."

"I'm getting better. Really, I am. I'm just excited."

"You are fortunate enough to have lovely hands with long fingers. Stop eating them."

To Maggie, Cate felt more like a little sister than a parishioner. Maggie could be herself with Cate. She could also boss Cate around, and that was fun. They continued the drive, chatting the whole way.

When they arrived at the airport, they waited in the cell phone lot for Bryan's call.

A few minutes later, Maggie's phone dinged, announcing a text. She remembered Mary Ellington's visit earlier in the day. Maggie never talked on her cell phone or texted while she was driving and she was grateful. There could be deadly consequences.

We just landed! I've got to get my bag.
Come and get me.

Yay! I'll be right there.

So are u alone? Is Jack with u?
Or anyone else?

Nope. Just me, your fav
sister. See you in a sec.

She turned to Cate.

"I think he was hoping someone else was with me."

Cate giggled.

When they pulled up to the baggage claim doors, Bryan walked out and then stopped. Maggie looked at her brother and smiled with pride. She still couldn't get over the change she had seen in him when he returned from his first trip to Ghana earlier in the year. He had gone from spacey kid brother to responsible, focused, mission-minded man.

In college, he wore his blond hair long and sported a patchy beard. He looked like a bum and smelled like one too. But now he was clean-shaven and had short, well-cut hair, and he had added bulk to his once scrawny frame. He was adorable. Maggie glanced at Cate and thought the younger woman might possibly start drooling.

Both Maggie and Cate got out of the car and went to him, but Cate hung back a bit to wait her turn. Bryan noticed Maggie's cane and her limp, so he carefully gave her a big hug. Maggie looked into the pair of eyes that were so like her own. Bryan took Maggie's left hand and admired the ring sparkling there.

"Whoo! Jack knows how to pick 'em," Bryan said.

"Yes, he does," Maggie said with a toss of her head.

"I meant rings."

"I meant fiancés," Maggie countered.

"Does he have a lot of those?" he asked, but his attention was clearly turning to the tall girl standing next to him.

Cate had been inching closer to Bryan as he bantered with his sister. It netted her a monstrous hug with a kiss added on at the end.

"Okay, you two. You can do that later. Let's get going."

Maggie was secretly proud that she'd brought Bryan and Cate together the year before. It was one of her better matchmaking schemes.

As she watched them smiling at each other like fools, Maggie had a flash of insight: *I'm going to have gorgeous nephews and nieces.*

She walked back to the car and carefully slid behind the wheel. Then Maggie noticed she was sitting in the front seat all by herself. She chauffeured the two lovebirds back to Cherish.

Once back at the parsonage, she remembered to punch in the code of her new alarm system before opening the back door.

"Sorry, Bry, but we have an alarm now. We have to put in the code before we open either door or a silent alarm will go off, and we will be swarmed with police."

Maggie had kept Bryan and her parents up to speed with the progress of catching the intruder. They were all relieved to hear Ann Arbor had been called into the investigation.

"No problem," Bryan said as he picked up his luggage and followed Maggie and Cate into the parsonage. "Do you think they'll catch the guy soon?"

"I do," Maggie said, thinking about Detective Crunch and his team. "You should have seen them yesterday at the church. All afternoon, the Ann Arbor police were taking pictures, swabbing things, dusting for fingerprints, and installing hidden cameras. It was like being in a *Midsomer Murders* episode. Then, when I went to the hospital to see Doris, they installed the security system here at the parsonage. I think whoever has been breaking in may find it more inconvenient now."

Maggie wondered how it would end. What would it be like to see the face of the person in black?

"Now, I know this isn't very nice," Maggie continued with a sly smile, "but I have to leave you two alone for just a bit." She looked at Bryan and Cate, just as they tried not to look at each other. "I've got to check in with Hank and then stop by the hospital and see if Doris is going home tonight."

"Why is Hank working today?" Bryan asked. "It's Labor Day."

"Oh, Bryan . . ." Maggie said with a long, dramatic sigh. "The work of the church is never done. We don't even get holidays." She shook her head sadly, then laughed. "It's sad, but the people of this church don't have a lot else to do. Hank was in first thing this morning, as usual. Oh, and by the way, I have a funeral on Thursday morning. Otherwise, this week we can plan and plan for your Ghana Extravaganza on Sunday."

Just then, they all heard a howl and a hiss. Cheerio slid across the kitchen floor right into the dishwasher. Before she could get her bearings, Fruit Loop leapt with all limbs outstretched, like a flying squirrel. He landed smack on Cheerio's back and began chewing on her ears. She screeched and wriggled away from her tortuous enemy. They both ran into the living room, running circles around the once-white-now-gray couches.

"That's Fruit Loop," Maggie said to Bryan.

"You're a Fruit Loop for adopting another cat," he retorted.

Cate looked at Bryan and fell into a fit of giggles as only someone completely in gooey love can do.

"I don't know why I let you come here," Maggie said disdainfully. "If you would have seen him at that gas station—"

But Bryan didn't let her finish. "I'm teasing. You saved a life. You're my hero."

Then he grabbed her around the neck and squeezed.

"Ouch! You are stronger than you think you are." Maggie squirmed away and rubbed her neck. "I'm getting out of here."

Marmalade walked in regally, flourishing his plume of a tail. He began inspecting Bryan's luggage, keeping alert to Bryan and Cate as he did so.

Maggie went to the freezer and pulled out a homemade veggie lasagna.

"I'll let this thaw, but if you two could go to The Sugarplum and pick up some bread or rolls and some kind of dessert, I'd appreciate it. Jack will be here around six thirty, but I should be back in an hour or so."

She left a twenty dollar bill on the kitchen table and hobbled across the lawn to the church. She could hear Irena playing and wondered how long she had plagued Doris and Chester at the hospital that morning.

"Hey, Irena," Maggie said as she passed by the organ.

"Hay ees for de donkeys," Irena snapped back without taking her eyes off the music.

Maggie kept moving with her cane. As she got closer to the office, she could hear Hank talking with someone. It was Julia Benson, the reporter from *The Cherish Life and Times*.

"Hi, Julia," Maggie said without enthusiasm.

Hank was standing behind his desk, looking harried.

"Pastor Maggie," Hank and Julia said simultaneously, then looked at each other indignantly.

Hank quickly spoke first. "Pastor Maggie, Miss Benson wants to know why the police were here yesterday. She's being quite *insistent.*"

"Pastor Maggie," Julia jumped in, "I'm doing an article for *The Cherish Life and Times*, and I need to know the facts of what's going on in this church."

"It's none of your business!" Hank spewed.

"My editor says it is!" Julia hissed back, her face red and pasty at the same time.

It looked to Maggie as if Julia hadn't brushed her hair in a good three days, and she was wearing the same bland suit she had worn for Maggie's interview the previous week. But Maggie could see that, if Julia would relax her face and smile, she could be almost likeable.

Distracted by Julia's demeanor, Maggie couldn't think of what to do. She didn't want Julia Benson to know anything about the church or the break-ins. Maggie quickly realized it was because she didn't trust her.

Bryan punched in the alarm code as he and Cate left the parsonage. They crossed the street to The Sugarplum and walked through the door to fairy bells.

"Well, hokey tooters!" Mrs. Popkin erupted as she bustled around the counter to give both Cate and Bryan hugs. "This sure is a treat. Cate, how is your dorm at the U? And Bryan, how is every single thing in San Francisco?" Mrs. Popkin laughed boisterously. "And just look at the two of you. You look like you were made for each other." She smiled knowingly.

Bryan and Cate couldn't help but grin under the affirmation of their true love.

"The U is great," Cate said. "I love my dorm, and I'm getting to know some of the other people on my floor. I miss being here, though."

It wasn't clear if she missed The Sugarplum or standing next to Bryan.

"Mrs. Popkin, you look great," he said. "Everything in San Francisco is as crazy as you would expect. There's nothing like The Sugarplum to be found anywhere in SF. Everyone eats kale and quinoa and seaweed."

Bryan took a deep breath and inhaled the aroma of sugar, butter, cream, and vanilla.

Mrs. Popkin stared at the couple, completely unaware that she had pink frosting on the left side of her nose.

"Too each his own. Haven't they heard about the health benefits of deep fried donuts?" She laughed long and hard at her own wit. "Well now, what can I do for you this afternoon?" she asked, wiping her eyes and smearing the pink frosting onto her cheek.

"We need some bread to go with lasagna tonight and a dessert," Cate said, peering into the different bread baskets hanging on the wall behind the counter.

"I've got just the thing. Hokey tooters! I made fresh soft pretzel breadsticks this morning. How does that sound?"

Bryan thought he could eat about five right then and there.

"Great," he said. "We'll take a dozen."

They also picked out a blueberry cheesecake.

"May I have a couple of those healthy donuts too, please?" Bryan asked.

"Hokey tooters, of course! I'll give you enough to get you all the way back across the street. It's good to see you both. Bryan, we can't wait to hear your presentation on Ghana this week. I'm sure you will open our eyes in many ways."

Mrs. Popkin wrapped up the baked goods and sent the two young people on their way. Bryan and Cate had done their chore for Maggie. Now it was time to talk Ghana. Bryan was glad to know people were excited to hear his presentation. Of course, Mrs. Popkin made everyone feel good about whatever it was they did. She just loved people.

Bryan and Cate each ate a *healthy* donut as they made their way back to the parsonage. Then Cate slipped her sticky hand into Bryan's. Knowing they would be together next year was bringing a new depth to their relationship. Cate was already studying and attending the requisite seminars to prepare for her semester abroad. Bryan was struggling with a halved heart—a piece planted in two different countries.

Bryan looked at Cate and said, "I want you to help me on Sunday with the Ghana presentation. I think the two of us can bring an excitement to the school project. What do you say?"

Cate became serious. "Yes. We need to give our church some hope and the orphanage in Ghana a promise. Even your dear sister could use a lift. What are your ideas?"

"Julia, we just can't tell you information about the church right now. It's police business and confidential."

Maggie was trying to sound as if she had a tiny bit of authority. It came out as pandering.

"I already know your janitor is in the hospital. Got hit on the head. This is the kind of story the public has a right to know about."

Julia matched Maggie's pandering with her own petulance.

"No, it's not a story for the public. And how did you know about Doris?" Maggie asked protectively.

"Well, there was an ambulance here early yesterday morning, and then you made an announcement in church about it all," Julia said brusquely.

"It doesn't matter. There is no more information for you here."

Maggie wished she had the magic power to make Julia disappear.

"Miss Benson, it's time for you to leave."

Hank came from around his desk and held the door open for Julia to make her departure. She stood still.

"What were the police doing here all afternoon yesterday? What were they looking for? Did they do anything here in the church?" Julia shot off her questions like bullets from a gun.

Maggie hated guns. And bullets. And unwanted questions.

"Go ask the police, if you're so interested," Maggie said dismissively. She knew Charlotte wouldn't say a word. "Please leave now."

Julia looked as if she might try another onslaught, but Hank's face was so serious that she turned with a huff and stomped out of the office and past Irena to the sanctuary doors. She glared back at Maggie before she stalked down the steps.

"Good grief!" Maggie said, looking at Hank. "What was that all about?"

"She's one angry woman, yesireebob!" Hank said. "She's doesn't like hearing the word 'no.'"

"She's not a pleasant person, that's for sure," Maggie said.

She felt a little shaky and noticed her hands were sweating. She hated confrontation.

"I just stopped by to see if you needed anything. And then I was going to go see Doris. Is she still in the hospital?"

"I believe so. It sounds like your Dr. Jack wants her to stay an extra night, just to keep an eye on her," he said while straightening his desk. "It will be good to have her back here, but I'm sure she'll need a few days to rest."

"She will. I'm going to head over there and see how she is. That's much more important than answering questions from a nosy reporter. Onwards and forwards!"

Of course, Maggie really didn't feel that way. The break-ins had taken a toll on everyone's well-being. And Julia Benson was just prying. *Why?* Then Maggie had another thought as she left the church for the hospital. *How did Julia know I made an announcement in church yesterday?*

As Maggie drove through town to the hospital, she saw Marla walking down Main Street. Marla opened the door to The Page Turner Book Shop. Maggie watched as Carrie and Carl Moffet entered the shop while Marla held the door. Maggie took a deep breath. There was another problem she hadn't had time to deal with.

20

Jack went into the emergency room with a sense of dread. He had been called from his office to care for a new patient being admitted to the hospital. He pulled the curtain aside and stepped into the tiny cubicle. The patient was lying on the gurney, eyes closed. Jack stepped back out and found the nurse assigned to the woman.

"When did she come in?" Jack asked.

"About an hour ago. She was in the waiting room but then passed out on the floor. We moved her in here, started an IV, and called you. She has been in and out of consciousness."

The nurse gave Jack the sleeping woman's vital signs.

"Was she able to tell you her symptoms?" Jack asked as he stepped back to the curtain.

"She said she had a treatment today but wasn't feeling well afterward. She actually drove herself here." The nurse sounded the tiniest bit judgmental.

"What kind of treatment?" Jack noticed the yellow pallor of the patient's face.

"Chemotherapy," the nurse replied. "At the U of M Medical Center."

Jack looked through the meager information in the woman's chart.

"When will she be moved to a room?"

"In about a half-hour."

Jack moved toward the woman and touched her arm.

"Can you hear me?"

His hand was gentle, but his voice firm. The woman didn't move. Her breath was shallow, and her body was still. Jack squeezed her hand. The woman began to stir, her eyelids fluttering. When her eyes opened, she looked as though she couldn't quite focus on whoever was talking to her.

"Mmm . . . what?" she mumbled.

"I'm Dr. Elliot."

Jack waited to see if she could respond. She struggled to open her eyes again, but it seemed too much of a strain. She lapsed back into sleep.

Jack left the cubicle and got to a telephone. He made a call to the U of M Medical Center, followed by another to the patient's doctor. He received all the information he needed.

On the other side of the hospital, Maggie entered Doris's room for the second time that day. Doris was sleeping while Chester sat on a hospital chair next to her. He was holding her hand as he watched her breathe. He barely blinked as he followed the rise and fall of her chest. Maggie could see that his eyes were bloodshot, his face white.

Chester looked up when he heard the soft thump of Maggie's cane.

"Oh, Pastor Maggie," he said, clearing his throat to let his words escape. "You're back. Doris is having a little sleep."

Doris stirred, and her eyes fluttered open. Maggie could tell Doris was trying to get her bearings. She looked around, confused at first. Then, seeing Chester's face, she gave a weak smile.

"How was your nap, Dorrie?" Chester asked with such gentleness and intimacy it made Maggie look away. She felt like an intruder.

"Good," Doris croaked.

She turned and, with a weak hand, gave a wave to Maggie.

Chester reached for the Styrofoam cup of ice water and held the straw for Doris to take a drink. When she finished, she sighed deeply with her eyes closed, her head resting back on the pillow.

"Hi, Pastor Maggie," Doris said. Her voice sounded fragile, her eyes remained closed. "I just need a minute to wake up my brain," she said with a slight smile.

"Hi, Doris," Maggie said softly.

She waited for Doris to open her eyes.

Chester spoke. "She's had a little nap. After keeping her up all night and most of today because of the concussion, they finally gave her the okay to have a rest."

"I will rest better in my own bed," Doris said, eyes still closed. "Pastor Maggie, now that you have that ring on your finger, you have some leverage with my doctor. Can't you tell him to let me out of here?"

Doris opened one eye and rolled it up to Maggie's face. She reminded Maggie of a parrot. Or a pirate.

"I have no leverage whatsoever," Maggie said in mock sadness. "I wish I did. But Dr. Elliot is a very mean and powerful doctor. I recommend you do whatever he says."

"Well, okay," Doris said. She and Chester both smiled.

"Irena was here earlier," Chester said. "She had a plan for busting Doris out of here and going back to church to do SSR."

Doris snorted and then reached for the back of her head.

"Oh, ow!" she said, her mouth caught between a wince and a smile.

"Good grief. What is SSR?" Maggie asked, wondering about Irena's secret life.

"Secret Staff Reconnaissance," Chester reported. "She was pretty adamant."

Maggie thought she had better mention that to Charlotte so that Irena didn't accidentally get handcuffed or shot. Or worse. The police wouldn't want to mess with Irena.

"I wanted to stop by because I didn't have a chance to pray with you earlier. I think Dr. Elliot is right in keeping you another night, don't you? Just have the nurses bring you lots of ice cream."

Maggie chuckled. She took Doris by the hand and then reached for Chester's free hand. In that little holy circle, Maggie thanked God for Doris and Chester. She thanked God for skilled doctors and nurses who were caring for Doris. She thanked God for Loving the Lord Community Church and asked him to protect the congregation and the building. In that order.

Then Maggie had one of her flashes of insight. She saw Loving the Lord as not just a building but a being. The walls, like arms, welcomed everyone in to listen to faith stories. The walls held all those who gathered within. The old wooden pews gave rest to the weary. The organ spilled music out from windows, doors, and bell tower, no matter who had played it over the decades. Loving the Lord heard every joy, hope, laugh, and kind word expressed by her people. Loving the Lord heard every cry, fear, worry, and pain suffered by her people. She was the place where people met God and the place where people said goodbye, then met God face-to-face. She bound the wounds of the people with her safe haven. She had held so many. Now she was under attack, the lovely old building that had stood so faithfully for so long.

Loving the Lord would not be damaged anymore. She would not become a sad old woman with a fearful story, abandoned. Maggie remembered the ugly and violent damage done to the front doors of the church. She felt a shiver make its way through her body with the new image of the church she loved so much. The frisson shook her back and shoulders while her eyes were still closed in prayer.

Then she heard the whisper.

I am with you. I will protect you. All will be well.

Maggie ended her prayer. She didn't lift her head until she was sure she wasn't going to cry. Then she took a deep breath, opened her eyes, and gave Doris a kiss on the cheek. She left the tired couple to another night in the hospital.

At the door, she turned and said, "Chester, Doris, everything is okay. With you, and with the church. All will be well."

They stared at her.

"I mean it. All will be well."

And Chester and Doris believed her.

Maggie drove away from the hospital more uplifted than when she had arrived. Her vision of the church as a loving being in need of protection filled her mind and imagination. It was like one of her dreams, except she was wide awake. She wasn't a victim, and neither were her congregants. The police were capable. She needed to trust them. God was good. She needed to trust God too. Feeling emboldened, she made one more stop before heading back to the parsonage. She headed east down Old US 12 to Freer Road. Within a few minutes, she pulled into Cassandra's driveway. It was time to do something about Cassandra's abdication of motherhood.

Maggie walked purposefully and carefully up the walkway with her cane. Toys were scattered everywhere. She made her way up the front steps and rang the doorbell. Cassandra's two Labradors, Black and Blue, began barking like crazy, but no one answered the door. Maggie could hear the television blaring. She could see the brightness of the kitchen light. She rang again. Then she knocked. The dogs kept up their vigilant yelping, but no one opened the door. Was Cassandra avoiding her?

Maggie finally got back in her car, a little more deflated than when she had arrived full of bravado. She drove back to the parsonage, determined to speak with Cassandra the next day and fix the daycare issue once and for all.

Bryan and Cate were brainstorming on ways to bring the Ghana project to life for the congregation on Sunday. Bryan had a PowerPoint presentation to share. It was his standard production for fundraisers, but it was much more personal now. People he actually knew were going to make the trip in January and see the work in action.

"How about, before I show the PowerPoint, you get up and talk about what you will be doing in Accra with the semester abroad program?" Bryan asked Cate.

"Okay. First, I can tell them about the city—that it's the capital of Ghana, it has nearly four million people, and it's located right on the coast of the Gulf of Guinea. Then I'll tell them a little about the University of Ghana and the hospital I'll be working at. But some of what I'll be doing will evolve with the different needs in the hospital. I'm preparing myself for constant change."

Cate chewed on her fingernail. The excitement of the trip, being near Bryan, and the fear of the unknown swirled in her like a small tempest. There was a possibility she would be fingernailless by the time she arrived in Ghana.

"Constant change works everywhere in Ghana," Bryan laughed. "It took me too long to figure that out. I thought I was going to oversee the building of a new orphanage. I got up early on the first day, ready to go, but the pastor, his name is Elisha, decided it was time for all-day-all-night church. I kept looking at my watch, wondering when we would begin building. He kept praying, and the people kept singing. For twenty-four hours! The next day, everyone was so tired, the building was delayed again. I was getting more and more upset until one of the other volunteers sat me down and explained 'Ghana Time.' All things get done when they get done. Sometimes there is urgency, sometimes there is waiting. It doesn't matter what my time frame is. It's Ghana Time. And then I took my watch off my wrist and threw it away. I finally got it."

Cate looked at Bryan's wrist. It was watchless.

Jack stopped in to see his new patient before leaving for the parsonage. She was still asleep. He asked the nurse to call him when the woman awoke. He needed more information, but only she could give it to him. She was in such a weakened condition. He was surprised she had gotten herself to the hospital in the first place. He needed to find out if she had any extended family. No one was listed on her forms at the Ann Arbor doctor's office, not even an "in case of emergency" person.

As Jack walked down the corridors of the hospital on his way out, he called Harold Brinkmeyer at the law office downtown.

"Harold, this is Jack. I need to see you sometime tomorrow. Are you available for lunch?"

"Yes," Harold said, sensing Jack's gravity. "Where?"

"How do you feel about the hospital cafeteria?"

"Can't say it's my first choice, but I'll meet you there at noon," Harold said, immediately thinking that after he met with Jack he could find Ellen and do a little flirting.

"See you then. Thanks, Harold."

Jack hung up, got in his car, and headed for the parsonage. He wouldn't tell Maggie this story. The situation would have to stay confidential for now.

Cate and Bryan animatedly shared their ideas for the Ghana presentation with Jack and Maggie over dinner. The lasagna, pretzel rolls, and salad were eaten efficiently, followed by Mrs. Popkin's fresh blueberry cheesecake. But the meal wasn't what Maggie was savoring.

As of that day, there were ten people signed up to go to Ghana in January. That was counting Bryan and Cate. Cate would spend weekdays as a student in Accra and all weekend with the rest of the group in Bawjiase, a tiny village in the countryside where the orphanage had been built. The rest of the group consisted of Maggie, Jack, Ethan and Charlene Kessler, Bill and Sylvia Baxter, Ellen Bright, and, to Maggie's delight, Addie Wiggins as the only high school student.

The group had formed after several announcements were made in church and small, informational meetings were held in the parsonage.

Then came the next challenge: money. Each person would need five thousand dollars. That would cover transportation overseas, along with money for the project of the new school at the orphanage. Each member of the team had paid fifteen hundred dollars of their own money, but now it was time for a little help.

Enter Bryan. He was equipped to light the church on fire, figuratively, and invite the people who weren't going on the trip to participate through giving. That coming Sunday was what they all had been waiting for: the big Ghana Extravaganza fundraiser.

Of course, Maggie had an annoying fear that the money wouldn't be raised and the trip would have to be scrapped. The fear hung over her like an angry little rain cloud. It had gone into hiding since all the ruckus with the church break-ins had begun, but now it was back. They had to raise the money and other needed donations of backpacks, school supplies, and playclothes for the children.

As she listened to parts of Bryan's prepared speech and Cate's enthusiastic hopes for her university studies, Maggie had an idea.

"Bryan, do you know how to make any Ghanaian food?"

"Why?" Bryan asked, not appreciating the interruption as he was waxing eloquently about his presentation.

"I was thinking, it would be a nice added touch if we could give the congregation a little taste of Ghana while you do your brilliant presentation," Maggie said.

She believed that nothing brought people together like food. Somehow, sharing a meal or a snack brought warmth to a conversation. What about eating something local to Ghana?

Jack had been very quiet throughout dinner. After greeting Bryan with a bear hug, Cate with a kiss on the cheek, and Maggie with both a hug and kiss, Jack had quietly helped with the last of the dinner preparations, lost in thought.

At first, Maggie thought he was just listening intently to the Ghana plans, but then she could see he was thinking about something else.

"What do you think, Jack?" she asked, squeezing his hand. She smiled at him.

Jack organized his face and said, "Food?"

"Yes. Something from Ghana? For Sunday? Just a taste. What do you think?"

Maggie looked at him expectantly.

"Wait, wait, wait," said Bryan. "I don't think so."

"Why not?" Maggie and Cate asked in surround sound.

"It's too much work. I just want to do my PowerPoint," Bryan said, deflated from his previous excitement.

"Can you make any Ghanaian food or not?" Maggie persisted. "Don't lie either." Her eyes bored into him.

"Actually," Jack said, finally joining the evening, "something Ghanaian might make it a little more festive."

Bryan shook his head in despair.

"What is your problem?" Maggie said, sounding like an exasperated mother.

Bryan looked at her. "I can make one thing."

"Well, go on," Maggie nagged.

"I can make jollof rice," Bryan said, sounding as if that was the most embarrassing thing he had ever said in his life.

The other three stared at him mutely.

Bryan took a deep breath. His cheeks were flushed with embarrassment. He ran his hand through his hair, making it all stand up on end. For just a moment, Maggie thought he looked like a very young Winston.

"Bryan," Maggie said evenly, "I'm going to punch you if you don't spit it out. Is jollof rice something you make with a dead human? Did you have to kill someone in order to make jollof rice?"

"No. A chicken," Bryan finally said.

"Ahh! What are you talking about?" Maggie yelled, punching him in the arm.

"I was supposed to kill a chicken. They told me it was part of my chores. You know, to help with dinner," Bryan said softly. "I couldn't do it. I just couldn't kill that chicken. It was probably the first moment of many when a light bulb exploded in my brain. I realized other people in other countries live so differently than I do in America." He took a breath. "Anyway, because I didn't kill the chicken, some of the older boys my age had a lot of fun at my expense and told me I had to make dinner with the women. That was the night I learned to make jollof rice around the fire with all the women."

Maggie wanted to punch herself now.

"Cultures are so varied, aren't they," Jack said. "I have a feeling we'll see many things on our trip that will surprise us about how people and genders interact. Is jollof rice good?"

How does Jack always manage to do that? Maggie wondered. He was able to take an uncomfortable situation for Bryan and clear away embarrassment or humiliation or whatever negative muck was hanging in the air. Maggie leaned over and impulsively kissed him. Then she leaned over to Bryan and kissed him too. Bryan smiled.

"Yes, it's good. The thing is, cooking jollof rice isn't done just by women. Men help all the time with a lot of the food preparation. The boys just wanted me to think it was humiliating. I had fun getting revenge as the weeks went on." Bryan was back to his old self. "But they got me good that night."

The evening ended on that quiet note. Maggie realized she was more exhausted than she thought. Her ankle was making itself known, and church issues began creeping back into her psyche. She realized she had been dreading going to bed the last few nights because of the vivid dreams she'd been having. Maybe, with Bryan in the parsonage, she would feel safe enough to relax. She looked up and caught Jack staring at her.

"It's time for you to sleep," he said. "How's your ankle?"

"It's yelping a bit. Too much sitting today. Or too much walking," Maggie said.

"We'll do the dishes," Cate volunteered.

She wasn't ready to leave Bryan yet.

Maggie looked at Bryan. "So about that jollof rice. What do I need to buy at the grocery store? I figure we can use little foil cupcake papers and give everyone a couple of big bites. Let's plan on seventy-five people at a quarter cup each. Do the math, and tell me in the morning."

She hugged Bryan and Cate together and then limped Jack to the back door.

"You have been busy in another realm tonight," Maggie said to Jack.

"Yes. Can you come to the hospital cafeteria for lunch tomorrow? Harold will be there too. We have a . . . well, a situation," Jack said.

"Sure. If I weren't so tired, I'd want to know right now. But I must confess, at this moment, I don't care one bit." She smiled ruefully.

"Go to bed, wife-to-be," he said as his arms slid around her.

"Yes, husband-to-be. Sir."

A very extraordinary kiss lightened both their spirits before they parted. Then Jack stepped out into the night.

21

Maggie stared across her desk at Detective Keith Crunch. He had come early Tuesday morning to give her the latest report. He had already briefed Charlotte and Bernie Bumble but felt Maggie also needed to know the update.

"We were able to track down Mr. Johnson's exact whereabouts in Montana. He stayed at the Mountain Peak Lodge from August twenty-ninth through the thirty-first. He was booked for three weeks but has left the premises. He destroyed a cabin there and then disappeared. We were able to get this information from a Clara Abbott, who seemed to have the most contact with him at the resort. She runs the front desk. She was the one who called the credit card company when she noticed he was using the Loving the Lord credit card." Detective Crunch took a breath. "May I ask why a church this small has a credit card?"

"I think the main reason began a few years ago when the stained glass windows were being refurbished. The glass company only took credit cards for payment. I guess some churches thought they could pay whenever they raised the money. The stained glass company got burned too many times. They wanted payment in full, up-front. But then it was discovered that having a credit card helped with things like church supper supplies and our summer barbecue and picnics. It makes it easier for Irena, our organist, to order new music and Marla, our Sunday school superintendent, to order curricula. Anyone who was authorized could purchase the basic products needed for an event. Otherwise, it was everyone throwing their receipts at the chair of the finance committee and waiting for refunds."

Maggie was able to explain it clearly since Hank had just explained it to her earlier that morning. When Hank had begun his work at Loving the Lord just over a year ago, he made it his business to learn the history and also the inner workings of his new place of employment. There was very little Hank did not know regarding his church.

"That makes sense. How many people have access to the credit card?" Detective Crunch asked.

"The members of the council and the staff. The unfortunate thing is that Redford Johnson is, or was, the chair of the finance committee. Right now we have no idea what he has or hasn't done with the finances of the church," Maggie said, beginning to feel sick to her stomach. "They all know the card has been cancelled and why."

"We are searching for Mr. Johnson, and I will have a warrant to search his residence by the end of the day. That may give us some answers regarding the church's finances. I take it you are not leaving any money on the premises?"

Detective Crunch had been jotting notes but glanced up whenever Maggie spoke. His eyes looked like sapphires.

"No, not anymore. We began to suspect Redford of stealing from the weekly offering. Now Harold Brinkmeyer, the chair of the council and an attorney in town, keeps the offering in his office safe until he makes the deposit on Monday mornings."

Maggie blinked but could not stop staring into Detective Crunch's eyes.

"We are monitoring all movements in and around the church. You can feel safe enough knowing someone is watching the cameras twenty-four hours a day."

His eyes crinkled at the edges as he smiled at Maggie. She smiled back.

"Thank you, Detective Crunch. It's been unnerving lately to have a place of safety and sanctuary turned into a place of fear and dread."

"You can call me Keith. And the fear and dread are going to end. I have no doubt."

Keith's eyes crinkled again. Then he stood to leave. Maggie rose too, leaning gently on her desk.

"Thank you, Keith."

As they walked out of Maggie's office, Skylar Breese was waiting in Hank's. She was seated in Hank's spare chair with her long legs all wrapped around each other. When she saw Maggie, she stood up, towering over both Maggie and Keith. Maggie heard the detective's intake of breath.

"Hi, Sky," Maggie said.

Maggie noticed Hank was sitting at his desk, pretending to do something on his computer. The only problem was, his computer was turned off. Maggie looked at Keith, who was captivated, and felt an odd sense of pride that the gorgeous Skylar was one of her parishioners. *Yes, we have freakishly beautiful people attending our church.*

"Skylar Breese, this is Detective Crunch from Ann Arbor. He's here on a routine visit, checking the building's safety standards."

Maggie lied easily with the assuredness that the ethereal Sky would believe anything she said but most likely wouldn't hear a word.

Sky stretched out her long, thin hand with her pale-pink-painted long, thin nails.

"Mmm . . . It's a pleasure to meet you, Detective."

Her gray eyes shone as her white teeth sparkled. The effect was dazzling.

Keith had to look up to meet her eyes. Sky, in her high heels, was about six inches taller than he. Keith slowly held out his hand while not taking his eyes off hers.

"It's a pleasure to meet you, Ms. Breese," he said much more smoothly than Maggie thought possible.

"Mmm . . . yes, it is. I hope our little church is . . . well . . . up to . . . mmm . . . code?" Her statement turned quickly into a question.

"Yes," Keith said warmly. "Everything is under control. Do you live in Cherish, Ms. Breese?"

Skylar focused her eyes on his. "Please, call me Sky, and yes, I do live back here in lovely Cherish. I was gone for a while . . . mmm . . . but it's always good to come home."

Maggie thought she might have to clean up Detective Crunch with one of Doris's mops. She looked sideways at Hank, who was barely able to control his amusement.

"Well, thank you for the good news about the inspection, Detective Crunch," Maggie jumped right on in. "I would like to invite you to worship with us on Sunday at ten o'clock, if you don't already have a church home of your own."

Keith dragged his eyes from Sky and pulled himself together.

"Thank you, Pastor Maggie. I may just do that." He turned back to Sky. "It's been very nice meeting you, Ms. Breese, uh, Sky."

Sky nodded her head like royalty. "Likewise."

Then Sky looked around, as if trying to remember why she was there in the first place.

Suddenly, the door to the office burst open, and Irena rushed in, looking cross. Her gold-plated eyes narrowed as she took in the scene before her.

"Who dis?" she asked Maggie, jerking her purple head toward Keith.

"Hello, Irena," Maggie said brightly. "Let me introduce Detective Keith Crunch from the Ann Arbor Police Department. He's here doing a building inspection." Maggie said the last sentence with emphasis to give Irena a warning. She didn't want Irena to give anything away with Sky standing there.

Irena was oblivious. She turned her sparkly face toward Keith like a satellite and laser-fixed her eyes on his.

"You catch de villain?"

Maggie noticed as Sky came back from the land of the flower fairies and carefully watched and listened.

Maggie was just about to speak, when Keith said, "And who are you?"

He smiled at Irena, who blinked rapidly, as if looking directly at an eclipse of the sun. Maggie couldn't believe it. Irena looked as if she were going to swoon.

"Oh, forgive me," Maggie said. "Detective Crunch, this is Irena Dalca. She's our brilliant organist here at Loving the Lord."

"Ms. Dalca, it's a pleasure to meet you." Keith held out his hand. Maggie thought for a moment Irena might kiss it. "And yes, I catch many villains in my line of work. I'm here today to check on your building codes. Everything looks good. Pastor Maggie has invited me to worship this Sunday. I look forward to hearing you play."

"Too bud," Irena said with a toss of her purple head. "I not play dis veek. Afrrica Day. You hev to come beck on not dis Sunday."

"Africa Day. That sounds interesting. Perhaps I'll come this Sunday and another Sunday as well."

As Keith spoke, he slowly led Irena out of the office. She nodded like a bobblehead the whole way. He turned back and gave Maggie a nod. If he wanted one more look at Sky, he didn't show it.

As for Sky, she seemed to be completely fixated on every word, but she couldn't seem to return to the reason for her visit. Hank just shrugged and pretended to work on his computer.

Maggie walked Sky slowly into the sanctuary. It seemed no one knew why Sky had stopped by the church, including Sky herself. Maggie asked a few questions about Pretty, Pretty Petals and then helped Sky through the sanctuary doors to the top of the outdoor steps.

Maggie shook her head. *How in the world does Sky run a business?*

As Sky floated down the front steps of the church, Marla was led inside by the rambunctious Carrie and Carl. As usual, they were overjoyed to see Maggie.

"Pasto Maggie!" Carl squealed.

He was grinning from ear to ear, and Maggie could see a milk mustache across his upper lip—left over from breakfast at Marla's house, she assumed. She set her cane against the church door and gave the two little urchins hugs and kisses. Looking over their heads at Marla, she could see Marla must not have had time to comb her hair or dress with care. She was wearing a pair of gray slacks and what looked to be a pajama top. Maggie did not need the reminder to know what she had to do. She had already decided to pay a visit to Cassandra before her lunch at noon with Jack and Harold.

"Hi, you two. And hi, Mrs. Wiggins. How are you all today?" Maggie asked cheerfully.

"We're good," Carrie said, laughing. "We get to play with Addie today when she gets done with school."

Maggie looked at Marla, who simultaneously raised her eyebrows and her shoulders in a symbol of defeat.

Why aren't Carrie and Carl in school? Maggie wondered to herself.

"Well, that sounds like fun," Maggie said.

"I love Addie," Carrie said dreamily.

Marla smiled at this and gave Carrie a pat on the head.

"Let's go inside for a bit and play in the nursery," Marla said, herding the two children into the sanctuary.

"I want to play in the spwinkleh," Carl exclaimed.

"Maybe a little later this morning," Marla said wearily. "May we use the parsonage hose, Pastor Maggie?"

"Of course," Maggie said brightly as she kissed the children.

Carrie and Carl tumbled into the church, ready to play.

"Marla," Maggie said, taking Marla's arm for a second, "I'm going to take care of this."

Marla nodded tiredly.

After giving Hank the order of the bulletin for Sunday, which was completely different from other Sundays due to the Ghana Extravaganza, Maggie took her cane and walked with a little more purpose and strength to her car in the parsonage driveway.

Within minutes, she was heading up Cassandra's front walk. Maggie rang the doorbell with a sharp jab of her finger. Seeing exhausted Marla with the children was the last boost of courage Maggie needed. She waited. Nothing but dogs barking. She rang the doorbell again. Finally, Maggie heard the lock click, and the front door opened.

Cassandra stood on the threshold wearing a dirty white negligee with fraying lace at the cuffs and hem. Her hair looked like it had had an unfortunate encounter with a hand mixer. Mascara was smudged under her eyes, and they looked sunken and hollow. Her face was white and drawn. She looked like she had been on a party bus all night long.

"Pastor Maggie, what can I do for you?" Cassandra spoke softly as her hand came up to hold her forehead.

The sight of a hungover Cassandra inflamed Maggie. She wanted to bang a drum or slam pots and pans together to add to Cassandra's pain. Maggie hadn't felt that angry in a long time. Not since Ed had died. But it was a different anger now.

Maggie pushed her way into Cassandra's house, not even noticing the inappropriate sniffs she was receiving from the dogs.

"Cassandra, I apologize if I woke you, but we seem to have an issue that has to be dealt with immediately. It has to do with Carrie and Carl." Maggie took a breath, then gently pushed the nosy dogs away.

Cassandra walked into the living room and silently waved for Maggie to follow. She sat on the couch—no, she *collapsed* on the couch. Maggie sat, perched on the edge of a chair, unsympathetically staring at Cassandra. She had a quick flash of Marla standing on the church steps in her pajama top, completely frazzled.

Cassandra slowly focused her eyes on Maggie.

"What about Carrie and Carl? Are they all right?" She was still speaking softly, but there was concern in her bleary eyes.

"They are fine. The problem is that Marla Wiggins is not. It seems she and Addie are the new caretakers of your children. Except they aren't. Cassandra, I don't know what you do with your time, but the church isn't your free babysitting service. Marla has her own family and a job. Addie is just a high school student with her own life. But more and more lately they have Carrie and Carl at church, in their home, overnight, on weekends, and on and on. They, of course, are too nice to say anything. I'm supposed to be too nice to say anything. Sorry, but I'm not. I think you have taken advantage of them, and it's not right. You have abdicated being a mother, and no one knows why."

"Do you have children, Maggie?" Cassandra had a little more firmness in her voice now.

"No, Cassandra, I don't." Maggie noticed the "Pastor" had been dropped from her name. She was glad. She wanted Cassandra to show some kind of emotion. "I'm not a mother, but I was raised by one. And I know enough to say with certainty that shipping your children off to others, when they need to be with you, is not good or effective mothering." Maggie was spoiling for a fight.

"Get out of my house."

Cassandra said it with all the force she could muster, which was very little. She put her hand back on her forehead and slumped down on the couch. Maggie wondered if she was on drugs.

"Cassandra," Maggie's voice softened just a little. "Do the children have a father?"

"Leave," Casandra hissed.

"I will leave," Maggie said more calmly, "but this has to be dealt with, Cassandra. I have a whole church to take care of. Marla is part of that church, and so are you. It's my job to make sure all is well for all of you, as much as I am able. Why don't you spend time with your children? Can we just talk about it?"

"My life is none of your business. And don't worry about me being part of the church, or Carrie or Carl. We won't be going back to *inconvenience* you all." Cassandra sounded whiny and petulant.

Maggie stood up and moved to the door.

"I hope that's not true. And if you ever want to talk about what's going on in your life, I'm willing to listen."

Maggie didn't know what else to say. She didn't want to lie and say Cassandra was loved by the whole congregation. And even though Maggie had the faint awareness that she had crossed the line by confronting Cassandra so harshly, she couldn't bring herself to apologize. All she could see in the moment was a drunk mother who was methodically abandoning her children.

Maggie let herself out amidst happy licks on her hands from the dogs. Cassandra stayed on the couch.

Once Maggie had left, Cassandra sank all the way down and began to weep.

Maggie got in her car high on adrenaline. She really hated confrontation, but evidence of injustice, no matter what kind, could rile her up and leave her mouth without control or filters. Her mother and Ed had both told her to stop and think before jumping into an argument. She had completely failed at that good advice today. If she had stopped to breathe and think for a moment, she would have seen clearly that her anger was not completely directed at Cassandra. She was angry at Redford Johnson. She was angry at whoever was breaking into the church. She was angry at herself for not knowing what to do about it all. Cassandra was the unfortunate recipient of the torrent.

Maggie drove to the hospital and arrived just in time for lunch with Jack and Harold. Her heart rate had relaxed somewhat by the time she made her way into the cafeteria. They were waiting when she walked in. Jack leaned down to kiss her cheek.

"Hi, Maggie," he said and then, staring at her, continued, "are you all right? You looked flushed. Or sunburned. Which is it?"

"Hi, Jack. Hi, Harold. Well, you caught me. I ditched work this morning and have been sunbathing on the front lawn of the parsonage."

They smiled as they made their way into the food line. After paying, they found a table in the corner. Maggie was slowly shaking off her meeting with Cassandra and felt her curiosity piqued. What was the reason for the little get-together at the hospital?

They settled in, removing their food from trays and setting the trays on an empty table. Maggie said a prayer, and they began to eat. She had a bowl of steaming chicken and rice soup and half a veggie sandwich. Jack had the soup with an egg salad sandwich and chips, and Harold had a huge hamburger with a pile of crispy, golden French fries. It was all surprisingly delicious for a hospital cafeteria.

Finally, Jack wiped his mouth with his napkin and proceeded.

"We have a problem," he began. "It's a problem for our church, which is why you're here, Maggie, and it will turn into a legal problem, I am certain. That's why I called you, Harold."

Maggie sipped her soup, her eyes glued on Jack. What in the world could he be talking about? And why didn't he just tell her last night?

Harold shoved a ketchup-covered French fry into his mouth and said, "What is it? I'm pretty busy right now, but things may slow down in about a month or so."

He grabbed his burger and took a huge bite, dripping ketchup and mustard.

"What I'm going to tell you is a breach of confidentiality," Jack said, "but we are all going to have to come up with a solution for this one. I'll take the lead, but you will both have to pitch in. Harold, this might have to take precedence over some of your other work, and I'm pretty sure it will be pro bono work for you too. Sorry about that." He turned to Maggie. "Maggie, you'll have to do what you do so well: pastor the flock. There will be a lot of pieces to pick up."

"Jack, just tell us," Maggie said, feeling frustrated. "You're being awfully cloak and dagger. We live in Cherish, for heaven's sake. Nothing happens here."

"Except for church break-ins, as well as someone abusing our church credit card and possibly someone stealing from the offering. And someone unexpectedly dying," Jack said carefully.

Harold stopped chewing. His mouth looked like a chipmunk who had just scored a pile of peanuts. Maggie slowly lowered her spoon. They both stared at Jack.

"People do die here, Jack. It's sad, but it's not unheard of," Maggie said slowly, but she felt a small shiver making its way down her spine.

"Who's dying, Jack?" Harold said after swallowing way too much hamburger. He began to cough and took a drink of water.

Jack waited for the coughing to pass.

"She came into the hospital yesterday, very ill. She had a horrible reaction to a chemotherapy treatment in Ann Arbor. Her diagnosis of cancer is terminal. There really isn't any hope. I admitted her, called her oncologist at the University Medical Center, and discovered she hadn't told anyone. She has no next of kin. And she's ours," Jack said, looking miserable.

"Who is it?" Maggie's patience was completely depleted.

"Cassandra Moffet."

22

Maggie felt the world slow to a stop. She couldn't see anything but the florescent lights in the ceiling of the cafeteria. She couldn't hear Jack speaking. She was floating gently away. Jack caught her before she slid out of her chair. The news of Cassandra's cancer diagnosis plunged Maggie to a place beyond reality.

Cassandra was dying. She wasn't drunk. She wasn't on drugs. She was dying.

Maggie's eyes slid shut.

Jack and Harold moved Maggie to a bench outside the cafeteria. Within minutes, her eyes were fluttering. Jack held her up and gave her some water.

"Do you feel all right to sit up?" he asked.

Maggie looked at him, trying to focus. "Yes, I think so." She paused and took a deep breath. Without looking at Jack, she asked, "Is Cassandra really dying?"

"Yes."

He waited. Maggie sat for a few minutes, sipping the water. Jack and Harold sat with her quietly.

Finally, Harold asked, "So she came here yesterday? Aren't you her primary doctor? Didn't you know about the chemo?" It was clear he wanted to begin putting the pieces together.

"No, I wasn't her primary care doctor, but I am now. Some patients in small towns don't want to go to a doctor they sit next to in church or see in the grocery store, so they see someone in a different town. I had no idea Cassandra was ill. Last night I treated her here and then admitted her. She couldn't open her eyes, and she certainly couldn't get out of bed. I have no idea how she even drove herself here from her house." Jack shook his head. "She knows her prognosis. She will have her records sent to my office. She decided she needed a doctor a little closer to home."

"So," Jack continued, "we have a young mother. She's terminal. She has two small children and apparently no relatives. We have to put a lot of things in order, and quickly."

Maggie listened, and then, taking a deep breath, she whispered, "But there's no way you admitted her. She's home."

"That's impossible, Maggie. I saw her at eight this morning. She was more alert, but I told her I wanted her to stay for more observation."

Jack was speaking to Maggie as if she were a child. She didn't like it.

"Cassandra is home," Maggie said definitively. "I just came from her house."

Jack looked concerned. Was Maggie going mad?

"I just . . . came from . . . her house." Maggie's eyes began to well-up with plump tears. "And . . . I made it . . . very clear . . . that I thought . . . she was a bad mother . . . who was abusing . . . the . . . church."

Maggie began to sob. She had never felt such self-loathing. She thought she might vomit.

Now Jack's head was spinning. He grabbed his cell phone and called up to the floor where Cassandra was located. He spoke quickly to one of the nurses. As he listened to her reply, his face changed. He thanked the nurse and hung up as he shook his head.

"You're right, Maggie. Cassandra left this morning sometime after ten without being checked out. The nurses discovered her gone when they went in to do routine tests. She had dressed and left her hospital gown on the bed."

Jack was stunned. How did Cassandra have the strength even to sit up, let alone drive?

Harold spoke up. "Okay, we have a snarl ball of a case here. Jack, I have to be crass. How long does she have?"

"Her oncologist said three months, at the most," Jack said. "She has ovarian cancer, but it has metastasized. It's very aggressive."

Maggie hung her head at the horrific words.

Harold continued. "I know what needs to be done from a legal standpoint. We'll need to know if she has a will and, if so, who is named as designated custodian of the children. That is, if there is anyone. We can help her get her finances in order. I can also draw up a living trust, if she wishes." Harold was clearly ordering documents in his mind and writing a list as he did so.

Jack had had the opportunity the night before and that morning to make his list of necessary medical choices and decisions he would discuss with Cassandra.

Maggie wanted to crawl in a hole and disappear. How was she going to repair what she had said and done? How could she have been so bull-headed, jumping to conclusions and judging without proper information? How could she ever apologize to Cassandra for being so cruel and insensitive? It was completely insurmountable.

Jack dragged Maggie back to the present.

"As her new physician, I'll speak to her immediately and begin the conversation. My intention is to direct her to you, Harold, for legal issues. If she is willing, I recommend you do as much as you can in her home. The less she has to move, the better."

"Of course," Harold said. "This will be my top priority. My assistant isn't going to like it, but too bad. We will make this work." Harold stood to leave, shook Jack's hand, and gave Maggie a pat on the shoulder. "It's going to be okay, Pastor Maggie. It really will. Our church takes care of its own."

Then Harold made his way down the corridor, leaving most of his lunch behind and taking away a new legal puzzle to solve. Harold was a man with a purpose but not overly encumbered with empathy.

Jack looked at Maggie's pale and devastated face.

"Maggie, are you feeling any better?"

"No. I mean, yes. I'm okay. I just can't believe what an idiot I am. I can't believe Cassandra is dying, and not just dying, she is suffering. I saw it in her face and thought she was drunk. I can't imagine the unbelievable pain awaiting her. And . . . Carrie and Carl." At that, she burst into tears again. "Oh, those precious children!"

Jack put his arms around her and let her cry. He loved her heart, and he knew she would mend from the misunderstanding of that morning. She would bring love like a salve to Cassandra, the children, and the church. Jack had no doubt about it.

"Shall we make a plan?" Jack asked carefully.

"Yes," Maggie said quickly. "I have to apologize. I must go back to her house and beg her to let me in."

"You can't do that yet," Jack said, trying to stop her speed-of-light thought processes. "How would you know about her diagnosis? I'll tell her I have been in communication with her oncologist. Then I will tell her there are people who care for her, and there are decisions that need to be made about the future, when she's ready."

"Why didn't you tell me last night? You knew she was dying. Why did you make me wait? That was unfair."

"Maggie, I didn't have any idea you were going to Cassandra's this morning. I didn't want you to have a restless night last night."

"This could be a hazard in our relationship," Maggie said quietly. "We can't fix it now, but we're going to have to talk this out. There will be times when one of us will know more about a parishioner or patient than the other. We will have to share information or decide to keep it strictly separate. What is happening with Cassandra, well, this won't work again."

At first, Jack didn't know what she meant. What was "this"? Then he saw her face crumple again.

"I said such hurtful things, Jack. I understand what you're saying about me having to wait to see Cassandra. I'm not a child. But I have hurt another woman, and I have to tell her I'm sorry. So do what you have to do, but I will see her before the end of the day." Maggie stood up, a little wobbly, and then turned to leave, pulling herself up very straight, gripping her cane with white knuckles. She turned back and kissed Jack quickly on the cheek. "All will be well. I hope."

Jack watched her leave. He realized Maggie had just taken control of the situation. She didn't need his protection in the matter of Cassandra. She had just given him marching orders. Jack called his nurse and asked her to cancel his afternoon appointments, with much apology. Then he collected his things from his office, got into his car, and drove to Cassandra's house. It would be a long afternoon.

Maggie went back to church and heard Irena on the organ. *Blessed familiarity.* When she entered the sanctuary, Maggie waved to Irena on her way to the office. The music abruptly stopped as Irena flew off her perch like an angry bird and grabbed Maggie's arm.

"Vere ees he?" she chirped.

"Where is who?" Maggie asked, staring into the elaborately sparkled eyes.

"Captain Crrunch," Irena said irritably. "Vere ees he?"

Maggie had to think for a moment. "Do you mean Detective Keith Crunch?"

"Ov courrse." Irena tapped her little foot in frustration.

"He's probably fighting crime somewhere. That's what he does," Maggie said. And then, as an afterthought, said, "You know, Irena, we can't tell people about what he and the other police are doing around here. We can't let the . . . the . . . *villain* find out there is surveillance. Right?"

"So?"

"So, don't ask him if he has caught the villain in front of other people, okay?"

Maggie stared at Irena's pinched face.

"I must prractice."

Irena turned, tottered back to the organ bench, and re-perched herself.

Maggie went into the office, hoping Hank had nothing of interest to tell her. But it was not to be.

"Pastor Maggie, I hate to inform you, but we received a phone call from a rental car company. Apparently, our man Redford charged a car in Montana an hour before he checked into the lodge. He used the church credit card for that as well. It wasn't until the lodge check-in that the card was suspended. They called to say the card has been cancelled, but Redford still has the car in his possession for another two weeks, apparently. The rental car company wants payment now." Hank reported this efficiently and with a slight FBI-ish tone to his voice.

"That's ridiculous," Maggie huffed. "The card is cancelled. We have nothing to do with Redford's crimes against the world. Harold or Detective Crunch or even Charlotte will have to handle this."

She sounded much more assured than she was. The church couldn't possibly replace a car. What did Redford think he was doing?

"Wait a minute," Maggie said. "Redford still has the car, but he's not at the lodge? Where is he?"

Just then the phone rang. Hank picked it up.

"Loving the Lord Community Church, Hank speaking. How may I help you? . . . Yes, Pastor Maggie is in."

He looked at Maggie.

"Just a moment please," Hank said into the receiver.

"Pastor Maggie," Hank whispered, covering the phone. "It's Clara Abbott from the Mountain Peak Lodge."

Maggie nodded, went into her office, and shut the door. She picked up the phone.

"Hello? This is Pastor Maggie speaking."

For some reason, Maggie was nervous. Was Clara going to yell at her for what Redford did?

"Hi, Pastor Maggie. My name is Clara Abbott, and I run the front desk at the Mountain Peak Lodge. How are you today?" Clara didn't sound like she was going to scream and yell.

"Hi, Clara. I'm fine. Except, of course, for the horrible experience you have had with one of our parishioners." Maggie thought she had better just get it out there.

"That's why I'm calling. I wanted to let you know personally that the lodge's insurance company is covering all the damages inflicted by Mr. Johnson. We just got word today. I thought it might ease your mind."

Clara's voice sounded like a gently rolling brook, calm and comforting. It was almost kind enough to make Maggie cry again.

Clara continued. "You know, I'm from Michigan."

"You are?" Maggie asked. "Where?"

"It's a small town just north of Lansing called DeWitt. I graduated from Michigan State University. I've been to Cherish before with my mom."

"Well . . . Go Spartans!" Maggie smiled back through the phone, taking a deep, pleasant breath. "Clara, it is so nice of you to call and give us this news. It's been a little tense around here, as you can imagine. We feel awful about what happened at your lodge. We had no idea Redford was capable of such violence."

"It takes all kinds of people to make a world, my mom says, but I always think there are a few the world doesn't necessarily need." Clara laughed.

"Yes, indeed," Maggie said ruefully. "But we are all stuck together, whether we like it or not."

"Well, I just wanted to let you know about the insurance. It's so nice to talk with you," Clara said, winding down the conversation.

"Clara, you have given me the best news of the week. Thank you. The next time you're back in Michigan, I would love to meet you. I'll have the rest of the story for you once it gets sorted out here."

Maggie hoped that was true.

"I'll do that, Pastor Maggie. You have a great day. Bye."

Redford pushed his glass forward for another whiskey. He was having the time of his life. It didn't take much to control another person, and Redford had mastered the art. Looking into his whiskey glass triggered thoughts of his own upbringing. Having been raised by a man who used a whiskey glass every day and who taught lessons by extreme punishments and humiliations, Redford had learned from the best.

His father had been an elder in their local church. He was well respected. He owned his own insurance business and was involved in the Rotary Club. No one knew that he regularly beat his wife and son. That occurred whenever Redford's father had gone to another town to drink. He made sure he was where church folk couldn't see him. After beating Redford's mother until she was unconscious, he'd turned his fury on Redford. That was how Redford learned to be a man.

Redford learned to steal and to lie. At first, his lying was for self-preservation. He told lies to try to get out of beatings. But it didn't take long for Redford to see lying, and then stealing, as devious challenges. He learned he could steal a dollar out of his teacher's purse while she was helping another student. Who would miss a dollar? In Sunday school, he was able to see where the offering was kept until the end of class. It was easy to steal a few quarters.

As he grew older, he watched for bigger opportunities, like the offering from the worship service. The people in the church were so stupid. Just leaving the offering plates on the altar while they drank their weak coffee and ate stale cookies. He'd learned to slip up to the plates and help himself. Redford believed the church was full of hypocrites anyhow. Why else would they allow his father to be one of them?

At school, he began seeking out the smaller children on the playground and tormenting them verbally and physically. He abused animals. His anger manifested itself into full-blown hatred and cruelty. Redford became brilliant at abuse and malice.

As an adult, he had to finesse his crude behavior into civility, but his father had set a good example. Redford had to play the role of smooth financier, a caring investor for his clients. He had watched his father for years with that sickening smile at church, duping the fools who were in the congregation.

Redford left his old life behind but never forgot what he learned there. He received a degree in accounting and finance at a local college. He moved to Cherish, set up an office, and began to wheel and deal with the other business people in town. He found a vulnerable church and joined it. He made sure to be elected to the council of the church. They were so desperate for members to serve on the council, it was an easy move. They were grateful to have someone in finance.

He pulled it off at the beginning. It was like playing a role. But as his drinking had escalated, his mask had begun to slip. His nastiness flared when the whiskey flowed. He had been getting sloppy with the church finances just before Pastor Maggie showed up. She and the council had set up some new rules and enforced old ones. He had to count and deposit money with another member of the finance committee. That angered Redford because of how hard he had worked to relieve the other members of the finance committee from any duty whatsoever. Now he was being watched. Stealing had become more difficult.

Damn that Pastor Maggie!

Gulping his whiskey as though parched for water, Redford would stay close enough to watch the happenings in Cherish. It sounded like trouble was raining down on that idiot pastor. It was delightful. But there was another person Redford had in his sights—his original plan and purpose. One more drink, and then the phone call. He laughed out loud as he thought of what was coming.

23

Maggie's spirits were a little lighter after her phone call with Clara Abbott. Somehow, church life would all get sorted out. All would be well, she hoped.

Then Maggie thought about the challenges they would face when she and Jack were married. They would each be helping people needing pastoral care and medical care at the same time. The situation with Cassandra showed Maggie just how bad things could get without communication. But was it right to share confidential information? Was it legal? Her brain went round and round. All she wanted to do was get over to Cassandra's and apologize, but she would wait a while and let Jack approach Cassandra with the medical concerns first.

Maggie looked down at her desk. On her list of things to do she had written:

Prepare for Sunday Worship – Ghana Extravaganza! (Goal: $28,000)
Write funeral sermon for Abe Jones
Visit shut-ins
Ingredients for jollof rice at grocery store

When faced with a list, Maggie usually chose the most difficult task first in order to get it over with. But not that day. She just didn't have the energy. She grabbed her purse and cane and walked into Hank's office.

"I'm heading over to Friendly Elder Care," she said to Hank. "I'll be back in a bit."

Hank gave a salute. "Yesireebob! I'll hold down the fort."

As Maggie was leaving the sanctuary, she saw Marla with Carrie and Carl on the parsonage front lawn. Marla must have changed her pajama top at lunchtime because she was wearing a short-sleeved blouse. However, her hair looked as if it desperately needed a brush. Carrie and Carl were in their bathing suits, running through the sprinkler attached to the parsonage hose. They were squealing with glee as the cold water splashed on their little bodies. Marla had towels stacked next to her on the lawn. She was cutting out giant letters for the Sunday school bulletin board, being careful not to let water from the sprinkler get on her large pieces of colorful construction paper.

Carrie and Carl saw "Pasto" Maggie come through the sanctuary doors and went flying toward her. She quickly sat on the steps and put down her cane before the two little human water bombs were in her arms and on her lap. Maggie hugged the children tightly. She felt the sting in her eyes as she looked into their sweet, open faces.

"Pasto Maggie!" Carl cried. "Look at us in the spwinkleh!" He laughed and shivered.

"Pastor Maggie," Carrie said with blue lips, "Mrs. Wiggins said we could play in the sprinkler. And then we get to go to The Sugarplum and get a cookie from Mrs. Popkin. And then we get to play with Addie."

Carrie bounced while holding her hands together under her chin, elbows tucked in tightly at her sides. Giggles came out of her like bubbles.

Marla began to get up and come after the children, but Maggie waved her back down.

"It's my turn to hug them, Mrs. Wiggins. You just stay there and cut out your bulletin board letters." Maggie smiled.

"Yes, Pastor Maggie," Marla said, smiling back.

Maggie helped the children off her lap, picked up her cane, and walked them over to where Marla was sitting.

"I'm just heading over to see the shut-ins. It sounds like you have a fun afternoon ahead of you."

"And night," Marla said. Carrie and Carl ran back into the sprinkler with more squeals. "We are keeping them overnight again."

"Marla, I need to talk with you. It's about Cassandra. If Addie's watching the children later, could you and I meet for a cup of tea? Maybe around four o'clock?"

Maggie searched Marla's worn face.

"Sure. I would like that," Marla said, obviously needing the break more than she needed the tea. "Where?"

Maggie thought a minute about a private place.

"How about right here at the parsonage? I'll kick Bryan out and make him run errands or something."

"I'll be here at four," Marla said, pushing her hair out of her eyes and turning back to her letters.

Maggie received wet kisses from the children and then got her soggy self into her car.

Maggie spent the next two hours making her way to the rooms of her older parishioners. They were all delighted to see her, even Marvin Green, who still pretended she was ruining his nap—or his lunch, or his life—every time she showed up. But Maggie knew better than that by the way he always barked as she was leaving.

"When are you coming back anyway?" he'd always say, his voice sounding like he had gravel in his throat. "I might be busy."

"I'll try not to interrupt anything too important."

Maggie would smile and then give him a kiss on the cheek, which was what he was really waiting for.

Visiting the shut-ins always lifted Maggie's soul. They had such wonderful stories of the past. They could tell her every piece of history regarding Cherish and Loving the Lord. They shared harmless gossip of pastors gone by. They were also wise. They had lived through many things and could see the future by looking at the past.

"So. What's this Africa thing you're forcing on the church?" Marvin rasped once Maggie was seated in his small living quarters for that day's visit. "I hear it's going to cost a fortune in donations that should be used for the church itself. Where do you get your ding-dong ideas?" He coughed a long, raspy cough and looked at her with watery eyes.

"Marvin, I have already told you about this," Maggie said with mock seriousness. "I'm raising money from the church, which I plan to steal and then run off to Africa to make a new life for myself."

"I believe it," Marvin growled. "And I suppose you're taking my doctor with you?"

"Actually, he's my doctor," Maggie said, waving her ring at him.

Then they both laughed.

"We are raising money, quite a bit of money really, and besides paying for our airfare to get there, the rest of the money will go right to the orphanage and the new school we're hoping to build. It will help buy food, medicine, school books, and uniforms. Things like that," Maggie said with a smile. "And I don't want to hear another word out of you about it. The church isn't just one little building. The church is the world. It's our job to do as much as we can, wherever we can. And that's that, Marvin."

"Well." Marvin coughed again. "I don't know about that."

"Of course you do," Maggie said patiently. "I know for a fact you gave Sylvia Smits, I mean Baxter, a donation to buy diapers and baby formula for the Cherish Faith in Action last month. Don't deny it."

Maggie looked down at her fingernails to avoid Marvin's face.

"Well, how did you know about that?" He tried to bellow but coughed instead.

"I know all. Don't forget it. Our Ghana trip will help make the world a little smaller. We'll be able to have a sister village for Cherish. Won't that be fun?" Maggie couldn't help chuckling.

Marvin tried to look perturbed, but it didn't quite work. Actually, Maggie thought he looked like he had colic.

"Well, I still don't know about all this."

Marvin was running out of steam. Maggie could tell. She reached her hands out to his, and he let her.

"I'm going to pray about all these things," Maggie said. "And I'm going to pray for you and thank God for your huge, generous heart. And that's that."

So Maggie prayed. While her eyes were shut, Marvin looked at her serious face and smiled.

Jack sat in Cassandra's living room, in the same chair Maggie had perched on earlier that day.

Cassandra had refused to let him come in at first but finally relented when he reminded her of the severity of her illness and his wish to help. She was wearing the same old negligee, but where Maggie had seen a drunk, neglectful woman, Jack saw a dying one.

"Cassandra, it would be best if you let me bring you back to the hospital. We can monitor you there and give you some needed fluids. Would you be willing to come back?"

"I can't," Cassandra sighed. "I need to take care of my dogs and cats. And I need to get my kids back here. Your little girlfriend made it clear my kids and I are no longer wanted around her church." Cassandra tried to say it with some venom, but it came out as a whine.

Jack was relieved Cassandra had so quickly brought up the subject of Maggie.

"I've spoken with Maggie," he said carefully. "She told me about her visit this morning."

"Visit?" Cassandra's eyes hardened. "Is that what she called it?"

Jack jumped in. "Cassandra, Maggie didn't know you are sick. I'm guessing Marla doesn't know either?"

Cassandra set her jaw and looked away.

"It's no one's business. I'm not going to be a piece of gossip for this town to chew on."

Jack knew she already was, or would be soon, but kept to the point of his visit.

"Cassandra, you are a very sick woman. I'm sorry for all you have suffered so far, especially yesterday's chemotherapy. It's obvious you are in pain. Unless you object, I want to care for you now. I also want to encourage you to be part of your treatment. But to do so, I need you to be honest with me. I want to help."

Cassandra looked at Jack. There was something in his voice that was working its way through the strong wall of protection she had so carefully constructed over the years.

"I'm going to die," she said calmly.

"Yes."

"The doctor in Ann Arbor tried to tell me that. I told him to shut up and get me cured. I didn't believe him. I can't die now." Cassandra's eyes were glistening with tears. "I've got . . . Carrie and Carl."

"Yes. I am so sorry you have had to deal with this alone, and I understand your wish for privacy. I also know I don't understand the depth of what you are feeling. But Cassandra, I want to help. Many people will want to help. We all care about you and Carrie and Carl."

He wanted to continue with his list of what needed to be done but waited. He could see she was absorbing the truth of her illness, her mortality, while the reality of leaving her young children constricted her heart. Cassandra was making a silent visit to hell, and it was hell to watch. It never got easier for Jack to share a deadly diagnosis with a patient. He waited for her to speak.

Finally, she looked at him with red-rimmed eyes.

"What should I do?"

Jack spoke slowly and carefully. He knew too much information would just be overwhelming, even though he was ready to dive in with his plan.

"First of all, we need to get you back in the hospital. Let's see if we can relieve some of your pain and give you some nutrition."

"What about Carrie and Carl, and my dogs and cats?" Cassandra pleaded.

"If you will let me, I will speak to Maggie and Marla about all of this. They love you and your family, Cassandra. Truly they do. If Maggie said anything hurtful to you today, it is because she had no idea you were sick. Everything will be cared for."

"Maggie said many hurtful things." Cassandra's voice cracked.

"May I tell her and Marla?"

Cassandra nodded her head. "I'm tired."

Maggie left the Friendly Elder Care and called Bryan from the parking lot.

"What are the ingredients for jollof rice?" she asked, pulling a pad of paper and a pen out of her purse.

She jotted down the ingredients as Bryan rattled them off, along with how much they would need. Bryan's voice was comforting. It was familiar.

"What time will Cate be over?" Maggie asked next.

"She has a class at two o'clock, so I guess about three thirty or so," Bryan said.

"I have a meeting with Marla at four o'clock at the parsonage. I'll need you to 'invisiblize' yourself."

"How about I go get the jollof ingredients while you and Marla meet? And hey, what's for dinner? I'm starving."

"I was thinking about tacos tonight. Does that sound good? I have some incredible Michigan sweet corn to go with them," Maggie said, her mind wandering to Cassandra, knowing another visit was next on her list.

"Great. I'm finishing up some more pictures for Sunday's Power-Point presentation. I'll go to the store while you have your meeting."

"All right. I'll be home in a bit."

Maggie hung up and then dialed again.

"Hello?" Jack said as he answered his phone.

"Hi ya. It's me, your fiancé," Maggie said quietly.

"Hi ya, yourself. I'm glad you called."

"I'm heading to Cassandra's now. I just wanted you to know."

"I'm glad, but she's back in the hospital. I brought her here after I saw her at her house. Can you come here, and I'll meet you in the lobby? I know it's after the fact, but I have her permission to tell you about her illness. And there's more, of course."

"Yes, I'm sure. I'll be right there, Jack. Love you."

Maggie hung up and headed back to the hospital.

She dreaded the visit, even as badly as she wanted to see Cassandra and apologize for her earlier behavior. Waves of humiliation had been rolling over her throughout the day. She had gone to Cassandra's purposely to be mean. She had made assumptions and come to unfounded conclusions. And then she'd attacked.

What kind of pastor am I? What kind of a person am I?

Then she thought of Ed. Her eyes filled with tears. She was so glad he was dead so that she wouldn't have to confess that ugliness to him. *What would he think? What could he possibly say? He never would have behaved that way. He loved everyone perfectly.* She needed a whisper. But in the midst of her self-pity and self-loathing, she was quite certain God had nothing to say to her.

"I'm so sorry. I'm so sorry. I'm so sorry." Maggie mouthed the words over and over again.

She pulled into the hospital parking lot, parked her car, and using her cane, walked to the front entrance.

Jack was waiting when she entered the lobby.

Maggie looked into Jack's eyes, and then her mouth opened. Thoughts and words flowed out in a waterfall.

"Something happened between us today. I didn't like it. Our work conflicted, and I felt angry with you for not telling me about Cassandra last night. But I'm mainly angry at myself for being hateful, cruel, petty, and impetuous. I'm glad I don't have to tell Ed. What do we do? What do I do? How does this work? Where is Cassandra?" She finally had to stop for breath.

Jack led her to a corner of the lobby and put his arms around her.

"Listen to me," he said. "We are okay. We are learning something about ourselves, and we'll make this work. I'm sorry I didn't tell you about Cassandra last night. I should have. Cassandra knows that you know about her cancer. Now you will do what you do like no one else I know. You will heal what is wounded."

Jack kissed the top of Maggie's head and walked with her to Cassandra's room. He stayed in the hallway as Maggie walked through the door and then shut it behind her.

24

Cassandra's hospital bed was positioned so she was partially sitting up, and her eyes were closed. An IV line was attached to her arm with clear liquid flowing through. It appeared she had been given some oxygen, although the mask was now resting down around her neck. She looked paler than she had that morning. What a difference the truth made when compared to assumptions. Cassandra wasn't a drunk. She was dying. Maggie inwardly cringed once again.

Cassandra's eyes slowly opened as Maggie crossed to the bed. She didn't appear angry. Instead, she looked defeated.

"Hello, Cassandra," Maggie said quietly. "May I sit here?" She patted the bed.

Cassandra nodded.

Maggie sat carefully next to Cassandra and gently took Cassandra's hand in her own. The two women regarded one another. Finally, Maggie spoke.

"Cassandra, I am so sorry for what I said to you today. I am so sorry you have cancer, and I am so sorry about the mountains of worries you have been carrying alone while trying to care for your children. I'm just . . . so sorry. I hope you can forgive me for being so . . . cruel and hateful this morning." Maggie bit the inside of her lip in an attempt to keep from crying. It almost worked. "How are you feeling? What do you need?"

Cassandra's eyes filled quickly, and tears began spilling down her pale cheeks.

Maggie reached her arms around her. Because of the bulky sweaters and flowing blouses that Cassandra usually wore, Maggie hadn't noticed the weight loss. She could feel the bones in her neck and back.

Cassandra let Maggie hug her, and the two women shook silently as sobs racked both their bodies.

When the tidal wave of emotion ebbed, Maggie sat back and reached for the Kleenex box. She offered it to Cassandra and then helped herself. Maggie waited for Cassandra to speak.

"Dr. Elliot has helped me get a grasp on reality today," Cassandra began. "Living in denial was working up until yesterday when I had my reaction to the chemo, but I have things I need to do now."

She paused and pressed the tissues against her eyes, stifling another sob.

"What can I do?" Maggie whispered.

Cassandra blew her nose and took a deep breath.

"There are many things I have to think about and make decisions about. Dr. Elliot has helped me realize some medical issues, I mean decisions, I need to be aware of, and also some legal issues regarding . . ."

"Carrie and Carl?" Maggie's throat constricted as she said the children's names.

Cassandra nodded, unable to speak.

Maggie could not imagine the depth of pain the mother was going through. It must be torturous.

"Dr. Elliot, Harold Brinkmeyer, and I, along with the whole church, are here for you," Maggie said earnestly. "Any need you have will be taken care of. You and the children are deeply loved. We will do whatever you wish, but we won't take over. You are in charge. Is that an okay place to start?"

Cassandra nodded at Maggie, sighing.

"Are there any family members you would like Dr. Elliot to call? The children's father? Your own parents?" Maggie tried to tread lightly.

"My husband, Cal, died shortly after Carl was born. He was in the military. My parents are both in a nursing home in Wisconsin. That's where we're from. I don't believe either one would know me anymore. They both suffer with dementia. Cal's parents are elderly too. They aren't ill, but they couldn't raise two little ones."

Cassandra said the sad facts as if speaking about someone else's life.

Maggie thought Cassandra was becoming too overwhelmed. She squeezed the sick woman's hand.

"I'll let you rest now. But I will be back. May I tell Marla what's going on?"

"Of course," Cassandra said. "I . . . I won't be home tonight. I gave Dr. Elliot a key to the house."

"Don't worry about it. The children will be well cared for. You need to rest now," Maggie said, standing. "And I'll take care of your pets on my way home."

"Pastor Maggie," Cassandra said, twisting the end of her sheet into a knot. "I know I should have told someone earlier. I shouldn't have tried to work this all out myself. I ignored my symptoms. When the oncologist told me what I was dealing with, I refused to believe. I was afraid that saying it out loud would make the cancer real. I wasn't even aware of how much time I was sending the children away. I was stupid."

Maggie sat back down and took both of Cassandra's hands in hers.

"You weren't stupid. You were trying to cope. You did exactly what you had to do to protect yourself. Now we want to help protect you too. You are a brave woman."

Cassandra leaned her head back on the pillow and closed her eyes. Maggie began to pray.

"Holy God, You hold all of our good days and our bad days. We are in some bad days now. Bless Cassandra as she makes decisions. Bless Carrie and Carl. Please make these very bad days manageable. Amen."

Maggie kissed Cassandra on the cheek and quietly left the room.

Jack was waiting outside the door for Maggie.

"Are you okay?" he asked, searching her face.

"I am," Maggie said calmly. "You were right at lunch today. We all have a lot of work to do. The only thing that matters is making each day easier for Cassandra and letting her know she is loved and supported. And, of course, caring for Carrie and Carl as they absorb what is happening to their mother. God help us."

Jack put his arms around her for a quick hug.

"I love you, Maggie Elzinga. I'm so glad you are my pastor."

"I love you, Jack." Maggie looked into his deep-brown eyes. "Did you talk to Harold? Does Cassandra know? I'm going to meet with Marla right now, and I will fill her in. Is Doris going home today? We're having tacos for dinner tonight with Bryan and Cate. What time can you be there?"

Jack tried to keep up again. "I did talk to Harold, and I told Cassandra. She's beginning to understand the legal issues. I'm glad you're talking with Marla. Doris has already been discharged with orders for two days' rest. Chester brought her home. Tacos sound great. I'll be there at six thirty." Deep breath.

Jack watched Maggie limp, ever so slightly, with her cane down the hallway. She was getting stronger. Probably because she was now laser-focused on Cassandra, Carrie, and Carl. She didn't need him to get her through this. She was very aware who the victims were. She wasn't one of them. She was their shepherdess.

Maggie's meeting with Marla took place in the parsonage study. Bryan had been dispatched to the grocery store with a list of food items. Maggie and Marla brought their tea into the study and sat staring at the three beautiful pine trees in the backyard. The small red wagon full of flowers was looking particularly cheerful.

The conversation was emotional. Marla felt the conflicting sensations of shock, frustration, sadness, guilt, the wish to shelter the children, and deep pain. The realizations hit her like icy waves. Her heart broke as Maggie slowly told her the story. Maggie somehow stayed calm as she shared what she knew from Jack, what Harold would be doing from the legal end of things, and how Cassandra was coping with the reality of it all so far.

When Marla had somewhat absorbed the news, she asked, "What about Carrie and Carl? Do they know? They can't possibly. They would have said something. What will happen to them?"

"Harold will help Cassandra make a will. She will have to choose guardians for Carrie and Carl. It doesn't appear there are any relatives near or able to take care of them." Maggie was struck again by what a horror the situation was. "We will all need to be the extended family of this little family. But," Maggie looked directly at Marla, "you are not solely responsible for Carrie and Carl. We have others who will help care for them."

Marla was thoughtful for a moment.

"I don't know if that's such a good idea, Maggie. Carrie and Carl have become used to Addie and to me. They are comfortable in our house and know how we function as a family. I think the familiarity and stability would be good for them." She began to tear up again. "And we don't know how they will be once they hear the news."

"You're right. They will need stability until everything is worked out," Maggie agreed.

The situation was a mountain of unknowns, except for the fact that Cassandra was dying.

"I feel guilty," Marla said, looking down at her teacup.

"For what?" Maggie asked, although she already suspected.

"I have felt so resentful toward Cassandra these last few weeks. I felt used. I had no idea what she was doing, and it seemed like I was turning into a nanny so that she could go do whatever she wanted. I was even beginning to resent Carrie and Carl."

"I know what you mean," Maggie said, remembering that morning in Cassandra's living room. "It would have been helpful to know she was sick or was at doctor visits. But she couldn't tell anyone. She hadn't accepted it herself. It's made me wonder what I would do." Maggie looked up at the pine trees. *Would I tell everyone or anyone?* She came back from her thoughts. "But now we know. Cassandra will make the decisions now. I think we need to do our best to keep this from becoming small-town gossip."

"Absolutely, especially for Carrie and Carl. May I tell my family? I think they should know. We'll continue to take care of the children until told differently. At least, if that's what Cassandra wants us to do."

Marla was already thinking of what the children might need for extra comfort.

"Of course. Addie has done so much for them already, and they are crazy about her. Tom and Jason have been so kind to them too." Maggie became thoughtful again. "It's amazing how quickly life has changed. I thought the break-ins were the worst thing that could happen to our little church. This is a million times worse."

The two women parted with a hug. They were both absorbing the news, both ready to do whatever was necessary, and both feeling helpless at the same time.

As Marla left, Bryan showed up with the groceries. Maggie felt herself switch gears again. Bryan was so excited for Sunday, excited to share his beloved Ghana, excited to see Cate for dinner, and happy to be near his sister. He was a ball of sparkly happiness. He began putting groceries away, except for the taco ingredients. He looked at Maggie with a wide grin.

"Shall I chop and dice, madam?"

Maggie laughed. It felt good.

"Yes, peasant. Chop, dice, mince, et cetera. I'll get the meat ready and begin frying the tortillas."

Bryan turned to the counter, smiling, when his eyes landed on Fruit Loop, who was attempting to help himself to some cheese from the grocery bag. His little teeth were doing a marvelous job of chewing through the plastic wrapper of the queso blanco.

"Hey!" Bryan exclaimed. "Fruit Loop, get down!"

Fruit Loop did just that, dragging the package of cheese along with him into the living room. He pulled it under the blue chair and continued his tearing and ripping exercises.

Bryan hauled him out from under the chair, but Fruit Loop had the package of cheese tightly locked in his small mouth. He wasn't letting go.

"Megs, do you ever feed this cat?" Bryan asked, carrying Fruit Loop back into the kitchen, cheese and all.

Maggie took in the sight. "I think he spent too much time starving. He doesn't realize he has enough to eat now."

"Well, he can't have our cheese," Bryan said, taking the package away and then handing the kitten to his sister.

Maggie gave Fruit Loop a cuddle.

"I guess we all try to hold on to what we think we need. Even when we don't need it anymore."

Maggie realized it was easier to hold on to a grudge or a hurt or a terrible misconception than to let go and move forward with a new focus and positive purpose.

"I'm glad you're home, Dorrie," Chester said.

He and Doris were sitting at their kitchen table, enjoying one of Chester's pot roasts with mashed potatoes and homemade gravy. A bowl of fresh Michigan sweet corn sat, piping hot, between them. Doris was eating gingerly. She realized chewing too fast was hurting her head.

"I am too," Doris said. "I've never liked hospitals. You can't sleep because they're poking at you all the time. The food is terrible unless you're a huge fan of green Jell-O and eggs out of a baggie. And there are some really sick people in there."

Doris put a small forkful of mashed potatoes into her mouth. Then she looked at Chester.

"I am so sorry, Chester. I'm sorry for being bullheaded and not being honest with you. I was stubborn and proud . . . and stupid."

"Oh, Dorrie, you weren't stupid." Chester smiled.

Doris caught on and laughed.

"You're an old dog, Dorrie, but maybe it's time to learn a new trick or two. Let's say, next time you have one of your bullheaded ideas, you try running it by me first. Then we can have a little vote about what to do." Chester reached for her hand and held it.

"I promise," she said.

The dinner table at the Wiggin's home was one of laughter and bouncing. The bouncing came from the two children scooping macaroni and cheese into their hungry and excited mouths. Carrie and Carl were telling the rest of the family about their afternoon at the Cherish Rock with Addie. The Cherish Rock was a huge boulder in town, right on Main Street. For as long as anyone could remember, the rock had been painted with different happy wishes for the citizens of Cherish. It often read "Happy Birthday!" with someone's name painted underneath. Each spring it would read "Congratulations to our Graduates!" For any and every occasion, the rock would be painted. There were times it was painted twice in one day, so the recipient of good wishes had only a short period of time to see their name made public.

That afternoon, Addie had wanted Carrie and Carl to help her paint the rock for the high school tennis team. Addie was one of the captains and wanted to highlight her team. The children had the time of their lives painting the background of the rock in bright colors, as they also commenced painting themselves. Once Addie had finished painting "Go Girls' Tennis Team!" in blue, over the Carrie and Carl masterpiece, they had all washed off back at the parsonage hose.

"I've never seen a prettier rock," Addie said, staring at the small artists now shoveling applesauce into their faces.

Addie's mother had had a chance to take Addie aside and tell her the news of Cassandra. Since Addie had inherited her mother's beautiful heart, hers had broken too, but crying and despair would have to wait. Carrie and Carl had needed dry clothes. Tom had just walked in the door, and Jason was grumbling about perishing if he didn't get food.

So Marla and Addie had let go of their own grief and made dinner.

In her hospital room, Cassandra was brought a covered plate from a tall rolling cart. When she lifted the lid, she saw chicken broth, a plain turkey sandwich, a carton of milk, and green Jell-O. Cassandra looked at the hospital volunteer, who had the pleasure of serving the sterilized and tasteless food to the patients. The volunteer could easily read Cassandra's disappointed face.

"I know," she said. "This meal is meant for people who may have nausea from their medicine. I'm sorry. It's what it says on your doctor's orders."

"Listen," Cassandra said, "I'm not dead yet. I'm not even in hospice. Is there any way you could get me some fried chicken?"

The volunteer laughed. She hadn't expected that from the pale woman sitting before her.

"We don't have any here, but do you like KFC?"

"Love it. Dark meat," Cassandra said, looking past the woman into the hallway for any hospital police.

"It will be in about an hour, but I'll be back."

The woman took Cassandra's plate back to the rolling cart.

Cassandra sat back and closed her eyes. *KFC.* Carrie and Carl loved going to KFC. She couldn't remember the last time she had taken them there, but she would take them again just as soon as she was feeling a little bit stronger.

The parsonage dinner table was uncharacteristically subdued, especially compared to previous meals when Maggie, Jack, Bryan, and Cate were together. The news of Cassandra's illness had been shared with Cate and Bryan as they picked at their tacos.

"Carrie and Carl will be orphans," Bryan said, taking in the fact their father was already dead.

Maggie thought of how that word was used about children in other parts of the world. Orphans in Africa, South America, India, Asia. It wasn't widely used in the Western world, but that was exactly what Carrie and Carl would be. Orphans. Her thoughts drifted to Harold. His legal expertise was a great gift to Cassandra and to her children, but there was so much work to be done.

They finished their meal and decided to go out to the parsonage backyard. They sat on the grass under the pine trees as the sun went down. The pine smelled fresh and spicy and perfumed the air.

Maggie silently thought through the day. The confrontation with Cassandra seemed like weeks ago. Now Cassandra was in the hospital, coping with a new reality, having to let go of all she held dear. It had been only one day, and life had completely changed.

Maggie reached for Jack and slid her shoulder under his arm. He held her.

The day was done.

25

Preparing the funeral service for Abe Jones—a complete stranger with a rude, angry daughter—was not going well. Maggie sat in her church office Wednesday morning listening to Hank tap away merrily on his computer, but she was in a bad mood. She knew it was the emotional hangover from the events of the previous day, but she couldn't move beyond the heaviness.

Maggie had spent the morning helping Bryan set up a screen in the front of the church and prepare the PowerPoint presentation for Sunday. Irena was gleefully blaring funeral dirges from her organ perch. Irena loved funerals. Unless they messed with other plans for her day.

Maggie was trying to stay focused on Abe Jones's funeral service, but her mind kept slipping back to Cassandra's hospital room. She would go for a visit later that afternoon.

The news of Cassandra's illness was already spreading in the community. That's what happened when one well-meaning person, often a visitor or volunteer to the small Heal Thyself Community Hospital, saw a patient lying in a bed or in the hallway waiting for tests to be done. That time it had been Pamela, Hank's wife.

It had been over a year since Pamela had "encouraged" Hank to get a part-time job after he retired from full-time work at the Skin-So-Tight hand lotion company. Her encouragement included the threat of her moving to Australia, alone, if Hank didn't find something to do with his time. That's when he saw the ad for a part-time position at Loving the Lord. Pamela was as thrilled as Hank with his new career path. The fact that part-time really meant full-time for half the pay was of no consequence. They both joined the church and became active members.

Maggie loved Pamela for her no-nonsense approach to life. Pamela was well-read, intelligent, and held strong views about many subjects. She also had the rare gift of being able to accept other people's strong views without picking a fight or trying to change that person's mind to coincide with hers. Pamela followed through with the promises she made. Her name was on every sign-up sheet at church, and she did everything her name was signed to. Maggie wished all parishioners had that kind of commitment.

Pamela enjoyed her work as a volunteer at the hospital. She loved to see faces brighten when she carried in vases of fresh flowers to the patients' rooms. She was happy to assist in every way when asked. Pamela was small, as well as thin, due to her constant activity. She rode her bike around town for errands and also to and from the hospital on her volunteer days. Her gray hair fell to her shoulders and was often up in a ponytail. She would never put her hair in a bun. That's what old women did. Pamela was a vibrant fifty-five years old. In her mind and body, she easily subtracted twenty-five candles from her birthday cake each year.

The previous day, Pamela had been volunteering at the hospital, delivering the evening meal from a large rolling cart, when she'd stepped into Cassandra Moffet's room. Pamela had kept her face in check, even though her heart gave a leap. Cassandra was sick. She was very sick. Although it was completely against protocol, Pamela could not resist doing something kind for the woman.

Hence, the undercover-fried-chicken plot was hatched. It would be their little secret—just Pamela's and Cassandra's.

Pamela had finished her shift, hopped on her bike, and ridden to the KFC near the highway. She brought her boxed treasure discreetly to Cassandra's room and watched with satisfaction as Cassandra devoured every bite of chicken, potatoes, corn, and biscuits. Then Pamela held the plastic bin as Cassandra threw up everything she had just eaten. Cassandra had cried while Pamela sat on the edge of the bed and held her hand.

"We'll try again once you're feeling better and all the chemo is flushed out of your body. I'm sure that's what it is," Pamela said lightly, although she was not sure of any such thing.

She stayed by Cassandra's bedside until the sick woman was asleep. Then she rode her bike slowly home to her husband.

Maggie reread the obituary for Abe Jones. She racked her brain about what to say regarding a man who had little more than a birth date and a death date. His daughter, Melissa, had been no help, and there were no other family members. Finally, she began writing the eulogy. Abe Jones was God's child too. There had to be some good news in that fact.

It took her four hours to wrestle with, grasp at, toss several drafts, beg God to help, then finally complete the eulogy and the rest of the service. Irena would be playing the piano at the funeral home. Maggie knew enough to let Irena choose her own music for church services— and also for weddings, funerals, and baptisms. The only time Maggie "interfered" was if a special hymn or piece of music was requested by the family. There was nothing to suggest that for Abe's funeral. Plus, she had already heard what Irena was planning. It was too depressing for words. *Perfect.*

So Maggie wrote and wrote and finally had a eulogy worthy of the poor man who didn't seem to have a friend in the world. Maggie listened to the machine shuffle paper and click rapidly along as she printed off the labors of her afternoon. Then she heard a knock on her closed door. She realized she'd had a full afternoon without an interruption. That in itself was a small miracle.

"Come in," Maggie said.

The door opened, and Jennifer Becker walked carefully into the office.

"Hi, Pastor Maggie," she said in her soft voice.

Maggie had buried Jennifer's mother the past year and had gotten to know both Jennifer and her sister, Beth. Neither sister had married, but they lived together in Cherish and owned The Page Turner Book Shop on Main Street. The sisters were in church every Sunday and were a helpful source for ordering books for the church library and adult Sunday school classes.

"Jennifer! What a nice surprise. Please come in and sit down."

Maggie used her desk as a brace to move around to the two cream-colored visitor chairs, where she sat gingerly.

"Oh, I don't want to bother you," Jennifer said as she moved across the room and sat down next to Maggie.

"It's not a bother at all. What can I do for you?" Maggie smiled at the older woman.

"I just wanted to let you know, I have taken the liberty of preordering the new G. M. Malliet book for you." Jennifer's face was animated, knowing how much Maggie loved Malliet's writing. "It's called *The Haunted Season*. Doesn't that just sound frighteningly delicious? It will be here next month, just in time for Halloween."

That little newsflash was like a cool waterfall pouring down on Maggie's parched soul.

"Oh! I can't wait," Maggie wiggled. "I haven't been keeping up lately. I didn't know there was another book on the way."

"I will personally deliver it to you the moment it arrives," Jennifer said, as if discussing some sort of covert mission. "Speaking of mysteries, has there been any progress in figuring out who has been breaking into the church?"

With some people, Maggie was vague and distant about the subject of the break-ins, not wanting to help the gossips and Nosy Nellies, but Jennifer didn't fall into either of those categories.

"We have the Ann Arbor police involved. And since they arrived, there hasn't been any trouble. Of course, they only became involved four days ago. Hopefully, they will get to the bottom of it all."

"I'm sure they will, Pastor Maggie. And they have our own Chief Tuggle to work with. She's a wonderful police officer. How is your ankle doing?" Jennifer asked kindly.

"I think I'm getting better every day. I can't wait to be rid of this cane," Maggie said, pointing at the long, brown candy cane leaning against her desk.

I really should give Charlotte a call and make sure she is doing okay with the extra police on the case, she thought to herself. She wanted to make sure none of Charlotte's feathers were ruffled.

"Well, I don't want to keep you," Jennifer said, standing up. "I just wanted to tell you our grand Malliet news."

Maggie stood slowly and said, "Thank you, Jennifer, for taking the time to stop by and tell me. You have no idea of your perfect timing. Say 'hi' to Beth for me."

Jennifer nodded on her way out.

Maggie gathered her funeral service from the printer, slid it into the three-hole punch, and then snapped it in her funeral binder, tucking the eulogy in the side pocket. She brought the whole thing home with her to look over again before bed.

The next morning, Maggie was up and actually feeling ready for the day. She had visited Cassandra the evening before and then had dinner with Bryan and Jack. Jack thought Cassandra would be going home in a day or two, which was good news for Cassandra but also meant that the hard work of preparing to die was something she was strong enough to do now.

But on that new morning, Maggie was focused on the funeral for Abe Jones. As she ate her oatmeal with banana and maple syrup, she went over the eulogy in her head. She had it almost completely memorized, which always gave her confidence.

Once in her black funeral dress, she grabbed her binder and cane. It was a short block down to The Porter Funeral Home. She would walk. She was arriving an hour early in hopes of meeting Melissa Jones. Maybe she could glean something personal about Abe if she could talk face-to-face with his daughter. Maggie would also be on hand to greet the other guests, and most likely, tone down Irena on the piano.

As she walked in the door of the now familiar funeral home, Maggie was greeted by Lynn Porter with ten-month-old Sammy in her arms. Lynn was placing the funeral bulletins on a small table near the door.

"Good morning, Pastor Maggie. It's so good to see you. Sammy and I are just getting a few things organized for the funeral."

Lynn worked side by side with her husband in the running of the funeral home. The people of Cherish relied heavily on the Porter family when death visited their families. Maggie thought Cole and Lynn did better funeral services than any pastor in town because they knew every family so intimately. Both Cole and Lynn had been raised in Cherish. As a teenager, Cole had worked with his own father in the running of the funeral home.

"Hi, Lynn," Maggie said. "I would love to hold Sammy, but I will have to sit down, I think. My ankle is still bothering me."

Sammy was the first baby Maggie had baptized, and she was quite smitten with the little guy.

"You'll be stronger soon. Then I will let you chase him around the yard of the parsonage for an afternoon." Lynn smiled. "Fortunately, he's still just crawling."

"Count on it," Maggie responded. Then, changing topics, she asked in a low voice, "Have you seen Melissa Jones this morning?"

"Yes. She just arrived and is in with her father."

Lynn and Cole both spoke that way when someone died. The family was "in with" their mother, father, sister, or child. It was a helpful way to assist the family in the grieving process. Maggie had learned that lesson well and copied it when working with families.

"Do you think I could step in and speak with her?" she asked Lynn.

"Yes. Melissa didn't seem to want to go in at all but finally did." Sammy began wriggling in Lynn's arms. "I'm going to take this little one home, but I'll be back for the funeral."

Lynn quickly went across the street and through the door to her house.

Maggie made her way to a small chapel set up in the funeral home. The doors were standing wide open. The first thing Maggie noticed was the smell of furniture polish but no smell of flowers. In fact, there wasn't one flower in the entire chapel. It seemed naked.

Then Maggie saw a woman standing completely still, straight backed, staring down at the open casket. She was dressed in a gray tailored business suit, and her hair was perfectly coiffed in a short, layered cut.

Then, as Maggie watched, the woman leaned over and spit on the dead man's face.

Maggie gasped. The woman quickly turned to face the pastor, her expression a mixture of anger and embarrassment.

"Who are you?" she demanded.

"I'm Pastor Maggie," she said, moving into the room. "And you must be Melissa Jones."

"Yes," Melissa clipped. Her face was completely flushed, and her brown eyes were shining with anger.

"I'm sorry for the loss of your father."

Obviously, Melissa wasn't.

"Don't be. I never knew him. In fact, this is the first time I've ever seen him."

Melissa was beginning to sound slightly hysterical. Maggie was at a complete loss as she tried to assimilate the information.

"He left my mother when I was an infant. I never knew him," she repeated.

"Oh," Maggie said quietly. "I had no idea. I'm sorry."

"I tried to make contact with him when I turned sixteen. My mother helped me find him. After all the pain he had caused her and the crappy life of poverty she was left with, she still knew the importance of me knowing who my father was."

She stopped to take a breath and grab a tissue from one of the many boxes in the chapel. Her tears were full of resentment and betrayal. Then more words boiled over.

"I wrote him a letter when we found out where he was. No response. I sent another letter. I sent *thirteen* letters. Then I called him." Melissa stopped to blow her nose. "I told him who I was and that I wanted to meet him."

She paused. Maggie was heartbreakingly enthralled.

"What did he say?" Maggie whispered.

"He said I meant nothing to him. He had completely forgotten I existed. Then he told me never to contact him again."

Melissa stopped, emotionally spent.

"Why are you here?" Maggie asked, dumbfounded.

"He put my name on a hospital document as 'next of kin,'" Melissa said simply. "Isn't that insane? I thought about not coming, but I had to see his face. I had to see the face of neglect and cruelty. Maybe now I can have some closure. I know that sounds like psycho-babble, but I think there is some truth to it."

Just then Maggie heard the trip-trap of Irena's stilettos coming down the hallway toward the chapel. *Oh, good grief!* Maggie thought.

Irena marched into the chapel with her tall stack of music balanced precariously on her arms. She stopped when she saw Maggie's face. Then she turned to take in Melissa's distress.

"Vat's going on herre?" she said through red lips and turquoise-shadowed eyes. Her purple hair was braided lavishly around her head.

"Melissa Jones, this is our organist, Irena Dalca. Irena, this is the daughter of the deceased," Maggie said, trying to figure out how to get Irena out of the way.

"Ahh . . . you sad," Irena said to Melissa.

"Irena, did you want to warm up on the piano?" Maggie asked, trying to get between the two women.

"No," Melissa said. "I was done being sad about ten years ago. I'm pissed."

Irena immediately warmed to that emotional, angry honesty.

"So, you not like yourr fatherr?" Irena said, looking at Melissa while setting her stack of music on a chair. "Vat he do to you? Beat you? Scrream and yell? Did he drrink da vodka?"

"No. He abandoned me," Melissa said, staring right into Irena's painted eyes.

"You sit vit me."

Irena sat down and patted the chair next to hers. Melissa sat.

Irena looked at Melissa and said, "Okey. So yourr pops, he left you. How old?"

"I was one week old," Melissa said.

"Yah. Okey. He is jackass. No one leefs a baby, rright? But den, some people do. Der is somting vrrong in de head sometimes. But mainly dey hev no hearrt. Yourr pops had no heart. Sick, sick, sick man. Okey. You not sick. You hev a heart orr you vould not be herre. You vanted yourr pops to hold you and giv you treats. You should be mad. But den, get done vit mad. You'rre de one valking around vit a hearrt and a life. You hev a mama?"

"Yes," Melissa said, now openly weeping.

"She luv you?" Irena snapped.

"Yes."

"Vell, goot. Den you know how to luv. You go do eet. Go luv!" Irena was clapping her small hands together. "But firrst, ve vill shut de coffin. Eet's time to say gootbye to de sick man who couldn't be a fader. And one day, you vill forrgiveness him."

Maggie was dumbstruck. She watched as Irena, in her five-inch heels, held Melissa's hand and toddled over to the casket. They both stared down at Abe Jones.

Irena said, "He ees not sick no more. He ees betterr now, you know?"

Melissa slowly nodded, wiping her eyes.

"He vill not hurt you. Or your mama. Or hemself. De sad storry ess all dun."

After a couple of minutes, Melissa took her tear-stained tissue and wiped the spit off her father's face.

Holding Irena's small hand, Melissa reached up and slowly closed the casket.

26

Dear Ed,

It wasn't a whisper this time. It was a loud, clear shout. I watched a miracle unfold before my eyes. Irena did more for Melissa Jones than I ever could have. I only had platitudes to go along with no life experience. I have been pondering this and realizing the charmed life I lead. I don't have trauma, heartache (except for losing you), or deep fears from past bad experiences. I had no idea what to say to Melissa after she spit on her father's face. It took my breath away. Then Irena just took over, and Melissa received the first layer of healing balm on her soul. Imagine—little, scary Irena!

After the coffin was closed, we sat and waited. But no one came. We waited an hour. Cole stopped in to make sure things were in order. But not one other person came to the funeral home. Can you imagine? I asked Melissa how she would like to proceed with the service, and she said nothing more was necessary. She wondered if there was a place to get a good cup of coffee.

Grief affects everyone so differently, doesn't it? You should have taught me that in seminary, by the way.

So, I found Cole and told him we were leaving. He was free to bury Abe Jones, but Melissa wouldn't be going to the cemetery. Cole was his amazing self and just smiled and nodded. I found out later that he never charged Melissa for the burial. He paid for it himself. What an incredible man.

Irena and I took Melissa to The Sugarplum. At first, I didn't know if Mrs. Popkin's joviality would be too much for Melissa's state of mind. You know, like big, jagged pieces of salt jammed in a gashing wound. But it turned out Mrs. Popkin was the second layer of balm for Melissa. For all her merriment, Mrs. Popkin understands loss. She gave us a table in the corner, then brought over a plate of heart-healing treats and strong black coffee. It amused Melissa to see Irena pour a shot of vodka into her own coffee from a small flask in her purse. It was a warm, comforting little table, Ed. A perfect funeral.

I have been pondering how people survive so many heartaches in life. How do they stay resilient? Earlier this summer, I stopped by Verna's house for tea. As we were sipping away, her cat Caroline jumped on her lap. You know, Caroline and Cheerio are identical sisters. Anyway, I finally got up the nerve to ask her why she named the cat Caroline. Verna very quietly shared with me her own story of abuse and neglect as a small child. It was a horrible story. Caroline was the woman who "accidentally" rescued Verna from her mentally ill mother. God used Caroline to save Verna, and Verna was able to grow, knowing that love existed. But then she had a terrible first marriage and was thrust into darkness once again. It was a mercy when that awful man died.

Ed, some people just need to die. There are some funerals worth looking forward to. I don't care. It's true!! I don't believe in murder, of course. Not the murder of anything. But sometimes I wonder why God doesn't just clean up the place a bit and get the wicked ones out.

Now, of course, Verna is the happiest woman in the world, besides me (ha!). She and Howard have so much fun and love together.

I don't know why abuse hasn't touched me, but I understand it has touched many. Some don't survive it, some repeat it, and blessedly, some overcome it.

I'm not going to write about my confrontation with Cassandra Moffet. I'm still much too humiliated. I'm sure you know all about it anyway, being where you are and all. I know that you would never have done anything so awful. I'm glad you can't look me in the eye right now.

Tell God thank you for the whispers but also for making things so abundantly clear when I'm in a muddle.

Love,
Maggie

Maggie had said goodbye to Melissa at noon. They were supposed to be standing next to Abe Jones's open grave. But sitting in The Sugarplum, with cinnamon buns and blueberry bran bars, along with honest conversation, was truly where they were meant to be.

Melissa asked about the church. They could see it across the street. Maggie and Irena talked about different aspects of the church's history and also its future. Maggie talked about the Ghana mission trip, and Irena almost talked about the break-ins, until she received a sharp kick from Maggie under the table. At the end of the morning, Melissa had one of Mrs. Popkin's pink bakery boxes filled with goodies to take with her.

"Hokey tooters!" Mrs. Popkin had bellowed. "You can't get on an airplane with no sustenance. You take this box, and don't forget us here in Cherish."

"I've never met people like you," Melissa said, looking at Mrs. Popkin, Maggie, and Irena. "This has been an unbelievable day for me. Certainly not the one I had planned or expected."

"God ees crrazy like dat," Irena said nonchalantly. "Eet happen all de time."

Maggie laughed to herself as Irena-the-prophetess/anger-goddess added to her not-so-profound annunciations.

"I appreciate what all three of you have done," Melissa said, misting up again. "I would actually like to come back one day and sit right here in The Sugarplum with you."

"Well, hokey tooters! You'd better, missy! Hey, does anyone ever call you Missy?" Mrs. Popkin popped.

"Yes, my mother does all the time. I should bring her here," Melissa said, smiling now.

"Did she want to come here for the funeral?" Maggie asked.

"She said she would so that I wouldn't have to be here alone, but I could tell she didn't want to. She was able to let go of him a long, long time ago. So even though I wanted her to come for me, I knew it wasn't necessary for her. I'm sure she didn't know that I saw the relief on her face when I told her she didn't need to come along." Melissa smiled. "Now I'm sorry she missed out on what really happened here."

The three Cherish women watched as Melissa put her pink treasure box into her rental car. They all waved as she drove down Middle Street and then turned, heading toward the highway. She had said she would be back. They all hoped she would.

Maggie limped with her cane across the street to church. Irena trip-trapped right behind her with her pile of funeral dirges.

"Vell. Dat's feeneeshed. Dun. She's goot voman, ees Meleessa," Irena said breathlessly.

Maggie turned to Irena once they stepped inside the sanctuary.

"Irena, you were remarkable today. You said just the right thing, and you gave Melissa permission to be angry and everything else she was feeling."

"Ov courrse. I git eet. I know dis feeling. My pops stayed arround to do all de damage he could do. He vas like, mmm . . . you know . . . Satan. One day, my mama, she says, no morre ov dis! Eet tek awhile, but she git us to U.S. and den to Detrroit. Okey. Ees goot. Eet happens. Okey."

Irena perched herself on the organ bench and shuffled through her music until she found what she was looking for. She set the sheets on the music holder and began to play.

Maggie limped toward her office, listening to the music. The familiar words began playing in her head.

Amazing grace! How sweet the sound,
That saved a wretch like me.
I once was lost, but now am found.
Was blind, but now I see . . .

Through many dangers, toils, and snares,
I have already come.
'Tis grace hath brought me safe thus far,
and grace will lead me home.

Maggie set her funeral binder in her bottom drawer. She hadn't even opened it.

Friday and Saturday kept Bryan and Maggie busy getting ready for the Ghana Extravaganza. The church was set up for the PowerPoint presentation. Bryan and Cate put up red, yellow, and green streamers—the colors of the Ghanaian flag—and placed small flags around the sanctuary. Bryan created a CD of traditional Ghanaian music that would play as the parishioners walked in. The whole sanctuary was bright, colorful, and exciting.

Saturday morning, in the church kitchen, Bryan and Maggie began making the first of five large batches of jollof rice.

Maggie's phone rang. It was Jack.

"What are you doing, beautiful?" Jack asked with a smiling voice.

"Oh, you know, bits and bobs, odds and ends, this and that," she said while pulling onions out of a mesh bag.

"So you're not going to tell me?"

"We're making jollof rice. I'm juggling onions right now."

"Well, I wanted to let you know that I saw Cassandra this morning."

Maggie set down the onions.

"You did?"

"Yes. And Maggie . . . she would like to talk with you. It sounds important." Jack's voice was tender and serious. "I think that she's ready to do what needs to be done. Make some decisions about the future."

Maggie felt a weight press on her heart.

"I'll go over this afternoon."

"Maggie, you're the right person for Cassandra to talk to."

"Thanks, Jack." Maggie could feel her eyes watering. "I've got to go. Bye."

Maggie hung up, taking a deep breath. *And grace will lead me home.*

She turned toward her pile of onions and started chopping. The air was filled with clouds of onion fumes. Before it was all done, both she and Bryan were sobbing like babies from the smell of the raw onions. Finally, the onions were fried in oil in big pots on the industrial stove as Bryan opened can after can of tomato paste. Then he added black pepper, Ghanaian red pepper, a shake of nutmeg, curry powder, and tomato bouillon powder. After that all cooked down and the onions were completely softened, Bryan deftly added the rice and water. Then the lids went on, and the pots were left alone for over an hour.

The entire church, and most of the neighborhood, smelled spicy and mouth-wateringly delicious.

∞

Later that afternoon, Maggie knocked on Cassandra's front door. Cassandra opened the door, took one whiff of Maggie, and began to wretch.

"Oh dear," Cassandra gasped, covering her nose and mouth with her hand. "You reek."

Maggie sniffed under her arms, but it was her hair, sundress, and skin that smelled like a tomato-onion pie.

"I'm so sorry, Cassandra. My brother and I have been making Ghanaian rice all morning. I guess I got used to the smell. Shall I come back another time?"

"How about we sit on the back porch? I would like to ask you some things, and Carrie and Carl aren't here right now."

Maggie wondered if they were at Marla's again but pushed the resentful thought out of her mind.

"Sure. That sounds good. I'll sit downwind."

The two women made their way to the back of the house. Cassandra was moving slowly and using furniture to keep her balance. Maggie was limping slightly with her cane. When they finally settled themselves on the porch, Cassandra began to speak.

"Mr. Brinkmeyer came over today. He was very helpful with the legal issues that need to be dealt with." She looked out over her backyard. Her two dogs were chasing each other and barking happily. "It was strange because we were talking about my death, but I felt as if we were talking about someone else. I became interested in the things he told me had to be done, but it seemed disconnected from me. Does that make sense?"

"I have no idea," Maggie said, once again at a loss. She wondered if it was some kind of coping mechanism. "Maybe it's a way to handle something so new and painful. Or perhaps it's because the focus is on Carrie and Carl. What do you think?"

Cassandra looked down at her hands. "I don't know. Maybe. Yes, we talked about their future and the legal steps I must take to ensure they have a guardian."

"Harold will help make sure the children are in the best place. And he actually cares," Maggie said. "He's not just being a lawyer."

"Yes. I picked up on that right away," Cassandra said. "So I have some things to think about and decide in the next couple of weeks. But I also have some more immediate needs right now."

"Of course," Maggie responded, leaning in closer to Cassandra. "What can we do as a church to help?"

Cassandra coughed and wiped her eyes with her sleeve.

"I know I have asked Marla to watch Carrie and Carl way too much."

"No. Don't say that now," Maggie said, feeling a wave of guilt.

"Okay. But I need help with the kids when I have doctor appointments and when I just need some rest."

"Yes. You can count on it. We love Carrie and Carl. I think a lot of folks will be happy to care for them. We'll try to keep it as stable as possible. What about food? And how about housecleaning and yard work? Maybe someone to walk your dogs?" Maggie's brain was flying.

Cassandra sat silently, and Maggie saw tears splash onto her lap.

Maggie snapped her mouth shut and sat silently.

After a few minutes, Cassandra looked up.

"I guess I hadn't thought of all those things."

"I'm sorry," Maggie said quietly. "I don't mean to make your list for you, and I'm sorry to jump ahead. How about you tell me what you need, and the church and I will make sure you and Carrie and Carl are cared for."

Cassandra nodded. "I guess you would have to make an announcement in church, wouldn't you?" She quickly went on. "It doesn't matter. I think everyone must know by now anyway. Some get well cards already came in the mail this morning. And I've had some phone calls."

"It's completely up to you, Cassandra," Maggie said. "You decide how you want me to tell people about what's happening. I won't do anything you don't want me to do."

"All those things you mentioned, I do need help now. As my cancer progresses, I know I will have to consider hospice care. And some final decision for Carrie and Carl's future has to be made. You, Dr. Elliot, and Mr. Brinkmeyer have given me some sense of peace that I don't have to figure this out by myself. I never knew a church could be an actual family." Cassandra tried to stifle a sob.

"We are your family," Maggie said gently. "If you want, I can make an announcement in church tomorrow and organize people to help in all the ways you need. I'm sorry something so personal for you is being made public. It can't be easy to have everyone know. I will not share personal day-to-day information with anyone. I will only get people organized to do the good work needed by members of our church family."

"Thank you. I have two other questions for you," Cassandra said, looking Maggie straight in the eyes.

Maggie felt a small shiver.

Cassandra spoke slowly. "Will you help me tell Carrie and Carl that I'm dying?"

Maggie stared mutely.

"I can't do it alone. I don't know how," Cassandra whispered.

Maggie nodded.

"And will you and Dr. Elliot consider taking them as your own children when the time comes? I know you aren't married yet, but I can't think of a better couple to raise my children."

Maggie blinked, not comprehending. She tried to breathe, but the air was gone again.

27

Maggie and Bryan were both up early on Sunday morning. Sunday school had been cancelled because of the special event, but Maggie had given each of her high school students a job for the Ghana Extravaganza. She didn't want them thinking that they needn't be in church. Each girl was going to wear a piece of Ghanaian fabric over her clothes or wrapped around her head. The fabrics were all brightly colored, and the girls had promised to stand around the sanctuary prior to the service and try to look interested. The boys were going to hand out bulletins and pass around the trays of jollof rice during coffee time.

Maggie had decided to "combine" the new members class with worship. She knew the service would capture everyone's imagination and would show what the church was really about better than attending a class in the nursery. She had encouraged all the new members to be present. It was also a selfish decision. Maggie's parents, Dirk and Mimi, along with Ed's widow, Jo James, and Maggie's best friends, Nora and Dan, were all coming from the west side of the state. She wanted to spend the afternoon with them, not leading a new members class.

As she made two bowls of oatmeal with banana and pure maple syrup, her mind wandered back to her visit with Cassandra the day before. Cassandra's request for Jack and Maggie to adopt Carrie and Carl had left Maggie speechless. She had finally said something polite and noncommittal and then left in a daze. She hadn't had a chance to speak with Jack, who had been at the hospital all evening delivering a baby.

"Hey, Megs," Bryan said as he breezed into the kitchen. "I could smell the oatmeal upstairs. Give me some."

He was grinning with excitement, and Maggie knew it had nothing to do with the oatmeal.

"Not unless you say 'please.' Were you raised in a barn?" Maggie said, drizzling maple syrup over both bowls.

"Yes. The same barn you were raised in." Bryan laughed as he popped a coffee pod into the Keurig. "It will be fun to see Mom and Dad today, speaking of the barn."

"I can't wait," Maggie said, handing Bryan his steaming bowl. "But I really can't wait to see what happens in church this morning. I think it is going to be one of those Holy Spirit days. You and I are absolutely out of control. Ha!"

"Good. If it goes badly, you can blame the Holy Spirit and not me," Bryan said, taking a slurp of coffee.

Two hours later, the congregation began filling the narthex of the church. Traditional Ghanaian music was playing, the high school girls were wearing their fabric, and they even began swaying to the music. Addie found herself the object of adoration by Carrie and Carl, as well as Penny and Molly Porter, Cole's daughters. They surrounded her like kids around a Maypole. Liz Tuggle had little Sammy Porter in her arms as she rocked back and forth to the music. He was enchanted with her fabric and kept trying to pull it off her head. The other girls were spaced around the sanctuary, resplendent in bright colors.

It probably had been because she was crying while driving back to the parsonage after her visit with Cassandra, but Maggie had quickly pulled into the drugstore and purchased several small boxes of Kleenex. She didn't know the whole of Bryan's presentation, but what she did know was that it would be quite moving for the congregation. When she'd returned to the parsonage, she had brought the Kleenex boxes to the sanctuary and spaced them around in the pews. Just in case.

Church that Sunday morning began with a buzz. Everyone was moving to the music. The smell of the jollof rice being warmed in the basement filled the air. The contingent from the west side of the state was present. Maggie's parents had brought Jo, and Nora and Dan had taken the Sunday off from their own church duties and surprised Maggie by bringing Mike and Kristy Brown with baby Matthew. Kristy blew Maggie a kiss.

There were many new faces in attendance. Marla had spent the last two weeks putting up posters in the shops around town to invite the community to participate in the Ghana mission, all with Carrie and Carl in tow. Her hard work had paid off. Maggie silently blessed Marla for the millionth time.

Lacey Campbell, from We Work Miracles Beauty Salon, was present, along with the new members class. Lacey was taking in everything. She even began clapping to the music, which spread throughout the whole congregation. Maggie noticed that William and Mary Ellington were present. She said a silent prayer for Mary. They must not have any guests at The Grange that weekend.

Ethan and Charlene Kessler were accompanied by their children, Kay and Shawn. Both children immediately left their parents and ran toward the high school girls. Liz was a regular babysitter at the Kessler home.

Dr. Dana gave Maggie a wink and a wave as she took a seat next to Ethan and Charlene. Sky Breese floated in wearing one of her harem outfits. Her long, blonde hair draped down past her shoulders, as if it were a wedding veil. Sky melted into the pew next to Lacey and smiled. Even Sky seemed to come to life and reality in the electric atmosphere of the church.

Maggie saw Jennifer and Beth Becker sitting in their pew, along with Max Solomon. Max had become a faithful member of Loving the Lord when his father died the past year. Maggie had done the funeral. It was her first. Max had met God on that day. He never missed church after that. He and the Becker girls sat in the last pew together every Sunday.

Cole Porter, being the only person in the church who knew what to do with all the buttons and levers of the sound system control panel, was standing next to the system at attention.

Mrs. Popkin was busy setting up the cookie table for coffee time. She was starting to worry that six dozen cookies might not be enough as she watched the church fill.

Howard and Verna, along with Winston, sat in their pew. Howard and Winston were enjoying the music. Verna sat ramrod straight, looking a little frosty as she wondered what in the world was going on in her church.

Maggie's mouth dropped open when she saw Irena enter the sanctuary. The organist had the Sunday off due to the recorded Ghanaian music. Her hair was wrapped like two purple cinnamon buns, one on each side of her head. She looked ridiculous, and her makeup couldn't have been more spectacular. The red on her lips clashed wildly with her purple hair. Sky-blue sparkles encrusted her eyes and, unwittingly, her left ear lobe. Her bright-gold peasant blouse could barely hold her overflowing breasts. The tiger-striped bra, clearly visible through her blouse, was apparently two sizes too small. As she trip-trapped toward a front row pew in her sky high heels, Maggie saw Detective Keith Crunch walk in.

He came! Maggie was thrilled.

Keith looked around at the crowded sanctuary and ended up making his way to the front pew, following Irena. Irena scooted in as far as she could, smashing two guests into one another, and patted the pew for Keith to sit down.

"Goot morning, Captain Crrunch," she said, her face looking somewhat electrocuted.

"Good morning, Irena," Keith said as he looked around the sanctuary. "I didn't know the church would be so full."

"Eet ees Afrrica veek. Crrazy musick. You come beck next Sunday. I play de goot musick."

Irena gave a glare in Maggie's direction for hijacking the service with foreign music.

Chester and Doris were in their regular pew. Doris still had a bandage on her head, but she was smiling and clapping along with everyone else. Chester had his arm protectively around his wife.

Maggie had never seen the church so packed.

Hank was running around like the proverbial headless chicken. He was in his glory, printing off dozens of extra bulletins and getting them lickety-split into the hands of the high school boys.

Bill and Sylvia Baxter were running up and down the stairs, busy checking on the rice in the basement and helping people find seats in the crowded sanctuary.

Maggie knew that Pamela had been at Cassandra's house that morning. She had offered to sit with Cassandra during the service so that the sick woman wouldn't be alone. Addie had picked up Carrie and Carl for church and the rest of the afternoon.

Charlotte was in her full police chief uniform. She and Bernie Bumble were at the back of the sanctuary, keeping an eye on things. Maggie imagined that Charlotte's pride was still somewhat bruised. It was good to remind people she was their chief.

But the biggest surprise of the morning was when Maggie saw Harold, Ellen, Jack, and Jack's entire family filing into the sanctuary. Jack hadn't told her that he'd invited them. He was grinning from ear to ear when she finally looked at him. There wasn't enough space for the whole family to sit together, so they scattered themselves, taking seats wherever they could find them. Jack gave Maggie a nod. She laughed out loud.

Finally, Maggie went to the front with her cane, which was completely wrapped in Ghanaian fabric, and welcomed the gathering.

"Before we begin our special worship service today, I have one announcement for our congregation." She looked down at Carrie and Carl cuddled up with Addie. "We have a need for a family in our church. If you can help with meals and other food items, childcare, and transportation, please meet me following worship. I will have sign-up sheets. If you can help in any way, it would be so appreciated."

She looked back down at the children and saw, thankfully, that they were completely unaware that she was talking about them and their mother.

"Now, some of you know my brother, Bryan, but some of you are new here today. So let me introduce Bryan Elzinga. Bryan works for Africa Hope and will be leading a group of us from this church on a Ghana mission trip in January. We are raising awareness, along with money, for this trip. Cate Carlson is also a member of our congregation and a student at the University of Michigan. Cate is going to Ghana the second semester of this school year to study. She will be there when we are on our trip and will be able to work with us on some of the weekends. Please welcome my brother, Bryan, and Cate Carlson."

Amid applause for her brother and Cate, Maggie limped down to the front pew and sat next to Addie, Liz, and the younger children.

Bryan welcomed the congregation and handed the presentation over to Cate, who looked beautiful in white, pink, and purple flowered fabric—a gift from Bryan. She explained the study abroad program she was part of, and her enthusiasm was contagious. All the high school girls—and boys, for that matter—were rapt with attention. Addie and Liz, especially, were enamored of the older girl. They wanted to *be* Cate.

Bryan spoke next, but Cate stayed at the altar with him. First, Bryan spoke about Africa Hope, and then he began sharing stories of the orphanage in Bawjiase, along with pictures of the children living there.

"They are a family," Bryan explained as he clicked through photo after photo. "This is a photo of Pastor Elisha and his wife, Marta. They heard God's voice call them to leave their home, their money, and their family to start an orphanage in a faraway village called Bawjiase. And that's what Pastor Elisha and Marta did. They have three children of their own and twenty-seven others. Pastor Elisha is a truly good man."

Bryan cleared his throat. Maggie knew that sound and watched her brother, holding her own breath. Cate watched him too. Bryan took a deep breath and continued.

"The older children help care for the younger ones. Everyone has chores to do. But I think you can see from their faces how happy they are to be where they are."

Just then a picture flashed on the screen of a young girl holding a baby. The girl was smiling as she held the little one close in her arms.

"This is Cynthia," Bryan said. "She is the oldest girl at the orphanage. She is thirteen. Cynthia goes to school every day, but she has to travel on foot to do so. She walks thirty minutes one way. When she gets back to the orphanage at the end of the day, she washes clothes in a bucket and lays them on the ground to dry. She helps cook the dinner. She chases the little ones around. After dinner, she helps wash all the bowls and spoons. She washes the children and helps put them to bed. Then she does her homework. If the electricity goes out, she gets up with the sun to finish her homework and begin a new day. Cynthia is one of the most cheerful, contented people I have ever met."

Maggie could hear the intake of breath from both Addie and Liz. Cynthia was younger than they and lived a life they couldn't imagine. The entire congregation was silent as Bryan continued.

"The baby she is holding is Leah. Leah was found at two weeks old, stuffed into a paper bag and left in an abandoned building. Fortunately, as Pastor Elisha passed the building, he heard her cry. He brought her back to the orphanage. He saved her life."

At that point, the congregation of Loving the Lord grabbed at the tissue boxes and sniffled loudly. Maggie hadn't heard the story of Leah before. *Drat, Bryan!* He could have given her some warning.

Addie and Liz had tears dripping from their young faces as they squeezed the smaller children on their laps. Sammy began to cry as Liz held him a little too tightly. Lynn came down the aisle and took Sammy back to her pew. She wanted to hold her baby.

Bryan looked at the people in front of him.

"I want you to know that I didn't tell you this story to make you cry. And I didn't tell you about Cynthia so that you would pity her. She doesn't need pity. No one at the orphanage needs or wants pity. They want a school closer to where they live. They want to plant a farm that will grow food they can eat and sell at market. They want a well on their property so they don't have to walk into town to get water. They want to share their water with people farther out in the countryside.

They want to share their food. They want to share their school."

Everyone stopped their sniffling and listened.

"There is a group of nine young men who live and work at the orphanage."

Bryan flashed a picture on the screen of nine laughing boys. They could have been in Maggie's Sunday school class, if her Sunday school class was in Ghana.

"This is Fifi." Another picture of one of the handsome young men filled the screen. "He saved his money and bought one pregnant pig. That began his pig farm. He now has so many pigs that he has had to build several more pens to house them. All the proceeds of selling the pigs at market go to the orphanage. He takes care of the children when they're sick. He helps cook. He is an amazing baker and bakes bread in the middle of the night to be sold each morning. He keeps the other older boys in line. But Fifi would be the first to tell you that he wants to do more. I'm hoping we can give Fifi and all the boys the materials to build a school. None of these nine boys had the chance to go to school when they were young, but they would love to give that chance to their little brothers and sisters at the orphanage."

Bryan grinned. "What do you think? Can we do that? Can we help build a school with Fifi and the other boys? A school for Cynthia and Leah and anyone else who wants an education? Can we?"

It was as if the whole congregation were holding their breath. All eyes fixated on Bryan.

Then a raspy voice came from the back of the sanctuary.

"Of course we can."

Everyone turned to look.

Sitting in his wheelchair at the back of the sanctuary, Marvin Green coughed once, then pounded his fist on the arm of his wheelchair.

"Of course we can. If we can't help build this school, we should all pack up and go home for good!" *Cough, cough, rasp.* "Being the church doesn't mean just sitting here Sunday after Sunday." *Hack, wheeze.*

No one seemed to know what to say. Even Bryan was dumbfounded. He looked at his sister.

Maggie stood up and said, "Marvin, you're absolutely right. We can do more. We can do more here in Cherish, and we can do more in Ghana. There is no shortage of places to take our hands and our hearts. We have to raise twenty-eight thousand dollars to make this miracle happen. That number has been hanging over my head for a while now. But Marvin just gave me the pep talk I needed." She looked around at the congregation. Some were holding tissues to their noses, some were smiling, but all were waiting. "I hope it's the pep talk you needed too. Will the ushers please come forward?"

The Ghanaian music began again as Howard, Sylvia, Harold, and Jennifer came forward.

The offering plates were passed up and down the aisles, and checks, dollars, and coins were dropped in with enthusiasm. Lacey got everyone clapping again as the music played.

Even Marvin was swaying ever so slightly in his wheelchair.

28

At the end of the worship service, Maggie asked the entire congregation to make a circle around the sanctuary. Everyone left their seats and made their way toward each other. Their circle was only broken by the front doors of the church, which were standing open and inviting a cool breeze into the sanctuary.

"Our church isn't complete within this circle. Our circle extends to a community far away, which is also part of our church," Maggie said over the Ghanaian music. "Our brothers and sisters in Bawjiase."

Maggie was surprised, along with everyone else, when Addie's clear voice called out, "Thank you for baby Leah. Bless her."

"Protect Fifi," came a voice from the front of the church. It was Bryan.

"Give Pastor Elisha and Marta wisdom," Maggie requested.

"God bless Cynthia," Liz said with a sniff.

Carrie's hand squeezed Maggie's as she said in her small voice, "Give all the babies milk and cheerios."

"Use us." It was Charlene Kessler.

"Forgive us for forgetting the needs of others," Jack's strong voice rang out.

"Thank you for our family far away," Verna Baker prayed succinctly.

The prayers continued—simply, lovingly, hopefully, thankfully.

The breeze continued. Maggie was pretty sure she recognized the Holy Spirit.

For a congregation who ferociously loved their coffee and cookie time, everyone seemed to love praying for their new friends a whole lot more.

Maggie finally gave the benediction, and the congregation gathered their belongings. But no one seemed eager to leave the sanctuary. They talked and laughed as Bryan slightly raised the volume of the energizing, spirit-filled music.

Small cupcake foils of jollof rice appeared on trays, and even Doris didn't worry about what her sanctuary floor would look like in the morning. The taste of the Ghanaian red pepper, tomato, and rice, along with the music and colorful fabrics, gave the entire congregation a moment of culture shock—in the best possible way. Dreams of Ghana and Bawjiase were seeping into reality.

Harold, remembering the reality of the church money, quickly gathered the offering plates and put them in the church safe during coffee time. He had no intention of leaving them on the altar with so many people mingling about, and he could tell it was a generous offering.

As Maggie looked around the crowded room, she was stunned to see Julia Benson, the pushy reporter. Maggie hadn't seen Julia in the worship service but could have missed her with the church so full. Julia was eating small bites of jollof rice as she spoke with Mary Ellington and Lacey Campbell. The sight of the three women made Maggie blink with disbelief. *What in the world can they be talking about?*

Just then, a herd of small children came racing through the gathering area, yelling and laughing. Kay and Shawn Kessler and Jack's nephew and niece, Garrett and Gretchen, joined the crowd. One little girl tripped over the footrest of Marvin Green's wheelchair and went sprawling on the floor next to him. She had long, red hair gathered in a black plastic hair clip. The hair clip broke when her head hit the floor. She lay still for a moment, then popped up and continued running after her friends, her red hair flowing behind her. Marvin tried to look annoyed, but to no avail. His smile was too broad.

Maggie didn't recognize half the children, including the little redhead. Addie, Liz, and the other girls were trying to wrangle the children outside to play on the parsonage lawn, but it was only semi-working. The cookie table turned out to be a huge distraction. Mrs. Popkin's cookies were disappearing faster than usual in the hands of the children.

Maggie started to make her way over to Julia Benson, Mary, and Lacey. She was almost there, limping with her cane and smiling at everyone, when she felt Jack's arm around her shoulder.

"What a morning," he said, giving her a chaste squeeze. "Bryan and Cate both did incredible jobs with their presentations."

"I know!" Maggie enthused. "And could you believe Marvin? That man has such a huge heart under all his crustiness."

"Marvin makes a colossal effort to be cranky. He's really a thoughtful and generous man."

Jack had known Marvin for several years. As Marvin's body had slowly given out on him, Jack had seen the weariness and depression set in. Marvin hated being trapped in his wheelchair, but what he hated more was relying on others for his care. Jack encouraged him to help others any way he could. After Marvin had set aside some of his self-pity, he'd asked Sylvia, on one of her visits, to let him know who was in need in town. She gave him the updates, and he gave her a check. But all of that generosity didn't deter him from the hard work of being cranky.

After talking with Jack, Maggie turned to look for Julia Benson, but she was gone. Maggie saw Mary standing alone in the corner. She limped as fast as she could toward Mary, who spotted her immediately and met her halfway.

"Pastor Maggie, how are you doing with your ankle?" Mary asked, staring at Maggie's foot.

"It's getting better." Maggie brushed off the question. "Mary, you're here today. How did that happen?"

"William told me about the Ghana program. I really wanted to hear what your brother is doing with his work. I'm glad I was here, and I'm glad there was no organ music."

Mary smiled wryly. Maggie remembered that the organ music caused Mary so much pain since her son Michael's funeral. Before Maggie could say anything, Mary spoke again.

"You mentioned a family in need here at the church. What can I do?"

"Oh, good grief," Maggie said. "I totally forgot about the sign-up sheets. Mary, can you help me get them from Hank's desk? I'll try to make an announcement in the midst of all this noise."

Mary moved quickly to get the sign-up sheets. She finally found them under Hank's blue tarpaulin. Maggie clapped her hands to get people's attention, but to no avail. Finally, Mason Tuggle, with thumb and index finger placed in his mouth, gave a loud whistle, and everyone immediately quieted down.

"Thank you, Mason," Maggie said, smiling. "Everyone, if you would like to help our family in need, please come to Hank's office for a moment to sign up."

Several people followed Maggie to the office. Mary had the sign-up sheets and several pens ready.

Maggie said to the group around her, "We have a family, the Moffet family, who is in need right now. They need meals, childcare for Carrie and Carl, housecleaning, pet care, and yard work. Cassandra will also need some transportation to appointments. If you can help, please put your name on the proper sign-up sheet and the days and times you are available."

Maggie refrained from saying anything about Cassandra's cancer, and no one standing in the circle had the bad manners to ask.

"What's the name of the family?" Mary asked.

"The Moffet family. Cassandra is the mother of Carrie and Carl." Then Maggie pointed toward the sanctuary doors. "There they are, Mary, the two little blondes."

Mary looked and saw the backs of their heads. She nodded at Maggie. Then she looked down and signed her name to bring meals and assist with childcare.

"I think William can help with transportation," Mary said quietly as she added his name to the appropriate sheet.

Others began signing up as well. Maggie tapped Mary on the shoulder.

"I'll be at The Grange Tuesday at ten o'clock, okay?"

"The tea will be ready," Mary said as she continued to sign the sheets.

Maggie returned to the gathering area. She concealed a smile as she noticed a little grouping in the corner. Lacey was chatting with Skylar and Detective Crunch. Irena was also in the little circle, glowering upward at Sky.

Maggie knew who would win in the competition for Keith Crunch. It wouldn't be the tiny, psychedelic-painted, vodka-drinking, brilliant-musician clown. No. Skylar, the Greek goddess of flowers and air, would win any suitor.

Poor Irena.

Poor Keith.

Finally, the church began to empty out.

Maggie was just kicking herself for not remembering to ask Mary if she knew Julia Benson when she felt a light tap on her shoulder. She turned to see a sweet face.

"We've brought three lemon rosemary chickens with roasted potatoes for dinner, Maggie dear." Bonnie's gentle voice danced into Maggie's ears. "Anne brought salads, including her heavenly fluff, and Leigh baked a German chocolate cake. Jack helped us get it all in the parsonage before that amazing worship service."

Bonnie was a woman who knew how to effortlessly prepare food for a large family. Her gentle spirit masked her endless hard work, meeting the needs of others. Maggie knew her future mother-in-law was a treasure.

"Thank you, Bonnie," Maggie said, impulsively kissing the older woman on the cheek. "I think we may all be floating on clouds for a few days after this morning."

Mimi and Jo had already gone to the parsonage to set the table and organize rolls, butter, and salads, and also to check on Bonnie's chickens.

The two women had been friends over the years through church and especially during Maggie's seminary training.

"Your daughter and son are gifted people, Mimi," Jo said as she hunted in the cupboards for napkins. "As overused at this sounds, you must be proud of them."

"Both Dirk and I are proud. Thank you, Jo. It's interesting to wait and watch what they'll both do next," Mimi said practically.

She loved her children but wasn't foolish enough to believe that they were the only two young people in the world doing good for others. But, yes, she was quietly bursting with pride.

"I wish Ed could have been here today," Jo said, opening another cupboard and finally finding a stack of linen napkins. "He would have loved the worship service this morning. I have a feeling he would have Bryan cornered right now, encouraging him to go to seminary."

"Maggie is the pastor she is due in large part to Ed. Your husband encouraged so many young pastors. I can't imagine the number of students you watched go through the seminary over the years—and also through your living room. Maggie always looked forward to the dinners you hosted for groups of students."

"Those were highlight days for us. Ed and I both enjoyed having the students over. And Maggie always brightened the dinner table."

"Thank you for saying that. Even if Ed were here, however, I don't think there would be a chance that Bryan would consider seminary. He loves his Africa Hope work."

Mimi glanced through the kitchen into the living room. Bryan was talking animatedly with Jack's brothers, Andrew and Nathan. She smiled as she glimpsed a memory of him as a three-year-old. She remembered little Bryan excitedly telling his father about feeding baby ducks at the lake for the first time. That afternoon, his face looked exactly the same.

Harold and Ellen went to fetch the offering plates from the safe before Sunday dinner at the parsonage. They took several minutes to count the offering, then they stared at one another with wide eyes. The congregation had been very generous, indeed. Then they bundled the checks and bills with rubber bands. Ellen took the many coins and put them in a Ziploc baggie. There was a banker's bag on top of the safe, and they used that to hold the money until Harold could get to the bank the next morning.

"Let's get this to the office," Harold said.

There was no way they would leave that kind of offering in the church. It would be asking for trouble with the vandal still on the loose.

Harold and Ellen made their way downtown. Harold's office was on Main Street, not quite three blocks from the church. Many people were downtown walking, shopping, and eating, but there was only one person following Harold and Ellen to the law office.

Maggie looked around the parsonage dining room table. It was crowded with family and friends—twenty-three, plus baby Matthew. Jack's entire family was there, with Gretchen and Garrett clamoring to go on the Ghana trip with Uncle Jack and Aunt Maggie. Of course, that gave Maggie a tiny thrill. She was an aunt, almost. Ellen and Harold were there, having arrived a little late, and Maggie realized there was a strong possibility that Harold was going to be her cousin-in-law. Maggie's own family was visiting with Jack's, as if they all had been neighbors and best friends for the past twenty years. Cate was next to Bryan, listening to as many conversations as possible. Jo, Dan, Nora, Kristy, Mike, and baby Matthew all felt like just more family.

As people lifted forkfuls of tender chicken, fresh fruit and vegetable salads, and buttered rolls to their mouths, the conversations replayed the events of the morning. Maggie helped herself to another large spoonful of Anne's heavenly fluff salad. She had to get the recipe. Then she heard Dan's voice.

"Cate and Bryan, do you think there is any way you could come to Holland and share your presentations with our church?"

Nora nodded wildly, her mouth unfortunately full of roasted potatoes.

Bryan and Cate looked at each other. After five seconds of silence, the table erupted. Nora'd had time to swallow and jumped right in.

"Yes! You have to come to Jesus Lives!"

Jesus Lives and So Do We! was the name of their church in Holland, Michigan.

Anne and her husband, Peter, both spoke at the same time. They were emphatic about Bryan and Cate coming to their church in Detroit as well.

Ken and Bonnie were able to get their hometown church in Blissfield into the conversation and make their plea.

Baby Matthew looked from face to face and held tightly to his mommy's thumb.

Why didn't we think of this before? Loving the Lord doesn't have to build the school alone. It's not up to me, or our congregation, to raise all the money. Why did I think it was?

Jack looked at Maggie's face.

"Are you okay?" he whispered in her ear.

She started, and then came back to the moment.

"It's a great idea. When more people know, the excitement will spread," Maggie said so loudly that the others stopped talking. "I feel selfish for thinking this was only our work to do. The more people who know and want to be part of this, the better for the orphanage. To be honest, I have been worried about raising all the money here at Loving the Lord, and to be more honest, I didn't think we could. We aren't a big church. Twenty-eight thousand dollars is a lot of money. No matter how much we pray."

"Maybe this idea of going to other churches is the answer to the prayer," Nora said quickly. "You can't keep all this good news and great mission work just to yourself, Maggie Elzinga." Nora smiled.

Ellen and Harold looked at one another. Ellen gave Harold a wink.

Maggie sighed deeply. She heard a whisper.

You are not in control. You aren't responsible for everything in and out of the church. You are responsible to share good news and care for the flock. Trust. All will be well.

Maggie looked up to see Jo staring at her.

"What do you think, Jo?" Maggie asked as the others continued their brainstorming.

"I'm just remembering a time when Ed was serving our first church. We had to raise money for a new roof. The church roof was falling in almost daily. We had buckets sitting around the sanctuary on rainy days. The church was small and poor, except for one man. He owned the bank in town. Ed went to ask him for help, actually to ask him for the bulk of the money to repair the roof. The man turned him down flat. He said he wouldn't give a dime because the church didn't deserve it. He said we would have to get a new roof some other way, not just by coming to the richest man in town for a handout."

The others were quieting down and listening to Jo's story.

"Ed was furious. He came home and told me all about it. He ranted and raved all around the parsonage. Before he had completely calmed down, he got in the car and drove back to the bank. He confronted the bank owner. From what Ed said, he came just short of hitting the man. Can you believe it?"

"No," Maggie whispered.

"Ed was young, remember. He told the man how un-Christian he was and talked about the rich not getting into heaven and camels not going through needles' eyes. Ed really let him have it. Misusing the Bible, of course."

"What happened?" Nora asked, entranced.

"The next day the banker was found dead in the back shed of his home. He had taken his own life. It turned out he had risked a lot of money, his and the people of the town, on bad stocks. He left a letter describing the scheme. His family was left with nothing, and the bank was shuttered."

Jo paused, looking back in time to that dreadful day.

"What happened next?" It was young Gretchen.

Jo looked at the child and then at the others around the table.

"Ed had to officiate the funeral. In our church. The banker was a member."

Maggie closed her eyes, imagining Ed's anger, pain, humiliation, and his need to make things right.

"He didn't blame himself, did he?" she asked.

"At first he did, until the letter from the dead man was found and printed in the local newspaper. It was obvious the man had already made his plan. For Ed, the worst part was that he never had the opportunity to apologize for the angry and judgmental things he'd said. It was a powerful lesson he took with him every day after that. He learned what terrible weapons words can be."

Everyone digested that last statement. Except baby Matthew, who was trying to digest his mother's finger.

"In the end, Ed went to the other churches in town and spoke with the pastors about our roof problem. The town pulled together and raised the money for a new roof in the wake of the banker's death. Ed never forgot that. He felt the connection with all the clergy."

Jack was carefully watching Maggie's reaction. He could tell that she had never heard that story about Ed before, and it certainly must be hitting home after her time with Cassandra.

"The point is," Jo continued, lightening the tone in her voice, "to involve other churches with the Ghana project can only benefit the orphanage and new school. Also importantly, it creates more community right here in Michigan. Bryan and Cate have a powerful presentation with options for everyone who hears it. I say, spread the news." Jo smiled.

"Bryan," Mimi asked, "would you either be able to stay here longer or make another trip this fall to do these services? It will probably take a little planning, I'm guessing."

No one had thought of that.

"You're right," Bryan said slowly. "Let me make some calls tomorrow and see what I can arrange. Maggie and I will call the rest of you and let you know what I find out. If it works, you can contact your churches for some possible dates."

Bryan's head was already spinning with how to approach Joy about the new fundraising plan. Joy Nelson was Bryan's boss at Africa Hope.

According to Bryan, she was the coolest person in the entire world. Although Cate seemed to be sneaking up on that title.

Everyone chimed in with options and ideas as they cleaned their plates.

Finally, the lunch dishes were cleared and dessert plates set. Everyone *oohed* and *ahhed* over the German chocolate cake that Leigh, Jack's little sister, had baked. They all helped themselves repeatedly to coffee that Maggie had made in the church's forty-cup urn.

The Ghana plan kept forming and expanding. So far, they had four churches to contact: Dan and Nora's, Anne and Peter's, Ken and Bonnie's, and Dirk and Mimi's. Jo said she would talk with the seminary president in Holland to see if Bryan and Cate could share their presentation with the students and professors there.

"What about us?" demanded Garrett, Anne's son.

"Yeah. What about us?" Gretchen chimed in.

Gretchen and Garrett were acutely aware they were being left out of the fun plans. They wanted something to do too.

"Maybe you could make some colorful posters with lists of supplies the children need for school?" Cate suggested. "You could glue Ghana flags to the posters or use pieces of fabric." She looked at Bryan. "What about some pictures of Pastor Elisha, Marta, the children, and Fifi?"

"Absolutely!"

Bryan wanted to give Cate a big kiss right then, but he refrained. There would be time for that later.

The afternoon ended after more dreaming and planning. It could have lasted longer, but Matthew needed to get home for bath time and bed. Kristy and Mike told Maggie they had never had a church experience like the one that morning. Maggie secretly hoped they would spend more time at Jesus Lives with Dan and Nora in the future. She marveled at how people were brought together under such different circumstances and the way joy and sorrow connected in different lives.

The families from east, west, and south Michigan hugged and kissed each other as if they were parting for life. The afternoon had cemented several families into one.

As Maggie watched them drive away, she took a moment to thank God for the whisper and the new plans.

She thanked Ed too. She now knew he would have understood perfectly, and without judgment, if she had told him about her confrontation with Cassandra.

Maggie was more thankful than ever that she'd had the chance to apologize.

29

Originally, the plan was for Bryan to go back to Zeeland with his parents, but Cate proved to be a roadblock. Not intentionally, of course. Cate was just being her delightful, winsome self, which Bryan could not resist. After making a plea to his sister and mother, Bryan was allowed to stay one more night in the parsonage. Maggie and Mimi would meet in Lansing the following evening, and Bryan would be passed from sister to mother.

After that was settled, Bryan and Cate walked down Middle Street towards Cate's house. Cate's family, longtime members of Loving the Lord, had been looking forward to getting to know Cate's new "friend" and Pastor Maggie's brother.

Maggie and Ellen loaded the dishwasher.

"What did you and Harold do with the offering?" Maggie asked.

It wouldn't have been appropriate for Maggie to ask in front of the whole family, but now it was just the four of them.

"Well, that's a story for Harold to help with," Ellen said with a smile. "It's safe in his office. Don't worry, Maggie dear."

Jack and Harold were putting the dining room back together and returning chairs to various places in the parsonage. When Maggie and Ellen found the men, they were in the basement, stacking folding chairs. Maggie looked at the chairs and cringed. She gripped her cane a little more tightly.

"Are you two almost done?" Ellen asked.

"Yes, master," Harold said, grinning at his girlfriend with all of his lovely teeth.

"Maggie was wondering about the offering today." She grinned back.

Once they were all seated on the once-white-now-gray couch and loveseat in the living room, Harold cleared his throat. But before he could speak, three whiskered noses appeared in the doorway. Marmalade, Cheerio, and Fruit Loop had been in hiding all day with the parsonage so full of people. Gretchen and Garrett had searched and searched in every room and under every piece of furniture, but the felines had stepped into their invisibility cloaks and disappeared. Now they were back. Maggie leaned down and began murmuring in kitty talk, sympathizing with their harrowing day.

"Oh, poor babies. Was it noisy in your house today?" Then she made some unrecognizable hums and cooing noises until Jack tapped her on the arm.

"I think Harold has some news for us, cat woman," he said, looking at Harold, who was waiting impatiently to share his news.

"Oh, all right," Maggie said, pretending nothing could be more important than her cats. She pulled the three up on the couch, and they snuggled in, purring.

Harold cleared his throat.

"This has been an extraordinary day, Pastor Maggie and Jack," he said with a dramatic flair. "Ellen and I counted the offering today before locking it in my office safe."

Maggie was almost afraid to know the outcome. She had figured that there would need to be more fundraisers before the January trip, and she and Jack had talked about how to offset the cost. Those going on the trip could be asked to pay more than the original fifteen hundred, but that might be a hardship for some. Perhaps they would have to cut the size of the group. But how? Maggie wanted to put in some of her own money. She and Bryan had both received inheritance from their two sets of grandparents. Dirk and Mimi had wisely told their children to keep the money until they needed it for something special or important. The mission trip seemed like something special *and* important. Jack also had money to add, but they had decided to wait and see what the church, and God, had planned.

After the conversation about other churches joining in the Ghana mission, Maggie had gained a tiny sense of hopeful relief. She took a deep breath and looked at Harold and Ellen.

"What was the total?" she whispered.

"We have a generous church, Pastor Maggie. The total was twenty-seven thousand, four hundred and thirty-two dollars, and twenty-seven cents."

Maggie was struck silent in shock, but Jack clapped his hands and whooped out loud. It was very un-Jack like.

"How can that be?" Maggie asked. "We don't have people with that kind of money. I was actually expecting a large offering today, but now I realize I also doubted the outcome. What's wrong with me?"

The other three just looked at her. They knew Maggie could be a jumble of conflicting emotions at any given minute.

Ellen started laughing first. Then Harold. Then Jack, who grabbed Maggie and kissed her. Finally, Maggie had a good, long laugh at herself.

"So how did this happen," she asked.

"It's pretty simple, when you get right down to it," Harold said. "I can tell you some specifics. There were two five-thousand-dollar checks. One from your parents, Maggie, and one from Jack's. So thanks to you both, on behalf of the council, for bringing your generous families to church this morning." Harold nodded his head while pretending to remove an invisible hat.

Maggie's eyes widened. She had no idea her parents were planning such a gift, but she realized it made sense. Both of their children were passionate about the project. Jack's parents really shocked her, but not because they weren't generous people.

"Jack, your parents . . . gave so much," she said.

"Yes. They must like you."

Maggie impulsively kissed the end of his nose.

"I think they love God," Maggie said.

"Jo James gave two thousand dollars. In the memo line of her check she wrote, 'From Ed and Jo. God Bless You,'" Harold said a little more quietly.

"She's an incredible woman," Ellen said.

Maggie nodded.

"Lacey provided a check for one thousand dollars," Harold continued nonchalantly, waiting for this little bit of news to register.

"Lacey?" Maggie gasped. She was stunned. *Lacey Campbell?*

"Your pastor friends, Dan and Nora, gave a nice check for five hundred dollars. And the congregation gave an amazing eight thousand, nine hundred and thirty-two dollars, and twenty-seven cents." Harold looked expectantly at Maggie and Jack.

"You're missing a big chunk," Maggie said, looking from to Harold to Ellen.

"Ah, yes, Miss Marple." Ellen laughed. "You're a smart one."

Harold cleared his throat one more time. "There was one other five-thousand-dollar check," he said, waiting in a dramatic pause.

"Who?!" Maggie demanded.

Ellen laughed out loud and said, "Marvin Green. Can you believe it?"

"Yes," Maggie said with glowing eyes. "Yes, I can."

Jack and Maggie were sitting in the kitchen, each sipping a glass of very good red wine from a bottle given to them by Anne and Peter as an engagement gift. When Anne handed her the bottle, Maggie was reminded that she and Jack were actually engaged. She had forgotten for a while.

"We have a lot to be thankful for," Maggie said, "and I don't mean the offering money."

Jack nodded. "Today was remarkable. I don't think anything like that worship service has ever moved our church in such a positive direction."

"Excuse me," Maggie said indignantly. "What about every Sunday since last June? I'm quite certain every service has been spectacular. Especially the preaching."

"Ahh, forgive me, Reverend Highness," Jack said, looking down with false deference. "You are correct. Nothing compares to Pastor Maggie. Except for her brother, of course."

Maggie rolled her eyes. "'Tis true. He and Cate were magnificent. I have to give God some credit too. There's a plan afoot."

She took another sip of wine and changed gears.

"We do have something a little more serious to talk about. I don't want you to be caught off guard the next time you see Cassandra."

Jack heard the tone in Maggie's voice and prepared to listen carefully. He sensed that it was Maggie's signal to him regarding how they would communicate going forward regarding parishioners and patients. It suddenly dawned on him: that kind of communication was a way of protecting each other. They weren't just sharing stories about others, but they were providing information in order to be better caregivers of those in their charge. And to be better caregivers of each other.

Maggie looked into Jack's eyes. Sometimes it seemed Jack did all his listening with his eyes. She took a breath and felt calmer.

"When I met with Cassandra, she made two requests," Maggie began. "The first is that she would like me to be present when she tells Carrie and Carl about her . . . her prognosis." Maggie used the sterile word as a kind of protection. Saying the word *death* was too difficult.

Jack placed his hand over hers. She didn't see the small wince in his eyes as he took in the gravity of Cassandra's request.

"I don't mind being with her when she tells the children." Maggie choked up just saying the words out loud. She swallowed hard. "Cassandra, Carrie, and Carl will need all the support we as a church can give them."

Maggie stopped and felt Jack's hand squeeze hers.

"I'm sorry for the entire situation," he said, "and I wish you didn't have to go through this, especially with the children. But I know why Cassandra asked you. She needs your whole heart. Hers is breaking."

"Thank you, but you give me too much credit, as usual," Maggie said, smiling wanly.

Jack was saddened by the work she would have to do with Carrie and Carl as they learned the one thing that frightened all children the most—losing a parent. But he knew without a doubt that Maggie would know exactly what to do and say as she watched and listened in Cassandra's living room.

Jack picked up Maggie's hand and led her to the living room. They sat down on the once-white-now-gray couch as he wrapped his arms around her small frame. Then he waited. She had said there were two requests from Cassandra. What was the second?

Maggie tried to figure out how to word the next request, but she finally just said it the best she could.

"Cassandra asked if we would adopt Carrie and Carl after she is . . . gone. You and I. The two of us."

Jack was silent. His arms stayed around Maggie, but she could feel his back stiffen slightly.

"What do you think?" Maggie asked Jack.

"What do *you* think?" Jack asked Maggie.

"Honestly, I would do anything for those two. But there is a jumble in my head. We aren't married. We don't even seem to have time to plan a wedding. We would be instant parents. I think we'd be great, but I think it would be hard. Is this what God is asking us to do because we will be the best for Carrie and Carl?" She paused for breath and stared at Jack.

Jack took it all in.

"First of all, we would be, and will be, amazing parents. I think about it a lot. I think about raising a family with you, Maggie. I guess I was stuck in the old-fashioned idea of you being pregnant, and we would begin with infants. Cassandra's request moves us right into preschool."

Jack's back loosened up, and he hugged Maggie so tightly she squeaked.

"This is a huge decision," she said. "I have gone back and forth since Cassandra asked. Of course we should say yes. We would be brilliant," she joked. "But seriously, how could we help two grieving children heal while trying to figure out how to be married and keeping up with two demanding jobs?"

She shook her head briefly and closed her eyes.

"Let's not do this tonight," Maggie said abruptly. "We are both such remarkably nice people, and we'll go back and forth with 'How do you feel?' 'No, how do *you* feel?' until the cows come home. I don't know how I feel about it. I know I love Carrie and Carl. I know I can't wait to be your wife. I know we're ready to be parents at some point. I think we need to speak with Harold." Maggie looked weary. "I just didn't want you to see Cassandra and have her ask if we had discussed the issue."

"Thank you," Jack said quietly. "This certainly isn't a decision we can make tonight or this week. We'll have to be sensitive to the fact that Cassandra is beginning to get her house in order, so to speak. I'm guessing she will have a sense of urgency regarding the kids, and I don't blame her. Let's talk with Harold tomorrow night."

"I can't," Maggie said with a sigh. "I have to meet Mom in Lansing with Bryan, the boy wonder."

"Then Tuesday or Wednesday. I'll set something up. Okay?"

"Yes. Thank you." Maggie yawned.

Jack took Maggie's hands in his. Staring into her eyes, he said, "God, we need your help with this. We need guidance, direction, whatever you want to call it. But you have to make it clear. This is Jack and Maggie, by the way. Amen."

The prayer made Maggie smile, which was Jack's intent. His prayer was sincere, but not polished. The situation was too raw for flowery words.

Jack kissed Maggie and said, "We truly will be great parents. I can't wait to watch you be a mother. I love you, Maggie."

"How do you do that?" Maggie said, perking up. "You look at a difficult situation and make it sound possible, even easy."

"I get to do everything with you now. What could be easier than that?"

Then Maggie was enveloped once again in his embrace.

All will be well, Maggie thought. And part of her actually believed it.

Jack was leaving just as Bryan came back from Cate's.

"How were all the Carlsons?" Jack asked.

"Great. I think I passed the inspection," Bryan said.

"Did you play Monopoly?" Maggie asked, smiling.

"How did you know?"

"Cate told me once that it's how her parents 'interview' new boy-friends. They pull out the Monopoly game and see how the victim—I mean, young man—plays the game. They see how he carries on a conversation *while* playing the game, and how he takes losing the game. They make sure the hapless lad never wins. It's genius, really." Maggie giggled.

"That's pretty rough," Jack said. "But I think we'll do that when our daughters begin dating." He kissed Maggie on top of the head.

"You have daughters?" Bryan asked casually. "Is that why you have to get married?"

"You figured it out," Maggie said, trying to stifle another yawn but failing.

But she thought to herself, *We may have a daughter and a son before the trip to Ghana.*

Harold arrived at his office before eight o'clock Monday morning. He didn't need his keys because the door was standing wide open. So was the door to the safe. Harold went to the office next door to use the phone. He dialed. The other line only rang once.

Detective Keith Crunch had been waiting.

30

Maggie awakened Monday morning from a particularly vivid dream. She slowly sat up and leaned back against her pillows and closed her eyes, remembering.

Harold was there, standing in front of the church. The congregation were all listening as he told them that they had given over three million dollars for the mission trip.

Then he said, "We have decided to move our whole church to Ghana. So we will pack up this church and get to the airport."

Maggie had tried to stop him, but everyone began moving, picking up pews and hymnals and filling boxes with office supplies and vegetable soup ingredients. Irena picked up the whole organ bench and carried it outside to a waiting truck. Maggie tried to speak. She tried to shout and tell everyone to stop. They certainly could not all move to Ghana. They were only going on a mission trip.

Her dream had quickly changed to a place her imagination said was Africa. Maggie was wrapped in brightly colored Ghanaian fabric. She was standing in front of someone she knew in her dream to be Pastor Elisha. He took Maggie's hand, and suddenly Jack was there. Pastor Elisha took Jack's hand and placed it in Maggie's.

"I now pronounce you are married," Pastor Elisha said solemnly in his best English.

Irena began playing a monumental pipe organ sitting on the red dirt road in the scorching sun.

Ken, Bonnie, Dirk, and Mimi all appeared, and Pastor Elisha had them put their hands on the tops of Jack and Maggie's heads.

"Now the parents bless you, the children," Pastor Elisha said. "Complete!"

Their parents were hugging and kissing Jack and Maggie. Bryan and all of Jack's siblings were there. Anne was cutting a cake that looked like heavenly fluff salad in the shape of a palm tree.

"You will have a happy life here," Mimi whispered into Maggie's ear. "We will miss you. Goodbye."

Mimi vanished. Slowly, everyone vanished. Jack and Maggie stood alone by the palm tree fluff salad cake. They turned as they heard the sound of rustling and squealing. Carrie and Carl came running from behind low bushes on the side of the road.

"You are our mommy and daddy now! You are our mommy and daddy now!"

They threw themselves into Jack and Maggie's arms with hugs and kisses exploding out of them.

Jack and Maggie began walking down the empty dirt road, each holding a child. They were walking with no place to go.

Awake now, still in her bed, Maggie breathed in deeply and exhaled. She opened her eyes and looked down at her engagement ring. It sparkled happily on her finger. With everything that had been happening lately, Maggie hadn't had time to think much about her engagement to Jack. She hadn't been able to do the things she thought brides-to-be should do. Wasn't she supposed to be giggling with girlfriends and looking at bride magazines? She absently shook her head. She wouldn't do those things anyway. And what about Carrie and Carl? She couldn't shake off the end of her dream, walking down a road to nowhere with a husband and two children. She shivered.

Just then, three furry bodies jumped on her bed. Marmalade stared and then gave her an award-winning head bump. Cheerio yawned. Fruit Loop let out a howl. Time for breakfast.

Maggie grabbed her cane and made her way to the kitchen, followed by three hungry kitties. She was glad they weren't fighting as much. It made for calmer mornings, not to mention calmer nights. She pressed the button on the Keurig and breathed in the comforting smell of brewing coffee. She pulled down the oatmeal cylinder but realized she wanted something besides oatmeal that morning. So she pulled out her toaster and slipped in two slices of Mrs. Popkin's homemade white bread. When the toaster evicted the toast, Maggie slathered butter on each slice, followed by generous spoons of cinnamon sugar over the top. She bit into the first slice of cinnamon toast and hummed with happiness. *The poor person's cinnamon roll,* she thought. She licked up every crumb, brewed her second cup of coffee, and felt much better with the caffeine, carbs, and sugar surging through her system.

Bryan came downstairs, awake and ready to work.

"Good morning!" he said loudly. "Mmmm, I smell cinnamon. Did you get something special from The Sugarplum?"

He searched on the counters for a pink box or a white bag.

"Nope. I made cinnamon toast. I needed a change from oatmeal today. What would you like?"

"Something from The Sugarplum."

"Great. You go get it. I'm heading to church, and then to Cassandra's, and then to the Friendly Elder Care, and then back here to do whatever you need me to do," Maggie said, sounding like a mother.

"Yes, ma'am," he said, brewing a coffee cup. "I will have news when you return. I'll wait until San Francisco wakes up and then have a long talk with my boss."

"Excellent."

Maggie took her cane and headed back upstairs to get dressed for the day. She felt emotionally hung over from the excitement of Sunday, the generosity of the congregation, her talk with Jack, and then her dream. She wanted to get moving and shake off the heaviness.

As she walked across the lawn to church, she was greeted by sounds and smells. Irena was making up for the fact she hadn't played the previous day. If the windows hadn't been opened, Maggie was sure they would have been blown out by pipe organ music. And because the windows were open, Maggie could smell onions frying and knew the soup committee was hard at work in the basement. *God bless normalcy.*

"Good morning, Hank," Maggie said, once in the office.

She had miraculously managed to slip past Irena, who was fully focused on her music.

Maggie had been happy to see Doris's rolling trash can in the middle of the sanctuary. Doris herself must have been down in the kitchen, overseeing soup preparation. Soon the sanctuary would have the diverse smells of boiling vegetables, Murphy's Oil Soap, and Pine-Sol.

Hank was getting his desk in order for the day. He said to Maggie, "I think yesterday was the best church service I've ever experienced. Your brother and Cate did a fantastic job. You must be proud."

"I am. It looks like they might be able to share their presentation in other churches, if Bryan's boss agrees. I don't know why she wouldn't. The more people who know the better."

She was already feeling restored, thinking of more projects in more villages. There just wasn't an end to giving.

Hank looked conspiratorially at Maggie.

"Do you know how much money we raised?" he asked quietly.

"I sure do. Twenty-seven thousand, four hundred and thirty-two dollars, and twenty-seven cents!" She beamed. "We will have to put it in the bulletin for this week so everyone can rejoice in the generosity."

"I will put it in bold numbers," Hank said, silently shocked at the total.

Maggie walked over to Hank's bulletin board. The sign-up sheets for Cassandra were pinned up side by side by side, covering the top of the bulletin board. She saw that every line had a name on it. The people of the church were generous in so many ways. Maggie didn't hear herself sigh.

"We're going to take good care of her and the little ones, Pastor Maggie," Hank said quietly.

"Just look at all the names. This church is jammed full of saints," she said, turning to look at Hank. "And you and Pamela are two of them. Look how many times your names are on these lists. Meals, transportation, childcare, yard work, housecleaning. Oh, Hank."

Maggie threw her arms around Hank's neck and hugged him. Hank just chuckled.

"Pastor Maggie, we're just being normal." He waited for her to get over the bout of affection. "Every human being has the responsibility to make sure other human beings are cared for. It's simple and indisputable. So we'll take care of our neighbors in the village in Ghana and our neighbors here in Cherish. And anywhere else there's a need. It's what good people do."

Maggie released Hank's neck.

"You are good, Hank. You and Pamela are two of the goodest." She smiled and looked back at the sheets. "It looks like today Mary Ellington is bringing dinner to Cassandra, and she's watching Carrie and Carl for the day. I bet they will have fun at The Grange."

"Yes. William has that small barn with a few animals roaming around to give The Grange a country feel. Those kids will have a lot of fun today, but they'll smell like the hind end of a cow when they get home." Hank wrinkled his nose.

"I'm having tea with Mary at The Grange tomorrow. I can't wait to see what it looks like, inside and out. But for now, I'm going to give the lectionary a look and see what I'm preaching on this Sunday."

She went into her office and spent the next two hours looking over Mark 9:30–37. Reading the last two verses left a lump in her throat.

> Then he took a little child, whom he placed among them; and taking the child in his arms, he said to them, "Whoever welcomes one of these little children in my name welcomes me; and whoever welcomes me does not welcome me, but the one who sent me."

∞

266

Detective Keith Crunch had been waiting for Harold's phone call. He made his way down Main Street to Harold's office with two Ann Arbor officers following him.

"Show me your office," Keith said to Harold, who was waiting for him in the parking lot. Keith, Harold, and the two officers went into Harold's office. The door had been forced open, the chair turned upside down, file cabinets flung open, papers everywhere. The safe was standing open and empty.

The two officers began their forensic work, searching for clues.

"It looks like the plan worked," Keith said to Harold.

"I did exactly as you said. I moved my important files into the business next door on Saturday. Then yesterday, Ellen and I came here with the money, but I used the inside door to the next office and locked the offering in the safe there. Whoever was following us was fooled. They found an empty safe and a lot of old files and blank pages. From the look of things, they didn't like the joke." Harold laughed as he surveyed the mess.

"Do you have the money?" the detective asked.

"I checked when I arrived, and it's still there, ready to go to the bank."

"Why don't you go now and make that deposit," Keith said.

Harold nodded and walked to the door leading from his office to the one next door by the inside wall. He knocked and waited. Keith watched from behind him.

Lacey Campbell opened the door to the business office of her salon.

"Howdy, Harold," she said brightly. "Are you here for your haul?"

"Hi, Lacey." Harold smiled in return. "The police are here now, looking for fingerprints and other clues. Thanks for helping out in this little scheme. The money certainly would have been stolen if I had left it in my office."

"Thank you for your cooperation in this matter, Ms. Campbell," Keith said.

"No problem, Detective," Lacey said, smiling, her red lipstick making her teeth look extra white.

Lacey opened her safe and gave Harold the banker's envelope.

"I'm glad to help. I sure hope you all find whoever is doing this hooliganism soon. I think we need our quiet little Cherish back."

"I agree. Hey, it was good to see you in church yesterday. I hope you come back," Harold said.

"I will. It was a great service. Since I cut almost everyone's hair who was sitting there yesterday, I figure I might as well join 'em in church. Plus, I like Pastor Maggie. Hey, when do you want your files back?"

"I'll come get them when the police say I can have my office back. Is that okay?"

"Of course, anytime. Just knock on the door. I'll be here. My first customer will be walking in the door in a few minutes, so I better get out there." She turned to go into her salon.

"Lacey, thanks. Really. We're going to catch whoever it is," Harold said seriously.

He went back to his office and was surprised to see Charlotte and Bernie Bumble standing in the office next to Detective Crunch.

"Hello, Charlotte, Bernie," Harold said, maintaining his composure. "Good to see you here. Quite a mess, huh?"

Keith quickly said, "I called Chief Tuggle and Officer Bumble and filled them in on what happened."

Charlotte looked as if she had been sucking on a particularly sour pickle followed by a shot of vinegar.

"The invitation to the dance is coming a little late, isn't it, Detective?" Charlotte said bitterly. "It looks like we've arrived for the cleanup."

Keith knew he should have called Charlotte before Harold had moved files and collected the offering, but he'd had the feeling that Charlotte, in her overzealousness, might actually have given the plan away by hanging out in front of the We Work Miracles Beauty Salon. What better clue would a criminal need? Charlotte was as subtle as a beagle.

"Chief Tuggle, would you mind accompanying Mr. Brinkmeyer to the bank with the church offering? I have a feeling we have a vengeful and angry felon out there. Let's protect the offering." Keith spoke with enough authority to make Charlotte move from her cemented spot on the floor next to Harold's overturned chair.

"Yes, sir," Charlotte said sharply.

Harold headed to the door with Charlotte, along with the hapless Bernie following behind. The bank was a block away. The two officers and the attorney walked wordlessly down the street.

Anger seethed from one in the alley who watched them walk away.

Maggie drove to Cassandra's house for a visit, but when she arrived, she saw a car in the driveway. It had a large car magnet on the side that read:

THE GRANGE
CHERISH BED AND BREAKFAST

There was a phone number printed beneath the sign. She concluded it must be Mary Ellington's car.

Maggie drove on past the house to let Mary and Cassandra organize the day. She kept driving until she reached the Friendly Elder Care Center, and then she parked under a shady tree. Taking a deep breath, she marched into the building and up to Marvin's room. She knocked but didn't wait for an answer.

Marvin was asleep in his wheelchair, his head lolling to the right, and there was a small line of drool making its way down to his shoulder. He snored softly. Maggie walked closer and took a tissue out of the box. She gently wiped the drool from Marvin's mouth and chin. He didn't move. She threw the tissue away, then patted him softly on the hand. His eyes fluttered open.

Marvin was disoriented at first, erupting with snorts and snuffles. When he finally got his bearings, he looked at Maggie. Just as he opened his mouth to bark, Maggie quickly spoke.

"Marvin, how was your nap? You look rested. I'm here to thank you for your motivation in church yesterday."

Marvin tried to interrupt, to no avail. Maggie just plowed on through.

"It's clear you were the inspiration for everyone sitting in the pews," she said joyfully. "I almost think you should be up preaching every week. I think we would have a full sanctuary consistently. But as for yesterday." Maggie paused quickly to breathe. "Your voice led the charge to build a new school in a faraway village, and your check will help make it happen. And I want you to know I love you."

Maggie bent down and kissed the old man on his bristly cheek. Then she turned and walked out the door. She didn't hear a single sound from Marvin's room as she walked down the hallway and out the sliding front doors.

31

After leaving the Friendly Elder Care Center, Maggie headed back toward Cassandra's house and was surprised to see Mary Ellington's car still there. Maggie drove past and went back to the parsonage.

Bryan was sitting at the kitchen table surrounded by his computer, several calendars, his phone, and a pink box from The Sugarplum. Fruit Loop was curled up on the calendars, his nose suspiciously close to the pink box. Bryan was stuffing a caramel pecan roll into his mouth when Maggie walked in. He grinned a sticky smile.

"Glad to see you found sustenance," Maggie said as she helped herself to a ginger scone from the box.

"I've got good news," Bryan said, licking his lips. "Joy said I can stay in Michigan for three more weeks. But I'll have to head back to San Francisco on October fifth to train the new advocates. She thought it was a great idea for me to visit as many churches as possible with the presentation. And she suggested we add stories and pictures from some of Africa Hope's other sites in Kenya, Tanzania, and Uganda."

Maggie thought quickly. It was September fourteenth. Bryan and Cate would only have three Sundays to work with before he had to leave.

"That's a great idea. Who can I call? How can I help?" Maggie blurted, putting down her scone.

"We need to get in touch with Jack's sister and his parents. I'll ask Jo if Cate and I can visit the seminary, then Dan and Nora's church, and of course, our own church in Zeeland. Maybe we can visit the east side of the state the following two Sundays. What do you think?" Bryan looked at his sister.

"It sounds perfect. How about you call Jo, Nora, and Mom. I'll call Anne, then Ken and Bonnie. They will have to get in touch with their pastors and hopefully arrange a time for you and Cate."

Maggie jotted down Jo's home number and Nora's office number.

"Here are the numbers you need. You can probably catch Mom at work."

Then she grabbed the rest of her scone and went into the study to track down Jack's family. It was so exciting! She was just a tiny bit jealous she wouldn't be able to see the upcoming presentations because she would need to keep everything running steady at Loving the Lord.

Two hours and a dozen phone calls later, Bryan and Maggie had come up with a schedule. Bryan and Cate would present their talk at the Elzinga's home church in Zeeland on September twentieth. The next weekend they would speak at the seminary in Holland and at Dan and Nora's church. Then the final weekend, October fourth, they'd drive to the other side of the state and speak at Jack's sister's church in Detroit in the morning and at Jack's parents' church in the afternoon in Blissfield.

Just looking at the schedule was exhausting.

"Jack and I can come to hear you in Blissfield since it's in the afternoon," Maggie said. "C'mon. Let's get ready for the big Bryan tradeoff in Lansing."

Just as Maggie and Bryan were getting ready to leave, Jack pulled up in front of the parsonage.

"I was wondering if I could ride along to Lansing?" he asked.

"Yes, please." She smiled. "Get in the back, Bryan."

"Well, I see how I rate," Bryan said, hopping in the back of the car.

"It's about time." Maggie giggled.

∞

Tuesday morning was normal with cat chaos, Keurig brewing, and oatmeal thickening in the microwave. But there was no Bryan. Maggie knew she would have to get used to the highs and the lows of seeing her brother and then having him gone again. He'd be back next week. *Quit your whining, Maggie!*

After stopping in at the office, giving Hank her sermon title for Sunday, and being grilled by Irena regarding the whereabouts of "Captain Crunch," Maggie was ready to leave and head to The Grange. But she didn't escape in time. Hank popped his head into her office.

"There's a certified letter here for you, Pastor Maggie." He lowered his voice, sounding conspiratorial. "It could be important."

Sometimes Hank doesn't have enough to do, thought Maggie.

She opened the letter, noticing from the envelope that it was from Melissa Jones, the daughter of dead Abe Jones and a possible best friend for Irena. A small piece of paper fluttered to her desk.

Dear Pastor Maggie and Irena,

Thank you once again for your hospitality and kindness on the day of my father's funeral. I came to Cherish wanting to hate everything about the people and the town. It was childish. I am embarrassed by my actions that day.

But the two of you gave me the freshness and forgiveness I needed to carry on with my life. My good life. You reminded me of what and who to be thankful for. You showed me how to laugh again. Sometimes I wonder if I was really there in Cherish. It seems like a magical day in a magical place.

Please find enclosed a check for Loving the Lord Community Church and the Ghana mission. Accept it with my gratitude and my hope to return to Cherish one day for an afternoon in The Sugarplum and a morning in worship.

With love and appreciation,
Melissa Jones

Maggie reread the letter. *What a kind thing to do.* Then she picked up the check that had dropped on her desk.

"Hank!" she shouted.

Hank was in the office in less than a second since he was waiting just outside the door.

"What is it?"

"Melissa Jones has just sent our little church a check for ten thousand dollars! Can you believe it?"

Irena trip-trapped into Maggie's office, having overheard Maggie's proclamation.

"I beleaf eet. Dat voman needed to git dat rock off herr shoulder. She hed to stop hating. Eet had been brreaking herr soul for too long. Ve just give eet de leetle push." Irena brushed her hands together. "Dun and dun."

As Maggie drove into the circular driveway at The Grange, Mary was outside the old Victorian home, watering the overflowing flower pots on the wraparound porch. She was dressed in blue jeans with a long-sleeved flannel shirt. She waved as Maggie pulled up and got her first view of the bed and breakfast.

The house was extraordinary. The main part of the building was slate gray, with sage green and deep plum adding to the cupolas, turrets, and trim. Just looking at the earth-colored house was soothing. Maggie stood gaping, taking in every detail from architecture to flower petal.

"Good morning, Pastor Maggie," Mary said warmly. "I take it you haven't been here before, not even for a little peek."

"No. I haven't. Now I wonder why not. This is breathtaking. I can't imagine that you ever have a second when this home is not full. You must turn people away constantly."

Mary laughed, took Maggie by the elbow, and ushered her inside.

"Tell me all about this place," Maggie demanded, looking at the large chandelier hanging in the foyer. She had heard that everything in the house was traditional Victorian.

"Well, there are seven bedrooms, each with its own bathroom. There is a parlor, a library, a large dining area, a television room tucked away in the back, a conservatory, and the kitchen, of course. Through here is the formal living room."

Maggie followed Mary like a puppy dog. Every detail of every room was perfect. The air smelled lightly of citrus and a hint of vanilla.

"Why in the world would you ever leave this place?" Maggie asked, astonished. "This is like walking into a magazine of the perfect home. It smells so good too. Mary, you are quite a secret keeper, and a talented one."

Mary smiled. "I'm glad you like it. I'll show you around, and then we can have tea in the conservatory."

"Are we in England?" Maggie asked.

Mary gave Maggie the complete tour, minus one of the bedrooms.

"We have a guest staying here for a few weeks."

"That's nice for them," Maggie said, "but it must be, uhh . . . expensive to do that."

"We sometimes have ways to help," Mary said cryptically.

Just then, a little girl and a woman came out of the closed bedroom door. The little girl had long red hair and ran right into Mary's legs. Maggie inhaled. It was the little redheaded girl from church on Sunday. The one who tripped over Marvin's wheelchair.

"Oh, excuse me, Hannah," Mary said, catching the child.

Maggie looked up from the child to the woman behind her. It was Julia Benson.

"Julia?" Maggie said softly.

Julia just stared at Maggie blankly.

275

"Hi, Mrs. Ellington," the little girl said. "Mommy says we can go look at the cows. Is Mr. Ellington by the barn?" She had a sweet voice, and she clearly adored Mary.

Mary knelt down in order to look Hannah in the eye.

"Yes, Hannah, he is. I think he might need some help feeding the animals."

Maggie couldn't take her eyes off Julia.

Julia nodded stiffly, took Hannah's hand a little too abruptly, and walked down the stairs.

Once they were gone, Maggie asked, "What is she doing here? Is that her little girl?"

Mary nodded. "I thought you knew. Julia and Hannah came here about three and a half weeks ago. She told us she needed a place to stay for the weekend. That has quickly multiplied. She had no credit card, so no hotel would take her. We couldn't let her and Hannah leave with no place to go. So we worked out a little deal. It's fine. She's got a job now and pays on time."

"Yes, she's a reporter at *The Cherish Life and Times*," Maggie said. "She interviewed me."

Mary laughed. "No, she's not a reporter. She gets advertisements from local businesses for the paper. She only just got the job a week and a half ago. Her hours are sporadic, but she's having some success. And we bought an ad for The Grange."

That news floored Maggie. *Ad work? A child?* Who was this Julia Benson? And why had she lied? She had fiercely grilled Maggie in a false interview. *Why?*

Maggie was confused but knew that talking to Mary about all of it was not appropriate. She would need to call Detective Crunch. Maybe he would have a way to find out who Julia was. She took a deep breath.

"Hannah is a sweetie," Mary said. "I watch her sometimes if Julia has to go in to work."

"Why isn't she in school?" Maggie asked. "Is it because she and Hannah are not staying in town permanently?" That was unlikely now that Julia had a job.

"We're working on that. Apparently, there is some paperwork Julia doesn't have in order. As soon as that's taken care of, Hannah can start school. Whatever the reason was for Julia and Hannah to come to Cherish, something has changed. Julia mentioned finding an apartment as soon as she saved up enough money. She obviously wants to stay in Cherish."

Maggie was floored. Then she said lamely, "Well, that's nice. I hope she can do that soon."

Mary and Maggie made their way down a winding staircase banked with green ferns and into the kitchen. It wasn't Victorian, but it was large, airy, and functional. The floor was laid with large, white, square tiles. There were black granite countertops, white cupboards, and a black-and-white checkered backsplash. Everywhere were splashes of bright red. The coffee pot and teapot were cherry red. Utensils were in a large red vase near the five-burner stove. Red hand towels hung from the double ovens. Bright-red pots hung from hooks in the ceiling above the long island in the middle of the room. Red dishes showed through the clear glass of the cupboards. Small red rugs were in front of each doorway leading in and out of the kitchen.

"I could live in this kitchen and never leave," Maggie said in her typically overstated way.

"Thank you, Maggie," Mary said appreciatively. "I designed this myself. I've always wanted a kitchen exactly like this. Now I have one."

They finally settled themselves in the conservatory. It was a miniature glass house. The slanted glass of the roof joined floor-to-ceiling windows all the way around. It was full of soft, peach-colored furniture with an abundance of plants, which Maggie decided must take up a great deal of Mary's time.

"I'm beginning to run out of compliments," Maggie said, sipping her tea. "Mary, you and William have a treasure in this home. I wonder if you know how welcoming it feels to step through your front door."

"That's our goal. We want to create a place where whoever stays here feels comfortable and relaxed," Mary said, slicing something covered in pink icing.

"By the way, I saw your car at Cassandra's yesterday."

Maggie put a bite of angel food cake in her mouth and moaned with happiness.

"Yes," Mary said, a little more subdued. She put her fork down on her plate. "I wanted to bring some food for them, but I also thought it might be a good way to get to know Carrie and Carl, you know, in their own home. So I brought a few little things for them to play with. I hope they will enjoy visiting here."

"Of course they will," Maggie said. "It's generous of you to be doing so much."

"William and I talked a lot about it. We have quite a few bookings coming up this fall, but I can still find time to help Cassandra with the children in-between cooking and cleaning."

"Hey," Maggie said quickly. "You said something about Hannah needing to get into school. What about Carrie and Carl? Shouldn't they both be in school as well?"

"Yes, they should. I spoke with Cassandra about getting them both registered. I'll help with whatever she needs. I think Cassandra's original plan was to home school the children."

Mary was obviously finding any way possible to help Cassandra. And Julia too, for that matter.

Maggie was grateful that, although Mary's heart had been devastated when her son Michael died, it had not been destroyed. *How fortunate for those she so easily wraps it around.*

"Mary, you seem like a different woman than the one I first met. Cassandra and Julia are blessed to have you in their lives. And personally, I loved seeing you in church."

"Cassandra is a special woman." Mary began to choke up. "For so many reasons. Some people die without knowing they're going to die, like Michael, but Cassandra will have to work hard to die. I want to do anything for her. And Julia is trying to live. She has a hard life. I want to do anything for her as well." Mary struggled to keep her composure.

Maggie was becoming more and more aware of the intricate and fractured layers of concerns being brought harshly to the forefront of her church. There was no choice but to gather up all the people and pieces and hold them carefully. Then hang on as life and death continued to play their eternal game.

32

For a while on Wednesday morning, Maggie forgot about Julia Benson, Cassandra, and their children. She was in her office at church, making notes for her sermon while listening to Irena blast "Great is Thy Faithfulness" on the organ and watching Doris dust Hank's office. As usual, that wasn't working so well for Hank, who was trying to print a new church directory with the addition of all the new members. Doris was spraying, wiping, pushing, shoving, and generally being annoying. But for Maggie, watching it all, life was great.

Then her phone dinged, announcing a text.

How is my betorthed?
What are you doing?

Bits and bobs, odds and ends,
this and that, my love.

I just want to know that
you're okay.

I am. And you?

I'm the luckiest guy alive.

Love you.

Love you the most.

Maggie clicked off the phone and sighed. Jack's texts were exactly what she needed to remember she was not alone. Then she wondered how they would ever get from "betorthed" to married. *Oh dear.* But that was another problem for another day.

When Maggie left after lunch for Cassandra's house, she was once again surprised to see Mary's car in the driveway. This time, Maggie parked on the street and went to the front door.

The door opened, and two blonde bombs exploded out of the house. Carrie was in full tutu regalia. Slippers, crown, and wand were all coordinated with her lilac-colored tutu. Carl was in a simple pair of shorts and a T-shirt. They both went slightly insane when they crashed into "Pasto Maggie." Squeals of delight erupted as they threw their little arms around her legs, cane and all. Mary was right behind them.

"Good morning, Pastor Maggie," Mary said as she began to peel the children from Maggie's legs.

"Pasto Maggie," Carl said. "We ah going with Miss Mawy to see the cows."

"Yes!" chimed in Carrie. "We are going to see the cows and the chickens. And we even get to go to school and see what's going on there."

Maggie thought the tutu might not be the best choice for visiting a farm. But then again, so what? Princess Carrie should be able to wear whatever she wanted.

"I think you are going to have the best day ever," Maggie said, bending down and hugging the squirming little bodies. Wet kisses were smashed onto her cheeks. She returned them in kind. "I hope you enjoy visiting school. That was always my favorite place to go. There are so many nice friends just waiting to meet you."

She smiled at Mary as the children ran to the car.

"I think we are on the right track," Mary said quietly to Maggie. "Cassandra is seeing the importance of getting them registered and beginning a new routine. I hope you two have a nice visit."

Mary walked quickly to settle her charges into the car seats she had borrowed from Cassandra.

Maggie walked into the living room. Cassandra was sitting on the couch, looking smaller than when Maggie had seen her just five days before. Maggie sat next to her.

"How are you doing today?" she asked, taking Cassandra's hand.

"I'm feeling a little tired today," Cassandra said, just above a whisper. "I think the kids will have fun at the farm."

"And school. What a good day they will have."

"I always thought I would home school my kids. I didn't want them under someone else's influence. That seems so foolish now."

"It made sense to you at the time. You had no idea how things were going to go. You aren't foolish." And she meant it.

"Dr. Elliot has been here. It looks like I might need some hospice care here at home soon. He's getting it set up. So I think it's probably time to tell Carrie and Carl about what's going on. What do you think?"

Maggie swallowed. "Yes, of course. You tell me when to be here."

"Would Friday work for you?" Cassandra sounded like someone making a date for coffee. "I want to have Marla here too, I think. And maybe Mary."

That surprised Maggie.

"Of course. The children love Marla so much. And it seems they are getting to know Mary. She's a lovely woman."

"Yes," Cassandra said. "You know about Mary's son, I imagine?"

"I do. It's a terrible story."

"It's horrendous."

The two women continued their conversation and then set a time to tell the children. Maggie would contact Marla and Mary and ask them to be at Cassandra's at six o'clock on Friday.

Before leaving, Maggie said to Cassandra, "I want you to know that Jack and I understand your request of us and the adoption. He and I have not had enough of a chance to discuss it, and we would also like to speak with Harold. I can't imagine how difficult this is for you."

"As you like to say, Pastor Maggie, all will be well."

Cassandra laid her head back on the cushions of the couch and closed her eyes.

The rental car had been reported unpaid for in Montana. The police were trying to track it down. Covering the license plate with mud helped.

Redford was feeling secure. He had just placed another phone call. It was so fun to hear the fear in the voice at the other end. He had set the final plan in motion. That called for a drink.

After leaving Cassandra's, Maggie decided to do something mundane and drove to the We Work Miracles Beauty Salon to buy some shampoo from Lacey.

The bell at the door jingled cheerfully as Maggie walked in. She saw Lacey behind a chair in the salon, working on cascades of long, blonde hair. Sky Breese.

Lacey turned when she heard the bell.

"Well, hi there, PM. How's it going?"

Sky immediately looked up from a magazine and gazed at Maggie.

"Hi, Lacey. Hi, Sky."

She had wanted to thank Lacey for her donation on Sunday, but not in front of Skylar.

"Come on in and have a seat," Lacey said, pointing a curling iron at the salon chair next to Sky.

"Actually, I just came in for some shampoo. I love the smell of whatever you used on my hair last time," Maggie said.

"Ahh, yes. I do that on purpose, you know. If you like the smell here, you'll probably want it at home too." Lacey laughed. "Just a little beauty salon trick."

Sky allowed a tentative smile.

"Mmmm . . . I never thought of that. You have me hooked too, Lacey. I love the smell of this stuff."

She pointed a long finger at the shampoo and conditioner on a shelf above the sink.

Maggie looked at Sky. "Of course, you get to smell flowers all day long, Sky."

Maggie was pretty sure Sky actually lived in a large pink rose.

"So, I was just telling Sky about the trick you all played on the . . . What's Irena call him? The villain?"

Lacey looked over at Maggie, who looked as if she might throw up.

"What?" Maggie said shakily.

"Yes, you know, how Harold hid the church offering in my safe here. And some of his files. It was brilliant. That Crunch guy is a smart one. He's pretty good-looking too."

Lacey continued making soft, lovely curls flow down Sky's thin back.

"What?" Maggie shouted. "What are you talking about, Lacey?"

Lacey was stunned out of her story by the tone of Maggie's voice. She held the curling iron in Sky's hair until it began to smoke.

"Lacey!" It was Sky's turn to shout. "My hair!"

Maggie had never heard Sky sound so alert. Or real.

Lacey unwound Sky's hair from the curling iron. Then she looked at Maggie.

"I'm sorry. I thought you were part of it. Harold hid some things here because Keith Crunch wanted to see if anyone had followed Harold to his office next door with the church offering. Apparently, someone did. They tore Harold's office to pieces. No one would have seen him bring the papers and money in here. We have an inside connecting door. I just helped out a little."

Lacey stared at Maggie, who was experiencing that pesky lack of oxygen once again.

"I'm guessing it's not a good idea to talk about this while you're working. The investigation isn't over because we don't know who the . . . the villain is yet." Maggie wanted to end the whole conversation. "I'll come back later for the shampoo, but please don't talk about this anymore."

Maggie turned and left. She felt her anger rising. She was angry at Harold and Keith Crunch for not keeping her in the loop. She didn't know why exactly, but she was mad that Sky Breese had heard the whole story. She was mad because the bell on the salon door rang so sweetly as she pushed through it to walk out onto the sidewalk.

Maggie didn't know what to do. She left her car in front of We Work Miracles and began walking up Main Street toward Middle. She cursed her cane with every step. She wanted to run. To run away. She couldn't handle any more crises, or gossip, or death. Or people. Maggie was sick of people.

Her cell phone rang. It was Jack.

"Hello," Maggie said as she continued limping.

"Hi, wife-to-be."

Jack was in a good mood.

Silence. Jack's good mood was making Maggie cranky.

"Are you there?" Jack asked, wondering if they had been cut off.

"Yes. I'm here. I'm . . . I was just . . . I'm on Main Street," Maggie said lamely.

"I miss you," Jack said sweetly. "May I take you to The Cherish Café for dinner tonight? Please?"

Jack was learning Maggie's moods. He could tell she was in a bad one and wanted to cheer her up.

"Yes. What time?" Maggie asked.

"Six o'clock. I'll pick you up early. Maybe we can have another glass of that good wine from Anne before dinner. I don't know if this is the best timing, but Harold can meet us before dinner and fill us in on the legal progress with Cassandra. Is that okay? Around four o'clock?"

"Yes. Okay. Can he just meet us at the parsonage?"

Maggie didn't feel like going to Harold's office.

"I'll call him. Just plan on it unless I call you back."

"I'll see you then." Maggie was about to hang up, then remembered. "I love you."

"I love you more." Jack clicked off.

Maggie limped along, turned down Park Street, and found herself on Marla's doorstep. Maggie rang the doorbell.

"Pastor Maggie! Wow, you look tired. Where's your car?" Marla asked, looking in the driveway and on the street.

"I left my car downtown. I thought a little walk would be nice." Maggie smiled wanly.

"What about your ankle? Should you be walking this much?" Marla went into mother mode, which irritated Maggie.

"I need to talk with you regarding Cassandra. May I come in?" Maggie was trying to be polite. It was painful—both on her manners and her ankle.

"Of course. Please, come in and sit down. How about some lemonade?" Marla asked gently.

"Thank you."

Maggie sat in the living room and realized the mistake of her trek on foot. Her ankle was throbbing.

Marla's sun-filled living room, along with the cool glass of lemonade, helped ease Maggie's soul. And attitude.

"Marla, will you come to Cassandra's house on Friday night and help us tell Carrie and Carl about their mother's illness and her . . ." Maggie paused.

"Her death," Marla said quietly.

"Yes. I'm going to ask Mary if she will come as well. She has been over at Cassandra's non-stop, and today she has the children at The Grange for the day. The more support and love for the family, the better."

"Of course." Marla sighed. "I will be there. What time?"

"Six o'clock."

Maggie took a sip of her lemonade.

"It's truly wonderful how Mary has suddenly come out of the woodwork," Marla said. "She's on every sign-up sheet at church for food, childcare, transportation, and cleaning. It's nice since it didn't seem like the new members class was working out for her."

Marla said that, not wanting information, but just as an observation. Maggie warmed to the goodness that was Marla.

"I'm glad you are getting a break too," Maggie said sincerely. "I don't think any of us were completely aware of how much time you were spending with the children."

"I have to admit, I have enjoyed these last few days to just clean my house and help Addie and Jason adjust to school. I had forgotten how much work little ones like Carrie and Carl can be. They need constant attention, and they move much faster than I do." Marla laughed. "Someday, I'll enjoy being a grandma, but it's nice to have my kids the ages they are right now."

That struck Maggie. She realized that she had assumed that, if she and Jack felt unable to adopt Carrie and Carl, the children would automatically go to Marla and Tom. Maggie shook her head slightly. *Good grief! How could I have made such an assumption?*

"Are you okay, Maggie?" Marla asked, watching Maggie's face.

"Yes. Of course," Maggie said quickly. "I'm just thinking of all the pieces to Cassandra's situation. I think Carrie and Carl are our first concern. Jack is dealing with the medical side for Cassandra, and Harold is working on the legal. It's just a lot to take care of in a short amount of time."

Marla nodded her head. "Hey! Remember last year when I was putting together the Sunday school curriculum for when children lose a pet or a loved one?"

Sadly, Maggie did remember. Maggie had done everything possible to keep Marla from going forward with her "death curriculum."

"Maybe I should pull out those books for Carrie and Carl. What do you think?"

Marla was already pinpointing in her brain where she had stored the books at church. Maggie cringed, remembering some of the titles.

No, Johnny, Grandpa Isn't Asleep
You Can Be an Angel Too Someday!
Heaven Really Isn't as Boring as It Sounds

"I think we should wait and see how Carrie and Carl react on Friday night," Maggie said.

She might have to hunt up those books and burn them before Friday.

Marla and Maggie finished their lemonade. Marla insisted on driving Maggie back to her car. She relented.

"I'll see you at Cassandra's on Friday," Maggie said.

When she got into her car, she found a package on the front passenger's seat. Inside were two bottles of shampoo and two bottles of matching conditioner. A note read:

Dear PM,

I'm sorry if I spilled the beans about the offering. I won't be discussing it anymore with anyone. Please accept these humble hair gifts as my apology.

Your Miracle Worker,
Lacey

Maggie laughed out loud. Lacey was such a nut, and she was so good. Maggie drove home with her hair treasures. And a lighter spirit.

33

Jack was at the front door at four p.m. with a large bouquet of red carnations from Pretty, Pretty Petals.

"Oh, Jack!" Maggie exclaimed. "They're beautiful."

"It sounded like you weren't having a very good Wednesday when we spoke earlier. Of course, I knew it had nothing to do with me, so I forgave your rudeness and bought you these."

He kissed Maggie as he handed her the bouquet.

"I apologize profusely for my rudeness earlier. I was a silly little wench and certainly don't deserve such lovely flowers. But I'm keeping them anyway."

As Maggie brought the flowers to the kitchen table, there was a knock at the back door.

"Hi," Harold said when Maggie opened the door. "Hey, how is this alarm working?" he asked, looking at the key pad.

"It's been working great. I also think having Bryan here last week was another deterrent for our villain. By the way, I hear there was a bit of a kerfuffle at your office Monday morning."

She ushered Harold into the kitchen.

"How did you hear about that?" he stopped smiling.

"I'm pretty sure anyone who sat in Lacey's salon chair this week heard about it. You and Detective Crunch probably should have said something to her about keeping the story quiet. When did you two hatch your little plan?"

Maggie was still miffed that she had been out of the loop, but Harold looked concerned enough to satisfy her. Jack listened intently. It was all news to him as well.

"I approached Detective Crunch," Harold began. "I told him I was going to take the offering to my office, but that I was pretty sure this wasn't a secret anymore. I thought, if Ellen and I brought it there, but really switched it to Lacey's safe, I could throw our thief off the scent. Keith was the one who suggested I also move some of my most private and important files. Lacey let me do that as well. It turns out it was a smart thing to do."

"Why?" asked Jack.

"My office was broken into Sunday night, but there was nothing to take."

He filled in a few more details, and after their surprise at the story, they were both grateful that the plan had worked. Losing that offering to the villain would have been devastating.

"Why didn't you tell us?" Maggie asked, tired of all the secrecy.

"We don't know who's doing all of the stealing and break-ins, but he or she seems to know what's going on around church enough to keep up the bad behavior. Keith and I figured the fewer people who knew about me switching the money to Lacey's office, the better," Harold said practically.

Lacey would be the last person to tell any secret to, Maggie thought uncharitably. But she had to remember that, after all, Lacey helped save the offering.

Harold, efficient lawyer that he was, had already switched gears and moved on to the business at hand. He opened the file he had brought with him and cut right to the chase.

"Cassandra owns her home outright. It turns out, when her husband died, there was a substantial insurance policy. It made it possible for her to stay home with the children. Carl was an infant at the time, and Carrie a toddler. Cassandra had a will and trust set up after Cal's death. She has the money she needs for medical care. And quite a bit more than that."

Harold looked up at Jack and Maggie. "In her will, she had designated Cal's parents as guardians for Carrie and Carl. That won't work now, due to their declining health. If the two of you are willing to adopt Carrie and Carl, a new will stating you as guardians will be drawn up immediately. Her situation isn't complicated, from a legal standpoint. That's all I have." Harold closed the file.

"How much time do we have to decide?" asked Maggie.

"Jack might be able to answer that question better than I," Harold said, looking at him.

"I've called hospice. They will be coming to the house beginning this weekend. Cassandra is a very sick woman. I don't think she will be here for Christmas," Jack said soberly.

"Will she be able to stay home until . . . the end?" Maggie asked.

"She will. But she's thinking through the effect of that on the children."

The three sat quietly at the kitchen table, each pondering the situation. Finally, Jack spoke.

"Maggie and I haven't had a chance to really talk about the possible adoption. We'll need some time."

"Of course," Harold said. "This is a serious matter."

"I'm just curious," Maggie said, "but has Cassandra mentioned any other possibilities besides Jack and me?"

"She hasn't, but I have to believe she knows it might be a possibility. Take time to talk it over. I'll be seeing her again on Friday. I can ask her then about other options."

"I'll be seeing her on Friday as well," Maggie said. "Marla, Mary Ellington, and I are going over to help Cassandra tell the children."

That was news to Jack and Harold.

"Mary?" Jack asked.

"Yes. I'm guessing Mary shared the story of the death of her son, Michael. She has an understanding about death. It's different from Cassandra's, but it is a horrible loss. She has also been helping with

Carrie and Carl this week. I think . . . I think Mary needs to help, just as much as Cassandra needs to be helped. I don't know that Cassandra has many friends."

Harold looked down at the kitchen floor, then back up at Maggie.

"I'll be praying for all of you on Friday night."

He cleared his throat and stood. Both Maggie and Jack stood up and walked him to the door.

"Thank you, Harold, for everything you're doing for Cassandra," Maggie said.

"And for all of us," said Jack, who knew how important the legal side was in life-and-death situations.

"Jack, you were right last week when you said that we would all have work to do to take care of this family. I'm honored to help. Now, I'm going to go pick up your cousin for dinner. I need to hold on to a different reality tonight."

As a young attorney, life had been easy and lucrative for Harold. The whole situation with Cassandra had brought him to a new awareness. People were not just billable hours.

After Harold left, Jack sat back down at the table while Maggie took two wine glasses out of the cupboard. She poured the remainder of the wine from Anne and Peter into the two long-stemmed glasses. The red flowers and red wine made a pretty picture on the table. That is, until Marmalade jumped up to investigate the vegetation. Marmalade loved eating flowers.

"Scat, cat," Maggie said as she tenderly lifted him from the table and kissed the top of his furry head. Her words were always harsher than her actions when it came to the felines.

"I better move these to higher ground," she said, placing the vase of carnations on top of a kitchen shelf.

"So now I understand some of what was happening today at the unfortunate time I called you."

He took a sip of wine, and Maggie added a few more details of her day. The visit with Cassandra. The confrontation with Lacey. The whole Harold-hiding-the-offering with Detective Crunch. Her realization regarding Marla and Carrie and Carl.

"I'm upset with myself for even thinking that Marla could adopt the children. When I put the whole day together, it felt like too much sadness and more lack of information. I'm trying to figure that out. What is important to know, and who should know it?" She was frustrated.

"I'm sorry," Jack said. "This is heavy work. We have life, death, break-ins, gossips, detectives. It's a lot to deal with, and it's not all connected. That makes it even harder to switch gears."

"How do you do it every day? All you do is life and death."

"That's the thing. *Life* and death. There is always good to celebrate. I remember that every time I deliver a healthy baby or watch a disease disappear or see a broken body mending after surgery. You have the same thing, Maggie. Think of Sunday's worship service and the new school that will actually be built in Ghana. Think of how the church is being the church by loving Cassandra and her children. And you are engaged to the most intelligent, handsome, loving man in the whole world."

Maggie laughed.

"Well, now that you mention it, Lacey left some delicious-smelling shampoo in my car as a gift."

Jack grabbed her by the waist and pulled her in for a hug, chair and all. "You smell delicious."

Maggie melted into Jack's arms. He held her close, burying his nose in her hair. She let herself be completely held.

Maggie looked up at him and said, "I don't want tonight to be heavy. Today was soul-crushing."

"We have much to celebrate and a big question to answer. And we have each other. So lighten up just a little bit, Pastor Maggie."

He kept holding her.

Dinner at The Cherish Café tasted delicious, as always. Jack and Maggie enjoyed their meal of lobster macaroni and cheese as they began the discussion of adoption.

"We should probably think about a wedding too," Jack said.

"It's amazing how the engagement excitement has dissipated," Maggie said. Then she saw the disappointment on Jack's face. "I mean, all of a sudden we might be parents. We'll have little ones who will be going through quite a trauma. The wedding seems almost frivolous. We already know we're a great couple. I wonder what kind of parents we'll be. I hadn't thought of being a mother quite yet. Like you, I thought the wedding should happen first." She smiled.

"Maybe we should think about calling Dan and Nora and taking a drive over to Holland," Jack said seriously.

That made sense to Maggie. Elopement was the smartest answer now.

At six o'clock on Friday night, Maggie, Mary, and Marla stood on Cassandra's front step. Maggie rang the bell.

Carrie answered the door in pink pajamas with an orange tutu around her middle. Carl came running in his pajamas—cotton shorts and T-shirt with fire engines scattered in all directions. They both smelled like bubble bath.

Cassandra sat in the living room on the couch with a blanket over her lap. She looked exhausted. She smiled at the other three women, who took seats around the room. There was one standing lamp in the corner that gave off a cozy light.

Carrie and Carl climbed onto the couch and cuddled with their mother. She gently kissed each one on the head.

"I told Carrie and Carl that you would be coming tonight and that we had something to tell them that might be hard to hear. It might hurt," Cassandra said, somehow keeping her composure.

"But not like a shot," Carrie assured the women.

They smiled at her with clenched hearts.

Cassandra began the telling of the tale of life and death. The four women did their best to stay calm and supportive of Carrie and Carl. Cassandra stayed focused as she slowly explained how sick she was. She explained that her sickness would not go away.

"What will you do? Call Dr. Elliot?" Carrie asked hopefully.

"Dr. Elliot has done so much to help me, Carrie, but there isn't any more medicine that can help my sickness," Cassandra said, holding back tears.

"Are you going to . . . What will happen?" Carrie asked.

She and Carl each cuddled a little closer to their mother, looking up with solemn blue eyes.

Maggie, Marla, and Mary held their breath.

"I'm going to die."

Maggie bit her lip so hard to keep from crying that she tasted blood.

"Like the mama kitty?" Carl asked slowly.

Maggie remembered last summer when she had first met the little family because of a dead mother cat that had been hit by a car. Cheerio was one of her three orphaned kittens.

Cassandra couldn't hold it together any longer.

"Yes," she said with tears filling her eyes. "Like the mama kitty."

"I said her funeral," Carrie whispered to the other women.

Carrie and Carl's voices lifted, one after another, with their simple questions.

"Who will take care of us?"

"When are you going to die?"

"Where will you go when you die?"

"Where is heaven?"

"What about our kitties and Black and Blue?"

"Where will we live? Can we stay in our house?"

Cassandra answered the questions as she was able. Maggie helped when she could, keenly aware of the concrete thought processes of young children. No, there were no exact directions to heaven. At least not how to get there by car.

Reality began to set in for the children. The warmth of the lamp light softened faces and words, but not the harshness of the truth. Carrie began to cry. Frightened by it, Carl began weeping with his sister. Cassandra was too weak to hold them. Marla quickly moved to the children, sitting on the floor in front of them. She helped Carrie, then Carl, slide into her arms. Maggie watched as Cassandra patiently answered a few more of her children's questions. She told Carrie and Carl that they would keep talking about all their questions.

"Yes, I will be alive tomorrow. Yes, I will make breakfast for you. Pancakes. I'll love you always."

Then she told them how much the nice people at church—Pastor Maggie, Mrs. Wiggins, and Miss Mary—loved them.

"And Addie?" Carrie asked.

Marla shivered and looked into Carrie's tear-filled eyes.

"Addie loves you so much. Addie will always love you, darling. You too, sweet Carl."

She squeezed Carl's small foot.

Maggie and Mary moved down next to Marla, Carrie, and Carl. Cassandra slid down and pulled the children into her arms. It felt natural. The four women made a safe circle on the floor. Carrie and Carl were in the middle, holding on to their mother. The other women hugged them and rubbed their backs and held Cassandra.

Maggie had never experienced anything like it before. There were no words, just raw grief. Each woman carried different degrees of the pain. There were murmurs, runny eyes and noses, and strong arms holding, holding, holding.

Mary began to sing quietly in a beautiful alto voice. "Jesus loves me, this I know . . ."

It was as if all four women were laboring together to carry, protect, love, and safely bring the children through the peril awaiting them. Into a new life.

They held each other until Carrie and Carl both slipped into sleep in the midst of the circle. Marla and Mary gently carried them to Cassandra's bed and tucked them in.

The women stayed with Cassandra until she also was ready to sleep. Maggie prayed. With hugs and kisses, they left Cassandra to slumber with her children.

Maggie drove home and walked straight to the sanctuary of church. She unlocked the large wooden front doors, removed her shoes, laid down her cane, and limped down the aisle.

Then Maggie crawled up the few steps and curled herself on the altar.

She waited for a whisper.

34

Maggie didn't know how long she had been lying on the altar when she heard the loud thump, followed by a scream. Maggie gasped, then froze. The sounds were coming from the church basement.

She sat up and felt around in the dark for the steps leading down to the aisle. She scooted toward the first step as a brick came flying through the window. Maggie looked up at the beautiful rose window at the back of sanctuary and watched in horror as it crumbled in the moonlight. More shattered glass rained down with a second brick.

Maggie crawled away from the aisle toward the secret door. She went through to Hank's desk and picked up the phone to dial 911, but she heard the sirens before she finished dialing. The police were already alerted.

There was another scream from the basement. Maggie hurried to the stairs and began the descent. She had completely forgotten about her ankle now. The sounds were louder as she got closer to the basement. Maggie had almost made it to the bottom of the stairs when she heard the sounds of booted feet rushing behind her.

Maggie screamed. Someone tripped over her, pushing her down the last two steps. The police officer who had tripped over Maggie lay splayed on the basement floor. Three more officers followed closely behind, but Maggie pulled herself out of the way before getting stampeded again. She crawled around to where the light switches were and stood up. She flipped on the lights, illuminating the basement.

Maggie and the police officers stared at the sight in front of them. Two people were wrestling on the floor. One was wearing all black, including a mask. The other was wearing an orange miniskirt, fishnet stockings, and red stilettos. Long purple hair was covering her face. She was lying on top of the person in black, hanging on for dear life.

"Get off me!" the person in black growled.

"Irena!" Maggie screamed.

Two of the officers moved in and pulled Irena off the other person.

"Lit me go!" Irena cried. "I caught de villain! I caught de villain!"

The other two officers grabbed the villain.

Maggie noticed for the first time that Charlotte and Bernie Bumble were two of the officers. They were the ones who now had hold of the person in black. The other two officers holding Irena must be from Detective Crunch's division.

"Charlotte? Bernie?" Maggie said, shocked.

"Good evening, Pastor Maggie," Bernie said shyly while restraining the culprit.

"Pastor Maggie, what are you doing here?" Charlotte asked in her police chief voice.

"I, well I . . ."

She couldn't tell them that she came to church after the experience at Cassandra's house. She couldn't tell them how full her heart was and how her soul was aching so badly she could physically feel it. She couldn't tell them she came to church to wait for a whisper from God.

"I came to the sanctuary to pray," she said simply. "But then I heard noises from the basement, and then," her eyes welled up, "someone broke our rose window. Someone smashed it. I was in the sanctuary when it happened. Our window."

"Then what happened?" Charlotte asked more gently.

"I went through the secret door to call the police, but the sirens were already coming. You must have known. How did you know?"

"The front doors had been opened. The officer in Ann Arbor, watching the security cameras, saw someone enter the church. Why, it must have been you. Good work, Pastor Maggie." Charlotte grinned. "We received a phone call to get down here while Crunch's men began combing the neighborhood."

There was a strangled gasp from the person in black.

"Let me go! I haven't done anything wrong!" The voice was familiar.

Maggie stared at the masked face.

"Lit me go!" screamed Irena. "I am nut de villain. I am de herro!"

"You can let her go," Charlotte told the other two officers, looking at Irena.

Irena gave them each a death glare as they released her. Then she took a moment to straighten her stockings, smooth her skirt, adjust her breasts, and get her hair untangled. It was a process.

More steps were heard coming down the basement stairs. Detective Crunch and two more officers joined the group downstairs. The officers were dragging a man in handcuffs, who was refusing to walk.

It was Redford Johnson.

Maggie leaned against the wall, breathless. Then she looked at Keith Crunch in wonderment. If Redford was with Keith, who was in black across the room?

"Get your hands off me," Redford growled, struggling to get away. Then he spit on the floor. "You don't got nothing on me."

Keith remained calm. "On the contrary, Mr. Johnson. We've got many things on you, as does the state of Montana."

Redford tried to kick Keith, who was not within kicking range.

"Who is that?" Maggie finally said, after getting some air into her lungs, pointing at the person in black.

"Let's see," Keith said.

He walked over and pulled off the mask.

Julia Benson gazed around the room, her eyes resting on Redford.

"Finally," she hissed.

∞

Keith began his own interrogation in the basement before deciding who would be going downtown. Redford was handcuffed and held in a chair by Charlotte, Bernie, and an Ann Arbor police officer. Julia was also being guarded but was not handcuffed. Maggie had asked if she might call Jack to come to the church. Keith understood and conceded.

Jack arrived within ten minutes. As he approached the church, he saw the jagged pieces of stained glass hanging precariously in what used to be the rose window. He carefully entered through the wooden doors of the sanctuary and was surprised to find Maggie's cane and shoes lying on the floor just inside the door. He carried them to the basement. Once down there, he regarded the roomful of people, found Maggie, and went immediately to her.

Everyone waited for Keith to speak.

"I'd like to begin by thanking Police Chief Tuggle and Officer Bernie Bumble. We couldn't have finished this operation without their full support, particularly this evening." Keith gave a nod to Charlotte and Bernie.

"Now," he continued, "Pastor Maggie, I need to know what you were doing here this evening."

Maggie repeated what she had said to Charlotte and Bernie earlier, choking up when she mentioned the rose window again.

"One of my officers saw Mr. Johnson throw the first brick that shattered your window. That was how he was apprehended, but not before the second brick was thrown. I'm sorry for that terrible act. Mr. Johnson will have restitutions to make."

"I'm not restituting a damn thing. You'll never get a dime out of me."

It looked as if Redford was ready to spit again, but the officer near him jerked Redford's head back.

"You bastard!" Redford yelped.

"Take him upstairs to the nursery and hold him there," Keith said quickly, knowing not to let the suspects hear each other's stories.

Charlotte and Bernie half-lifted, half-dragged Redford up the stairs to the nursery. Foul language spewed from the handcuffed man.

"Irena," Keith said, "let's go into the kitchen." Another officer led the organist, followed by Keith, into the kitchen. Keith shut the door. "I need to know why you were here this evening. I can't imagine you were practicing the organ this late on a Friday."

"Play de orrgan? Ov courrse nut. But yess, maybe sometimes. Vatever. I vas herre to cetch de villain. Okey. I know how dis verks frum my countrry. I ask Dorris to help, but she had a bunk on de hed. So I do eet myself. I ben herre to churrch everry night forr two veeks now," Irena said with gleeful smugness.

"Irena, how did you get in without being spotted by the cameras?" Keith asked.

"Eezy. I am small. I leaf de bar unlucked and go through de vindow Pastooorr Maggie fell through in de basement. I crawl under de cameras to de kitchen. I vait."

"What about sleep and food?" asked the other officer, who was taking notes.

"I hev naps. My ears, dey are verry goot. I hev de vodka. No prroblem."

Irena was having the time of her life.

"What happened tonight?" Keith asked.

Irena turned her full gaze upon Keith and smiled.

"Vell, I'm herre vunce again," she batted her lashes, "and I almost am sleeping, ven I hearr de door by de vindow unluck! I sneeek frum de kitchen. I see de villain! I jump! I land on de villain and yell. Den she yell. I don't let go." Irena tilted her head down while gazing up with a simpering look at Keith. "Dat ees eet, Captain Crrunch."

Keith smiled. "Good work, Irena. We didn't know you were on the team, and I have to say, it was a dangerous thing for you to do. But if I were a villain, I certainly wouldn't want to tussle with you. But next time, please let the police do this kind of work. We sure would hate for you to hurt your hands and not be able to play the organ."

Irena looked as if she might possibly shinny up Detective Crunch and permanently attach herself to his body. Her red lips curved into a smile.

"And now, Ms. Benson, why are you here?"

Keith was back in the large basement room speaking to Julia.

Maggie and Jack were allowed to stay with Julia and the officer guarding her. Maggie had told Keith she would stay as Julia's pastor, even though that was stretching the truth like a piece of saltwater taffy.

"I came to meet Redford," Julia began.

Maggie realized her own mouth had flopped open, but she quickly closed it.

"Why?" Keith continued.

"Because he promised to give me money he owed me." Julia looked at the ground.

"Money for what?" Keith pushed.

"Child support. He owes me five years of child support," Julia said, angry tears springing to her eyes.

"Hannah?" Maggie whispered.

"Yes." Julia looked at Maggie. "Hannah is Redford's daughter. Redford is my ex-husband. I left him when Hannah was born because of . . . of . . ." Julia turned and looked at Keith Crunch. "He beat me," she said. "I didn't want him to hurt the baby. So I left."

"She's a stupid bitch. I've been having fun yanking her around for the last three weeks. She's an idiot." Redford's face was red, and his eyes were blazing. "Ever since she left me, I've been waiting for her to come crawling back. And she did," Redford snorted.

Keith left the nursery and returned to the basement.

"So you came here tonight because Mr. Johnson told you to?" Keith asked Julia.

"Yes. He told me to be here. Again. He said to come through the back door in the basement, and he would have my money," Julia reported.

"'Again'?" Keith asked.

"Yes. When I figured out where he was, I came here to Cherish. That was at the end of August. I called him to let him know that I was in town and that I had a court order for him to pay child support for Hannah. He told me to meet him at his church, through the basement door. He said he would have the money for me." Julia shook her head. "I believed him."

"So you came to receive the child support back payments?" Keith continued.

"Yes. He said to come at nine o'clock on Friday night, August twenty-eighth. He told me to wear black." Julia shook her head in disbelief of her own words and then continued. "When I arrived in Cherish, I found The Grange bed and breakfast and checked in, thinking it would only be for a weekend. But I was on a goose chase." Julia's faced flushed. "Mary Ellington was kind enough to watch Hannah when I was trying to meet with Redford to get the child support. She thought I was working for the paper. Of course, those meetings with Redford never happened. Until tonight."

"Why don't you tell us how smart you are, Mr. Johnson? You certainly planned an elaborate scheme."

Keith Crunch kept his voice reasonable, encouraging. He knew psychopaths had to share their own tale. They exalted in telling of their faux brilliance. They had to show how clever they were. He gave Redford the opening he needed.

"It was so easy," Redford sneered, "when you're dealing with an imbecile. I told her to meet me at church. I told her I'd had a conversion." His laugh was cruel. "I made my reservations in Montana and made sure people knew I was leaving for a long vacation. I unlocked the back door of the church before I left. I knew no one would notice. A bunch of trusting fools.

"I made sure people in Montana knew I was there," Redford continued with a harsh chuckle.

Keith knew what happened during Redford's visit to Montana.

"Then I drove back. It's only a twenty-five-hour drive. I drove straight to Ann Arbor and got a room at the Holiday Inn." He sighed condescendingly. "Everyone thought I was in Montana. Ha! I could do whatever I wanted around Cherish. Many a night I was right outside the parsonage door. I could have broken in any time I wanted. The police never saw me once!"

Keith's face was immovable.

Redford continued. "I was able to come into the church, in the daytime no less, and listen in on conversations. It was so easy. I knew exactly what they were up to around here and could put a stop to whatever I wanted to. When you police showed up and installed the cameras, I had to figure out different ways to get information. I had already been using Julia, the chump. So I just kept making times for her to meet me. Then I wouldn't show up. She is so stupid. When she began to demand the money, I reminded her I was engaged and had to pay for a wedding. That got her riled up. She hated Maggie almost as much as I do."

"Redford told me you were his fiancé," Julia said to Maggie.

Maggie thought she might vomit. "Julia, you didn't believe him, did you?"

"I believed him, and I ransacked your house because I was so angry. I thought you had messed up my life. I had been sneaking around inside the church without anyone seeing me. Even listening in behind doors. Then, when I pretended to interview you, I saw your engagement ring, and I was sure you were in a relationship with him. The same kind of relationship I'd had with him. You looked beat up, you were limping, and you had bruises on your face. I recognized that. It all confirmed what he had told me. I'm so sorry." Julia put her head in her hands.

Maggie reeled. Then she remembered something her mother had told her once. Mimi had worked with students at the college who had suffered mental and physical abuse. Many of them had been abused by family members. Some of the young women were battered by boyfriends. Mimi had explained that when a person suffers physical abuse for a long period they sometimes begin to believe they deserve the abuse. Often they're told by the abuser it's their own fault. Some women, men, and children who suffer that way can't break out of the cycle of self-hatred. They can also believe that the abuse will stop if they behave differently. Or they hope the abuser will change miraculously. Miracles that never happen.

Maggie didn't know enough about the issue to diagnose Julia. It was hard not to judge her for continuing to show up at church whenever Redford barked. But Julia and Redford had a history that Maggie knew nothing about. And a child that Julia was wise enough to protect.

"Don't worry about the parsonage," Maggie said. "You had been lied to, and you were under a lot of stress. That's over now." Maggie added impulsively, "I think you're brave. And you're a good mother to Hannah."

Julia began to cry openly.

Keith handed her one of the ever-present boxes of Kleenex.

"I want to know how you got into the church after we had installed the cameras. That was quite a feat." Keith played into Redford's narcissism.

"Easy. It's funny how smart police think they are. Bunch of gorillas." He smirked.

Keith did not react.

"After I knocked Doris unconscious in the basement, I moved the bookcase in the gathering area. That's where the real secret door is. It leads to the back of the organ pipes. It was simple to hide there and watch through the pipes where you idiots were putting the cameras, both in the sanctuary and the gathering area. After I stole Marla's key and calendar, I could come and go as I pleased because I knew the entire church schedule. And by the way, it's called 'not walking in front of the cameras.'" Redford finished with a flourish of sarcasm. "Oh, and in case you're wondering, I kept calling Julia and telling her when to come to church and that she had to wear black. Which she did. I figured, if anyone caught her, she'd be too scared and stupid to tell the truth."

"Julia, how did you know about Doris getting attacked and the police coming to church?" Maggie was curious. "You mentioned it the second time you came in for a . . . well . . . an interview." Maggie didn't want to embarrass Julia.

Julia wiped her nose with the back of her black sleeve. The Kleenex was tattered by now.

"William and Mary had been in church the day you announced Doris had been hurt in the basement. They told me about it. I heard about the police being here from Lacey Campbell when I went in to get an advertisement from her for the newspaper." She took a deep breath. "I also knew about Doris because Redford told me he had put her in the hospital, and he would do the same to me if I said a word."

Keith listened intently. Maggie's questions were bringing more pieces of the puzzle together.

"The rose window?" Maggie whispered.

Julia shook her head. "I knew nothing about that. I swear."

Redford laughed. "I had a bit of a setback when Harold switched the money out of his safe Sunday night. But I knew even the money they got on Sunday wouldn't be enough to pay for a new window. No window. No Ghana. No nothing. I've made sure they are as poor as . . . Ha! Poor as *church mice*! As poor as those orphans in Ghana."

"All of this was to destroy the church?" Keith asked.

Redford ignored him.

"Well, it might not be completely destroyed," Keith Crunch said lightly. "We've had the opportunity to visit your home, Mr. Johnson. Don't worry, we didn't break the law. We had a search warrant. We found many helpful and interesting items. Some muddy shoes that matched a shoe print we found outside the church's back door. A crow bar with fragments of the sanctuary doors on it."

Redford's face went slack. Then hardened.

"What? You were in my home?"

"Mmmm, yes, we were. And it appears you don't trust banks much. You like to keep an eye on your cash." Keith kept the light tone in his voice, enraging Redford.

"Of course," Keith continued, "we did find some information on your computer regarding stocks, bonds, investments, those sorts of things. We had the court freeze those accounts. You used to be a wealthy man, but we will help relieve you of the burden of your wealth. You have new bills to pay, Mr. Johnson. You're done terrifying Julia Benson. You're done terrifying this church. You're done terrifying this community. You have been read your rights. There will be only one arrest tonight."

Keith looked at Charlotte and Bernie and the other officers.

"You can take him away now."

It was close to midnight when the small group left the church. Maggie had spoken with Detective Crunch about not pressing charges against Julia for breaking into the parsonage. Maggie thought the council would agree, once they heard of Redford's abuse and manipulation.

It was too dangerous to leave through the sanctuary doors due to the broken glass. No one seemed to know what to say to Julia as they walked out of the basement door at the back of the church.

Maggie looked at Julia. "I'm so sorry for all you have been through with Redford."

"Yes," Julia said. "I'm embarrassed by my actions and for thinking I could believe him. I made stupid decisions by marrying him and thinking he would change if I did. I've worked hard to overcome that mindset. I should have let the court take care of finding him, but I wanted to see his face when he handed over the money he owed me.

I should have known he never would. My goal now is to take care of Hannah."

Julia was sounding a little stronger with Redford gone. He was like a cancer, spreading toxins and disease to whomever he came in contact with.

Maggie, tempted to pity Julia, remembered Bryan's words in church: *I didn't tell you about Cynthia so that you would pity her. She doesn't need pity. She wants a school closer to where she lives and a well.*

Maggie considered that. Pity was a wasted emotion. It was demeaning to another person. Pity was a way of looking down on another, instead of looking them straight in the eye. Empathy and action were what mattered. Helping someone achieve a goal or get relief from a difficult situation was positive, forward action. And no one made it through life without receiving help from others at one time or another. No one.

"You are a great mother," Maggie said. "You need a chance to make a living and continue to care for Hannah. Redford can't do any more damage to you or anyone else. What would you like to do next?"

"I don't know," Julia said thoughtfully. "I don't think anyone has ever asked me that question before. I've just tried to get by."

Keith Crunch joined the conversation. "Redford has fooled many people for a long time. He won't be able to fool people where he's going now."

"No. Hee's going to de dungeon."

Irena put in her two cents' worth, eyeing Keith as she spoke. Julia laughed at Irena's comment.

"I like you, Irena," she said. "You get things done. I think I will have a few bruises from our skirmish tonight. I wish it had been Redford you attacked. You could have taken him down."

"Ov courrse. He ees weakling een everry vay," Irena said with a toss of her small purple head.

Jack and Maggie moved toward the door with the others. Jack had given Maggie her shoes and her cane, but her ankle was protesting somewhat after the evening's events. Jack took Maggie's arm, holding her back behind the others. Then he asked softly, "Why did you take your shoes off at the sanctuary doors?"

She looked into his dark-brown eyes.

"I was on holy ground. I came looking for God tonight."

"Did you find Him?" Jack asked.

"I did. In the midst of broken glass and broken lives, God is still here." She sighed. "I'm tired."

35

Maggie was up early Saturday morning. The volunteer fire department was coming to do the cleanup of the shattered rose window. Maggie would watch from the parsonage lawn with, she felt sure, many curious folks. She and Jack were also going to spend part of the afternoon making wedding arrangements with Dan and Nora. Maggie felt no excitement about that. It was a purely utilitarian event. If Jack and Maggie were going to become parents to Carrie and Carl, they needed to be married. They also *wanted* to be married, of course. Maggie had thought it would be different, but it was their new reality. A fluffy wedding party made no sense in a world of life and death. Terrible death.

At nine o'clock, the Westminster chimes rang. Jack was at the front door. Maggie was so relieved to see his face.

"How are you feeling this morning, my Maggie?" Jack said, sounding somewhat muffled as he kissed her. "How is your soul?"

"My soul is still a bit weary, but on the mend. I'm so glad you're here. I can't imagine going through this Redford situation, along with Cassandra's, without you. If you are still interested in marrying me, this may be your life on a more regular basis. How do you feel about that?" She blinked at him.

"I have to admit, you lead a pretty crazy life. But I'm seventy-five percent sure I still want to marry you," Jack said, walking toward the Keurig.

They settled in with coffee at the kitchen table and watched out the window. The volunteer fire department showed up in their red fire truck, which looked as if it had driven right out of the 1950s.

Fred Tuggle, Bill Baxter, William Ellington, Chester Walters, Tom Wiggins, Winston Chatsworth, and Dana Drake descended from the truck. They were all wearing protective gear.

"All right, crew," Fred Tuggle yelled. "Bill, Dana, and Tom, you head inside and begin the cleanup in the sanctuary. William, Chester, and Winston, you stick with me out here. There's some glass in the grass and bushes."

They mobilized and brought large, industrial-sized vacuums out of the truck. The cleanup began. It didn't take long for members of the church and the community to show up and watch the proceedings. There were also unhelpful shouts of unhelpful tips.

"Watch out! That glass is sharp!"

"You missed a piece right there. No, right there. No, to your left!"

Mrs. Popkin had set up a table in front of the parsonage with baked goods and several carafes of coffee. She had asked Addie and Liz if they would make sure everyone had refreshments throughout the day. For free.

Jack and Maggie watched for a while, then sat back down in the kitchen to call Dan and Nora.

"Well, we're thinking about October third," Maggie said when Nora asked about the date.

"You mean two weeks from today?"

Nora was not a hopeless romantic, by any means, but since her own wedding, she had contracted the ability to adore true love. The fact that her best friend was getting married was cause for celebration. The fact that the wedding would take place in Dan and Nora's living room, with only Maggie's family present, was not.

"You haven't even had any premarital counseling. How do you want the service to be ordered? What are you going to wear?" Nora sounded sad because she wanted her best friend to have a fairy tale.

"Jack and I will try to muddle through without any counseling. Who knows, we'll probably be divorced by Christmas." Maggie tried to joke. "As for the order of the service, short and sweet. Traditional vows. We probably won't have time to get rings, so just pronounce us married. And I'll probably wear my kitty pajamas. Easier to be ready for the honeymoon that way."

Even trying to keep it light and happy, Maggie was beginning to feel cranky. It was not the wedding of her hopes and dreams.

"Listen, we have to focus on Carrie and Carl. I know you understand that. The wedding is a formality so we can get on with being parents."

Maggie looked at Jack. He nodded but was looking tired too.

"I understand," Nora said immediately. She could understand the gravity of the situation and immediately changed her attitude. "We're going to have a wedding in two weeks, my dear friend, and it will be beautiful. I promise." Nora kept her voice cheery but looked at Dan and shook her head. "Try to think of anything special we can do to make the ceremony personal for you and Jack. A favorite poem, or a song, or a scripture reading. Something that means something to the two of you."

"Okay. We will," Maggie said with just as much fake cheeriness. "I'll call you in a few days, and we'll solidify the date."

Maggie clicked off with a sad sigh.

Nora looked at Dan once she hung up.

"We've got a real problem," she said seriously.

"What?"

"Maggie thinks she needs pajamas for the honeymoon."

Dan shook his head and smiled.

Nora immediately clicked her phone back on and dialed a familiar number.

"Hello?" Mimi said.

"Dr. Elzinga? This is Nora calling. Do you have a minute?"

It was Saturday evening, and the cleanup had taken all day. It finally ended with Fred Tuggle and Tom Wiggins climbing up the huge ladder connected to the fire truck and securing thick, clear plastic to the outside of the window. The sanctuary would be protected from rain. Everyone was trying hard to look at the positive. At least it wasn't December. But at the end of the day, smiles had all been used up, and tired bodies went home bedraggled.

Earlier in the day, Maggie had gathered a few of the council members together to tell them about Melissa Jones and her very generous check. She only shared the best parts of the day she spent with Melissa and also highlighted Irena's uncharacteristic kindness. No one believed her.

"I want to pass this on to you, Harold," Maggie said, handing over the check. "We'll discuss at our next council meeting how to use the money. We should also let the congregation know."

"Well," Charlotte said, astonished, "people never stop surprising."

"That should be a bumper sticker, Charlotte," Maggie said.

Maggie and Jack were just sitting down for some quiche and salad after the cleanup day when the Westminster chimes rang. Maggie went to the front door and opened it.

William and Mary Ellington were standing on the porch.

"May we come in?" William asked.

"Of course," said Maggie. "Have you had dinner?"

"No," William said. "But we don't want to interrupt yours."

Mary was silent.

"Please, eat with us. It's spinach quiche and salad. We have plenty."

Maggie smiled but could sense the tense mood of the couple. She led them into the kitchen, pulled two more plates out of the cupboard, and set them on the table.

"Hi, William, Mary," Jack said.

He grabbed silverware. Maggie thought Jack would do very well as the pastor's husband. They would have many interrupted dinners in the years to come.

Once they were all seated and had filled their plates, Maggie said a prayer. Then she waited for someone to speak.

William dove into his dinner. It had been a long day for him, helping with the cleanup and all. He was tired and hungry. Maggie looked at Mary, who was completely uninterested in what was on her plate.

"We've got something to share with you." Mary tumbled into the reason for their visit. "I have been talking quite a bit with Cassandra lately. I know she is worried about the children and who will be their guardians. I also know she has asked the two of you to consider that role." Mary breathed deeply. "But here's the thing." At this, William put down his fork and took Mary's hand. "We would like to have Carrie and Carl live with us. We would like to be their guardians, their parents." Mary said the last part as if she were running out of breath.

Maggie and Jack sat and stared in profound silence.

"Because," Mary dove back in, "our son Michael, when he died, he hit another car with his car. Another man died. I told you that, Pastor Maggie. Remember?"

Maggie nodded. "I do."

"The man was Calvin Moffet, Cassandra's husband."

Maggie and Jack were dumbfounded.

William spoke. "We never saw Cassandra at the time of the accident. Insurance companies took care of the policies. We just knew the name, Moffet. But we were living in Ann Arbor at the time, and Cassandra was living here in Cherish. It wasn't until we came to church. Actually, I figured it out first . . . because Mary had a hard time coming back after the first two new members classes."

Maggie remembered the first time she and Mary had tea in the parsonage, and Mary had poured out her story.

"Cassandra had just had Carl when Cal died," Mary continued, "but we didn't know any of that. After being in church, William put it all together. The name Moffet and her two children with no father. And then Cassandra's cancer diagnosis was shared, and the sign-up sheets were made available. When William told me who she was and who Carrie and Carl's father was, I wanted to help. I wanted to help her, this woman whose husband was killed by ... by ..."

"Don't you dare say it was you!" Maggie blurted, surprising everyone. "It was a horrendous accident. You lost Michael, and Cassandra lost Cal. People know now about cell phones and the danger they pose while people are driving. But you have to stop blaming yourself. Mary, get out of Michael's grave. There's no room for you there."

Now it was Mary's turn to stare. Her mouth opened, as if to respond, and then closed again. William looked down at his plate, shaking his head. Mary let out a long sigh.

"You just slapped me with the truth," she said. "No one has done that before. I think I needed it."

William looked up at his wife. Then he began speaking slowly.

"Mary and Cassandra have been, well, working through a lot of this the past few days," William said. "Michael being our son has come as a shock to Cassandra. She hadn't been in church for a while and hadn't heard our name. She would have known who we were right away because of the newspaper articles after the accident. But we've all come to realize there isn't time for regret or anger now."

"We told Cassandra that we would like to be Carrie and Carl's guardians. We know they don't know us well yet, but we will love them," Mary said painstakingly. "God has been silent in my life since the day Michael died. I feel like he's speaking for the first time since then. Hopefully, we can help Carrie and Carl heal, and they will help us heal as well."

Whispers. Thank you, God, for whispering to Mary.

"What did Cassandra say?" Maggie asked.

"She asked us to speak with you," Mary said softly. "All of this is weighing heavily on her, of course. She said she would like to know what the four of us decide. She trusts us to know the best answer. I know my own grief, but I can't begin to imagine hers."

"And it's not even just the four of us," Maggie said. "Everyone at Loving the Lord will help love and raise those precious children."

William and Mary looked at Jack and Maggie imploringly.

"The two of you are doing a great thing," Jack said seriously. "Maggie and I have been talking about the guardianship of Carrie and Carl since Cassandra asked. We don't want to disappoint Cassandra, and we do love the children, but we have struggled with this request somewhat. We thought we just had to plan a wedding. We didn't know we would have an immediate family." He smiled and lightened the mood.

Mary's deep sigh was felt by all of them.

"This could be the beautiful ending to a tragic story," Maggie said. "May we babysit once in a while?"

"Of course," Mary said. "For Cassandra's own well-being, I think we should let her know there is a decision. She must be so worried about her children and their future."

Mary picked up her fork and took a bite of quiche, finally able to eat.

"Shall we call her now?" Maggie asked.

Jack said thoughtfully, "What if the four of us drive over to her house?"

Leaving dinner on the table, the two couples got in their cars to make the short drive to Freer Road.

Three naughty cats enjoyed a spinach quiche dinner.

36

It was Saturday morning, and Maggie was in her church office, pondering life. She replayed the events of the past week and felt her brain jumble around and around.

The decision had been made. Jack and Maggie had joined the Ellington's at Cassandra's home, and they told her of their conversation. Cassandra felt peace, as well as relief, about where her children would be when she died. She shed no tears. She could make the next step in her journey. Having held her children since before they were born, Cassandra now had permission to begin the process of letting them go. She could tell her children where they were going to live.

Mary would bring Carrie and Carl to The Grange several times a week to help the transition. Marla and Addie were also spending time with the little ones. Maggie visited Cassandra every day. Pamela also made daily visits to Cassandra, often with KFC. Cassandra could take small portions of the food Pamela brought, and it was always an act of love on Pamela's part.

Redford had been in court for his preliminary hearing. His rudeness toward the judge added a contempt of court charge to the long list of charges and felonies he had racked up over the past five years. It all began with not paying child support to Julia. Maggie knew about that news thanks to Keith Crunch, who had decided that quirky little Loving the Lord Church would be his church home. Maggie added him to the new members class, even though he hadn't been a part of it. She figured he knew more about the church than just about anyone. And if the members didn't like it, they could take it up with Irena.

Keith was pleased to assure Maggie that for a new rose window, which was priced at ninety thousand dollars, there would be complete restitution from Redford's frozen accounts. Maggie was relieved they wouldn't have a piece of plastic attached to the front of the church for all eternity. She was also relieved they wouldn't have to use Melissa's check for part of the new window.

Bryan and Cate had led Bryan's church in Zeeland in meaningful worship with their Ghana presentation. The church had given generously to the orphanage, which could now consider a larger school building than originally planned. Dirk and Mimi graciously received the praise heaped upon them by their fellow parishioners regarding Bryan and his lovely girlfriend.

That very Saturday afternoon, Bryan and Cate would be sharing their presentation at the seminary, with Jo introducing them. Maggie believed the group of students and faculty who heard about the Ghana project would be inspired and leave with new knowledge and dreams of different kinds of ministry. Tomorrow, Cate and Bryan would be in Dan and Nora's church in Holland.

And in one week, Maggie and Jack would be driving to Dan and Nora's house to be married in their living room. Jack and Maggie had had a long discussion about changing the wedding plans now that William and Mary were going to be the legal guardians of Carrie and Carl.

"Maggie, we can have a real wedding if you want to," Jack had offered.

"I really can't imagine it. Our church has almost been destroyed, Redford is going to prison, and Cassandra is dying. It would feel frivolous to plan something big. I want to be your wife. I want us to have a life." Maggie sighed heavily.

"Then let's stick with our plan. We'll call my folks, and they can come too. How about that? When were you going to let your parents know? And what about Bryan?"

"I thought I'd wait another week. I want Bryan to enjoy his presentations and not be distracted by our big, uh, *little* day," Maggie had said practically.

"Our happiest day. And our celebration."

Jack had been determined to make Maggie smile. He himself was almost giddy with the prospect of marrying the woman of his dreams in less than two weeks.

"I would love your parents to be there," Maggie had said, uplifted. "I'll let Dan and Nora know."

One other piece of good news for Maggie had been putting her cane away for good. Jack had checked her ankle and watched her walk around the parsonage.

"I give you permission to walk among the normal folk once again. I banish the cane!"

Every once in a while, Jack adopted a little of Maggie's dramatic flair.

So Saturday morning, one week before her secret wedding, Maggie had awakened early and walked to the cemetery, her usual destination for her morning run. She went on her own two feet with two strong ankles. She wouldn't be running for a while, but the walk had felt like pure freedom. Then she had headed over to the church to finalize the service for the next morning.

A knock on Maggie's office door quickly brought her out of her ponderings. She could hear Irena blasting the organ and wondered who would be at church on a Saturday morning, besides Irena and herself. Doris had already done the cleaning for Sunday.

"Come in," she said.

The young woman who opened the door didn't look familiar. She was small in stature. She had short, brown, tousled hair, blue eyes as bright as marbles, and a striking smile.

"Pastor Maggie?"

Ahhh . . . that voice.

"Yes. Are you . . . are you Clara?" Maggie asked.

"Yes, I am. I'm Clara Abbott. We spoke on the phone."

Clara's smile was radiant. Maggie got up from her desk and happily walked without a cane to the cream-colored visitor chairs.

"Please, sit," Maggie said. She grasped Clara's hand and shook it as the girl joined her. "It's so nice to meet you."

"It's nice to meet you too," Clara said.

Maggie thought she had an easy way about her.

"What are you doing back in Michigan?"

"Well, to be honest, all the happenings at the lodge with Mr. Johnson and all were a little wild. My boss said I could come home for a couple of weeks if I wanted. You know, just for a break. So I took her up on it. My mom was glad too." Clara smiled again.

"I'm sure she was. Is it good to be back?" Maggie asked.

"Yes. I love Michigan, and the longer I'm away from home, the more I appreciate it. Have you heard any news about Mr. Johnson? I've been wondering. Actually, we all have been at the lodge. We couldn't believe what he did to the cabin."

"Fortunately, I do know some of what has happened," Maggie said, pleased to report the information that Keith Crunch had given her. "He's been charged with committing felonies with regard to theft and damaging the church. Because he was trying to keep our church from helping an orphanage in Ghana, they are now charging him with a hate crime as well. Extradition to Montana seems to be too expensive to pursue, but our detective says that, if he's found guilty, he will go to prison for a very long time."

"It's crazy, isn't it?" Clara said thoughtfully. "What makes a person want to destroy for no reason? With so much hate or anger, they can't help but destroy themselves."

She was thinking again of the cabin Redford had demolished.

"I had a good friend," Maggie said, "and he would have said that some people aren't redeemable. But only because they don't want to be."

Clara thought about that. She had met so many different kinds of people in her work at the lodge. So many personalities and behaviors to observe. Mr. Johnson had been someone who seemed intent on hurting others from the outset.

"I think your friend is right," Clara said.

"Would you like to get some coffee or something?"

"That would be great."

They walked across the street to The Sugarplum for a little bit of Mrs. Popkin's cheerful magic. It was delightful in every way.

The next morning during Sunday worship, the new members were welcomed by the congregation. They had all met with the council the previous Thursday evening for a homemade soup-and-sandwich supper, hosted by Bill and Sylvia Baxter and Howard and Verna Baker. The four of them had made soup all day in the church.

Maggie had been happy to see Mary and William walk into the supper together. Harold greeted them warmly. The three of them had been working with Cassandra on the legal side of things. Harold's heart had perhaps grown a little softer over the past few weeks.

Detective Keith Crunch had walked in with Sky right behind him. Keith was looking fabulous in a blue cashmere sweater that made his sapphire eyes pop. Maggie took personal pride in having him join their church. At first, she wondered how it would all work out with Charlotte, but Charlotte had come to realize that being part of a bigger team had its advantages. Maggie knew how Keith had deftly made sure Charlotte's ego was properly in place throughout the Redford debacle.

Maggie had watched as the lovely butterfly who was Sky floated her way in to the gathering area. Sky had several daisies encircling her blonde head and was wearing a white gauze pantsuit. She looked like the love child of Greek gods.

Lacey Campbell had been another happy surprise for Maggie. Lacey had made it to only one new members class, but her presence at church was enjoyed by all. She had asked if she could join. The only answer was a resounding "Yes!"

Dr. Dana Drake had gone right up to Maggie and given her a hug.

"Pastor Maggie, it's so good to be part of this church. I was thinking of the animal blessing service coming up in October. Don't you think I should bring all the sick and abandoned animals at the hospital to the service? I think they need more of a blessing than anyone else. And maybe a few might even find a home with people here at church."

Dana tossed her black ponytail. She had more energy than any adult Maggie had ever met.

"I love that idea," Maggie said. "We'll get the announcement in this week's bulletin. I'll tell Hank first thing in the morning."

Winston Chatsworth had arrived with his white hair sticking straight up and his shirt buttoned one button off. Maggie had no qualms about rebuttoning his shirt. Winston loved every second of it.

"Did you do this on purpose, Winston?" Maggie laughed.

"Maybe," grinned Winston.

Everyone had chortled when Kay and Shawn ran into the church. They were laughing and chasing each other around the chairs. Of course, Shawn pushed Kay, and she fell into the folding chairs. They all began to fall like dominoes. Ethan and Charlene looked at their children in horror. Kay began to cry. Ethan picked her up and grabbed Shawn by the arm.

"Shawn! Kay! Get over here right now!" Charlene had commanded. "Pick up those chairs and set them back around the tables."

It was obvious Charlene ran a tight ship. The children obeyed immediately.

Maggie looked at the folding chairs and sent a curse out into the world for their existence. They were "deth trups," as Irena would say. Maggie had gone over to Shawn and Kay and given them each a hug.

"I know these church dinners can be boring. I have some baskets in my office that need to be filled with candy. They're for our shut-ins. Right after dinner, could you fill them for me? I'm pretty sure there will be some leftover candy."

"Sure, Pastor Maggie," Kay said with no sign of tears.

"What should we do with the extra candy?" Shawn said, looking slyly at Maggie.

"Well, I don't want any left in my office, that's for sure," said Maggie. "We'll ask your mother if you can find a way to make sure there are no leftovers."

Maggie had taken a moment to look at the faces in the room. All the council members were helping to ladle soup and serve sandwiches. People were visiting and laughing. Her first new members class was a success.

"Hullo," came a familiar voice.

Maggie turned around.

There stood Irena. She had outdone herself with her makeup. Her purple hair was braided with small gold cymbals tinkling down her back. Her red fishnet stockings looked as if they had been stolen from a prostitute, along with her sky-high heels. Long dangling earrings were pointing down to her breasts, which were bulging out of her black silk blouse. Her black leather skirt must have been glued on with industrial-strength adhesive.

"Irena," Maggie said, trying not to look horrified. "What are you doing here?"

"De dinner for de new memberrs? I come for dis."

Irena scanned the room until her gaze landed on Keith Crunch. She made a beeline to his side of the room.

Keith had been visiting with Sky and Charlene and Ethan Kessler. When he saw Irena, he chuckled.

"Good evening, Captain Crrunch," Irena said with a batting of her lashes. She completely ignored the others.

"Good evening, Irena," Keith said jovially. "It's nice to see you here tonight."

"Ov courrse eet ees," Irena said coyly. "Come vit me. Ve git some soup."

Irena had slipped her arm through Keith's and led him to the soup tureen.

Maggie had found Jack and whispered, "Love ees een de airr!"

"It certainly is. Next week you will be Mrs. Reverend Pastor Elliot."

37

On the morning of Saturday, October 3, Maggie awoke to a head bump from Marmalade.

"Oh, Marmalade. That one hurt," Maggie said, rubbing her temple.

Then she remembered it was her wedding day. She and Jack had successfully kept their secret. She could hardly believe it. She had worked with Hank on the bulletin for church, and she had prepared a sermon for Sunday. She and Jack would drive back to Cherish that night after the ceremony. Then they would tell the congregation of the elopement Sunday in worship.

Marmalade, Cheerio, and Fruit Loop led Maggie downstairs, then began meowing incessantly for their breakfast.

"You all get extra treats today. It's my wedding day! Jack and I will be back tonight. Please don't head bump him, my dear Marmy. We don't want him to leave the first night, do we, kitty darlings?"

Maggie decided she would have a quiet wedding morning of oatmeal and coffee. Then she thought she might take a walk with her two good ankles. At noon, Jack would pick her up, and they would drive to Dan and Nora's house. She had decided to wear her cream-colored suit, the one she wore when she officiated other people's weddings. What could be more appropriate?

Jack and Maggie had made the top-secret phone calls to the Elzingas, including Bryan, who was staying with Dirk and Mimi, and also

Jack's parents. All were invited to the small ceremony. Everyone registered surprise, followed by excitement. Fortunately, none of them had any plans for Saturday afternoon. They would meet Jack and Maggie at Dan and Nora's at three o'clock. Dirk and Mimi offered to take the wedding party out for a celebratory dinner following the ceremony. Bryan had planned to drive back to Cherish Saturday morning to see Cate and get ready for the two presentations set for Sunday on the east side of the state, but he wouldn't miss the wedding for anything. He would call Cate and tell her he'd be there Saturday evening, without giving the real reason.

Maggie had finally felt the first blush of excitement at being a bride.

She was just drizzling maple syrup on her oatmeal and banana when the Westminster chimes rang. She was still in her kitty pajamas. *Drat!*

She walked to the front door and cracked it open. On the front porch stood her mother, father, and brother.

Bryan pushed the door open, grabbed Maggie around the neck, and said, "Good morning, Margaret. Happy wedding day! Want a donut?" He was carrying a pink box from Mrs. Popkin.

Mimi and Dirk followed their children into the parsonage. They both had their arms full of clothing and gifts. Maggie looked at her parents as Bryan continued with his friendly chokehold.

"What . . . umm . . . What are you doing here? Now?" Maggie asked.

"We're coming to your wedding, Maggie dear," Mimi said, patting Maggie on the cheek, then removing Bryan's arm and giving Maggie a kiss. "You didn't think we would miss this day, did you?"

"But, Mom, we're getting married at Dan and Nora's at three o'clock. You're in the wrong city," Maggie said sensibly.

"No, Maggie," said Dirk, giving his daughter a bear hug, "we are right where we should be. A wedding in Cherish."

The parsonage phone rang. Maggie felt as if she were having one of her vivid dreams, and she needed to wake up.

"Hello?" she said into the receiver.

Jack had woken up in his condo to a loud knocking on the front door. He jumped out of bed, the way he used to when he was a resident in the hospital, ready for an emergency.

When he got to his door, he was amazed to see his entire family staring happily at him and then pushing their way into the condo. They had clothes and packages, and Gretchen was carrying a large pink box from Mrs. Popkin. Their announcements were the same as Maggie's family's had been.

"Happy wedding day? I've got to call Maggie," Jack said in a daze.

"Maggie?" Jack's voice sounded strange.

"Jack!" Maggie said a little too loudly.

"Maggie, how are you?"

Maggie wondered for a brief second if Jack was being held prisoner. He was talking formally, as if someone else was very close to him, listening in.

"Jack, you'll never believe—"

Suddenly, Maggie heard familiar voices coming through the phone line. She heard Anne and Leigh. She heard Gretchen and Garrett. She heard Bonnie's soft voice in the background.

"Jack, your family? Is your family at your condo?"

"Hi, Maggie," came Ellen's voice.

"Yes. They all showed up a few minutes ago. I was still sleeping." There were more squeals and laughter coming through the line. "I think someone blew our secret." Jack laughed.

"My family is here too," Maggie said.

Happiness was beginning to tingle its way through her body.

"Look out your kitchen window. Is there any evidence of other wedding infidels?"

Maggie ran to the kitchen and looked out the window. Jack heard her intake of breath and had his answer.

"Jack, they're all here. Everyone is here. They're getting out of their cars and carrying things. Wedding-type things. What's going on?"

Mimi finally took Maggie's arm. She spoke so Jack could hear her too.

"Maggie, Jack, you are getting married today. No one wanted to miss it, so we have all made the plans you haven't had a chance to make. Congratulations!"

Jack and Maggie hung up to attend to their families. The surprise of their wedding day began to sneak around their consciousness and erupt in pure joy.

Maggie stared through the kitchen window and watched. She saw Cole and Lynn Porter, Bill and Sylvia Baxter, Marla and Tom Wiggins, along with Addie and Jason, Howard and Verna Baker, the Becker sisters, Harold, Bernie Bumble, Charlotte and Fred Tuggle, Sky Breese, Julia Benson along with Hannah, Mary and William, Hank and Pamela, Doris and Chester, and tiny Irena, who was herding them all inside the church like a possessed shepherdess. Irena's hair had been self-dyed white-blonde for the occasion. They all carried a variety of bows, ribbons, flowers, several pink boxes from Mrs. Popkin, and a five-tier wedding cake covered in flowers on a huge platter as big as a card table. Mrs. Popkin was happily barking orders as the cake made its journey from across the street. They all laughed and talked and carried their treasures into Loving the Lord.

Maggie, these are your treasures. Each and every one. Enjoy the day. Keep loving your people. The way I love you.

Maggie closed her eyes and breathed in the whisper. As she exhaled, she said softly, "Thank you."

Maggie's wedding day had begun.

Soon there were more sounds from the Westminster chimes. Lacey Campbell was standing on the porch with two baskets of hair supplies.

"Pastor Maggie, congratulations. Now, I need you to sit right down. We have a miracle to perform on your head."

Lacey pushed Maggie into the kitchen.

Bryan, Mimi, and Dirk had made their way to the church to watch the preparations. Cate was already there, helping with the decorating.

Jack's family, except for his brothers, had also made their way to Loving the Lord.

Ribbons and bows were being strung on the outside of the pews. They were white with sparkles and looked like something out of a Walt Disney princess movie. Perfect. Sky Breese was in complete command of the flowers. Everyone was a bit surprised by Sky's coherent orders and authoritative presence. It appeared she could awaken from her normal fairy-land existence and work with military precision.

Irena was practicing piece after piece of wedding music. It was loud but helped set the mood for what was to come.

The soup committee was busy in the basement, setting up chairs and tables. Verna had lovely pink linen table cloths ironed and ready to place on each table. Howard was setting matching linen napkins and silverware at each place. They had all been secretly planning for two weeks. They'd had to keep it a secret from Pastor Maggie and Dr. Jack. It wouldn't do if the lovebirds had found out about their wedding ahead of time.

Mrs. Popkin bustled over from The Sugarplum to oversee the placement of the cake. Sky had brought her the fresh flowers under cover of darkness last night. That morning Mrs. Popkin had finished the cake with the lovely petals.

Hank was busy in the office retrieving the wedding service bulletins he had secretly hidden for over a week. He had been a basket of nerves every time Pastor Maggie set foot in his office. Nora had called Hank two weeks ago to ask him to help with the secret plans. They had made a pact. A real live pact! Hank had been beside himself with secret glee. He and Pamela had had secret meetings in their home with church members, planning and plotting each detail of the wedding. And now their hard work was coming to fruition.

Back at the parsonage, Maggie's hair was covered in foils as the highlights took hold. Lacey took it upon herself to do Maggie's makeup as well as her hair. Maggie had to ask Lacey to tone it down just a bit. She wanted Jack to actually recognize her.

Nora, Dan, Jo, Mike, Kristy, and baby Matthew all arrived at eleven. Maggie grabbed Nora and hugged her friend.

Then she said sharply, "You did this! Admit it, Nora. You gave away the secret."

"Of course I did. You were being a little idiot and letting the darker days of church life eclipse the lighter, lovelier days. I figured you needed a reminder of joy."

Maggie felt the stark truth in Nora's statement.

Nora watched as Lacey finished Maggie's hair with soft curls and small pearl encrusted clasps. Maggie looked in the mirror and gasped. *Is that really me?* Maybe she should put a little more effort into her appearance on a daily basis.

"Lacey, I had no idea I could look this good. You really do work miracles." Maggie smiled.

"You have a good base to work with," Lacey said practically as she packed up her hair paraphernalia. "But yes, I do work miracles each and every day of my life."

More chimes at the front door. Maggie opened it and saw Anne standing on the porch with a large box in her arms.

"Anne!" Maggie gave her almost sister-in-law a hug around the box.

"Hi, Maggie! May I come in?" Anne walked through the door as she asked.

Lacey said goodbye, adding she would be at the back of the church to touch up Maggie's makeup before she walked down the aisle.

Walk down the aisle. Maggie hadn't even thought about that.

Anne led Maggie upstairs to her bedroom.

"I have something for you, Maggie. I hope you don't mind."

Anne's eyes were looking a little watery, which unnerved Maggie. They sat down on Maggie's unmade bed, and Anne handed Maggie the large box.

"This is my wedding dress," Anne said. "I think it will fit you if you have some tall shoes." At this, Anne laughed lightly. "I know you haven't had time to plan anything for your wedding, and I'm sorry for that. But it would be such an honor for me if you would wear this dress. It . . . it is the dress I wore into my true love's arms. And today, you will wear it into yours."

Maggie opened the box.

Layers of white satin felt soft to the touch. The pearl beaded neckline glimmered in the sunlight shining through the bedroom window. In a separate dry cleaning bag was a long veil attached to a delicate pearl headpiece. Maggie stood up and held the dress up to her and twirled slowly.

"I love it, Anne. I couldn't have picked out anything more lovely than this. It means so much to me that it's yours, that we will both share our wedding days in this dress."

Maggie was beginning to feel a trickle of the emotion that would hit like a waterfall as she walked toward Jack in the amazing dress.

Anne helped Maggie put on her wedding dress. It fit beautifully, even if it was a little long. Maggie pulled out her cream-colored pumps. The height was just right. The dress just dusted the floor. Lastly, Anne put the veil on Maggie's coifed head, gently placing the headpiece as a small crown.

"You look like a princess," Anne said, eyes shining.

Maggie looked at Anne.

"Do you know what time I'm getting married?"

"Oh! Hasn't anyone told you? Three o'clock," Anne said. "I wonder if Jack knows."

Anne pulled out her cell phone and called her brother Andrew.

"Hey," Andrew said to his sister.

"Hey, yourself. Does Jack know when he's getting married?"

"I don't know. Let me ask."

Andrew covered the phone and mumbled something to Jack.

"Nope. What time is he getting married?" Andrew asked.

"In an hour and forty-five minutes, you moron. Is Jack dressed?" Anne was in teacher mode.

"No, but he will be. We'll all be there in fifteen minutes."

Andrew hated it when Anne got bossy, which had been almost every day of his life.

"Good. Make it happen, Andrew." Anne clicked off and looked at Maggie. "You're marrying into a family of dumb boys."

"I can't wait." Maggie laughed.

"Well, I'll leave you now," said Anne. "But I'm so happy we will be sisters, Maggie. I mean that."

"I am too, Anne. You're not as scary as you were when I first met you." Maggie grinned.

Westminster chimes.

Anne went down to answer the door. It was Dan.

"I need a few minutes with Maggie," Dan said. "Nora is looking for your brother. Do you know where he is?"

"He is frantically getting dressed. He should be here in a few minutes," Anne said. "I'll call Maggie."

Maggie came down the steps looking radiant.

"Hi, Dan. What are you doing here?"

"Don't you know?" Dan asked, smiling.

He pulled out a small index card.

Maggie knew. The waterfall began to trickle.

"Maggie," Dan said, "in a little while you will walk down the aisle to Jack. Tell me what you love about him. Maggie, what do you love about Jack?"

The words poured out. Dan could barely keep up with the torrent of loving sentiments. He filled up both sides of his index card. Then he handed Maggie a Kleenex to mop up the mess her eyes and nose had made of the rest of her face.

"Maggie, this is such a wonderful day. Nora and I love you. We'll both be waiting at the end of the aisle with Jack."

Dan hugged his friend, then made his way across the lawn to church.

Westminster chimes.

Maggie opened the door. It was Sky Breese. She was holding an exquisite bouquet of flowers.

"Pastor Maggie, I created this for you today. I hope you like it."

Sky was speaking in complete and whole sentences.

"I know you love carnations because I asked around. I also added roses, fern, peonies, Queen Anne's lace—I know it's another favorite, even though it's a weed—lily of the valley, and at Mrs. Baker's insistence, a zinnia. But I hid it pretty well."

Sky stopped and took in Maggie's appearance.

"Wow, Pastor Maggie, you are a beautiful bride," Sky said sincerely. "Mmmm . . . I have seen many . . . brides. You are the most . . . mmm . . . peaceful bride. I can feel it." Sky was slipping back into the land of fairies. "Your . . . beauty comes from . . . your heart."

Maggie was moved by this. She also had to laugh at sweet, beautiful, smart, flaky Sky. Maggie had never met anyone like her before. Sky leaned down and gave Maggie a gentle hug.

"I'll see you in there," she said, pointing at the church. Then she left out of the kitchen door.

The front door opened again. *Thank goodness, no more chimes.* Mimi and Dirk walked in. Maggie had wiped her eyes, and now they glistened at her parents.

"Are you ready?" Mimi asked. "Are you ready for your last walk of maidenhood?"

Mimi definitely had a way with words.

Dirk looked at his daughter with pure love.

"Maggie, you are beautiful. What an honor it is to call you my daughter."

He gave her his elbow, and she slipped her arm through his.

Before Maggie and her parents stepped out the back door of the parsonage, Maggie looked once again through the kitchen window. She gulped hard when she saw Cassandra leaning on Pamela's arm and walking slowly to the sanctuary. Carrie and Carl must already be inside. The two women were alone.

∞

Nora had been searching for the groom. Jack finally arrived with Andrew, Nathan, and Peter. Nora grabbed him and dragged him into Maggie's office.

"Jack, did you not know what time you were getting married today?" Nora asked.

"I thought three o'clock at your house. That's the last I knew."

Jack smiled. He looked over at Maggie's desk and saw a framed picture of himself and Maggie at the beach. His heart thumped.

"It's at three right here in the sanctuary of Loving the Lord," Nora said, perturbed. "Anyway," she changed her voice tone, "Jack, why are you going to wait at the end of the aisle for Maggie today? What do you love about Maggie, Jack?"

Nora had her index card and pen poised.

Jack paused. Then he carefully gave Nora his answer.

Irena was perched on the organ bench, her white-blonde hair covered in a short pink veil in honor of the occasion. She regularly glanced over her shoulder, watching for Maggie and her parents. She played piece after piece, with the Pachelbel's "Canon in D" at the ready.

Finally, she spotted them. She changed chords, and just as Dirk and Mimi, with Maggie between them, stepped into the sanctuary, Pachelbel's canon filled Loving the Lord Community Church. And the great outdoors.

Maggie and her parents paused at the back of church. When Maggie looked down the aisle, she saw Penny and Molly Porter in their best Sunday dresses. She saw Kay and Shawn Kessler, also dressed up for church. Hannah Benson was standing with Carl and Carrie, who was resplendent in white leotard, tutu, crown, and wand. Gretchen and Garrett smiled at Aunt Maggie. Sammy Porter and Matthew Brown were in their mother's arms in the choir loft, along with all of the high school students. Addie and Liz waved at Maggie. She waved back.

But then Maggie looked down the white-ribboned aisle. And she saw Jack.

Jack and Maggie only had eyes for each other.

Maggie walked her parents down the aisle.

Because she had someone to get to.

Once everyone was seated, Jack and Maggie stood before Dan and Nora. Nora began.

"Sometimes there is a happily-ever-after story that plays out right before our eyes. Today, we are all witnessing that story."

There were smiles and nods all around.

Dan continued.

"We've all been entwined in two weeks' worth of secrets, haven't we?" He smiled. "Jack and Maggie thought they had a secret, but we have all been planning to thwart that idea. Jack and Maggie, welcome to your wedding day!"

Spontaneous applause erupted from the congregation.

Dan and Nora took turns with prayers and readings, but right before the vows were pledged, Dan had the couple face each other and said, "I asked Maggie before this ceremony began why she was walking down the aisle to Jack today. What does she love about him? It was hard to keep up with her, but here is what she said about you, Jack:

'I love his eyes. They are full of wisdom.

I love his sense of humor. No one has ever made me laugh like he does.

I love the way he loves his family and the way he loves mine.

Jack loves God. Everything he does reflects that sentiment.

He likes my cats.

I love his mind.

I love him because somehow he doesn't mind my emotions and impetuousness.

I love his arms and the way he holds me.

I love how he smells.

I love how he cares so deeply for his patients.

He finds the silver lining in any cloud.

Jack is the most handsome man I have ever seen or known.

I love his heart.
I can't wait to be his wife.'"

Dan stopped. The many Kleenex boxes in the pews were being used well, but Nora hadn't shared her index card yet.

"Here's what Jack had to say about why he loves you, Maggie." Nora cleared her throat.

"'I love her smile.
I love her spirituality.
I love her beauty, both inner and outer.
I love the way she cares for others.
I love the way she cares for me.
I love how family is so important to her.
I love her love for God's creation and creatures.
I love that health and healthy living are important to her.
I love how she's willing to share her thoughts and feelings with me.
I love her intelligence.
I love her skills as a pastor and preacher.
I love her heart for the less fortunate.
I love her passion.'"

Dan handed Maggie a wad of Kleenex. The beautiful makeup rapidly slid down Maggie's cheeks.

It was time for their vows. Nora read each traditional vow for Jack and Maggie to repeat to each other, which they did. But it happened, when he said:

"To have and to hold . . ."

Jack paused, then took Maggie in his arms and held her as he repeated the familiar words. Then he whispered them a second time in her ear.

Her eyes shone up at him, as she mouthed, "To have and to hold. Forever."

And then it was done. They were husband and wife.

Dr. Jack and Reverend Maggie Elliot.

Maggie and Jack looked around to see cell phones staring back at them. Hometown photographers marked an incredible day for the bride and groom. And a more incredible day for Loving the Lord.

Irena played as the congregation stood and applauded the new couple.

All but Marvin Green, who was sitting in his wheelchair at the back of the church, smiling and crying like a baby.

38

Following the ceremony, Maggie and Jack were led down to the basement, wrapped up in friends. Days before, the basement had been a place of fear, destruction, and mysteries revealed. But it was a new day. The basement had been transformed into a large, pink cloud of sugar and spice and everything nice. Maggie stopped at the bottom of the stairs, causing those behind her to haphazardly crash into one another amidst bubbling giggles.

Maggie wanted to take in everything about the day. Without having the nuisance of planning it, she could be surprised by every detail. Tables were set with delicate pink cloths. Church china was elegantly set at each place. Pink tulle was scalloped along the windows and across the room from corner to corner. Pink, white, and red carnations were exploding from vases on every possible surface. Maggie wondered how Sky could have procured so many carnations. Their spiciness filled the air and Maggie's nose.

She also smelled beef and pork roasts, rosemary chickens, cooked onions, and vegetables. Maggie knew where all the delicious vegetables had come from and found Sylvia in the crowd and gave her a wink. Spicy cinnamon applesauce was steaming in bowls on each table. Someone must have just made it that very morning.

As Maggie moved into the reception, her arm through Jack's, she saw the ribbons tied on each chair ending in a large cheerful bow. Pink and white name cards were at each place.

"Can you believe all this?" Maggie whispered to Jack, who seemed slightly dazed himself.

"Do you know what I believe?" Jack asked, looking into Maggie's wide blue eyes.

She shook her head.

"I believe this church full of good people has learned how to love because you have loved them, I mean loved us. You taught us how to care for each other in brand-new ways."

They both looked around and watched Verna, Mary, Marla, Ellen, Sylvia, Bill, and Mrs. Popkin putting baskets of fresh baguettes and clover leaf rolls on the tables. Howard, Winston, and William were standing by a huge punch bowl full of green punch topped with melting sherbet, ladling cups for all the guests. The children were sneaking handfuls of nuts and mints.

Maggie looked at the walls of the basement, the strong doors and shining windows.

You are going to be all right. You have held firm. We will repair you and make you whole, and you will hold us within your loving walls as we worship and dance and sing. Maggie closed her eyes for a moment and thanked God for Loving the Lord Community Church and for all the days to come in that lovely, holy place.

Mrs. Popkin had outdone herself with the wedding cake. Fives tiers of fluffy goodness reposed on a silver platter. The layers were alternating pink and white. Sky's exquisite flowers were growing out of the frosting in bursts of brightness. The tiny top tier had a gold cross resting atop its frosted swirls. *Perfect!* thought Maggie.

People began to take their seats, due to the fact that Irena was shouting at them to do so. She was poking and prodding people with a fork to get them to shut up and sit down. The whole time she had one golden-green eye on Detective Keith Crunch. Irena had made sure their place cards were side by side.

Just as everyone was settling down, Kay, Shawn, Carrie, and Carl raced out of the kitchen in a mighty game of tag. Shawn went left toward the stairs, followed by Carrie. Kay circled back to the kitchen once she saw her mother's face. But poor little Carl ran right into the cake table.

Everyone watched as Carl's forehead slammed into the edge of the table. The blood was immediate. As were Carl's howls of pain. Charlene Kessler quickly got to Carl and staunched the bleeding with her pink napkin. But by the time she reached him, all eyes were on the cake, which seemed to be falling, falling, falling in slow motion. The gold cross clanged on the floor, as the top layer of the cake tumbled after it, followed by the rest of the lovely layers.

Detective Crunch dashed to the table, grabbed the silver platter to salvage whatever he could of the cake, and managed to slide the platter with the first two layers back onto the middle of the cake table. Unfortunately, he was wearing the tiny top tier as a hat on his perfect hair. The other two tiers were resting in an unbecoming heap on the floor. Everyone gasped.

Except for Polly Popkin. Polly began to chuckle, then snort, then guffaw, and then she was in a full-blown laugh. She walked over to the cake and took a peek at Carl's forehead.

"Dr. Kessler, he may need a couple of stitches there, but you know that. You're a doctor. And Carl honey, we will never forget this wedding reception or your amazing running capabilities. Hokey tooters! I expect to see you on the track team, young man."

Polly picked up Carl and kissed him on the nose. She and Charlene took Carl to Charlene's office for a quick stitching procedure. Pamela, Cassandra, and Mary followed along.

"I'm not even embarrassed," Cassandra said dully. "I suppose I should be, but Mrs. Popkin seemed to make it all okay."

"We just want Carl to be okay. And we also want to eat cake," Pamela said with a smile.

Cassandra's eyes glistened. She looked at Mary.

"My children will be fine. I know that for sure now. They will be fine. This church is so . . . so much like a family."

Mary squeezed Cassandra's hand.

"Yes, Cassandra, that's exactly who we are. Your family."

When the women returned to the church with a bandaged and Ty-lenoled Carl, the reception was in full swing. Heaping plates of roasts and rosemary chicken, whipped potatoes, roasted vegetables, and the homemade cinnamon applesauce were being enjoyed by all. The two tiers of cake that had made their way to the floor had been cleaned up, along with Detective Crunch's head, but he still had pink frosting sticking to strands of his hair, which gave him the peculiar look of an aging punk-rock star.

Jack and Maggie danced to Frank Sinatra's "Like Someone in Love." Everyone smiled when the refrain was sung about bumping into things like someone in love. They thought of their clumsy little pastor, now dancing with her new husband, sans crutch or cane.

Everyone clinked their glasses to signal Jack and Maggie to share a kiss. Again and again and again. The children were especially enthusiastic about this new power and clinked with great gusto, although it completely grossed them out to see Pastor Maggie kiss Dr. Jack.

On the other side of the room, when the glasses clinked, Irena grabbed Detective Keith Crunch by his frostinged lapels and planted a kiss directly on his mouth. He didn't seem to mind. It probably didn't hurt that some of the vodka from Irena's ever-present flask had made its way into Keith's green punch throughout the afternoon.

The evening finally came to an end with an abundance of hugs, kisses, and more hugs. Maggie's beautiful wedding dress had been delightfully covered in small frosting fingerprints, sticky pats on the back, and at least fifty kinds of perfumes.

She looked at Anne and said, "I will have this dress dry cleaned and resealed first thing on Monday. Then we can put it away for Leigh, or Brynn, or maybe Gretchen."

When Anne heard her daughter's name, her mouth pursed to keep her lip from wobbling. She hadn't ever thought about the dress going to little Gretchen. The day had been way too full of emotion. No more mushy talk.

The soup committee finally kicked Jack and Maggie out of the church and watched as Jack picked up Maggie and carried her across his new lawn and into his new home. Their new home.

Epilogue

Maggie was dreaming.

She was swimming in a vanilla wedding cake, her arms slicing pieces that fell down onto giant plates for everyone in the church basement. She was laughing with Cate and Bryan, who were spraying pink whipped cream on the pieces of cake. As she continued to cut cake with her arms, she knew she was missing someone important. Where was Jack?

She could smell his cologne. He must be near. Her eyes fluttered as Jack's cologne filled her nose. She turned to slice another piece of cake.

As she turned, Maggie's nose bumped into Jack's shoulder and woke her up. Her blue eyes opened and stared into Jack's brown eyes.

They were in her bedroom in the parsonage.

They were married.

"Ow!" Jack said as Marmalade head bumped him with loving ferocity.

"It means he loves you, and he thinks you're safe. And also, he now owns you," Maggie said sleepily.

"Well, I only want you to own me," Jack said, wrapping her in his arms, "for as long as we both shall live."

"Okay," Maggie agreed as she nuzzled her nose into his chest.

It was Sunday morning. Maggie had a sermon to preach in two hours. Oh wait, no she didn't. Nora was preaching that day. She'd told

Maggie last night at the reception. Jack and Maggie could sit together in the pews as husband and wife.

"Would you like some oatmeal?" Maggie asked.

"Sure. But only if it has banana and maple syrup on top," Jack said, refusing to let go of his brand-new wife.

The church was still decorated for a wedding. Both Jack's and Maggie's families had stayed at The Grange the night before, reliving the fun of the day and the enjoyment of giving Jack and Maggie a true, celebratory wedding.

Anne and Peter were heading back to Detroit that morning to welcome Bryan and Cate to their church.

The rest of the family members, including Jack and Maggie, would all meet in Blissfield for Bryan and Cate's final Ghana presentation that afternoon.

But that morning, Maggie had to get ready for worship. Not to lead it, but to experience it.

After breakfast and a third cup of coffee, she stepped into her parsonage study. She could hear the shower running upstairs and liked the new sound that would soon become familiar.

There was a wicker basket with a soft-pink bow wrapped around it sitting on her desk. It was full of wedding cards. She didn't know who had placed it there, but she sat in her chair and casually thumbed through the many white and pastel envelopes. One caught her eye. The familiar handwriting invited her to take it from the basket. Maggie carefully slit the envelope open and pulled out the card. When she opened it, a rectangle of soft lace fell into her lap. Cross-stitched on the lace in delicate stitches was Shakespeare's *Sonnet 116*. Knowing that Ed had used that sonnet when he officiated weddings, Jo had made the delicate piece of lacey poetry for Maggie and Jack with Ed's silent blessing.

Maggie had loved the sonnet since the first time Ed had shared it with her.

"... love does not alter when it alteration finds ... love is an ever-fixed mark ..."

Holding the soft fabric in her hand, she closed her eyes.

Thank you. Thank you for the gift of Jack. Thank you for the gift of marriage. Thank you for fixing my heart on love. But what about everything else? What will these next weeks and months hold?

She listened patiently. She gazed at the three beautiful pine trees standing tall outside her study window. She listened some more.

Maggie, you are loved. You're loving. Believe your days are cared for. Believe I hold each day you live in the palm of my hand. I hold you, so you can hold others. All is well, and all will be well.

And God meant it.

And Maggie believed.

To Have and To Hold
Discussion Questions

1. Who did you think was breaking into the church? Were you right?

2. What was the most surprising part of the book to you?

3. At the beginning of the book, after Maggie and Jack got engaged, church members immediately started spreading their news before they had a chance to tell their families and good friends. And church members even started making decisions about the wedding (the cake, music, flowers, etc.) without consulting Maggie and Jack. While this is humorous (and even a little sweet), what are ways that communities (churches, towns, families) ignore important boundaries related to "their own"?

4. How is humor used in the book? How does humor work alongside tragedy, conflict, and crisis? Is humor a humanizing element? Does humor help make seemingly perfect things imperfect?

5. What did you think of Redford's behavior throughout? What motivates him?

6. What was your initial response to Maggie and Jack deciding to get married quickly in a small ceremony in her friends' living room? Did

you think it was a wise decision? An unwise decision? Did you think Maggie was missing out on something she would later regret?

7. The story deals with some serious topics. For example, Mary Ellington was dealing with severe guilt, loss, grief, and anger. Cassandra was dealing with illness, denial, parenthood, and negligence. How are these two women's burdens somehow carried and/or resolved?

8. A number of characters in the story take risks for others. Name some of these situations. Does someone's willingness to take risks make you see that person in a different light?

9. Abuse and abusive relationships play a large role in this book—from the very first scene to the dramatic reveal in the church basement. How does Maggie's response to finding an abandoned kitten at the gas station foreshadow future events in the book?

10. Cassandra is first seen as potentially an abuser because of the appearance of her taking advantage of babysitters and neglecting her children. What does this say about caring for others that we might consider unsafe?

11. Another theme of the book is not reaching out when in need (Cassandra, Mary, Melissa). Have you ever held back from asking for help when you needed it? Why? Was it for privacy? For independence? Was it out of stubbornness? Have you experienced someone close to you doing that? What were the results?

12. Mary says to Maggie: "Some people die without knowing they're going to die, like Michael, but Cassandra will have to work hard to die." What did she mean?

13. There are a number of parenthood issues: Mary losing her son, Carrie and Carl losing their father and now their mother, Maggie

and Jack considering instant parenthood, baby Matthew Brown being baptized, the orphans in Ghana. Do you believe "it takes a village" to raise children, whether it be an actual village, a church family, or neighbors? How does this play out in your own neighborhood or church?

14. At the beginning of this book is Shakespeare's *Sonnet 116*. Shakespeare writes that "Love is an ever-fixed mark." Where did you notice the "fixed mark" of different characters through their words and actions? Love is all-consuming. Where did you see love of vice and virtue?

Recipes

Maggie's Cinnamon Pecan Pie

Place 2 cups halved pecans in an unbaked single pie crust.

In a sauce pan mix together:

¼ cup brown sugar

2 ½-3 teaspoons cinnamon (depending on how much cinnamon you enjoy)

¼ cup sweet butter

½ cup halved pecans

Simmer for four minutes over low heat. Let cool.

In mixing bowl mix:

3 eggs, beaten

¾ cup white sugar

1 cup light corn syrup

2 teaspoons pure vanilla extract

½ teaspoon salt

Pour cooled cinnamon mixture into egg mixture and combine.

Pour combined mixture over pecans in pie crust.

Bake at 375° for 45-50 minutes until almost set in the middle, but still with a wiggle.

Mrs. Popkin's Fruit Bran Bars

In large bowl mix together:
2 boxes of bran muffin mix, equaling 30 oz. total
1 cup whole wheat flour
3 teaspoons cinnamon
2 teaspoons allspice
1 teaspoon ground nutmeg
1 ½ cups chopped hazelnuts, pecans, or walnuts
1 cup brown sugar
2 cups chopped dates, currants, dried cranberries, golden raisins, dried
    cherries, or dried blueberries
In another mixing bowl mix:
1 cup applesauce
¾ cup canola oil
3 eggs, beaten
¼ cup molasses

Pour wet ingredients over dry ingredients and mix well.
Pour mixture into greased 9x13 pan and bake at 350° for 50-60 minutes
until top is golden brown.
When cool, you can make them more decadent by drizzling the Yummy Drizzle over the top (with scone recipe).

Anne's Heavenly Fluff Salad

Mix together thoroughly:
One 8 oz. Cool Whip
One 16 oz. sour cream
One large box (6 oz.) of dry Jell-O (strawberry, cherry, lime are all good)

Add:
1 cup finely chopped pecans
3-4 cups fresh fruit (depending on how fruity you want it, blueberries,
sliced strawberries, chopped peaches, raspberries—make sure the fruit
isn't covered in excess water or the salad will lose its consistency)

Refrigerate for 2 hours.

Mrs. Popkin's Ginger Scones

In mixing bowl, mix together:
2 cups all-purpose flour
1 teaspoons baking powder
½ teaspoon salt
¼ cup sugar
2 tablespoons chopped candied ginger

Rub in with fingers until crumbly:
4 tablespoons of sweet butter at room temperature

In small bowl, whisk together:
2 eggs

Enough milk to make a smooth dough

Add milk/egg mixture to dry ingredients. Knead dough on very lightly floured surface. Pat out into a circle that is 1 ½ inches thick.
Use a scone pan to mold or a thin-rimmed glass to cut circles.
Brush tops with heavy cream.
Bake at 375° for 20 minutes or until lightly golden on top.
When cooled, drizzle with Yummy Drizzle:
1 cup powdered sugar
1 teaspoon vanilla
½ teaspoon ground ginger
2 tablespoons milk
Whisk together, drizzle.

Decorate with a piece of candied ginger on top of each scone.
These scones are delicious warm and plain or with butter, honey, or orange marmalade. Of course, you must also have a cup of Lady Grey tea with your scones.

Acknowledgements

God still whispers. I'm so thankful.

Duke and Kimberly Pennell and Pen-L Publishing, you are a constant blessing.

Head editor Meg Dendler, thank you for taking this book to the next level. You are invaluable and make me a better writer.

Editor Susan Matheson, thank you again for your expertise, straightforward critique, and constant encouragement. It is a joy working with you!

Author G.M. Malliet, thank you for your wisdom, advice, and encouragement.

Marsha Rinke, dear friend, you know Maggie so well. Thank you for all your insight and thoughtful suggestions.

Dr. William G. Marx, your meticulous proofreading and copy editing is an incredible gift. Thank you.

The Reverend Stanley Jenkins, thank you for taking the time to read this book, even though you have millions (more or less) of obligations demanding your time and attention.

Police Chief Bruce Ferguson of the DeWitt, Michigan, Police Department, your help was invaluable to this book.

Dr. Charlene Kushler.

Ethan Ellenberg.

Anne Duinkerken, thank you for your excellent proofreading, once again.

First readers: Mom, Uncle Craig and Auntie Vicki Hubbell, Auntie Judy Ann Elzinga, Mitsuko Marx, Ann Sneller, Judy Teater, Marianne Grooters, Lynn Samuelson, Lacey Campbell, Priscilla Flintoft, Mary Jenkins, and Leanne Harker.

Those who graciously allowed me to use their names: my mother, Dr. Mimi Elzinga Keller, Howard Baker, Joy Nelson, Ken and Bonnie Walter, Lacey Campbell, Pastor Elisha, Marta, Fifi, Cynthia, Promise, and baby Leah (who is actually too small to know if I used her name or not), along with so many others at United Hearts Children's Center.

Alli Edema, dear daughter-in-law, who gave exceptional creative advice for a very special dress in this book.

And most of all, my husband, Doug. Not only do you patiently answer every medical question I throw at you, you also make writing romance so very, very easy.

If the fictional organization Africa Hope caught your attention, please visit the website of the organization it's based on:
www.MamaHope.org

About the Author

The Rev. Dr. Barbara Edema has been a pastor for twenty-three years. That sounds astonishingly boring. However, she is a great deal of fun with a colorful vocabulary used regularly out of the pulpit. Barb has spent decades with people during holy and unholy times. She has been at her best and her worst in the lives of the people she has cared for.

Now she's writing about a fictional church based on her days serving delightful and frustrating parishioners. Pastor Maggie is a young, impetuous, emotional, clumsy, and not to mention, a crazy cat lady, who steps into ministry full of Greek and Hebrew, but not much life experience. She learns quickly.

Barb lives in DeWitt, Michigan, with her husband, Dr. Douglas Edema. She is the mother of Elise, Lauren, Alana, and Wesley. Like Maggie, Barb is an avid feline female. Hence, she has collected an assortment of rescue kitties. Barb enjoys date nights with her husband, watching her children do great things in the world, a glass of good red wine, and making up stories about the fun and fulfilling life in the church.

Enjoy visiting Cherish, Michigan, and Loving the Lord Community Church. Pastor Maggie will delight you!

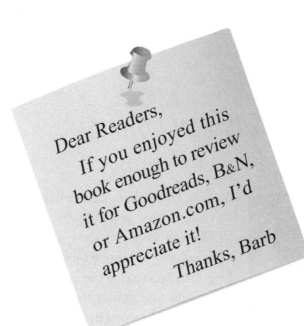

Dear Readers,
   If you enjoyed this
book enough to review
it for Goodreads, B&N,
or Amazon.com, I'd
appreciate it!
         Thanks, Barb

Find more great reads at
Pen-L.com

Made in the USA
Monee, IL
28 February 2022

92017022R00203